FRESH FEAR

AN ANTHOLOGY OF

MACABRE HORROR

KING BILLY PUBLICATIONS

Wellington, New Zealand

Fresh Fear © 2016 King Billy Publications
(2nd edition)

Edited by William Cook

Front/rear cover photography (C) 2016, Louis Blanc
http://loublancphotos.com/
Cover design © 2016 William Cook
Interior design: Cyrusfiction Productions

ISBN-13: 978-1534864276
ISBN-10: 153486427X

Internet: http://www.williamcookwriter.com

*Note: the astute reader will notice that both US/UK English have been employed in the telling of these tales. There is a varied mix of stories from all parts of the globe; herein you will find tales from as far afield as New Zealand and Australia alongside work from England, Canada, The Netherlands, and the United States. The hope is that you will enjoy the differences in the respective styles and voices that these fine writers use to weave their tapestries of terror!

CONTENTS

KING BILLY
PUBLICATIONS

Dedicated to the memory of author J.F. Gonzalez

FRESH FEAR

EDITED BY WILLIAM COOK

WHY WE TURN TO HORROR

W.J. RENEHAN

A selection from W.J. Renehan's
*The Art of Darkness: Meditations on the Effect of
Horror Fiction*

Why is it that we so often turn to works of horror fiction as a source of entertainment when they should, by all rights, turn us off completely? Why should we pay good money to be scared out of our wits? The most obvious answer to this would be the adrenaline rush we get from it, but to chalk up the attraction of horror to this alone would be to only skim the surface of the genre's dark waters. Works of horror have myriad implications when considered from psychological, sociological, and philosophical stand-points, and perform numerous functions in regard to both personal and collective experience. Allowing for the simultaneous gratification and abreaction of tabooed desire, the simultaneous fracture and reinforcement of social, sexual, and moral codes, such fiction has persisted in cultures the world over as a stabilizing force—a means of fostering both individual and collective growth while also acting to maintain the status quo. The benefits of horror are undoubtedly subtle and largely overlooked, yet their value cannot be overstated.

As a state of intense physical and cognitive agitation, horror is capable of temporarily inducing what is known as regression, in which one reverts to an earlier, more primitive stage of psychological development as a means of coping with overwhelming fear/anxiety. Horror fiction provides a kind of psychic relief in this manner, in that it allows for the experience of fear without presenting any actual physical or psychological threat. Valdine Clemens notes that "Such fiction provides an antidote for the excessively cerebral consciousness, the devitalized state that Thomas Hardy called 'the ache of modernism' and to which D.H. Lawrence referred— anticipating modern media jargon—with the term 'talking heads'" (*Return of the Repressed*, 2). As an atavistic experience, horror serves to reconnect us with our primal selves, provides temporary respite from the droning conditions of modern life, and facilitates a process of self-reevaluation in regard to the conditions of our existence. The initial shock is merely the tip of the iceberg.

Images of horror fascinate due to their effect as representations of what psychoanalysts term the "uncanny"—repressed desires of the personal and collective unconscious. As Noël Carroll asserts, "the horrific images of this genre represent compromise formations. Their repulsive aspects mask and make possible various sorts of wish fulfillment, notably those of a sexual sort" (The Philosophy of Horror, 170). Shock and repulsion are simply the price we must pay in order to play out these repressed desires, and thus horror fiction generates a kind of cognitive dissonance, in which we find images/situations to be foreign, yet familiar;

repulsive, yet attractive; disturbing, yet somehow intriguing. This paradox is essential to understanding the various benefits of the genre's effect, as it explains why we would subject ourselves to such material in the first place. Unhealthy impulses/desires are effectively discharged in a controlled manner through vicarious stimulation.

But horror fiction acts not only as a release valve for underlying psychical pressure; such works also address everyday fears common to the human condition—areas of unease such as mortality, Apollonian/Dionysian conflict, social strife, anxieties concerning sexuality and reproduction, etc. By affording us the opportunity to confront these subjects in a controlled manner, horror fiction acts as counter-phobia, focusing fear as a means of overcoming it. This is akin to the process of habituation, in which a person comes to respond less intensely to a stimulus in the wake of repeated exposure to it. Many variables come into play, and there is no guarantee that such exposure won't result in further sensitization—therefore some people find nothing beneficial in the effect of horror fiction. But assuming we do respond in a positive manner, it is within the power of such works to help us become better adjusted, happier individuals.

Aside from its cathartic aspects and ability to renew personal and collective perception, horror fiction also works on a more obvious, unsettling level. At the forefront of consciousness, even though we aren't likely to admit it, we know we like to participate in the weirdness—even if only in a passive sense. Stephen King acknowledges that "[Horror] offers us a chance to indulge in deviant, antisocial behavior by proxy—to commit gratuitous acts of violence, indulge our puerile dreams of power, to give in to our most craven fears" (Danse Macabre, 43). On a base level, the attraction of horror is not unlike that of a sexual fetish—deviously intriguing. Therefore it seems no coincidence that such fiction frequently expresses themes of sadism, masochism, unnatural and seemingly insatiable lust, physical and emotional degradation, and so on. In fact, our most firmly established horror figures and conventions are absolutely loaded with sexual energy. Ever found yourself rooting for a monster/violator? Sure you have. Now ask yourself why that is.

Continuing this line of thought, while horror fiction effectively lifts the constraints of social, sexual, and moral codes for our entertainment, it simultaneously reinforces the established order as well. (This should come as no surprise, as fear has been employed throughout human history as an effective means of control, both oppressive and motivational. Right wing employment of fear of the outsider or "other" is a classic example.) Appearing in cultures the world over and frequently corresponding with Jungian archetypes, horror images and narratives have roots in various mythical and spiritual belief systems. By depicting the horrific consequences of indulging in unproductive, tabooed behavior, such fiction is socially instructive; a mechanism for perpetuating the laws and values of the collective. Thus the young woman who becomes a bit too familiar with the men folk finds herself deceived by a demon in disguise. The man who attempts to play God deludes himself, his efforts resulting in abomination and ruin. Those who push too far beyond the boundary of that which is known come to pay a terrible price. James B. Twitchell notes that "these sagas, while not necessarily making the right predictions about future life, are memory banks of social and sexual possibilities both for the individual and the group. They show exactly what will melt down the nuclear family" (Dreadful Pleasures, 104). In that they are prescriptive as well as entertaining, works of horror present themselves as a fascinating means of maintaining societal order.

But works of horror fiction act not only as a means of coping with the anxieties of a particular culture or era; they also function as a means of responding to such anxieties. As Michael J. Collins points out, "[Horror] acts as the voice of every successive generation, and tailors its approach accordingly" (A Dark Night's Dreaming, 121). For example: more recent works of horror clearly reflect a heavy postmodern influence. These stories have become increasingly self-referential, emphasizing a sense of tradition in response to the ever more fragmented and compartmentalized conditions of modern life. Also, the ever more graphic depictions of violence and gore in such fiction can be seen as representative of the devalued conception of the individual in the modern world. The focus has turned more and more toward the complete and utter helplessness of the individual in the larger scheme of the universe, existing at the mercy of forces beyond control.

If anything is absolutely certain about works of horror fiction, it's that they touch us in a very personal way, and what we take away from that experience—whether positive or negative—is very much our own. (This is a very special phenomenon in a day and age when people go about their lives in a relatively numb and detached state. To feel anything, even fear, is like a breath of fresh air—invigorating, rejuvenating. Fear is a wonderful reminder that we are indeed alive.) Aside from allowing for escape from the confines of modern life, and providing an outlet of release for underlying psychical pressures, horror fiction has the power to facilitate personal and collective change in anticipation of the future. Such works have a great deal to teach us if we are willing to open ourselves to the experience, and if the price of that knowledge is a little scare, then so be it …

… but enough pontificating. You'll forgive me; my love of horror is surpassed only by my love of talking about it. But that's not why you're here—you're here for some fresh fear. Well, dear reader, that's exactly what's in store. *Fresh Fear* is a tour de force in both scope and variety, comprised of voices both old and new the world over, striking a fine balance between tradition and innovation. Here we have a dreamy mingling of the real and the unreal, the natural and the supernatural, the sane and the insane. There is something for everyone in this collection, and it is my distinct pleasure to help raise the curtain on it. Happy reading.

– W.J. Renehan
(editor at Dark Hall Press)

J. F. GONZALEZ

LOVE HURTS

I suppose it really all started one evening late at work when, during a break, conversation drifted to the greatest unsolved crime in the history of Los Angeles: the murder and mutilation of Elizabeth Short, also known as The Black Dahlia.

The reason this came up was because one of our co-workers, a guy named Brian Denison, told us about a case his brother was working on regarding the litigation between the city of Santa Ana and the Board of Directors of the old Laguna State Mental Hospital. The Hospital, which had been closed and abandoned for what seems like forever, had been converted into an industrial warehouse that was hardly ever used and was largely abandoned.

In its heyday, Laguna Hospital housed only the seriously mentally ill; the real crazies, the people who mutilated themselves, the psychos. It had been built in the late 1930's far enough away from Los Angeles at the time to give the citizens of that city some relief that the crazies were far away. It continued to operate as the urban sprawl spread south and eventually surrounded the hospital. Now it's closed, the building all but condemned. The city was trying to close the building down for good—they wanted to raze the place and give the go ahead for another mini-mall to be erected. Brian's brother had given him the sordid history of the place, and that's when the subject changed to the murder of the Black Dahlia.

If you don't know much about the annals of true crime, here's the story in a nutshell: in early January of 1947, Elizabeth Short, a 22 year old woman who had drifted to Los Angeles from Massachusetts to be an actress, was last seen at the Biltmore hotel. She made a few phone calls, then exited the hotel and walked down the street. She was never seen alive again.

A passerby discovered her five days later. Lying just a few feet from the sidewalk in a vacant lot off 39thth and Norton in Los Angeles, Elizabeth Short's body had been cleanly cut in half. The killer had posed the body with both parts resting just a few feet from each other. Her legs were spread in an obscene invitation. There were numerous slash wounds on her body. Her ankles and wrists bore rope burns, suggesting she was tortured horribly while bound. The most ghastly wound, aside from the severing of her torso, were the deep cuts from the tips of her mouth all the way to her ears, making a grim smile. In 1947 the murder of Elizabeth Short was the media sensation of the day. Over fifty years later the murder remains officially unsolved.

What does all this have to do with Laguna State Mental Hospital? What does it all have to do with the story I am going to tell you, which is essentially my relationship with Susan Thompson, my co-worker? What does it all have to do with why I do what I do?

As Brian explained, legend has it that Laguna Mental Hospital housed only the most dangerous, most psychotic patients. He later learned that a mental patient by the name of Victor Johnson, who was committed to Laguna Mental Hospital in 1962 for the mutilation murder of a twelve-year-old boy, claimed to have killed Elizabeth Short. Reading about what Victor Johnson had done to the boy made him a prime suspect for Short's unofficially unsolved death in Brian's book: he liked to torture and kill young women, girls, and boys, filming the atrocities on a super 8 millimeter camera. The police apparently found 25 such reels of 8-millimeter film in Victor's house.

Remember that. It becomes important later on.

Like I said before, it really started when Brian related that story, but the wheels didn't really grind into motion until Susan Thompson and I had already become lovers.

We were both working for a large consulting firm, and we were stationed in the high rise offices of our latest client, a large international financial firm. Susan and I were thrown in together as teammates, and we spent countless late nights in the office going over data sheets and flow charts while we wolfed down endless cartoons of take-out Chinese and junk food. I liked her the moment I met her. She was pretty, with large brown eyes and dark chestnut hair that fell to her shoulders. She stood about five foot five and was petite, favoring fashionable, but conservative business suits. She looked like she could have been a cheerleader in high school. And her personality? Not bubbly, but lively with laughter. She was great to work with, and more fun in a social setting. Sometimes after work we went out to a nice little piano bar on Jamboree Road where we would sit and talk until well after midnight, sipping drinks and picking at complimentary munchies. It was a good way to relieve the stress in our high-pressure corporate lives.

Like I said, for two years Susan and I were friends, nothing more, nothing less. We became really close, like surrogate brother and sister, really. She had family in Kansas, and she had few friends in Orange County where she had moved upon completing her MBA. I know she flew home for holidays like Thanksgiving and Christmas, and that she treated herself to a three-week vacation every summer in Hawaii, but beyond that her life was devoted to her work as a Financial Analyst for the firm. I was identical to her in many ways. It was inevitable that we later became lovers.

It happened late one night in the conference room where we were working. Normally we worked with a team of at least three other people who stayed as late as we did. On this night, though, we were alone. We were sitting at the table crunching numbers and I leaned back in my seat. I was tired. Susan stopped typing into her laptop and looked at me. "We've really put a lot into this phase of the project today. What you need is a massage."

"You can say that again," I said.

Susan stood up. "Come with me." Intrigued, I followed her out of the conference room and down the hall to the darkened executive lounge. Once there, Susan made me lie belly down on the plush sofa where she began to massage my aching shoulders. It felt great and I groaned in pleasure. She smiled down at me. "Another little tidbit you are just learning. I used to be a massage therapist in college."

To make a long story short, one thing led to another. We began talking more, relaxing more together, and then I gave *her* a shoulder massage. The atmosphere seemed to be just right, and before we knew it we were making love. I think it took me by surprise as much as it did her.

Susan appeared to regret it almost immediately after we slipped back into our clothes. She smiled in the darkness. "That was nice, Jeff. Really, it was, but—"

"I know," I said, thinking the same thing. "You don't have the time to get into a relationship."

She nodded, her lips set in a frown. "I hope you understand."

"I do." I tried to smile to reassure her. "And it's fine with me. Hell, I don't have time for a relationship, either."

"Just because I don't have time to commit to a relationship doesn't mean that changes my feelings toward you, Jeff," Susan said, touching my arm. "You're my best friend."

"I feel the same way."

She smiled. "And I had a great time."

Confessing to each other that we didn't have time for a committed, normal relationship but that we still respected the hell out of each other as friends and that we enjoyed the sex made it easier to become lovers. Susan was my fourth lover ever; in fact, I had only lost my virginity two years before. I know that's weird in this day and age—losing one's virginity in your mid-twenties—but I had always been shy around women when I was younger. In fact, I was always nervous around them. I was picked on a lot as a kid in school, and as a result always had an inferiority complex. I was the perennial geek in school that nobody wanted to bother with. In fact, I suspect that the woman who took my virginity (who was twelve years my senior and an executive at a banking firm I did some consulting with) did it as a mercy fuck. The other three were women I'd met in bars after gaining a little self-confidence in myself, and to tell you the truth, I didn't see what was so exciting about sex once I had it.

Susan and I had sex again the following night and it was more intense this second time. I could feel her nails digging into my back as she urged me on. Afterward we lay in a crumpled heap on the floor of the executive suite, catching our breath. I reached out and touched her; it was like touching a live wire. We looked at each other in the darkened suite, and I think we both knew then that we had crossed that barrier. This was turning into something more than just a casual, carnal relationship. The question was, how far would it go?

The following night was a Friday, and instead of staying late at the office we took our work to her apartment, a luxury high-rise in Newport Beach. When we had sex again, this time in the comfort of her king-sized four-poster bed, we did so in darkness.

Our bodies and souls came together that night in an orgy of ecstasy. When it was over I held her in my arms and kissed her shoulder where I had bitten her (she had actually begged me to bite her while we were having sex, and I was so wild with lust that I complied—she loved it!), and she sighed. "Sorry I hurt you," I said.

"You didn't hurt me." She turned to me and kissed me. "It felt great. I loved it."

"Yeah?"

She nodded, her dark eyes deep and penetrating, gazing into mine. "Have you ever had intense sex and afterwards noticed bite marks on your neck of which you had no memory?"

I thought about it. To tell you the truth, I hadn't, but I wasn't going to tell her *that*. "Aren't those, like, hickeys?"

"In a way. What happened was your love partner bit you, hard enough that it bruised you, and all you felt was another jolt of pleasure. If they bit you that hard when you *weren't* having sex, you would scream 'ouch!' because it would hurt. But when you are sexually aroused your pain tolerance goes way up, and stimulation that you usually feel as pain is now actually pleasurable."

"I never thought of it that way."

"Another usual explanation is that the brain produces endorphins, natural opiates, to compensate for pain. You actually get high off the sensation. It's the same rush you get after eating chili peppers. It all comes from the same source, and that's what makes it enjoyable for S&M players to be whipped or spanked or whatever. It's not pain, it's pleasure."

A thought occurred to me then. "Have you ever … participated in S&M?"

She wouldn't answer me that night. She merely smiled and kissed me, snuggling closer to me. "Let's just say I've had some experiences and I really enjoyed them."

I left it at that. Still, there was a part of me that had been excited about what we had done.

I noticed the next morning that Susan was very apprehensive

about allowing me to see her nude. She was dressed in a robe, standing in the kitchen making pancakes. She turned down my request that we shower together and instead pointed the way to the second full bathroom on the other side of the apartment. I shrugged and walked naked to the living room couch, gathered up my clothes and headed for the shower, puzzled by her refusal.

The puzzlement grew as the day progressed. We had about nine hours of work to do to complete the first phase of our project for Monday morning, and we worked out of her apartment that afternoon. It was a nice warm day, and Susan opened the windows of the apartment, letting in a cool ocean breeze. I went_home quickly for a change of clothes and returned wearing a pair of shorts and a tank top. Susan was dressed in shorts and a T-shirt that covered up too much of her body for such a nice day. I didn't think much of it until later that night when we were together in her darkened bedroom under the covers.

She was laboring over me, leaning her breasts in my face and begging me to slap her ass. Exhilarated and strangely turned on by her request, I did. I kept slapping her ass until my hand stung. She came with a shuddering gasp and collapsed on top of me. We both lay like that for a while, catching our breath.

"Sorry about that," I said as she rolled off of me.

"For what?" She rolled onto her back.

"I slapped you pretty hard. I'm surprised you can lie down on your ass after that."

She grinned at me. "Remember what I told you last night? The rush you get from pain in conjunction with sex? Come on, you were into it as much as I was."

I grinned back. "I guess I got a little carried away."

"See? Our chemistry is working together to form a synchronized fusion of energy. You're a natural dom for someone like me."

"Dom?"

Susan sat up in bed. Without my glasses on, I could make

out a fuzz y image of her smiling face. The rest of her was blurry. "Maybe I should rephrase that. You're as much a bottom as I am, but you're having a hell of a time playing the sadist. In fact, I think you've been a dominatrix for a long time but you've never known it." She touched my arm. "Don't you see, Jeff? We were meant for each other. I never thought I'd be saying this, but—"

I stopped her with a kiss. "I love you."

That sealed it. We spent the rest of the evening expressing our love to each other. It even got a little rougher sex-wise. Susan had to encourage me to go forward, but whenever I complied I felt this rush that helped carry me on. Hearing her scream in ecstasy rather than pain boosted my confidence that I wasn't hurting her seriously. She really enjoyed the pain. And I found that I was enjoying it as well. Although I couldn't admit it at the time, I was beginning to get excited by dominating her and inflicting pain on her.

Three hours later we were lying in a sweaty stupor. It was probably well after midnight and my fingertips traced patterns on Susan's belly. She rolled over and sat up on her side of the bed, looking toward me. "You meant what you said when you told me you loved me, right?"

I nodded.

"Put your glasses on." She reached slowly to the lamp by the nightstand on her side of the bed and flicked it on. I blinked as I put my glasses on, slightly dazed by the sudden intrusion of light, and then by what I saw. It's strange how lack of light and being near-sighted will fail to make you notice certain things about a person.

The skin along Susan's back looked like one big scar. It was paler than her normal skin tone, and puffy in spots. The scarring went all the way from her ass to just below the shoulder blades. She turned around and my eyes widened in shock. Her entire torso was covered with the same scarring, less so around her breasts, but heavily scarred around her stomach and groin. The scarring was so bad she looked like a burn victim.

I tried to hide my revulsion, but it was painfully obvious what my reaction was. She smiled at me and took my hand. "It's okay," she said softly. "In time you will come to understand."

I somehow found my voice. "Were you in an accident?"

She shook her head. "No." Then she smiled and I suddenly knew. It was in her eyes, the way she told me that pain was pleasurable, and I knew how she had gotten so scarred up. I wanted to heal her from the self-abusive part of herself, but part of me was also strangely turned on by what I saw. I imagined myself scarring her like that. She must have noticed it turned me on; she glanced down at my rising cock.

"Kiss me, Jeff." She stretched her body out, offering herself to me. "Kiss me."

And I did. I moved toward her and tenderly kissed her scar-ridden body.

As horrified as I initially was, I was also strangely excited. Our getting together was really a godsend. For if it wasn't for Susan I would still be this shy, inhibited creature afraid of my own shadow. And I would still be holding my own yearnings in.

You see, before I met Susan I was repressed. Taught at an early age by my parents that sex was wrong, that it was only for procreation, warped me at some point in my adolescence. I had normal sexual urges, but I felt guilty whenever they arose due to my upbringing. I would relieve my urgings through masturbation. Because of my fear of the opposite sex, and because of my upbringing, I never pursued relationships with women; I was constantly afraid I would be laughed at, rejected. Don't get me wrong: my parents never beat me, they never abused me in any way, but they did have a way with getting their message across. Knowing I had let my parents down, that they were disappointed in me, was probably the greatest punishment of all when I was a child. And when they taught me their values about sex and other issues, I was already hard-wired to not disappoint them in this area. It was the fear of bringing home a girl they wouldn't approve of, or of getting a girl pregnant, that kept me from fully acting out my sexual urges. I never felt in control of myself. I never felt that I had power over my urges and my feelings. Instead I let it all bottle up inside, letting it transform me into a complete workaholic.

It was at this moment when I finally admitted to myself that the fantasies I sometimes had from adolescence till the time I met Susan were really fantasies I *wanted* to have. The fantasies in question involved me dominating every single woman or girl that turned me on in high school, college, and the few years after I obtained my MBA. Sometimes I had fantasies about doing similar things to men, but men don't excite me sexually; the only way I get turned on by homoerotic thoughts is if I'm torturing another man. I had tried to deny I was thinking such thoughts. I thought that I could never act on them—normal people didn't give in to such urges, much less have them. So for ten years I would occasionally think about what it would be like to strangle the head cheerleader of the high school football team, or castrate the homecoming king and stuff his cock down his throat, or cut my secretary's fingertips off with a paring knife and force-feed them to her. And then I would deny that such thoughts excited me. I didn't realize that inflicting pain on these people would be like music to my ears.

As our relationship progressed, it got wilder and wilder. Susan drew me out of my shell; she encouraged me to experiment, and with her at my side lovingly encouraging me, I did. Somehow, I knew that as long as I had her that she wouldn't let anything happen to me. I was safe with her. I later came to realize that this is what true S&M is: the complete surrender and trusting of your body and emotions to another person. I came to realize it was the truest expression of love I have ever experienced. I no longer saw it as deviant sex practiced by perverts. Of course what I'm describing to you now … if a regular S&M practitioner were to hear this they would be horrified. What I'm describing—the whole extreme hardcore scene—is a very brutal, very underground scene within the S&M world. Most S&M players are either ignorant of the more forbidden aspects of the extreme hardcore world, or they don't want to admit it exists. But it's there. The more you get into S&M, the more you dig into its various sub-cultures - you'll soon start finding people that are into some pretty extreme shit.

Our work schedules stayed pretty much the same, only now we were an item. We hid this very well from our co-workers, but alone we were a couple. We didn't need to send each other roses, or exchange rings like everybody else did to proclaim our love to each other. We just knew. And with that knowledge came power, both in our personal lives and in our unity as a couple.

Our sex life accelerated into something I had never experienced before and never knew existed. Previously, I was merely content to play my part in a wham-bam-thank-you-ma'am role. I suppose most guys are. With Susan I was becoming more confident in myself, and in pushing the limits with her. Our sessions accelerated rapidly until we were getting into some heavy stuff, things I wouldn't have even imagined participating in. She demanded that I hit her harder, bite her harder, whip her harder. And I complied. The harder our sessions got, the more I would feel that I shouldn't be doing this, that what I was doing was wrong, but then Susan would coax me on. "You can do it," she'd purr up at me, her limbs tied to the bed on her hands and knees, barring her red ass at me. Her eyes gleamed at me. "Use me and abuse me. I *want* you to do it, Jeff!"

And the more she pulled me in, the more I found myself liking what I was doing to her.

We began having regular intercourse less and less. It never really did much for me anyway.

But what we did together? Me playing the sadist to Susan's masochistic fantasies?

That's what got me off.

She introduced me to the underground extreme hardcore scene. She explained that it was at such functions, usually held in private homes, where she had to go to be satisfied sexually. I was apprehensive at my first party, but in time relaxed around the other couples, people who shared my desires. Susan introduced me to an underground hardcore porn filmmaker named Alex Johnson who sometimes filmed the parties for private video collections. He looked like he could have been one of our senior executives. A real friendly guy, though. He even asked me permission if he could film Susan and I. By then I was feeling totally uninhibited and thought *why not?*

Her first earth shattering orgasm with me was when she introduced me to blood sports. It was also the first time I seriously thought we were going over the edge. She opened a slim, mahogany case that was lined with red crushed velvet and showed me the scalpel. "Just make a small cut on the top layer of the skin on my lower back," she said, flopping her nude body down on her stomach. She turned back to me. "But first, I want you to do what I love to do most."

She really had to pull this out of me. First I tied her up, then I inserted a ball gag in her mouth. I flogged her back, and she cried out in pain and pleasure. I teased her pussy with my fingers as I whipped her and she writhed in excitement. Then came the *coup de grace*. She signaled for me to take the gag out and she panted. "Cut me! Do it now!"

I don't know what possessed me to do it, but I did. I drew the scalpel along her back, slicing into her skin effortlessly. As I cut I kept my fingers inside her and she had the most earth shattering orgasm I've ever seen any woman have. Then she cried. I thought she was crying because I had hurt her, and as I untied her I kept whispering "I'm sorry" over and over. I realize now as I'm telling you this that I was apologizing to her because it was something I felt I should do; inside, I knew that's what she wanted. In fact, I wanted to cut her some more. Cutting her had turned me on tremendously.

"Oh Jeff," she said, melting into my arms, kissing my face.

"You were so good. You did that to me so good."

That cut on her back was the first I put on her, and it wouldn't be the last. This session represented another milestone, and she pledged her undying love to me even more now. In her eyes I was the man of her dreams. She would have no other. She began to open herself up more, and for the first time she shared her past experiences with me that night in bed. "I've been into the raptures of pain for so long now, I can't count the years. I don't know why I enjoy it, but I do. My parents didn't abuse me, daddy didn't try to have his way with me, I never had abusive boyfriends. I just enjoy pain."

She told me about the people she had met at the underground parties like the one she had taken me to. "We were simply feeding off each other, a symbiosis if you will. They needed something from me, and I needed something from them. Only I had to get what I needed from the more hardcore freaks, the people who are into mutilation. The more I played out scenes with them, the more hardcore it got for me. Now it's to the point that I can't really get off unless it's *really* hardcore." She pulled the covers down over her belly and pointed to a large scar that ran from her belly button to just below her breasts. "See this scar? I got that from a burn. Most people who are into heat playing won't burn the skin due to the danger, but it just wasn't doing anything for me. I had to literally scream at my partner to put the flame on my skin and hold it there while my other partner fucked my ass with a dildo." She smiled at me. "Next to tonight, that was the best fuck I ever had."

I thought about the people I met at the underground parties we attended, the scenes we witnessed them playing out. I remember watching as a man in a black leather hood drew blood from his partner with a syringe and then fed it to her; I thought about what it would be like to be him. I remember watching a gay couple, the dom cutting his bottom with a scalpel and then sucking the blood from the wound as his slave writhed in pleasure—I wondered what the slave's blood tasted like. I thought about the extreme hardcore films that were screened, watching women scream in pain as their doms pulled at their pierced labias, stretching the fragile skin to the point that the skin began to stretch and bleed and they began to beg for mercy—I imagined myself as the dominatrix, doing that to a slave. I thought about the first snuff film I saw at the last party we attended in which a young black girl, who looked like a homeless junkie, was fucked to death with a baseball bat in an abandoned warehouse; I had watched with bated breath, unable to take my eyes from the screen, imagining myself doing what her killer was doing.

I thought about the rush I was now getting by satisfying Susan, and how good it made me feel, the rush of power it gave me when I tortured her. And then I thought about the story Brian Denison told us and the man Laguna State Mental Hospital had once housed. Had he felt this same pleasure? Was this what drove him to do what he did?

What finally broke it off with us was what happened six months or so into our relationship. After that last session things got even heavier. I was enjoying it more. When I cut her skin with the scalpel and she screamed in a mixture of pain and ecstasy, it made me feel good. When I brought the whip down on her back again and again, making new scars on her already scar-ridden body, her cries brought shudders of pleasure through me. When I branded my name into her flesh with a hot piece of metal and she literally passed out from the intensity of the orgasm, I felt an extreme sense of power. And it was a *good* power. I've never had power over anything in my life before, and with her giving me blanket permission to indulge in her freely, knowing it pleased her so much, gave me a sense of empowerment I never thought I would feel. It seemed to unlock all the inhibitions I had been holding inside myself. Susan changed me, irrevocably, forever.

What happened later occurred at the end of a particularly brutal session. I had tied her up to a pair of hooks constructed in the ceiling of her apartment and had gone crazy on her. She was swinging back and forth, her body bruised and bloody, a smile on her face. She looked down at me as I lay on the floor on the blood and sweat drenched plastic tarp I had placed there, trying to catch my breath. "Take me down," she said. "I want to tell you something."

"What?"

She kissed me softly, then nuzzled close to me. "What I have to tell you I've never told anybody except one other man, that film maker I introduced you to. It's a fantasy of mine, but it's a fantasy I only want to do with the man that I love. You're that man, Jeff."

I looked at her and knew she was speaking the truth. She leaned closer to me and whispered her fantasy in my ear.

That's what broke us up. I couldn't do what she wanted me to do. That was my first reaction. I also wanted to satisfy her, because what she wanted was something I *wanted* to do.

But then balking at her wishes had always been my first reaction. I always stepped over that line later, after much coaxing from her. She tried to draw me out that night by explaining that I was the only man who could grant her this ultimate pleasure and I refused to listen. I got angry. I got up and reached for my clothes, dressing as she rose to her feet and followed me, pleading with me to hear her out. But she had gone too far. What she was asking—I could never do that. If I did what she wanted, it would be over; no longer would I have an outlet for what I had come to find as pleasurable. As I left her apartment the last thing I heard were her sobs; it was the crying of a broken-hearted woman.

The next two weeks passed slowly, almost dreamlike. We continued seeing each other at work, but we weren't social at all. Where before we always sat together around the big conference table at meetings, now we poised ourselves on opposite ends, barely even glancing at each other. Susan had a hurt, wounded look to her; betrayal. That look got to me; I had hurt her in a place worse than I had hurt her through all our S&M play.

Where I had hurt her would scar much deeper than the scars along her back and stomach. She had opened her soul to me and I had shattered it. Wounding the soul was always more devastating than wounds of the flesh.

That's really what decided it for me. I loved her very deeply. Thinking of how much I had hurt her was painful to me.

But I also wanted to grant her wish. I wanted to experience the power.

When I called her late one night at her apartment two Fridays later, she sounded surprised to hear from me. I thought she was going to hang up on me but I told her I had a birthday present for her—she turned thirty that Saturday. I told her if she wanted her present that she was to go to an address in Santa Ana the following day at two p.m. I would be on the second floor, in the back. I gave her detailed directions. Then I told her I loved her, and I hung up.

I can still see the smile on her face when she walked into that abandoned asylum on the outer fringes of Santa Ana, what had once been Laguna State Mental Hospital. Thanks to some discreet investigation on my part, I got a very detailed map of the hospital, and from that map gave Susan and her old S&M acquaintance Alex Johnson a call and passed that information on.

I know Susan must have remembered the story Brian told us about Laguna State Mental Hospital, because when she walked into what had probably once been the recreation room of the facility and saw me, she smiled. I was wearing a pair of black leather chaps, my ass exposed to the wind. I wore a black leather vest over my shirtless body, a black leather hood over my head. There was an old mattress placed in the center of the room, laid out on top of a large roll of plastic tarp. A table stood nearby with knives of assorted sizes and sharpness. Alex Johnson hefted the camcorder up on his shoulder. He looked at me and nodded. "I'm ready to roll whenever you are."

I'm sure it was hard for her to see it, but Susan knew I was smiling beneath the hooded mask. "Happy Birthday, honey."

And now I have it all on tape; her final, most pleasurable orgasm ever. I paid Alex ten thousand dollars for the privilege and the secrecy. I watch me and Susan playing out our scene on tape every night. And the more her screams of pain echo in my ears, and the more I sit on the couch with my eyes riveted to her last few torturous moments on earth, the more happy I am that I was able to give Susan her one last wish: to be tortured to death in a snuff film, so her final moments of pleasures will live on.

Granting Susan this one last wish was also my breakthrough. Watching it over and over in the months following her death gave me a power I never thought I could imagine. I now live for nothing else but fulfilling my desires. My high profile position as a consultant, the money and prestige that comes with it doesn't matter now. I still go to work every day and do my job well, but it is no longer the beacon of my life the way it once was. Apparently it never was with Susan, either, for she had known this day would come eventually. I found her letter of resignation on her computer the day after I immortalized her and I knew what to do with it. I printed it, dated it, scrawled a perfect imitation of her signature, and mailed it to corporate headquarters. Then I took care of her things. To everybody at the office, she just suddenly quit for no apparent reason and moved back to the mid-west.

But she's always with me, immortalized on videotape. And she has joined many others. Thanks to Susan, and in a way thanks to Alex Johnson, I'm now hooked. I had the next one lined up six months later. She was a sixteen-year-old runaway I met in Hollywood. I brought her to my place to sleep off a heroin binge in my spare bedroom. You see, I found a few others who share this new fetish of mine. I'm not alone. Thanks to them, and some other people in the circle who are well-off financially who actually pay for this stuff, I was able to indulge six months later. I raped and slashed that sixteen-year-old runaway deep in the bowels of the Laguna State Mental Hospital. An executive for a large HMO bought it. He and people like him all over the world have bought and paid for the privilege of watching other films I've been in. They'll pay a handsome price for the privilege of watching another person be hacked to death, or to listen to their pain-wracked screams.

It gives you a strange sense of power.

SCATHE MEIC BEORH

GOD OF THE WINDS

The world is a predator, yet some places prove friendlier than others. Ireland, for instance, with all of its blood and sorrows, brings a comfort in its woesome gales that I have found the American West never to afford. The lords of the two lands do not know one another, both rising from the places they serve, and remaining constant in those arenas. The kings of Ireland (a green place of wet terror) are made cordial through humble service to the land and its people. The Mesa Lords of northern New Mexico rage fierce, and dry, and require an affronting ferocity to appease them—if such strength is available. I was in no way prepared for that which would unfold as these rulers took fresh lie of their land, discovered me, and set forth to challenge my presence.

I had temporarily relocated from my home in Hollywood to Mora, New Mexico, in an effort to escape a vampiric relationship where I had become the selfish aggressor—and to study the shamanism of the *Greasy Eye Cavities of the Skull* clan of Hopi; the extinct *Wikurswungwa*. I arrived on a nameless ranch the day after Halloween. The snows had already come—intermittently, but heavy, and wet when they fell.

Mora is not particularly known better than any other place for Hopi shamanism. It is, however, one of the more silent places of the continent, where bloodshed cries out in its meek way still, but the whir and stir of humanity is altogether absent. This is the land of the *mesas verde*—the great, green tables once mountains in times not remembered. An unparalleled climate for sustained academic research, and potential healing of the heart and mind.

"Here today, gone to Mora," I said to no one as I popped the lock on the heavy front door of my log house and entered the dark main room that smelled of cinnamon and pine. I laughed at myself, then said the phrase again as I rolled the 'r,' and adopted it as my motto. I soon had the hearth roaring and inviting, and a cast iron pot of curried lentils bubbling away on the wood-burning stove.

After a restful third night's sleep, I arose at dawn, dressed in warm clothing, and hiked the five miles to the abandoned monastery where the bravest of the Spanish monks had crucified themselves in the attempt to make the Hopi and other local natives understand their message. During this *épouvante*, hundreds of Indians were baptized into the Faith. Because of this, it was thought that the monks were being effective in the sharing of their religion…until it was discovered, some years later, that the long-awaited Hopi savior, *Bahana*, comparable to the Aztec *Ehécatl*, was a crucified sun-god who had required no human sacrifice—and that the Indians believed the monks to be emissaries of their beloved lord. Nevertheless, the Catholic authorities continued with their missionary work, heathen salvation not their actual goal, but power through land and populace ownership. The natives made good, humble slaves in the name of the Lord Jesus Christ.

It began with the chimney swifts. I noticed them flocking in unusual numbers to the ranch. At the same time, blustery currents of air, warmer than the November temperatures, commenced. I knew, though, that these New Mexican *chinooks* were animated with something more than air currents.

After the winds began in earnest, at night I would recline on my longsettle near the fireplace, done with my studies for the day, and listen to them howling down from the nearest mesa like feral creatures on the hunt. Too often I allowed myself to fall beneath their enchantment, and became so unnerved that warm milk infused with valerian extract was all that would calm me.

I began finding the glassy-eyed bodies of the swifts, untouched by hawks and unmolested by beetles and other scavengers, their wings fully outstretched. There were dead swifts by the river. I also found them scattered around the barn garret, behind my house near the generator, inside the outhouse, and, yes, in the chimney (when suddenly the flue wasn't working properly). Each bird died in the shape of a cross, with a worm in its mouth—the international icon of the sun-god…the eagle with the serpent in its beak.

One crisp morning, just after a new snow, I fueled up on 'cowboy coffee' and rock-hopped across the greenish-clear river to get a better look at an ancient juniper clawing the sky like a severed hand.

There is something about the way the piñon-juniper landscape smells after is has been moistened. It comes to life—all the fresh conifers and red earth activated by water. *Zesty* might best describe it, like sea spray or sitting by a waterfall—a secret of the high desert only unlocked by a cold rain, or wet snow.

When I stepped from the river into the fresh snowfall, with no warning my legs turned to rubber, and breathing became difficult, as if the wind had been knocked out of me. The brisk, sunny day became overcast as if gargantuan fingers covered it, and the Mesa Kings, who had previously come with their most forcible antics after dusk, began to roar down from the heights with such velocity that I was forced to lean into them to stay upright.

As I fought for balance with my newborn legs, fallow earth surrounding the old juniper began to rupture and push upward, shifting and swirling, forming a maelstrom of stinging sand, snow, and natural debris. From the loosened, flying dirt emerged carrion talons, and human digits, and undersea feelers, and waving antennae.

Then, breaking the surface of the land, around and around the juniper as if swimming, or drowning, moved creatures dead, and dying, and things of bone—howling like starving felines as they swam. The lacerated heads of those still wearing flesh oozed, open and raw—and as they moved in a quickly increasing diameter, they reached for my feet with their appendages.

One gruesome humanoid, smelling of rotten meat and trailing a matted, black mane behind him, leered at me with yellow lemur eyes as he passed. I was struck by his evil gaze, crumbled, and went down. I was then yanked into the hideous multitude by a corvusian deathling trailing my vascanian assailant.

Fire and ice tore into my right kidney, and then my left, soon filling my flanks with molten agony. Feeling as if I were being torn asunder by the monsters that were now punctured children, now quivering hags in their death throes, I writhed and screamed and kicked, but my aggression only caused more of them to sidle toward me, grab me, and pull me into the cold, disturbed earth. My mouth filled with sand and gore. I choked, and purged. The lemur-eyed thing mounted me then, gyrating as we bathed in the whirling charnel. The undulating ground then opened, and I plummeted with those ministers of horror into a dank, pitch blackness.

I awoke dazed. As I held my throbbing head, I saw that I lay alone in a room of indiscernible size, as the place was illuminated by one candle set in an earthenware dish three paces away. Panicking, I checked myself over to see how badly I had been clawed, and bitten. My fingers pushed into a thick death-smelling seepage that I knew was not my own, and I gagged. Relieved that my unwanted companions had deserted me, I pulled to my feet, stumbled, took up the candle, and began a slow exploration.

I had not crept far into the gloam of the building when I knew that I was, indeed, underground. Twisted tree roots pushing down from above decorated the walls like heathen serpentine icons. Water dripping from them formed intricate webbing designs as it trailed away to the floor. Was I in a *kiva* of some sort? Though not as cleanly designed as those I had witnessed before, soon enough I saw that the place was something akin to the *kiva*—the underground ceremonial room of the Hopi—for to my right I discovered a wooden table whereupon three *kachina* dolls had been displayed: a *Wiharu*, a *Soyoko*, and a *Nata-aska*. Oddly enough, this display disturbed me as deeply as had my convulsions beneath the juniper, for these are the evil spirits of the Hopi.

"*Taaqa.*"

I jumped backward at the voice, inadvertently blowing out my candle. My spine iced over. I could see nothing—not even my fingers which I brought up only centimeters from my eyes.

"*Taaqa.*"

The voice was addressing me in Hopi, as *man.*

"*Taaqa!*"

"I…I don't speak…I…"

"*Taaqa.*"

"I don't speak Hopi…I maybe *should*, but I…"

"Well, you speak *something*, you filthy dog!"

I clamored sideways, searching for where the root-covered wall to my left had been. It was not where I remembered. I fell, cracking my wrist on the solid clay floor. The pain was excruciating. I knew I had fractured my ulna.

"*Taaqa.* Welcome to Flesh-House."

I froze, not knowing how to answer the voice. I patted the immediate area for my candle, but it was gone. I then felt something warm, and wet, and reached around me to see what I had fallen into. I didn't know until I lifted my fingers to my face. The metallic scent of new menstrual blood.

I rolled away, only to thump against something solid, yet soft. Knowing intuitively what I had hit, I screamed, and as I did so, as if my voice were some kind of light switch, a yellow glow interrupted the darkness, and I saw my verbal assailant: a baboon.

I screeched like a child on a playground. Survival instinct alive and electric, I threw myself behind the body.

No. Could it be? At first I saw it to be Miriam, the woman I had been with in Hollywood, her large violet eyes unmistakable. She was bloodless and dying, and beckoning to me with her full lips, yet no sound came from them. Then I saw her to be a beautiful Indian girl who had been tortured by having her hands cut off. Or had they been gnawed away? I could not tell. I vomited my breakfast over her shoulder and long raven hair, wiped it away from her face, told her I was sorry, and collapsed, hanging over her waist, spent and laughing. I laughed so hard. I laughed, and then I wept, and then I laughed again. A voice from inside me said I was losing my mind, but I didn't care. The scene was horribly hilarious; deliciously demented.

Then my thoughts turned downward. Should I strip the girl and gloat upon her obvious loveliness? Should I penetrate her (with my abrupt, throbbing erection) and so give my soul fully to all that is debased in the world? Should I then eat her after our thanatophilia? Bite off her nipples? Chew at her pudendum filled with my salty gift? I didn't know. I climbed upon her and pushed on her solar plexus. She expectorated blood, which I kissed away from her before I roared, horrified, a madman now. A lunatic. I lay there thrilled, and revolted, and terrified. I felt my core temperature cooling, my body shaking. I was freezing to death. I was dying. In

Hell.

"Leave the girl, *taaqa*," the baboon said as he blinked sightless grey eyes. "Leave her or do your desires, you foul thing. This is Flesh-House. Your will is your command."

My will is my command? What did he mean?

"Frig the girl, flay the girl, or flee the girl," the beast said as he ambled over, took one of her stumps in his hands and pushed it between his lips, sucking. "This is Flesh-House. Your will is your command. Get up. Stop being so indulgent, or you'll die where you lay, *taaqa*."

Of a sudden I was sane again, or so I thought. I knew that I was warm again. I stood, the blind baboon turned, and we walked together toward the source of the egg-yellow light.

I awoke in my bed crying out for Miriam, wet with sweat though the night outside had grown frigid.

"My god, what a nightmare," I remember saying, and all day long I was disturbed by the infernal visions remaining fresh in my memory. As before, valerian root tea was the only thing I found to sufficiently calm me for sleep again that night.

"You've returned, my fiend," said the benighted monster. "This is good. Let us continue our walk, will we?"

I screamed, thrashed about in my bed, and clawed at my eyes, trying to gouge them out.

"You silly little *taaqa*," the simian said. "Believing blindness to be a deterrent to the visions. Keep your eyesight. You are already damned. This is Flesh-House. Follow me."

I followed the beast, who moved as if sighted, and as we walked, he somehow became the dead girl. I was ashamed, and held back. She sought to gather me to her, to help me along, but her bleeding stumps could only grab me like kitchen tongs. I pulled away from her, mewing like a kitten, which only further shamed me. She held me tighter, yanking me toward her. She then kissed the corner of my mouth, her pretty upturned nose brushing mine, her big black eyes wet and shining.

"You are mortified by your base thoughts toward me?"

"Yes, Miriam," I said, but I knew she wasn't Miriam.

"Have power over your mind. You are its lord and king. Ready yourself now. We enter the Hall of Pleasures."

We squeezed through a slimy passage allowing us only to turn sideways as we went, the girl ahead of me. I found that I had hold of the long braid she now wore—like Miriam had worn. As I tugged, she moaned as if in great pleasure. Though I fought it, I again became aroused, and imagined her doing things to me with her stubs.

"You have an iniquitous soul," she said as we pushed through the tight corridor. "You would sleep with your own mother, and beg her to call you daddy."

I said nothing in reply, but I flushed with shame and went rigid with horror and anger. I shut my eyes against the fresh knowledge of my deviant lechery. When I opened them again, we were in a room reminding me of a hospital ward, but the beds were stone slabs carved with deep blood-catches and serpentine drains, like those found at Peruvian Wari sacrificial sites.

"What is this place?" I heard myself ask. The Indian girl pushed a bleeding limb to my lips and held it there until I wretched. As I wiped my mouth on my shirtsleeve, before us, on the dozen tables, there appeared apparitions of sacrifice victims. I turned to the girl, questioning this scene. I wish I had not, for behind her loomed a coven of translucent, hollow-eyed things.

"What..." was all I could say. She turned.

"Oh. Those are the Old Seers. They are the most potent humans on Earth. Or at least they *were*. Their abode is Flesh-House, and from here they move outward, to usurp energy from those unaware. Their time of gleaning is dusk. Only the impeccable warrior can defeat them."

Forgetting—or not caring—that my guide was hideous

without her hands, I pulled close to her. Hot tears streamed down my face.

"They will not harm you while I am here," she said. "Look," and she pointed a ragged wrist to the row of slabs.

I turned away from the Old Seers, and as I watched, the vague shapes of the sacrifice victims took on bone, and then flesh, and soon lay whole and shuddering in the cold of the evil room.

Then from the plant roots crawling down the walls slithered black vipers that, as they came to the floor, morphed into endowed nude priests wielding curved knives of obsidian. Nodding to me as if I were somehow part of their ceremony; each of them then climbed upon the slab and penetrated his prey with his engorged equine-like phallus. I stood aghast, unable to turn away from the debauchery as the orgy reached a heightened frenzy. The moment each pair climaxed together, the priest plunged his knife into the abdomen of his partner, twisted it, and laid his mouth upon that of his lover—I assume in order to catch all of the escaping life essence.

"Hide your face, you whore," the girl said to me.

I did as I was told. When I looked again, we were in a new place.

"This is the Room of Idiots," she said. "You should feel welcome here, *taaqa*."

My face must have revealed my anger at her words.

"Ah, I see," she said as she walked to a bench and with her mouth lifted from it a cat-o'-nine-tails made of black leather and pieces of jagged stone. She then slid out of her purpled buckskin dress, spread her legs in a wide horse-stance, and pushed the long leather handle deep into her dewy genitals.

"Don't you want to pleasure me?" she asked. "Come here, big white man what studies our culture like a big hero. Don't you want to make me scream, big man? Don't you want to eat me? You said you wanted to eat me. You sucked my blood. Didn't you like my taste? You disappoint me, big boy. I bet your tuber spurts good, yellow milk. Am I right? Why don't you come over here and show me. Push your big tuber up inside my hot oven, hero-man. I bake it good for you."

I was on my knees, hiding my face in pure humiliation, every inch of me flaccid and trembling. The first sting of her whip was like ice, followed by flame. I bellowed, but could not move. I wondered how she was holding the lash whose fiery tails came down again, and again, and again. She had soon flayed my back to rags, and I knew that if I did not escape her, she would kill me. The smell of my visceral fluids covered the room.

"Enough, *wùuti*," I heard a familiar voice say, and peering up through my own blood I saw the baboon creature enter the room. Removing his red Phrygian cap and tossing it aside with an air of carelessness, he retrieved the whip from the girl, who had somehow tied it to her left wrist. She dressed again, walked over to me and, sliding her gory arms beneath mine, lifted me to my feet. I felt no more pain, and realized that I had not been hurt in the least. My torture had been some kind of cruel illusion.

An arduous trek of a quarter mile or more through the blackness of yet another narrow passageway (with the terrible, grunting baboon following behind me) led us to a gargantuan door opening onto an ancient sports arena. As we stepped out into the open night air, the winds with which I was now so familiar growled all around us, and seemingly *through* us.

"*Dios del Viento*," the blind creature said. I quaked. *God of the Wind.*

"He has come for you, *taaqa*," the *wùuti* said, *wùuti* meaning *woman*. "He does not like your spirit, and he has come to kill you. *Es la Casa del Aire y tu no eres bienvenido.*"

"The…God of the Wind? I…am not welcome in his House of Air?" I asked, my voice feeble, shaking. I received a cutting blow across my mouth from the simian devil for an answer.

"Damn you!" I screamed as blood and saliva filled my mouth.

"Damn *me*? Damn *me*?" the primate replied. "Oh, *taaqa*.

You are so full of pride I fear you are lost forever. Damn *me*, he says, *wùuti*." And he laughed. And the girl laughed with him, and coughed, and spat phlegm at me, and laughed again, her eyes widening in a demonic glee, her tongue rolling in her once-pretty mouth.

"Christ," I said.

"You think your Christ can save you now, *taaqa?* Yes, he *could* save you, if you knew him as you claim to. But you have no lord save yourself, though your mind spins with delicious religious head knowledge. You are a lazy academic buffoon."

"How much…how much more of your insults do you think I will take?" I asked, finding strength to step away from the sadistic duo, preparing to run.

"Where will you run, little man?" the Indian girl asked. "You cannot run from *Bahana*. Your *hisatsinom* Adam and Eve tried to run from him; your Simon Peter tried to run from him; many have tried to run from *Bahana*. None is ever successful. *None*. This is Flesh-House. There is no running from Flesh-House."

Bahana swept down into the arena with a ferocity causing his antics at the ranch to seem as if they had been light breezes. The skies above us revealed themselves to be a deep indigo each time an onset of lightning flashed and crackled. I looked, and the baboon was gone. I was left with the handless girl, and for some reason, this frightened me to the core of my being. I fell where I stood, and was blown over to my side, my broken wrist pinned beneath me, making my arm explode with electric agony.

The girl walked forward a pace, turned, and faced me. Blood dribbled from her lips. "I will always love you," she said. *Miriam's last words to me.*

The Lord of the Mesas then manifested himself in human-like form, and what little sanity I held left me.

One might expect *Ehécatl* to appear as a glowing warrior of tremendous strength, feathered with colorful plumes, a bronzed and handsome king of his ancient culture; a destroyer of the Anasazi vampire god *Huitzilopochtli*—the 'Blue Hummingbird from the Left.' Oh, if I could erase the image of *Ehécatl*, of *Bahana*, from my mind forever, I would gladly give anything I own to do so. But, was it his image I saw? Even today I am not sure, yet, after all, what color is the wind? Are not the heavens our mirror? *Do we not make God in our own image?*

Before me and the Indian girl, stooped a naked Caucasian man with no hands. His eyes had been scraped out, and his back had been shredded, as if with a whip. His complexion was sallow—almost dead in appearance. As the winds continued their outrage, he mouthed words I could not understand…

LILY CHILDS

STRANGE TASTES

She's so bloody *articulate*. I want to slice out that petty tongue and lay it on my leather strap. I will – later.

These corporate get-togethers are too dangerous. So much flesh, getting pinker and pinker as the booze soaks in. It adds to the taste, indubitably, but I never risk the bite. Tonight however, she's pushed me too far. Droning on and on about projects and sales, percentages and profits – shit, this world is at the mercy of grey, characterless accountants. When I boil her brain later I'm going to dig through that OCD-ridden mass until I find where her imagination has been hidden, or suppressed, or whether it even existed in the first place.

She slides closer along the table, squeezing her breasts higher between the spindly arms until her chin practically rests on them. Her tightly-bound hair slips in wisps around her face, fingerous tendrils licking her skin.

It starts. The roar in my ears. Saliva dripping from my teeth. And God help me, however much I despise the woman I'm just going to have to eat her.

"Let's get out of here," I say. She doesn't need asking twice, grabs her bag and follows me through the double-doors. No-one notices.

My rooms are over two floors. I'm here alone most of the time. I pay low rent because I caretake the rest of the building. Sometimes I sleep in the owners' bed, and play with their … things. I'm always careful to wash what I use.

The kitchen is a designer job; clinical white units and walls with worktops of black reflective marble – great slabs of it. And glinting everywhere, blades of sharp expensive steel.

As we arrive at the house I question whether to impress my guest or get straight to business.

What the hell.

She staggers up the steps behind me, breathless, grabbing for me. I couldn't risk a cab-driver remembering us so I'd made us walk, keeping her interested along the way with teasing kisses and hands that stroked.

I pull out the Pearsons' key card and let us in through the front door. We're barely into the hallway when she falls on my throat, sucking at it as she tears at my clothes. Gently I push her away and peel off my coat. She moans in disappointment.

"C'mon." I incline my head with a smile. "I'm hungry."

Her brow trembles, but she follows me despite her annoyance. I don't look back, and hear her clip clop in those ridiculous heels; heels I'd made her run across the park in. Metal gleams in the darkness of the kitchen as she catches up with me at the door. She tries to take my hand. I don't do romance but let her linger a moment so that I can feel the meat on her bones. There's nothing of her; she's barely worth the effort.

Lights flash on with a low hum. I stand back for impact.
"Wow."

She looks around without moving. Me, I'm already at the centre caressing the cold, waiting stone. I stare into her face as she crosses the room and I can see she's nervous. She giggles, a tremulous high-pitched sound.

"Well, we obviously pay you too much."

Even at times like this, it's all about the money for finance monkeys like her.

"I have sidelines," I reply, watching her try to hide how she'll check my tax declaration when she's back in the office.

But she won't be going back. Not now.

I run my fingers down my front and slowly start to undo buttons, my eyes locked on hers. She kicks off her shoes, a lurid grin on the pinched face. She's on me in seconds.

I throw back my head. She's done me first so I'm alright Jack. But I don't reciprocate; I'm not into women. I take her hair in my hands and pull her to her feet, avoiding her kiss.

"My turn," she laughs and pulls herself up onto the counter. I push her onto her back.

"Close your eyes."

Her cheeks are delicious. The best feature in that dour face.

After slitting her throat - very neatly I thought – I left her dripping whilst I nipped downstairs to grab a box of herbs, oils and extra ingredients for the feast.

It will be a long night. I have much to do. As I only have myself to entertain I don't bother to dress the dining-table, instead I eat in situ. I have pan-fried the cheeks in unsalted butter then glazed them in sweet Marsala wine. Just a spoonful of cream lifts the flavour, with a pinch of cayenne to add to the bite. I serve and consume them immediately with some perfectly steamed French beans.

I check the skull. I'm poaching her brain after scalping the head, skinning it and removing the facial extremities. It's a long process to get the cranial consistency right so I leave it to bubble at leisure.

I have the Pearsons' cleaver in my hand; it's always the biggest question – which cut of meat to freeze now, and which to prepare dishes from straight away, to store in meal-size portions for later. I start with the toes. They're easy to cut off once you've snapped them back and forth to break the little knuckles. These bear a scarlet nail polish which will ruin a stew, so I dedicate a little time to peeling the nails away. Then it's CHOP – ankles, CHOP – knees. The thighs have to be sliced upwards and removed at the buttocks. Despite the sinews, hardened in a woman that spends too much time at the gym, I'm able to gather enough decent meat to feed me for a few weeks, and while I pack her away into neat boxes for the freezer I nibble at the deep-fried right hand and wait for the brains to finish simmering.

I spent most of the early hours extracting the marrow from the bones; they're the hardest remains to get rid of so it's fortunate the Pearsons' waste disposal unit is top of the range. The leftovers were fed to the bay; the sea around here is viciously tidal – nothing dropped into its murky green maw ever returns – tried and tested.

There is no evidence of slaughter at the Pearsons', or indeed my own humble abode. I am clean to the point of obsessive – which is why my employers chose me. The meat, several pounds of it is now stored in freezers in a lock-up garage two miles out of town. If anyone should ever ask to look inside the brick construction, all they would see is my vast collection of Royal Family memorabilia – useless, cheap tat that is available in bulk and can be stacked high enough to reach the garage ceiling. My eyes would fill as they judge my tastes, and I'd let a single tear drop, telling them how I'd inherited most of it from my late mother and felt I needed to keep adding to it, in memory of her. They would nod sadly and retreat, leaving me to laugh inside.

My mother was a bitch. She'd have sooner spat at *the scroungers*, as she referred to our monarchy, than have any reference to them in her house.

Meat aside, personal effects are a different matter. Clothes can be burned – they already have been. Phones can be traced. After the travails of a long but fruitful night with no sleep, I got into the office early this morning, as is my habit. I dropped the phone – untouched by my bare skin – into the accountant's desk drawer before taking my usual seat, and chewed over how to complete the essential disposal plan.

They call it serendipity. In the rush to get her tongue into my mouth, Fielding and Burke's Chief Finance Officer had neglected to inform me she was about to take a three-month hiatus – alone. I learn this valuable titbit from the usual sources gossiping at the drinks vending machine; a passing comment about how no-one would notice *the shrew's* absence. I reward myself with a smile. Turns out I was off the hook before I'd even started.

It's only now as I head back home after a full day's work surrounded by people pale with hangovers and stinking of coffee breath, that I count myself lucky. The woman won't be missed, and I will continue to behave in my regular way, getting off on eating home-made accountant sandwiches within laughing distance of my colleagues at lunchtime.

It's been a long day. I'm busy grinning at my cleverness when I turn the corner into Cranleigh Avenue to find police crawling all over the Pearsons' house. Ice pierces my gut and I reach out to steady myself against a flint wall. Before I can back away I'm spotted by a sneering copper.

"Clear the area please. This is a police-only zone."

I have to act fast; I walk towards him, hoping my face is stricken enough for him to be concerned.

"What's happened?" I tell the truth. "I'm the Pearsons'

caretaker. I live in the annexe." The young officer looks me up and down; apparently I don't look the part.

"Wait here."

He returns with his sergeant. There is a curious duality about her – good cop/bad cop in a single face.

"DS Philps. So you're the neighbour?"

The question throws me.

"Yes. No." The officer frowns at my inability to answer a simple question. "What I mean is, *yes* I live next door but it's part of the same building. I act as caretaker to the Pearsons and pay a low rent in return. They're away a lot – it suits us all."

Philps jots my ramblings down; I've said too much. I try but fail to read her scrawl.

"You're the cleaner then?"

Blood rushes through my ears at the indignity. I am far, far more than a cleaner; I mend, I repair, I stoke, I mow, change light bulbs and fuses, I dust, I wipe … I clean.

"Yes," I say. "What's happened? Are the Pearsons alright?"

Philps shakes her head.

"No, they are not alright. What's your name?"

If I had to describe the difference between the thrill of the chase – the danger in scouting and trapping a meal – and the terrifying panic at being discovered, I'd say there is little between them. It's all about needles. When I'm *hunting*, the needles stab at my groin. Here - right here and now - they are stabbing at every other part of my body and bursting out through my sweating skin.

Fuck it, I think I'm going to pass out. Sergeant Philps catches my arm as I sway, but she asks again. "Name?"

I tell her. My heart flips in my chest as I nearly, oh so nearly give her my real name; the identity I'd sloughed off over ten years ago when I couldn't put up with mother any more, and fed her – part by part – to the scavenging wildlife on Rimley Heath. Another decade. Another county. Another me.

I catch a movement at the window. Mrs Pearson peers through

the blinds, eyes caked in fat mascara, sunken into a face of over-tanned orange skin. I catch my breath. "Mrs..."

"...Pearson is currently being held on suspicion of a variety of serious offences," the sergeant finishes for me. I stare at the officer, a wary calm melting the nagging needles.

"She's killed *Mr* Pearson?" I pluck the idea from nowhere, believing it immediately. Yes, the old goat had affairs – but so did she. I used to watch them through the webcams I'd set up in their bedroom; dirty old buggers they are, the pair of them. I gave up after a few weeks – pensioner porn is no turn on. But I also quickly discovered they had 'an arrangement' with a variety of partners of differing ages, and sexes. Before I can ponder further, Sergeant Philps flips her notebook shut.

"No," she frowns, as though my suggestion - whilst outrageous - bears some consideration. I wish I'd kept my mouth shut. In the circumstances, my words could reveal more about me than my employers. "Mrs Pearson hasn't killed her husband. He's under arrest too. Come with me."

I am taken up the steps into the vast hallway of the house where Mr Pearson is being cuffed. He nods at me as though I am just passing through on an errand for his wife. I hear voices in the kitchen and we head in that direction. Mrs Pearson stands beside the herb rack, casually smoking - a cigarette held aloft in her hand. She looks with disdain at the various people emptying her cupboards and drawers, dusting surfaces with wide brushes. I don't know what they're looking for but they won't find anything; I'm as thorough as it is humanly possible to be.

"Ah, Haynes," my employer says as she spots me. "There's been a little misunderstanding. Alleged tax evasion last week, and now - would you believe it, attempted murder! It's all rubbish, of course."

A plain-clothes policeman steps towards her. "Please Mrs Pearson, may I remind you that anything you say will be..."

"Yes, yes. I'm aware of my rights. My lawyer will be here

shortly. I just wish to speak with my caretaker."

I utter silent thanks to her for re-elevating me to my correct job title. She ignores the cop telling her she will have to speak openly – that is her intention anyway.

"Haynes. These people believe they have found evidence of wrong-doing. They are mistaken. However, I have no doubt they will want to interview you about Mr Pearson and any activities in our home..." She turns to the officer who is taking notes beside her. "Haynes has no knowledge of our affairs outside of this house so I would appreciate it if my staff are not pestered unnecessarily."

Staff? There's only me. I manage to avoid reacting as she looks at me once again, and continues her instructions.

"Whatever the police do ask, Haynes, I want you to be completely honest."

"Of course."

She has taken on such a high and mighty tone I feel as though I should bow or curtsey. I turn to leave the room with Detective Sergeant Philps at my back. I still don't know what the Pearsons are supposed to have done.

"Oh, and Haynes?" The *grande-dame* calls out to me. "These people are taking us away now to be formally interviewed. I'm sure we'll be back for dinner. Would you be so kind as to prepare us a late supper? Say … nine? Nine-thirty? There's plenty in the freezer."

I am whisked away before I can respond but I hear her tell the police, "At least I know my kitchen will be in safe hands with Haynes."

I watch the Pearsons being driven away in two separate vehicles, then I lead the police around the side of the house to the annex. I have nothing to hide, nothing to incriminate me. I let them roam through the small rooms, picking up and opening whatever they wish.

"Can I stay here?" I ask. The young officer I originally spoke to nods. "But don't expect the Pearsons to be back for *supper*." He sneers over the old-fashioned term then leaves me to the silence of my rooms.

The Pearsons *have* done something, I'm sure of it. Their arrogance was nothing unusual but I had noticed the spikes in my landlady's words, her lips tightening around them as she spoke, and her tone far more clipped than usual.

I stare out the window, wondering how long it will be before the investigators stop fishing and leave; I've a supper to make.

The phone rings, and I jump. No-one knows my number here.

It's the Pearsons' lawyer. Apparently they feel they should apologise further for the inconvenience, and want me to feel safe in my own home. They still hope to be *back between nine and nine-thirty* for supper, the lawyer reiterates in a slow drawl.

That's it.

But it's enough.

When I first moved in, some eight years ago I was waiting tables at the Pearsons' Golf Club house. They were friendly, and not as condescending as most of the golfing fraternity. In retrospect, I realise I must have told them quite a bit about my made-up life. When I got the job at Fieldings they openly congratulated me, and when I mentioned I'd be searching for accommodation they gave each other a look that turned into an offer of the caretaking position. I couldn't believe my luck when Mr Pearson showed me around the annex, a sparkling-clean, mock-Georgian addition to the original house.

"You'll have plenty of room to do your own thing," Pearson had said before taking me to a small corridor that connected the annex to the house. The hallway was, and still is lined with bookcases, brimming with faux-distressed classics. We stopped and I eyed the titles, eager to declare my interest, until Pearson reached up to the top shelf and pulled a handful of Thomas Hardys from their resting place. In the space vacated by the books I could see a dull-metal cabinet, the dial black, with white numbers around its edge.

"This is our second safe, should anything ever happen to either of us, or to the house." He reached up to turn the combination then pulled out a sheet of paper - the only contents of the box as far as I could see. "This document contains a list of important contacts, starting with our lawyer, and gives instructions on what you should do and say in an emergency." He put his hand on my shoulder. "Can I trust you?"

I took a deep breath. "Yes, Mr Pearson."

He studied me for a moment, his eyes cold but kind then he returned the list to its hiding place and locked the safe.

"Sorry," I said. "But shouldn't I be given the combination?"

"It will be made available to you if and when you should require it." He handed over a key to the interconnecting door. "This is for your ease of access only. You have a double-lock and bolts this side so you'll have no concerns that we might break in!" He chortled at his own joke before correcting himself. "We simply want you to feel secure and happy in your new home."

The arrangement has worked well until today, but I now know what is 'required' of me. The Pearsons have obviously already spoken with their lawyer but I need to contact the rest of the people on their list. I head for the corridor. The Hardys that I pass every day and never bother to read fall quickly to the floor; I ignore the crack of spines and the musty waft of old pages.

My hand is on the safe dial in seconds. Zero Nine Three Zero – supper time. But I can't get the bloody thing to accept it. I try different combinations of numbers, my skin heating up as I become obsessed with the urgency. Blood pumps in audible beats and I panic – I *almost* panic. Then ... I wonder.

Two One Three Zero – 24-hour clock. It's obvious. I bite my tongue to halt the whoop as the safe clicks open and I plunge my hand in to pluck out the document. My fingers slap hard into a rattling pile of plastic ... video tapes, old-fashioned video tapes.

My emotions shift.

Morbid excitement curdles into unease. The Pearsons *had*

come into my home after all, despite their assurances. I finger the tapes, pulling at them one by one until they slip out. There's something else in there but I can't get to it. The Hardys come to my rescue again; piled up, there are just enough of them for me to stand on. Teetering, I peer into the back of the safe. A large white envelope has been lodged there, its corners curling and creased.

My name is hand-written in large black letters on the white surface.

It's my real name.

KATHERINE MORLEY

My ankle twists and I slip from the books, falling to my arse with the envelope in my hand. Bile stirs in my gut, and my hands shake as I tear the envelope open to drag out a single sheet of paper. It carries today's date.

Dear Katherine

Circumstances beyond our control mean that we must reluctantly let you go. We regret the inevitable intrusion by the Police – you will discover soon enough what we are accused of. Please take your time to watch the video tapes, especially if you are under any doubt about whether to speak out.

Do accept our apologies for this short notice. Our lawyer will be in contact soon to confirm your 'obeisance' and to provide you with financial assistance in obtaining new accommodation.

Sincerely, your landlords

Greta and Stephen Pearson

The acid in my gullet gives way. Puke shudders from my throat, covering the Hardys with a steaming mess. I gather up the tapes and the letter – and shaking – make my unsteady way into the living-room. I pull the curtains shut before turning on the TV and switching on the ancient VCR. It whirs into life with a spooling roar before quietening to an idle tick.

The tapes are labeled. I pick up *No. 1 Pearson Vacation (copy)*. The innocuous title suggests harmless holiday fun; Spanish cocktails and wrinkle-tanned, half-cut toffs. I'm partly right; the tape begins with the Pearsons raising a toast. A cheer goes up and I can hear a clatter of voices and laughter behind the camcorder. All seems well, and then the camera pans down to the dining table. Strapped across the heavy oak, a man - oriental in appearance - bucks and strains, his skin tearing from the leather at his wrists. His mouth is taped but I can just make out the muffled screams. His beautiful black eyes, long-lashed and staring, bulge from their sockets. I can taste his fear and my own begins to stir. The film judders for a moment as the camera zooms out and is placed on a steady surface, facing the inevitable carnage.

"Who's first?" someone calls. From the back of the room comes the click, clickety click of a ball rattling around a roulette wheel.

"Red six!"

A woman leans forward. I can only see from behind her but she has a muscular back, her skin bare in a halter-necked dress. "Someone hold him down," she purrs. "I want his arm."

The camera wobbles with the number of diners rushing forward to taste the living feast. The bound man writhes and twists, beneath guests in black tie and evening dress until the bare-backed woman calls "*Quiet*" and holds up a gleaming stiletto dagger.

I am as enraptured as the waiting crowd. She toys with them, stabbing around the victim's forearm in playful jabs until the game has gone far enough, and she slams the knife in deep, severing sinews and arteries.

She skillfully removes the flesh with a ripping *pop* and I almost join in the applause at the perfect execution, scanning the screen at the same time to look for pans and cooking utensils – but there are none. Instead, the woman turns to the camera. Her face is familiar, one of Stephen's regular bed partners. She takes the dripping muscle to her lips, caresses it with tiny kisses, then starts to suck the raw meat, moaning in pleasure as her tongue licks at it. Gradually other mouths join hers. Teeth tear the fillet apart and the faces chew noisily as they kiss one another, sharing the delicacy between them. I am orgasmic with horror when beside me, the phone rings.

"Have you watched it?" the lawyer whispers.

I grunt a reply. "Now. Doing it now." And I hang up. I *know* he already knows.

The tape plays on for another ten minutes, descending from a tissue-tearing feast to an orgy of blood, the guests insane with the ecstatic pleasure and taste of raw human flesh, and of each other. When the filming eventually fades out, I am ravenous; spittle slides down my chin. Juices lap at my knickers.

Panting, I reach to remove the tape but a message blares across the screen.

Katherine. Destroy this copy of the tape in your usual place.

Shit. They've really thought about this. They obviously have another copy somewhere, they know my true identity and – by giving me a glimpse of the cocktail party – they've let me into their secret. But to what end?

My sleeve is sticky as I wipe the drool from my lips and replace the tape with another. The vodka bottle calls to me; I can't get lashed - it's too risky and I have instructions to follow, but by fuck I need it.

No. 2. Katherine Elizabeth Morley.

A gallery of photos plays across the screen, fading in and out with old-fashioned transition effects. There are lots of me waitressing at the Golf Club, starting with my first day, before I even met the Pearsons.

Fuck.

Here's a photo of my pay packet. "Sarah Haynes" – how the hell did they get that? And then, rippling into view ... almost translucent images of me as a child, in school photos, at discos. They'd got them all from my only photo album, except for this last shot. The portrait fills the screen, her face lined and raging, glaring at me, scaring me. I can hear her, "*You wicked little bitch. Clean the floor. Clean the fucking floor.*" My mother, disgust oozing from her permanently scowling mouth. I fall back in my armchair and the screen turns black.

I slug back the vodka and top the glass up, just as a grainy video film starts playing. It's me again. A year after my mother disappeared, her skull washed up on a pebbled beach twenty miles away. The police said they could tell from her teeth and bones she was a chronic alcoholic – just like I'd told them. They believed me at the time, when I said she'd staggered out for booze; they'd picked her up from the docks more than once.

I snort back a laugh as I watch. If only she hadn't taught me to clean so well, the cops might have found out the truth. The little film whirs on. There I am, standing alone at the cheap marker in Portland cemetery. The camera just catches me dropping a wreath of nettles before I spit on the grave, and walk away.

I wait. This can't be the end … and I'm right.

I don't recognise the voice that speaks through the darkness but its message is clear.

"People like Helen Morley don't just disappear, Katie."

I shiver. No-one has called me Katie since I was a child. The voice continues. "We know what Katie did. And we're proud of you - a lesson learnt early is a lesson learnt well."

I stare through my pale reflection in the black screen. It fades, replaced by a photo of a huge detached house; Curlews. I recognise it immediately. My mother worked there when I was young, before she started to drink. The house hovers, shaking on the screen before being rapidly replaced by a succession of images – dinner parties, guests in evening dress, familiar faces. Oh. Christ. People I've seen *here* – in this house, fucking and getting fucked by the Pearsons. And here – here it is, my mother strapped to a bed, the Pearsons slavering over her – and she is laughing with joy.

Fuck the glass. I pick up the bottle and swig. I'm not here by chance. I've been theirs all my life.

The tape ends and ejects itself. I grab the last one from the floor and shove it in the machine. What comes next is no surprise.

Everything. All my indiscretions and delectations. From my first clumsy feast – a pretty homeless boy I'd picked on a train – right through to last night's accountant, filmed in perfect detail for prosperity. The sex, the murders, the cooking … the banquets-for-one.

I knew the Pearsons' house inside out; how could I not have found their own cameras, tiny webcams slotted into places I'd never look – or even clean?

There I am, in my bedroom in the annex, eating human breakfast in bed before pleasuring myself with the memory of the kill. They'd watched me all those years...

Now. They're watching me now. I scan the room but seeing nothing, reach for the phone. It rings before I get to it.

"I wouldn't have said anything," I say. I'm whining; it's horrible. "I didn't even know."

"That may well be the case, dear." The woman's voice is confident, and familiar. "But you would have been discovered soon enough. In fact..." She pauses for effect, and it works. My legs grow weak and the pounding of my heart is louder inside my ears than her words. "We would have revealed ourselves to you sooner rather than later. But as it happens, we're moving – all of us – to new shores."

I know what she is going to ask - that I destroy all the evidence, of which they have copies for their own insurance - in case it goes tits up. And she'll ask me to forget what I know – permanently.

"Don't worry." I say. "I don't tell tales. And even if I wanted to, you've already got enough to get me lynched." I sound like a criminal; I don't like it – the words are odd in my mouth.

The woman, she of the stiletto dagger and Scandinavian proportions barks a deep, throaty laugh into the phone. I hear her suck on a cigarette.

"You're quite wrong Katherine … Katie. Have you been told what Greta and Stephen have *actually* been accused of yet?"

I shake my head, knowing she can see me, that I don't need to speak. How am I to know if Greta's tax and murder spiel was true? The police didn't acknowledge it.

The voice sighs.

"This morning, Stephen phoned the police to tell them he'd found a handbag in Blethyn Park – after some joggers spotted him there *acting suspiciously*. Do you know who the bag belonged to? Of course you do. It belonged to Susan MacAllister, Chief Accountant at Fieldings."

My mind reels. "What?"

"The bag, a cheap thing for a woman loaded to the expensive teeth – did you find the gold one, by the way? Tooth, that is?"

"Yes, it's in a box above..."

She snorts. Of course she knows, and I find it difficult to hide my irritation. "What about her bag?" I ask.

"It had been emptied," she replies, her voice full of false intrigue. "Its belongings were found strewn all around the public toilets. MacAllister's wallet was recovered a few hundred yards away, also empty except for a gym membership card." That sucking again, a deep drag. I wonder how she knows so much detail, so much inside information. But most of all, I want to know how the accountant's personal belongings ended up back in the park, when I'd stored them so carefully for later use or disposal.

My lock-up garage blazes onto the TV screen. Vodka-soaked vomit fills my mouth with the thought of all those carefully-packed body parts.

"Watch," the woman says in my ear.

Mr Pearson – Stephen – comes into shot. It's dark, the light poor. It must be around the witching hour of this morning, long after I'd packed MacAllister away and returned home with some pickled lights for breakfast.

I watch Mr Pearson draw out a key – my key? He opens the

rusted, screeching garage door and I can barely contain the nausea.

It's empty.

Almost empty.

I swallow bile as Stephen walks toward the freezer at the back of the breeze-block-built room. He has my second key in his hand and slips it into the lock to open the container.

Nothing.

It is an uncharged, gaping cavity.

No meat.

No bones.

He turns to face the camera, arms folded over his slight paunch. He smiles.

"Do you understand?"

I jolt, forgetting I'm holding the phone.

"No. I don't … unless the Pearsons deliberately set themselves up?"

A single clap is joined by a growing round of applause. I hear voices chattering, light laughter and glasses clinking in discordant harmony. When the woman speaks, there's a smile in her reply.

"Precisely," she says. "There's nothing like a scandal to hide the meat from the bones."

People in high places scratch backs, and more.

The charges are dropped. Apologies made. The Pearsons are suitably compensated for the indignity of such accusations and decide to leave the country for good.

No tax is paid.

No body is found.

I am on a boat. We're three miles off the French coast – a dozen of us. We'll meet Stephen, Greta and the others in Bordeaux later this evening.

We have new names, again, and I am no longer 'staff'.

Tonight we'll be having dinner on board "The Curlew". Chef

is preparing one of my favourite dishes - *filet cru, sauce financière* – raw tax man with morchella mushrooms, white wine and cream. You'd think the meat would be tough and wiry but the trick is to pulverise it while still alive, before marinating it in truffle juice. As such, it's only fair that we all assist in such a delicate operation, even down to the skinning and boning. We're not afraid of getting our hands dirty.

Chef selects the most perfect cuts for our palates.

It's going to be quite delicious.

They might have to strap me down, I'm so hungry.

ROBERT DUNBAR

HIGH RISE

The other ghosts didn't like her.

"Why are you making that noise?" She would accost them in the hallways or just come gliding into their apartments with some rude remark. "That's just stupid. Why are you doing that?" She challenged everyone and had no time for traditional haunting behavior. The wailing; the bleeding: it all bored her. Her scorn fairly blasted them, and the other spirits complained incessantly.

Even more appallingly, she always wanted to fuck them.

Not surprising really. She thought about almost nothing but sex – an old problem that had kept her from accomplishing anything much while alive. (Brief though her life had been, people had stopped speaking of her "potential" long before it ended.) The other ghosts recoiled in disgust but soon grew a bit afraid of her as well. None of them had encountered so strong a spirit before. Possibly, her lifelong involvement with the occult accounted for some of this power. Plus she had always seemed somewhat otherworldly, always, a feature exaggerated by her abnormally intense intelligence. Such intellect had its downside. She could focus on only one thing at a time, and all else ceased to exist for her, everything, the whole gray universe.

That single focus had generally been reserved for sex. Sex in general. Only toward the end had it become sex specifically, as in sex with a particular guy. Then he became everything. When he took off, she had nothing.

Nothing.

So she stalked the halls now, abusing other phantoms until they all drifted away from her, and she wandered alone.

Not that any shortage of ghosts existed here. Older people were forever getting robbed and (almost incidentally) stabbed or bludgeoned. Young women got raped and strangled. Young men shot each other, and toddlers got caught in the crossfire. The elevator alone housed eleven spirits who manifested between different floors (on those rare occasions when the elevator worked). And the more sinister areas of the stairwell positively teemed with revenants.

Still, she found herself increasingly isolated. The others congregated elsewhere, often dissipating altogether at her approach. But this only made her angrier. And hungrier. By no means had death gentled her. Sometimes she paced like a lunatic in a cell. Sometimes she cried out wild things that the others could not comprehend.

They waited, assuming she'd subside in time, which proved correct. Soon, she stopped leaving 11D so much, but this was not because she had settled down. It was because Tyrone and his family moved in.

"This place looks … okay," Brandon hazarded. "Better than the last one."

"Yeah, it's a fucking penthouse." Ty dumped out a garbage bag full of laundry, making a big soft pile in the middle of the parlor.

"Lots of sun anyway," replied Brandon, still trying to keep it cheerful. (In reality, ashen light barely filtered through the security gates over the fire escape.) "Hey, don't leave those clothes there. Mom will freak."

His brother ignored him as they explored the dusty gloom of the place, Brandon in a hopeful fashion, though with increasing trepidation, Tyrone with disgust. "It's bigger. I don't know though," announced Brandon as even *his* optimism sputtered. "I don't like the way it … feels."

"Don't be such a fag. I ain't like the way it *smells*."

"Yeah. What is that? Gas?"

They'd spent all morning lugging their possessions up the stairs, armload at a time from their ratty old place on the second floor. A couple of cardboard boxes one trip, then a plastic basket or an overstuffed shopping bag. Of course, Ty could carry a lot more than Brandon, not that he usually bothered, but at least he pitched in this time. Their sad-eyed mother had been at work since before dawn, but she trusted her boys to handle the move. They'd had enough practice.

Tyrone got the only room with a door of course. (It almost closed too.) And their mom would be down the hall near the bathroom. Brandon would sleep in the parlor. He was used to it. And to being picked on.

Tyrone was six one or two maybe – and at sixteen years of age not above pounding on his little brother's head. He was too short for basketball though, which pissed him off some. But not as much as he let on, Brandon suspected. Basketball would have meant hard work and hustle, and Tyrone moved pretty slow most of the time. No, he just liked having an excuse for acting surly … at which he excelled. Weird how much girls went for that combination of sleepy eyes and sneering mouth. Even their mom cut him lots of slack because of his looks, Brandon believed.

The two boys couldn't have looked less alike. No justice in this world. Only two years younger, Brandon had more or less given up hoping for a growth spurt. He remained skinny and short, serious and studious, all qualities that the other guys in the neighborhood would have happily beaten the crap out of him over. Worse, his voice could sound distressingly high pitched. Good thing his big brother stuck up for him. Sometimes.

Putting stuff away in the bathroom, Brandon called out as his brother ambled by the doorway. "Did you see that?" Behind him, shadows, provoked by a ceiling bulb, gathered where a broken windowpane had been replaced with plywood.

"What?" Ty stuck his head back in.

Foul vapors issued from the blue stained sink. "I don't know. Something in the mirror." Brandon stared.

"Man, you can't see shit in that mirror, it's so old."

But Brandon knew. Right away he knew. And all the rest of that afternoon, while he fetched and dragged and unpacked, he kept looking around as though he heard footsteps, and once he thought he felt hair brush his face. Ty had stopped helping, which didn't surprise him. While Brandon found places in the little kitchen for dishes and spoons, he heard Ty yell, "What?" from his room, sounding really irritated.

"What?" Brandon yelled back.

No answer.

Instead, Ty just made a surprised sort of noise. Brandon ignored him and kept unpacking. Later, while putting away the laundry that Ty had dumped on the floor, he realized he could hear him talking. With pauses. Like a conversation. Weird. Ty never had whole conversations. Did he have a new cell phone or something? Brandon listened but couldn't make out any words.

His brother's door slammed, then drifted open again.

That first night, Brandon lay on a sheet on the couch. He squirmed. Strange visions clouded his sleep until he woke suddenly, convinced his mother stood over him in the dark. (She used to do that sometimes, though mostly she got home too tired anymore.) For a moment, he panicked in the strange room, until moonlight through the bare window oriented him.

Floorboards creaked slightly, as though with the memory of weight, and for an instant, he almost saw something moving away, a kind of pale stain in the darkness. Then the door to Ty's room squeaked.

Fear kept him from getting up to check on his brother.

"Aren't you going to school today?"

Tyrone always slept late, but the next day got ridiculous.

"Yo?" Not a sound. Hurrying out the door, Brandon just yelled from the hallway, still too afraid even to go in and look. All through the day, his gut stayed clenched, and he barely heard a word in any class.

When he finally got home, he found the apartment still quiet and dim. Ty's door stood open. Without even putting his books down, Brandon rushed in.

Ty sprawled like a derelict across the mattress on the floor.

"Please, do something so I know you're not dead."

His brother obliged.

Brandon stumbled out of the room, doubled over. When he could talk, he said, "I'm telling Mom you punched me in the stomach."

"Fuck you."

In the days that followed, Tyrone got meaner. A lot meaner. He even slapped their mother one night, and Brandon threatened him with a kitchen knife. But the night he beat up his girlfriend had to be the worst. Sasha went out on a stretcher, her little nightie black with blood.

She only wore it in the first place because she wanted to fix things up between them. Normally, she sat around in one of his old tees. But she loved Ty ... and lately just couldn't seem to get his attention. Had he met somebody else? She kept pestering him.

Mistake.

Standing on the sidewalk, Brandon watched them load the stretcher into an ambulance, while a whole bunch of people nearby laughed and called out crude things. Crusted with blood, Sasha's face had swelled so badly he could barely recognize her. (He felt bad, because he'd always liked her – she used to sit and talk with him a lot until Ty wanted her – and now he figured he'd never see her again.) With no particular urgency, the ambulance pulled away. Afterwards, cops questioned him about Ty, but he just kept saying he didn't know anything about his brother's whereabouts. True enough.

Ty didn't come home till the middle of the night.

"You okay?" Brandon lifted his head.

"Shut up. Go back to sleep."

"Sasha's in the hospital."

"I told you once."

"Cops are looking for you." He closed his eyes and turned over. If he got punched, he didn't want to see it coming. Since early childhood, closing his eyes always made him feel safer, especially around his brother.

His brother wasn't safe though. He knew that.

He heard grunts from the next room all night long.

Ty started not to look so good.

She was merciless. Every night. All night long. And mornings too lately. Then – after he stopped going to school altogether – all day long as well. Or so Brandon assumed.

No, Ty didn't look so good at all. Not that anybody saw him much anymore. Seemed like he never got out of bed.

Brandon woke in the dark with the sheet tented over him. It ached. He took care of himself in a sweat but couldn't seem to get any relief. He knew the cause. He could feel heat pulsing out of Ty's room. Physically feel it. If he held out his hand, it was like *almost* touching a radiator. It had never been this bad.

Quietly, he slid off the sofa and stood for a minute in his underwear, just listening. Then he crept toward Ty's door and peered through the opening.

He'd seen his brother naked before but not like this.

A fat white candle guttered on the floor, and dim luminescence filled the room like floodwater, lapping at the walls and pooling around the mattress. Moaning, Ty lay on his back, his whole body clenched. His muscles glistened, and his sweat might have been oil on a wooden carving. Everything looked hard. It struck Brandon as especially weird when Ty started heaving, because statues shouldn't be able to do that.

Ty made a drowning noise with his mouth as his whole body arched. Judging from the expression on his face, it must have hurt. Bad. He spurted, and it hung in the air like smoke. Not much for a guy his size, Brandon thought, but then this probably wasn't the first time today. Or even the second. Then it faded as though something absorbed it. For a long moment, Ty gasped so heavily it almost sounded like weeping.

When he started to writhe again, Brandon backed away and tried to close the door.

He had to tell somebody. "She's killing him."

"Man, this is the weirdest thing you ever came up with." Ash had been Brandon's best friend since middle school. About a million butts crusted the curb at their feet, along with dirty condoms, a couple of needles, a broken bottle of Jack Daniels and some bullet casings. (Slow night.) Ash shook his head slowly. "And that's saying something."

"I'm serious."

Ash blew out a cloud of clove-scented smoke.

"You still working those?" asked Brandon. "Stinks bad."

His friend shrugged with what he clearly hoped would be perceived as sophisticated boredom, but his appearance rendered the gesture merely bizarre. The beige frizz of hair framed a softly cream-colored face, not fat exactly, just baby-round. With the cigarette in his mouth, he resembled a debauched infant.

"I'm telling you," Brandon persisted. "If I don't do something soon …"

"Why bother? How many times he hit you over the summer?"

Brandon's face screwed up while he tried to keep his eyes from leaking.

"Chill, man, chill" Ashley relented. "Let me nose around some. I know some people."

"Ash?"

"What?"

"I know he's a shit."

"Got that right."

"But he's my brother."

"Whatever."

When he came home that afternoon, he found Ty awake and sitting on the sofa, drinking something in a mug.

"What is that?" asked Brandon.

"What it look like?"

"I don't want to say."

"You funny."

"Is it supposed to be coffee? Where'd you get it?"

"Da fuck you think?"

"You make it yourself? Since when you cook? Don't drink that," said Brandon. "Let me make you some."

For the first time, his brother's gaze flicked toward him, and he almost smiled. "This is fine."

"Okay." Encouraged, Brandon took a deep breath. "Listen,

I've been wanting to talk to … to say … I mean … " He started over. "You've got to stop."

"What you talking 'bout? You think I'm on something?"

"I don't mean that. I mean … her."

"I ain't seen her."

"I'm not talking about Sasha," said Brandon. "The other one." In the silence that followed, he watched deliberation roll behind the hot glitter of his brother's eyes.

At last, Ty just smirked. "Crazy shit, huh? It feels like … feels so … like nothing else."

"You know what it is," Brandon continued. "What she is."

"So?"

"So you got to stop. You want to throw everything away?"

"What? You want I should give up the ghost?" Ty barked a laugh. "All right for you." He set the mug down on the table so hard it splashed everywhere. "Mr. Smartest-Kid-in-School. Mr. College-Bound Scholarship-Boy, and not for bouncing no balls neither. What I gone throw way?"

"What about your life?"

"Shit."

They sat quietly a moment. Then Brandon sensed a change in pressure. "She's here, isn't she?" But Ty had already gotten up and sauntered toward his bedroom.

Brandon wiped up the mess on the table.

A couple of mornings later, Brandon left for school as usual but returned within forty-five minutes and just stood in the doorway until Ash arrived.

"Thanks for coming, man." He closed the door. "Anybody see you?" He hoped none of the neighbors had noticed them sneaking back in (none who would mention it to his mother anyway), but Ash – hard to overlook at the best of times – squelched that prospect. He had done something to his hair so that it stuck out even higher than usual today and had a piece of spotted cloth tied around his forehead. Plus a new earring. He looked something like a chicken in a pirate costume. "You find out anything?" asked Brandon.

Ash peered around. "He here?"

"Asleep."

"Good," said Ash. "It was a white girl lived here. Died here, I mean."

"Get out."

"Stuck her head in the oven. About a year ago. Weird chick. Into fortune telling. Candles and incense and all that scene. I asked around. Turns out she hooked up with some big gang dude. Funny she couldn't read that card."

Brandon thought about it. "You find out her name?"

"Maya something."

"So she's the ghost? Has she done this before? Fucked guys to death, I mean? How come we don't hear nothing about it?"

"Might be something new." Ash shrugged. "People go through different stages in life. Maybe ghosts do too."

"Ghosts?" asked Brandon. "There's more of them?"

"This project was built on a cemetery. Everybody knows that." Ash pulled out a red bandana and wiped his neck with it. "Hot for October. Ain't you got no air in here?"

Brandon shook his head. "Cemetery? Ghosts don't haunt where they're buried, do they? That don't make no sense. Doesn't. Any." He stepped back. "What's with the hands? Fight it, man. That's her."

"Oh. Sorry." Abashed for a moment, Ash observed the phenomenon. "Couldn't you tell? About the ghosts, I mean. I thought you were supposed to be so freaking sensitive."

"Yeah," Brandon nodded thoughtfully. "Place is crawling with them. You're right."

"When you see one," Ash agreed, "you know there's zillions more in the walls."

"So what do I do now?" Brandon wondered. "Holy water? An

exorcism?"

"That's for devils. You got to lay the ghost, buddy."

"I think my brother's got that covered."

"You know what I mean. You got to get her to go into the light and all that shit. To move on."

Brandon pretended to be asleep on the sofa until it got dark and quiet, or as quiet as this tower ever got. He could hear Ty snoring a little.

She'd be here soon.

Sitting up, he lit the candle he'd stolen from Ty's room and stuck it on the coffee table. As the glow brightened, shadows danced, and tension seemed to sludge through the room. It wasn't that she arrived so much as that – gradually – he became aware of her.

"You can see me?" he asked, though his throat immediately closed up.

He felt a corrosive ripple in the dark, a kind of silent laugh.

Yeah, he figured that had to be about the single stupidest thing a person could ask a ghost, but he recovered. "What are you doing to my brother? No, don't answer that. I know what you're doing. Why are you doing it?" In melting shadows, he glimpsed a darker shade, then a lighter one, until he could almost see her, pale and slender and insubstantial, molded by the shifting gleam, her breasts softly luminous.

"We're in love."

The girlishness of the voice surprised him. And he could sort of make out her face now too, sharp in the shadows. Pretty enough, he thought, but creepy somehow, and not just from being dead. He figured she probably had looked much the same alive: a tangle of yellow hair, milky eyes that stared and stared, the soft, hungry mouth.

"Please," he said and stopped. This wasn't going the way he'd imagined it. No confrontation. No banishment. Just conversation.

"What if he dies?"

"I'll still have him."

"One ghost haunting another ghost?"

"Possessing." The voice grew fainter.

"Wait. Please."

But she had already disappeared like a pearl sinking in a bottle of ink. A glow, having nothing to do with candles, seeped from Ty's room now, and through the wall came a groan. Not a groan of pain. At least not entirely.

"Please," Brandon added uselessly. He stood in the dark and watched a fat bead of tallow roll down the side of the candle. "Got to do something. Got to think."

By the minimal morning light that bled through a sheet tacked over the window, Ty looked almost gray. Brandon stood over the mattress, gazing down at him.

Tyrone's eyes drifted partly open, unfocused, blind, and his breath sounded like plastic melting – it bubbled and hissed. He smelled like rotting meat.

"It's going to be all right, bro. I promise you. She ain't ... she isn't going to take you. I got a plan. I'll fix everything. I swear." Brandon backed toward the door. "Okay, you sleep. It's too hot to get up anyhow." At the doorway, he turned back, blinking against the sweat that dripped into his eyes. "It's gonna be all right."

Even in the dark, the tarred surface of the roof exuded a hot stench. Brandon never came up here. Never. He hated it. Hated the panoply of the blighted neighborhood spreading below, endless and ruined. How many shades of ugly could there be? And he hated how impossibly faraway the lights of the real city looked. Plus heights scared him some.

Yet tonight he found a strange peacefulness here. Street noises, dim and distant, penetrated the solitude to echo like the muted throb of surf.

"Ty's not here." A slight breeze seemed only to swirl heat around him as he propped the broken door with an old crate. "Maya? I know you can hear me."

Darkness stirred in the stairwell.

"I called the cops on him. About Sasha. They didn't care. So I told them he was the one shot that cop last week, and they came and grabbed him. They won't hold him long, but he sure won't be here tonight. No way. Come on. Maya?" He intoned her name like an incantation. "You got to deal with me now." He paused to listen. "Come up here. I know you. You're all restless and twitchy. Come up," he finished, squaring his bony shoulders. "I'm a boy too."

Did a bulb go on down there? No. Just a sort of gleam, like a shimmer of fog or the movement of water. For an instant, he glimpsed her face in the depths: a pale sliver.

Then she seemed to erupt at him, gushing up through the stairwell.

She covered him like a whirlwind.

"Okay. You're here." Shutting his eyes tight, he took a step back. "Stay with me." She whirred angrily in his ears as he took another step.

"You need to see this. Please." The edge of the roof must be here. Somewhere. He felt behind him with his foot.

"No. Stop touching me like that. Look up. The stars. So pure. So much better than here."

Teetering, he halted.

"The next step. Take it. Maya? You are ready. I can sense it. Don't you want it? You need to move on. You know you do."

He could feel the way her touch changed. Became more powerful. Purposeful. And she seemed to be agreeing with him.

They mourned him, though no one knew for sure what had happened. And once Ash came up to the roof and sobbed for like an hour.

They said it was drugs. Or that he jumped because of being

queer. Or maybe he saw something go down, and some of the gangbangers threw him off. (They did that from time to time.) Then everybody stopped talking about it. Too much other stuff going on.

In time, only the other ghosts kept gossiping. Sometimes they even came up to look, though they never stayed long. This cloud of energy shocked them, and they would hurry away, murmuring like dry leaves. Still, for the most part they approved of the changes. Maya had ceased to pester them and had, they considered, become a proper haunt at last: rooted, insensate.

Brandon knew little of this. Had she secreted some milky cocoon? It covered him, squeezed him tight. Through the sticky mesh that imprisoned him, he could hear nothing, see nothing, feel nothing but her spongy vibrations. For Brandon, there would be no prowling. He could only move inside her.

It felt like smoke.

It felt like music.

It felt like being swallowed.

It felt like being buried.

Things went on this way for a long time.

Was he cold? Crooning softly, she stroked him. Holding him inside made her feel at long last satisfied. Nothing else in the world existed.

Sometimes, when her attention seemed lax, Brandon groped about with his mind, and occasionally a dim sense of his brother penetrated through the slats and tarpaper. Tyrone had not recovered. Even before the funeral, he'd begun searching for other things with which to obliterate himself. So it had all been for nothing. Brandon felt this acutely.

Maya soothed him, whispering of devotion and of how the two of them needed nothing else, not while the sky spun and eternity yawned around them. What mattered the world? He shifted within her, pushing, rubbing. Sometimes he murmured that he would be with her always, even when she grew old. Then they giggled together in voices only pigeons and mice could hear, because they both knew this to be nonsense. Neither of them would move on. Neither would grow, old or otherwise. Did anyone anywhere still speak of his potential? No. Why should they?

Sometimes this thought made him sad; sometimes it filled him with bitterness. But it all fed back into her. Always. All of it. A closed loop. She petted him and rocked, while night faded into day and seasons withered. Despite winter winds and cold spring rains, warmth coruscated through them.

Motherhood was like that.

BRANDON FORD

SCARE ME

"Drive, bitch."

Paula froze, breath held. Lips parted, eyes wide, she wondered if she should scream. Quickly, she scanned the parking lot. Empty. The large building she'd just stepped out of. Dark. The road alongside of her. Deserted. Her instincts told her to run and so she reached for the door handle, preparing to flee, but something hard pressed against the back of her head before she had the ability to pull. Wincing in pain, she pinched her eyes closed and felt the fear paralyze her. She didn't have to see to know that the barrel of a gun was pressed against the back of her skull.

"Don't." His voice was deep, raspy. Frightening …

She wondered if she should recognize it. She wondered if she should *know him.*

Opening her eyes, she looked for the rearview mirror, but came to find it had been ripped out of the ceiling.

Breathing heavily, Paula struggled to think fast, to devise a plan. Wondered if there was anything in the car she could use against him. Anything *on her* she could fend him off with. But there was nothing. Taking a silent inventory, she counted her wallet, keys, and a knapsack full of books. A lot of good that would do her.

"You don't understand English? I said *drive.*"

She started, a gasp escaping her open mouth. The barrel of the gun pressed harder against the back of her head and a chill ran through her.

Paula wasn't even sure she *could* drive, but knew she had no other choice. With an unsteady hand, she reached for the keys, still resting in the ignition where she'd left them. She hadn't even had the time to start the engine before she heard his voice. Before she felt the gun …

Turning the key, she listened as the engine revved, felt the car's subtle vibration beneath her. With the touch of a tentative hand, she changed gears and pressed on the gas. Slowly, the car turned and emerged from the lot. The road, long and lit by a sea of orange lights, looked brooding and perilous. She'd driven up and down this road countless times before, but now, she saw it only as a path that would lead to unspeakable evil.

She saw it as a gateway to death.

"Pick up the pace," he said.

Paula had been driving only twenty miles per hour, well below the speed limit. Perhaps she'd subconsciously tried to draw the attention of others this way. Pressing harder on the gas, they accelerated to forty-five. Woods and trees on either side of them, Paula knew that unless someone happened to come upon this road and take notice of these dire circumstances, she was dead. Even if she leapt from the vehicle, there was no place for her to run.

"Where … " she choked, swallowing a lump in her throat. "Where are we going?"

"You don't ask questions. Do you understand me?"

She nodded, blinking and sniffling. Gripping the wheel, she passed another light and felt her insides tighten when a vision flashed in the windshield glass. She'd only caught a glimpse, so she wasn't sure of what she'd seen. Not yet. Turning towards the road, she saw another light not far ahead. As she neared, she allowed her foot to ease off of the pedal, decreasing the car's speed. As they passed beneath the light, she saw that vision again. It was the reflection of something so terrifying, she almost lost all sense of control. It was *him*, huddled in the backseat, a ski mask concealing his features, a black hood over his shoulders. She saw the gun in his gloved hands and the look of menace in his squinted eyes.

"What the fuck do you think you're doing?" he growled, pulling back the hammer. "I said *drive the fucking car before I blow your head off right here and now. Do you understand me?"*

Paula began to cry. The tears slid down her cheeks, past her chin, and down into the open neck of her sweater. She hadn't even had the chance to button her coat and she shivered in the icy cold chill seeping in.

She sniffled again. "Could I … Could I turn the heat on?"

"No."

"Please? I'm freezing. It's so cold out . . ."

"No."

She held tighter to the wheel, watching her hands shake.

Black ice and snow stood in large, shoveled patches on either side of the smooth, dry road. There wasn't much left from last week's storm, but the chill in the air was still strong. It was only the first week of December, still several days before the official start of the season, but already the temperatures had dropped and white flakes fell from black skies with some regularity.

"Where are we going?" Paula asked.

He didn't respond.

"Please ... Please talk to me."

Nothing.

"Please tell me why you're doing this to me."

Not a word.

She swallowed hard, focusing on the road. "You don't know me," she said. "You don't know who I am. I'm ... I'm no one. I'm nothing to you. Right? Just another ... another ... " The word *victim* spun around in her mind, but she wasn't yet ready to call herself that.

"Paula Sheffield."

She blinked. Her eyes widened.

"Eighteen forty-six North Woodbridge."

Her heart hammered inside her chest.

"Age thirty-two."

Oh God ...

"Graduate of Penn State."

No, this can't be happening ...

"Currently employed at the Hemdale Chronicle. Should I go on?"

She was at a total loss for words. Now more confused than ever, she tried to think. She *had* to know him from somewhere. A jilted ex? A former colleague? A friend from her past? Someone she'd wronged?

No, it didn't sound likely. She'd been married to Alan for close to nine years. They were college sweethearts. Most of her friends and colleagues were still in close contact. He had to be someone who'd been stalking her. Someone who'd been watching her for a while. Someone who'd planned this all out. Someone who'd probably been waiting a very long time for this night ...

But why?

Paula felt her shoulders slump and the tears fall once more as they passed her exit. They continued down this long, unwinding road for miles. And when the headlights came out of the distance, she felt her spirits lift, watching as a car quickly approached.

"Don't do anything stupid," he hissed, ducking down low, while still keeping the gun pressed against the back of her head.

Maybe she wouldn't have to do anything. Maybe the driver of the car would see her. Maybe the driver would see *him.* Maybe they'd call the police. Write down her license plate and send help. Maybe they'd swing around and follow. Maybe that driver would be her savior.

Oh God, please help me!

Focused, she watched as the car approached. She kept her eyes on the windshield, doing all she could to will the glance of this anonymous stranger. The anonymous stranger in the bright red sports car. The anonymous stranger who didn't turn or even blink as he passed her car and kept right on going.

Damnit!

That was the last car Paula had seen that night. The last opportunity she had for rescue. They were several miles down the road when he told her to pull over onto the shoulder and turn off the engine. She waited for what felt like a really long time for him to speak again. But he didn't. Instead, he opened the back door and climbed out. He stood before her window, a large beast of a man well past six feet, the gun facing her head-on now.

"Open the door," he said.

Paula didn't move. She sat there shaking, praying to God another car would emerge out of the blue. But there was no one around for miles. Nothing but the deep, dark woods and the icy cold winds. Nothing but the large, menacing figure standing outside the driver's side door.

"Open the door or I'll blow your fucking face off through the glass."

She knew there was no way in hell she could start the car and speed off before he had the chance to pull the trigger. It would be a miracle if she managed to get away in time. She was stuck. Dead. She had no choice but to do as she was told. Bracing herself, she reached for the door handle and pulled. She allowed the door to swing open all the way before stepping out.

"The keys ... " she said, shivering as the warm breath passed her lips and formed a full cloud that disappeared into the night almost immediately.

"Leave 'em."

She looked up and into his eyes, wondering if she should see something there. Some familiarity. Some hint that she knew him. Something that would tell her *why he was doing this to her.* But there was nothing but a cold, blank stare. His lips were pulled back, like a vicious animal, as he exposed his crooked teeth.

"Walk," he said, pointing towards the darkness of the woods past the shoulder.

He's going to rape me. He's going to rape me, shoot me in the head, and leave my body in the woods. Sweet Jesus, is this really the way it's going to end for me?

Paula took careful steps, snapping twigs and crushing dead leaves as she passed the thick trunks of two dead trees. The faint light of the moon guided the way as he stayed close behind. Antsy, she wanted to just run. Just take off and leave him behind. But there was no way she could outrun his bullets. No way she could outrun *him.* And the uncomfortable office shoes wouldn't take her very far.

She almost lost her balance several times as she tried to continue across the treacherous earth. Arms spread wide, the cold surrounded her, left her entire body trembling and fragile.

"Stop," he said when they were deep enough into the woods.
She did.

"Get down on the ground."

"No ... Please ..."

"Did I stutter? I said *get down on the fucking ground, Paula.*"

She fell to her knees, her back to him. Twigs and rocks dug into her bare calves and exposed legs. She winced in pain.

"Turn around and face me."

"Please don't do this to me … Please, I'll-"

"YOU'LL DO AS I FUCKING SAY! NOW TURN AROUND!"

So startled, she shook, letting out a yelp that echoed in the night with his sharp command. She made her way around to face him, but she couldn't open her eyes. She didn't want to know what was coming next. She didn't want to see his eyes when he savaged her. She knew that if she made it through this night, it would be wise to memorize all she could so she'd have something to give to the police. But that was a mere fantasy. There was no way she was making it through this night. She knew that from the moment she felt his gun in the back of her head.

He was going to kill her.

Good-bye, Alan. I hope you know how much I love you.

He stayed perfectly still. She wasn't even sure he was still there. Opening her eyes to thin slits, she saw the barrel of the gun pointed directly at her forehead. And when he spoke, she pinched them closed again.

"His characters are deeply flawed, the plot is unbelievably derivative, and the setting is something straight out of a direct-to-video slasher film used to scare adolescents out of pre-marital sex. The dialogue is unrealistic and the murders unintentionally comical. This book is not only a total waste of time and money, but it's also a waste of paper. Lionel Benton shows zero talent or skill and it wouldn't surprise me if he was never heard from again. He couldn't so much as scare a mentally challenged child with this nonsense."

Inside her, something stirred. Paula knew these words …

He was reciting a passage from a book review she'd submitted to the paper two weeks ago. Some ridiculous horror novel her editor insisted she bump to the top of her list. She couldn't even make it three quarters of the way through before chucking it in the garbage. When she wrote that review, she felt liberated. It felt good to hurt someone who'd wasted her precious time. Secretly, she wished the author was not only never heard from again, but that he never wrote another word.

When she opened her eyes, she saw that he'd lifted the ski mask. She recognized the face as the one smiling on the back of the dust jacket. He wasn't smiling now.

"Let me ask you something, Paula," he said, a crooked sneer lifting his thin lips. "Are you scared now … ?"

He pulled the trigger.

And when he did, a stream of water shot from the barrel, spraying her between the eyes. Startled, she flinched, mouth agape. The water mixed with her falling tears. Panting for breath, she watched him straighten, a look of sheer satisfaction on his unshaven face. He turned on his heels and started off in the opposite direction, leaving her kneeling in the darkness of the cold night, struggling to process what had just happened.

BILLIE SUE MOSIMAN

VERBOTEN

My sister Mira vanished. She's seventeen and threatened to run away a dozen times, so the police say that's just what she did. They promised to put out a missing person alert, but I could see in their faces they didn't expect Mira to turn up.

She didn't run away. That's the thing about Mira; see, she liked to drive you crazy with threats, but she never carried through. She was afraid of being on her own. She just kept getting tired of being trapped at home with me and Granddad. I'm nineteen and wanted to move to Nashville to sing songs after high school (I sing songs all the time.), but Granddad's got Alzheimer's so, hey, I had to stay here in Paryville, Arizona, a one-street desert town dying at the edge of Interstate 10.

I understand Mira's desire to run away. We both wanted to do it. But I know neither of us would, not until Granddad passes. He raised us after our parents died in a car crash so we have to stay with him to the end. We both know that and nothing would make us leave him anyway. He's witless now, but he did the very best he could to parent us and keep us safe while we were growing up. We'd both do anything for him.

So when Mira disappeared, I knew she didn't go of her own free will. Someone took her.

The only place Mira went without me was the truck stop. It sits like a humpbacked dinosaur on I-10 and it's the only place for miles we can go to get food or Cokes or packs of Marlboros. I went there after I called the cops and they wrote notes they knew they wouldn't consult again. I sat down in my favorite booth and waited for Carson Louetta to bring a glass of iced water and an ashtray.

"You seen Mira?" I asked right off. I put my lit cigarette in the tray and brushed brown hair from my eyes. Carson Louetta is forty-ish, hard-ridden and put up wet. She's got a temper sometimes too.

"Hell, when don't I see Mira? She's always hanging around in here."

"No, I mean in the past three days? She hasn't been home."

Carson Louetta knew our family well and she knew the circumstances. Despite her easy temper, she had a soft spot for two girls left to grow up in Paryville with an old man living on Social Security. She often let us have our Cokes without paying.

"What do you mean she hasn't been home in three days? You call the cops, Dorothy?"

I nodded and picked up the cigarette to take a puff. "They don't care. They're from over in Sidler and they think she's a runaway."

"Mira wouldn't run away."

"I know that. That's why I'm looking for clues."

"You think something bad happened?"

"I think it did. 'Cause if it didn't, Mira would be home by now."

"It's been three days since I saw her." Carson Louetta slid into the booth opposite me. The cafe was slow this time of day.

"Did anyone try to pick her up? Anyone sit with her?"

The old waitress's face creased with thought. "No..."

"But what?"

"But there was a trucker keeping his eye out."

"More than usual, you mean?"

"Yeah, more than we usually see. He sat over there." She pointed to a booth on the back wall. "He couldn't get his fill of Mira. She had a Coke and a Frito pie. He left before she did. I don't know what he did after that—I mean, if he hung around in the store or if he left."

I sipped the cold water. My stomach was feeling queasy. "What did he look like? You see his truck? He wear a uniform?"

"He was thirty-something, long dark hair, black eyes, mustache. I didn't see his truck, no uniform. Wore jeans and tee-shirt like they all do. Might as well be homeless the way they dress."

"You ever see him here before?"

"He might have been in before. I think I remember that mustache. It's big and bushy."

"You'll know him if you see him again?"

"Absolutely."

"Can I get a Coke, plenty of ice?"

Carson Louetta left for my drink while I thought about a trucker watching my little sister. He could have waited for her in the store and followed her out. He could have strong-armed her to his truck and...

I didn't want to think what a stranger might do. Strangers are *verboten*. That's what Granddad always told us about the truck stop and our frequent visits to it. At least he did when he could still remember what he was saying. "Strangers, they verboten," he'd say in his German accent. "They get you, keep you, then leave you in a ditch. Watch that place, those people."

At home that night, the third night of Mira's disappearance,

I made Granddad a frozen dinner of smothered steak, mashed potatoes, and corn. I added a green salad and a dish of peaches for dessert. I had to help him eat. He didn't really communicate anymore, not in any real sense. He often said things, but they were off-topic or odd things and we just ignored his mutterings.

I always talked to him anyway, hoping to keep a piece of his memory alive. "Mira's missing," I said, spooning mashed potatoes into his mouth. His eyes gleamed blue and clear, but behind the blue the mind was dim as dishwater. He grunted.

"I think she was followed out of the truck stop. A *stranger* took her."

"Verboten!" he shouted.

I reached to touch his mottled arm. There were little burst purple capillaries and bruises on the papery skin. He was almost a cadaver. My sweet Granddad, thin as spaghetti, weak of mind and body. It hurt me to look at him. "It's okay, Granddad, settle down. I'm going to find her."

I offered him a peach slice and his mouth came toward it where he slurped it in with a loud sound. I grinned at him. "You like peaches," I said.

"Mira," he said.

I nodded, getting another peach on the tines of the fork. "Yeah."

"Gone?"

Once in a while a little got through to him. I looked up. "Yeah, she's gone. I'm going to get her back."

"Ditch," he said.

"Don't say that."

"Ditch," he said.

I put the peach in his mouth to shut him up. I didn't want to think about ditches.

I went to the Human Resource office in Sidler and explained the situation. I needed help at home with Granddad. He had to be watched unless he was asleep and I couldn't leave the house at all. I showed them his bank account and the direct-deposited small Social Security check. "I can't pay for help."

They took pity and sent a girl called Teppy to spend days with Granddad. She swept the floors, did his wash, made him meals. She was a patient, rather dull girl and she even sat for hours with him helping him cut newspapers into strips.

With Teppy there, I spent my days at the truck stop. It was called Dillon's and the big sign outside was in white neon that lit up the front parking area at night, but there were no lights behind the building where truckers parked.

When Carson Louetta was on duty, she gave me my Cokes free. When she wasn't there, I paid and sipped slowly. I waited and watched. I was looking for a big, mustached man with black eyes.

It was a week later he came in. I knew it was him before Carson Louetta started gesturing. I took my Coke glass and walked to his booth. I sat across from him.

"You still got Mira?" I asked. I didn't see any point in beating around the bush.

He didn't even look surprised. He seemed to smile a little, but who could tell with that bush covering his lips?

"I knew a Mira once."

"Like last week? She just vanished after she was here. You take her? I want her back. She's my little sister."

He waggled his head and chuckled as if I were the funniest comedian in the world. Carson Louetta brought him a menu and he told her he'd just do the buffet. When she walked away, she gave me a warning look.

I knew what I was doing.

"You want her back," he said.

"I want her back."

"What if when you get her back, you're sorry you asked?"

"I'll handle it."

"You're a tough one, right?"

"Wasn't Mira? It runs in the family."

He seemed to think it over and then he said, "She wasn't tough enough."

I had taken to carrying Granddad's .25 caliber automatic and I almost pulled it on the truck driver. He was admitting she was dead. Tears came up my throat and my eyes burned. Then fury blocked them and I felt like a brick wall he'd never bring down, *never*. Not with his words, his confessions, and not with his black, evil deeds.

"I want her back."

"You'll have to come with me," he said, rising to go to the buffet bar.

I sat waiting for him to come back. I knew what going with him might mean and I had to be ready for it. Ready for anything.

I sat watching him eat while I sipped my Coke. I smoked and waited.

When he finished I followed him to the checkout counter where he paid. I saw Carson Louetta coming from the kitchen, her face all screwed up seeing me standing beside the stranger.

"Let's go," I said, taking his arm, angling him to the exit door.

His truck was an old Peterbilt with a small cab with a sleeping nook behind the seats. It smelled like body odor and rancid food. I saw empty potato chip bags on the floor and candy wrappers on the dash. Mira would have fought him. I looked for evidence of blood, but the rig was so dirty it would take a forensic team to find it.

"Where is she?" I asked.

It was barely noon and I had five hours before Teppy's shift ended with Granddad. I hoped Mira wasn't too far away.

"I'm taking you," he said, not really answering the question.

The .25 auto pressed against my spine where it hid beneath my loose denim shirt. I wouldn't pull it until it was time. I didn't know when that time would be, but I knew it was on the way. I didn't carry a purse. I wanted my hands free at all times and besides, it eased the stranger's worry thinking I had no protection.

"Why do you do it?" I asked. I really wanted to know.

He shrugged.

"Go ahead, tell me."

"Just something I do, that's all."

"Like taking a bath or eating a meal? Like driving a truck? Just something you do—taking girls?"

He looked over hearing my tone of voice. It hadn't been that hard before.

"You want to watch it," he said.

"It's just been me and Mira for two years. Our Granddad raised us when our folks died, but he's been sick and can't think anymore so it's just been us."

"Now it's just you."

I swallowed hard. "You going to let me have her? I just want to bury her body. It's the Christian thing to do. It'll be a grave I can visit."

"I don't know yet." He glanced over again, his eyes very still and threatening. "You might have to join her."

"You want to watch it," I said, mimicking his own threatening voice. "I'm tougher than Mira was. Write it down."

He chuckled. I hated when he chuckled.

He drove for an hour and then he pulled off the freeway onto an exit, and from the exit onto a dirt road leading away into the long desert. The sun flooded the land with white lava light, and sweat was rolling down my neck.

"Out here?" I asked. It was so empty. It was the moon. Mira didn't deserve this. She had only been seventeen and full of life. She slapped her knees when she laughed. She liked practical jokes. She treated Granddad with such respect and love, always kissing his grizzled cheek when she left him. She had one more year of high school and then she said maybe she'd go to beauty school because she liked hair.

"She's out here?" I asked again.

He nodded.

"You get off on it, is that it? There's gotta be a pay-off."

The rig bounced and jounced, rocking us in the leather seats. I'd never put on the seat belt so I had to hold onto the arm rest to keep from being thrown to the dash.

He hadn't answered. I prodded. "You even get an erection? Is it soft, like a sausage lying out in the sun on the porch all day?"

I saw his jaw clench. I was pushing it. So fucking what. He needed pushing. If he'd really abducted and killed my sister, he needed a lot of pushing.

"Women won't fuck you on their own, am I right? Women find you too creepy. You creep them out. They shy off. So you go hunting. You pick up pretty girls like Mira, just teenagers who won't give you a whole lot of trouble. I bet you've even taken old women, women who can't fight worth shit. And little kids, you take kids too?"

I expected it, but wasn't ready when it came. He hit me so hard in the face I felt my teeth slam together and a couple of them cracked to send instant lightning pain into my head. Blood ran from my nose and mouth. I reached up and wiped it off with the back of my hand. I needed time to get my mind back. The slap had made my brain rattle around in my skull and the whole world went gray for seconds.

I straightened in my seat. He was slowing down. I peered out the window, looking for something that shouldn't be in the desert. There it was. A mound of dirt about ten inches above ground-level. Mira's grave.

The truck stopped and he turned off the ignition. The engine ticked, ticked, and he didn't move. A hawk flew high in the azure sky, circling an air current.

"Get out," he said. He opened his door and stepped down, the metal step ringing loud in the silence.

As I got out, he came around the hood of the truck. He walked toward the mound. "Here," he said. "This is where she is. Now what's that get you?"

I stood over the yellow-tan dirt and the pebbles and the clots of brown earth and I almost went to my knees to dig her up.

"I don't do kids," he said, turning to leave me in the desert to die of thirst.

I turned to watch him while I pulled out the .25 automatic. He must have had a sixth sense for danger because he turned quick, frowning. He saw me pointing the gun.

"That's a pea-shooter."

"I'm a marksman," I said. And it was true. Granddad had taught us to shoot at bottles until we never missed.

"She came with me willingly. She was running away." I saw the sweat running from his temples to his cheeks like mind-tears.

"Bullshit." I pulled the trigger and the bullet caught him on the right side of his jaw and went clear through. He went to his knees like a bear falling. He stared up at me, his eyes frantic.

"She's not there. I lied. I can show you where she is..."

That's when I shot again, this time aiming for the space between his eyes.

"You don't get out of this with a lie," I said. "You die here."

With him dead, I slouched to the ground, shaking. I'd shot desert varmints, but never a man. It felt different, a lot different. It felt like changing into something not human—a panther or a scorpion or a rattler, something with a brain far less sophisticated. For some moments I was as mindless as Granddad. It was a bad place to be and it made me cry inside for my grandfather. No one should be lost in a place where your mind leaves you.

I dropped the gun and crawled to Mira's grave. It took me another hour to get her out, to dust her off, and to carry her to the truck.

I peeled an orange and pulled the succulent sections apart, the juice shooting out over my knuckles. I carefully laid one section at a time on Granddad's tongue. He chewed slowly, relishing the strong, beautiful taste. The scent of the orange filled the air and made it citrus.

"I brought her home," I told him.

He said nothing and didn't look at me. He had a newspaper in one hand and the scissors in the other. He hadn't finished making a neat pile of the strips on his tray yet.

"Man took her off and I shot him dead."

Granddad grunted.

Teppy came in the door and called out cheerfully, "I'm here!"

I handed her the rest of the orange to feed my grandfather. "I'm going to Dillon's for a Coke," I said. "Be back later."

She sat down in my chair and turned her attention to Granddad. "You like oranges, don't you? Me too. Oranges are good for you. All that vitamin C."

At the truck stop I knew Carson Louetta wanted to question me, but she never said a word. It had been weeks since the boss had the abandoned truck hauled out of the back lot. Carson Louetta knew it was all a secret. For Mira.

I had buried Mira in the back of the house, digging the grave much deeper than the one the stranger had put her into in the desert. I planted a wild red rose on it and ringed it with white rocks as if it were a flowerbed.

Granddad died peacefully in his bed. I woke one day in the autumn and found him looking so quiet, so cold. I had him taken to the funeral home and put in the Paryville graveyard.

After the service, I stopped by the real estate office in Sidler and signed up the house for sale.

They say my songs are beautiful, but sad, really sad. My voice, they say, sounds like it's been steeped in bitterness. "It sounds like green pecans taste," the producer said once.

My hit, "Mira," topped the country billboard and made me enough money to buy a nice place outside of Nashville. I had dug up Mira and brought her with me in a big old round-topped chest Granddad had owned when he'd been in the Navy. At my new house, when the moon was high, and everyone asleep, I pulled the chest into the backyard, dug Mira a new grave, and put her dry remains in it. I planted a rose over her and used bricks to fashion a flowerbed around the newly turned earth.

It was early dawn when I finished. I sang to her; I sang my little sister's song I'd written, and the birds twittered along with me as accompaniment, an owl called *whoooo,* and somewhere in the distance I heard a dog howl like it was dying.

She'd always be with me. She was not a verboten dead thing of bones and hanks of hair and flesh shriveling to leather. She was Mira and she was home. She'd never meant to leave me and now she never would.

Time passed slowly, age crept into my body on caterpillar feet. Having a successful singing career, I was on the road a lot doing gigs, giving concerts. I forced my driver to park for the night in truck stops. He tried to argue, but I paid his salary so in the end that's where we stayed on tour when we had overnight trips.

I drank Cokes in the cafes, looking at the truckers. When one approached, I smiled, and asked him to join me. I went with him when he wanted me to. My driver would wait. My band wasn't going anywhere without me. I'd already instructed them on the rules. "I don't come back to the bus some nights, just stay and wait. I'll return."

I was much too successful for them to question me.

In the cafes I wore wigs and no makeup. I was rarely recognized.

I dropped the truckers who tried to hurt me in deserted places and drove their trucks back to the truck stop. There must have been thirty of them over the years. Thirty bodies in thirty dismal out-of-the-way makeshift graves.

I retired when I turned fifty and my voice got too beat up

and worn out. I had enough money to last me until I was at least two-hundred years old.

I stopped going to truck stops. I didn't think I had enough years left to get them all. They were everywhere, the men with black eyes and blacker hearts, and they weren't just drivers of trucks. Some of them who took me with them and wanted me to vanish were travelers, those in cars and vans and old rusted motorhomes. People out on the road, looking for victims to lose in nameless graves in the dark.

I'd never be able to stop them all.

I'd have to be satisfied with what I'd done. Not the singing career. Not the escape from Paryville, Arizona. I'd have to be satisfied with the strangers I'd dispatched to hell. Who can say when enough is enough? I did my best.

They say now I'm losing my memory. They say I have to keep a girl in the house to watch over me. She feeds me oranges and peaches and I like her curly hair. Mira had curly hair. The other day I asked the girl to bring me a picture puzzle, but I couldn't put it together. Nothing fits. I said, "This puzzle is defective." She took it back to the store and bought another. Same thing. I played with it anyway, turning the pieces this way and that for hours, my mind wandering and calm, so calm.

I realize I'm a lot like Granddad was toward the end. Some of us go that way—with a whimper, not a bang. I don't mind. We all go some way. We all vanish in the end, taken against our will by Old Man Death.

I told them to bury me in the backyard, next to the rose garden...next to Mira. They think that's the name of the rose or something. They think I'm cracked. I called my attorney over and made out my will and my wishes. I told him if he has to get a special court order, then do it. If he didn't get me buried in the yard next to the rose garden and if he didn't have my house torn down per my wishes, I'd come back and haunt him.

I don't know if he'll do it. If he didn't, if he put me in the city graveyard, you have me disinterred and moved, okay? Pull the house down. Keep the land so you know where we are.

Men. I don't trust the lot of them. Never did and that's why I divorced your dad. My last advice for you, my daughter, is: You want to watch out for strangers. Tear up this diary when you've finished reading it, burn it, get rid of it. You just watch it. And carry a gun. I've told you this before.

Always carry a little gun and know how to use it.

Your loving mother,

Dorothy.

LINCOLN CRISLER

NOURI AND THE BEETLES

Marna watched as Nouri swished through the marketplace in her filmy skirts, appraising produce and looking over the various shopkeepers' wares. The looks on the men's faces as Nouri passed by them turned Marna's stomach.

"There are precious few prospects to choose from," she whispered to a girl standing beside her, "without having to compete with her for every single one of them!" Her complaint wasn't exactly unfair; the most popular and eligible men of the tribe were fighting a war with a neighboring people, and the ones left behind either knew their increased worth or were too dense to care.

"Well, what do you expect, Marna? She has everything," the other replied. "Look at the way her skirts cling to her hips! The way the wind moves in her hair! No man is going to look at us twice with Nouri around."

"Pendal did," Marna scowled, "for almost a whole day." Pendal had fallen into that latter category of men, as far as she was concerned.

"Well, I don't know what we can do about it, Marna," the other girl said. "Maybe you should just drop it."

"Maybe I just need to find better friends, Urie."

Marna turned her back on Urie, on the marketplace, on Nouri and stalked down the worn, dirt path to her family's hut. Her brother Mabek and his friends were gathered in a tight circle in the dusty front yard.

"What's so interesting?" Marna demanded, and the young boys broke apart to let her see. They had carved a circle in the dirt, and in the midst of it a large, black insect crawled over another, motionless one.

"We caught beetles and made them fight," Mabek explained, "And now the winner is eating the loser."

"Perhaps he heard the legend our people tell," one of the other boys giggled, "That if a hunter kills a tiger and eats its heart, he'll gain its strength!"

Marna shook her head and went inside to help her mother with dinner. To be so young again, she thought, and not as concerned with matters of substance. She was a woman now, and had to cast her eyes to the future. Mabek could still be oblivious to everything but his chores and schooling for a few more years. Gods, but she was jealous of everyone today.

"What can I help with, Mother?" But Risha, her mother, was already cooking. A large pot steamed over the fireplace, and she stirred it with a heavy wooden spoon. "I'm sorry I'm late."

"Oh, you're not late," Risha looked up. "This isn't dinner. This is a spell for our men at war." Marna looked into the pot. Flower petals, bones, scraps of skin and herbs swam in the repellent-smelling liquid.

"Is it to keep them from coming back?" Marna asked, waving her hand in front of her nose. "It's so awful, how can it do any good?"

"The best medicines aren't always pleasing to the senses, girl," Risha said gently. "And someday, like I am with this spell, you'll have to do things you may not like now because of the benefit they'll have later."

Risha watched the boiling spellpot a moment longer and then began making preparations for dinner. Marna worked alongside her, enjoying the thwack of her mother's sharp knife on the wooden block, the crunch of the vegetables and the scent of the seasonings they rubbed on the pig leg. As she helped her mother put the roast on the spit she heard her father come in from the fields.

"Those boys are still out there bug-fighting, Risha," he said, laying his cloak aside and taking his wife into his arms. "Do you remember me being so interested in insects at that age?"

"Not really. You had your mind on other things." She smiled at him and Marna looked away. It made her eyes burn to be so close to love after being forsaken by Pendal.

"Those boys should be studying their lessons, or working with their fathers," she muttered. Her father, Majab, laughed and pulled her under his arm.

"They're learning things, Marna. Mabek was just telling me the story of the hunter eating the tiger's heart. My grandfather swore he actually did it when he was a boy, and I spent a week looking for tigers when I was Mabek's age, after hearing that story. Of course there weren't any; they moved on to greener pastures, like we should if the hunting doesn't begin to improve. But he's learning history and the ways of our people, and I don't mind working the fields by myself while he does. I'm much happier with him playing with bugs than looking for a tiger to slay."

"It's just a silly story, though, and I don't see how it'll help him grow crops or raise pigs and chickens," she said, pulling away and pouring her father a mug of water from a jug on the ground.

"It's symbolic magic," Risha explained. "Like when I burn seeds for the fertility of our animals and crops. Seeds are a symbol of fertility, right?" Marna nodded. "So using them in a spell to bring life makes sense, doesn't it?" Marna nodded again.

"Our ancestors thought the same way," Majab continued. "Eating the most vital organ of the strongest, fiercest creature they knew in order to gain such power for themselves made sense." Marna shuddered.

"They must have been pretty fierce to begin with to eat a raw, beating heart."

She lay awake that night in her pile of thick, woven blankets. Every time she tried to sleep, images of Pendal and Nouri, wrapped around each other, flooded her mind. There had to be something she could do; she was better suited for Pendal and she knew it. He was strong, fast and smart; he'd make a good provider. Nouri was weak and soft and would be a drain on the resources he'd provide.

Marna knew she'd keep a better house, bear and raise stronger children and be of more assistance in the farming of crops and cleaning of animals than Nouri. Just looking at her, Marna could tell she'd shy away from spilled blood in an instant, and Marna had never seen so much as a speck of work-dust on her. The only thing she had going for her was her appearance. She was the most beautiful and healthy-looking girl Marna knew.

That gave her an idea. She needed to talk to someone about it first, and her parents were out of the question. She slowly put on her clothes and eased her way to the front door and out of the house. Despite her fight earlier with Urie, she knew her friend would be able to make sense of things.

She was at Urie's hut in a couple of minutes and stooped in the dirt a few feet away to gather small rocks, which she threw one at a time at the bundled-reed shutter covering her friend's bedroom window.

"What do you want?" The shutter flipped open just enough for Marna to see a glittering eye and tiny, brown fingertips.

"Come outside. We need to talk!"

"Couldn't find any better friends?"

"Of course I couldn't, and we both knew that when I said it. I didn't even try. I'm sorry. Now please come out!"

She heard Urie sigh and let the shutter fall back into place. A moment later her friend appeared, slipping out the back door, fully clothed, with a small basket in her hand.

"I have a bit of bread and meat, and some liquor in here," she said, smiling. "We can empty the basket and do some picking for my mother. If she finds me gone, this way she won't be upset."

They munched together in silence until they reached Urie's mother's berry bushes. Urie pulled the last item, a small bottle of liquor, from the basket. The girls shared a drink, then set it down beside the bush and began filling the basket with berries.

"So what is it you wanted to talk about?" Urie asked softly.

"I think," Marna hesitated for a moment, but her belly was warm from the liquor, and she felt more confident than before she'd left her house. This was a good idea, even if Urie said otherwise, so why not tell her? "I think I'm going to kill and eat Nouri." Urie dropped the basket and stared, gaping and motionless, at her friend.

"What kind of demonic talk is that?"

"Hear me out; we've been friends since we were babies, and you know I'm not insane. It's a principle of magic; you know those little spells our mothers sometimes do?"

"Sure," Urie said, nodding. "My mother does one the evening before each of father's hunting trips."

"Right. Mine was doing some kind of charm for our fighting men. Do you know the story about our ancestors and how they ate the heart of the strongest, fiercest animals they killed?"

"I think I know where this is going," Urie said. "You want to eat Nouri's heart so that you can possess her beauty."

"Exactly," Marna said. "Can you think of any woman in the village more beautiful, who can more easily ensnare any man she desires?"

"No," Urie agreed. "But to eat her flesh? To kidnap and murder her? Do you think you can do that?"

"I think I can try. Look at it this way, even if we can't bring ourselves to eat her, she'll still be out of the way. I'll have my chance at Pendal and you'll have your pick of anyone else."

"You want me to help?"

"I *need* you to help. Look, you'd help me kill her if she threatened me, wouldn't you?" She stared at her friend fiercely. Urie stared back, straight into Marna's eyes.

"You know I would."

"Then help me now. She is a threat, just in a different way."

They filled the basket with berries and walked back to Urie's hut. They stood beside the front door for a moment, sharing the last of the liquor and a handful of the sweet, juicy fruit.

"Tomorrow, we'll need to find a place to keep her," Marna said. "And think of a way to lure her."

"Let's find the place, first. Then maybe an idea will come to us."

"Agreed." The two girls hugged tightly and went their separate ways until morning.

The next morning, Marna rushed through her chores with even more than her usual efficiency, packed a sack with some of her mother's fresh bread, cheese and water and hiked over to Urie's hut. Her friend was outside, throwing feed to a small group of cackling chickens.

"Good morning," Marna called, waving away the cloud of dust the fowl were kicking up in their struggle for food. "I brought lunch. We can look for a secret spot when you've finished your work."

"I'm just about finished," Urie said, scattering the rest of the seed and going back inside. She returned with a bag slung over her shoulder and her little sister in tow. She knelt before the younger girl for a moment, whispered her some instructions and then stood, walked over to Marna and took her by the arm.

"What's in the bag, Urie?"

"You'll see when we get there."

They walked nearly two miles, well outside the village, over the hills that bordered it on the south side and through the grassy valley some of the herdsmen used to graze their flocks. There were a couple of young boys tending some sheep and goats, but they paid the girls no mind. On the other side of the valley were more hills, steeper ones. Marna and Urie climbed to the top and looked around. A short distance down one of the far slopes was a small cave mouth, partially concealed by brush.

"Let's try over there," Marna said. Barely a minute later they were at the mouth of the cave. The hole was barely big enough for one girl to enter at a time. Urie put a hand on Marna's shoulder to halt her and set her pack on the ground. She pulled out a thick candle, a piece of flint and a chunk of metal and struck sparks until the candle caught fire.

"You're not the only practical one," she said, grinning, and thrust the candle and her head into the cave. "It's a lot bigger in here than it looks."

"I used to play here when I was a little girl, with some friends," Marna said, "Before your family settled in the village. I was hoping it would be the way I remembered it."

"Well, come inside and see," Urie said, squeezing in the rest of the way and making room for her friend. Marna eased her way inside and looked around. The ground was flat and there was more than enough room. Urie reached back outside and pulled her bag in, then began clearing the center of the cave of pebbles and rocks.

"What are you doing?" Marna asked, helping her friend.

"If we're really going to do this, I want to do it right," Urie answered. When the dirt was smooth and clear of debris, she pulled a thick bundle of cloth from her bag. She unrolled it, and there lay inside four metal spikes, a hammer and some rope.

"You did think of everything, didn't you?" Marna said, helping Urie spread out the cloth.

"I'm still not sure about … eating Nouri," Urie said, shuddering.

"She does need to go though, I agree with you on that." She set the spikes at each corner of the cloth and began hammering them into the ground. "At least this way, we'll be ready for whatever happens. Tie these ropes to the spikes." Marna knelt and began tying the ropes off while Urie finished hammering the spikes. While her fingers worked, her mind did as well.

"I think I know how to get her here," Marna said when they were done.

That night after dinner, Marna asked her mother if she could spend the night with Urie. Her mother agreed, and after helping her clean up and saying goodnight to her father and brother, she took up her small pack and a water jug and walked to Nouri's hut.

She and Urie had discussed their plan earlier, and everything was ready. Urie would tell her parents she was staying with Marna and would be waiting at the cave. Marna was to bring the knife and the sacrifice. The knife was in her pack, and Nouri, gods willing, would be coming along shortly.

Nouri's hut was quiet, and dim light came from a couple of the windows. They'd just be finishing dinner themselves, more likely than not. Nouri's father was a farmer, like Marna's, and most farmers in the village kept the same schedule. She tapped lightly on the door of the hut, and Nouri answered.

"Hi, Nouri," Marna said, stifling the nervous feeling in the pit of her stomach. What if this didn't work? It was the only part of the plan that was entirely out of her control, and she couldn't be sure how the girl would respond. They knew each other from school, but they had never been friends.

"It's good to see you, Marna," Nouri said, smiling. Her graciousness made Marna feel even worse. She really was a nice girl, not stuck up at all. Marna pushed her feelings back. *Sometimes you have to do things you may not like now because of the benefit they'll have later.*

"I found a new spring on the other side of the valley," she said.

"I'm going there to fetch some water, and I thought maybe I'd show you were it was."

"That's really nice of you," Nouri said. "I could use a walk. Let me grab a jug." She went back inside and Marna breathed silent gratitude to the heavens. Maybe she was meant to do this. Nouri returned a moment later and the two girls set off for the valley.

"What did your mother say when you told her about the water?" Marna asked as they walked.

"She wasn't home, actually," Nouri said. "She's visiting with the priest to discuss my brother's puberty ritual." Marna shivered with anticipation. This was even better than she had expected. The two girls walked in silence and Marna played what was to come next over and over in her head until they reached the crest of the hills of the far side of the valley.

"It's right down the other side," she said. "You'll be able to hear it soon." Nouri looked at her and smiled.

"Thanks for thinking of me, Marna." Marna fought back the pain in her heart.

"I think you can see it, if you look over there," Marna said, pointing down the slope. Nouri turned and looked.

"I think I can . . ."

Marna picked up a sharp rock and smashed it over Nouri's head, and the other girl dropped without a sound.

It was hard work dragging Nouri down the hill, even with gravity on her side. It took her endless, nervous minutes to reach the mouth of the cave, but when she did, Urie was waiting inside to help her, just as planned. Marna slipped in after and huddled on the ground, catching her breath, while her friend secured the ropes to Nouri's ankles and wrists.

"What do we do now?" Urie asked when she was done.

"Now, we need to pray, and offer sacrifice," Marna said. She wasn't sure about this, and she didn't have anyone to ask, but it just seemed right. She took the knife from her pack and cut off Nouri's silky dress. Then she tied a bit of Urie's rope tightly around Nouri's

thigh and stuffed a wad of cloth into her mouth. She took a deep
breath and drove the sharp, cold blade into Nouri's thigh.

Blood oozed thickly from the cut and she heard Urie gasp
as she cut deeper, all the way to the bone. Nouri woke up, tried
to scream through the gag and struggled against the ropes and
Marna forced herself not to look at the girl's face as she drove the
knife through the bone, breaking it. She sawed the rest of the way
through Nouri's leg. Blood spurted as she severed the artery, but
stopped quickly; Marna had tied the rope well. When the leg was
severed, Marna was relieved to discover that Nouri had passed out
again.

"Honored gods," Marna said, lifting the dripping leg into the
air, "We honor you and ask you to give us the gift of this girl's
spirit. Make her vitality and beauty one with ours, as we make
her one flesh with us." She licked her lips, tasted the salt-copper
of Nouri's blood, and looked up at Urie. Her friend was in shock,
staring off into space, and spattered in blood herself. Marna laid
the leg back on the cloth and sawed off two chunks.

"We need to save most of it for the wild dogs when we throw
her down the hill," she said, "But this is for us." She raised a chunk
of quivering, red flesh to her mouth and bit into it. It wasn't as bad
as she thought it would be. Quite good, in fact, as long as she didn't
think about where it came from. She chewed slowly and imagined
Nouri's soul soaking into her, trickling through her body as the
blood trickled down her chin.

"Eat," she said to Urie, offering the other piece. Urie sat still on
the ground, motionless. Marna stroked the meat across her friend's
lips, and Urie's tongue flickered out to taste the blood. Slowly, Urie
took the flesh from Marna's hand and placed it in her mouth.

The girls sat there for a while, in silence. Marna savored the
taste of Nouri still on her tongue and spread across her mouth. She
licked her lips and looked over at Urie. She was doing the same.

"Not as horrible as I thought it would be," Marna said. Urie
nodded, plucked a scrap of meat from Marna's cheek, and popped

it into her mouth.

"I wonder what the heart will taste like," Urie said. "You're flushed. Magic or not, I swear I can see a difference already."

"You look different, too. And I'll tell you what the heart tastes like in a few minutes. Morning will come soon, and we still have to get rid of the body."

"What do you mean, you'll tell me what the heart tastes like?" Urie frowned at Marna. "We're sharing it, aren't we?"

"I'm not sure it works that way," Marna said. "It's not like I could ask anyone. To be on the safe side, I'm going to eat the whole thing. This was my idea, after all."

"No!" Urie rose to her feet. "You couldn't have done this without me. I brought the ropes, and I … I ate a girl's *flesh!* I didn't do that for nothing!"

"We'll find you another girl," Marna said, licking the knife clean and appraising Nouri's naked chest. "And you can have the rest of the leg, if you want. The dogs will gnaw the bone and no one would be able to tell anyhow, even if she's found."

"She's the best! And you're no better than me, that you should get her spirit all to yourself! Besides, we'll be lucky to get away with killing her. You want to make things worse by murdering two?" Urie picked up a large, sharp rock and sprang at her friend.

Marna threw herself backwards and pushed her legs up to fend Urie off, but the angry girl thrust her way past her friend's defenses and brought the rock down on her skull. Marna's head spun from the shock, and she slashed the knife up in a wild arc at the three Uries, each raising a rock over her head, hovering above.

She struck air. Urie didn't. The last thing Marna heard was a fierce scream, and then everything went black.

It took Urie an hour to drag Marna and Nouri down the hill and into the brush for the dogs to find, and she was dirty, sweaty and covered in blood. As she climbed back to the valley and over the hills bordering her village, she swore she could still feel the girls' hearts quivering in her belly. They had tasted quite good, even better than Nouri's flesh.

She reached the riverbed as the sun was coming up, and the small wading pool at the river's mouth beckoned her with its still, cool depths. She stopped and washed her dress, then wrung it out and stretched it across some rocks before kneeling at the pool again. Her reflection *was* improving already. Her skin had never been as clear as Nouri's, or Marna's, even, but it now had a healthy glow and was smoother than before, if her eyes could be trusted.

She slid into the chilly water and washed away the dust and gore. Then she settled against the bank and relaxed, taking in the orange hues of the new dawn. When she began shivering from the cool air, she rose, tugged her half-damp dress back on, and walked upstream to pick some aloe and lavender for her skin.

She had to look her best, after all. Several heartbroken young men would soon be seeking comfort.

SHANE MCKENZIE

SO MUCH PAIN, SO MUCH DEATH

"What the fuck do you want me to do? What else can we do?"

Erin glared at him from the kitchen table, her eyes rimmed red and sunken. She pointed at him with a shaking finger, the nails chewed down to slivers. "You're ... you're glad this happened. Aren't you?"

Shawn had been pacing, but at the sound of his wife's words, he stopped. His eyes burned from lack of sleep. "What did you say?"

She jumped to her feet, throwing her coffee cup to the floor and shattering it. The coffee had grown cold, and it crawled across the linoleum until it touched the tips of Shawn's toes.

"I said you're glad. *She's our baby! Where … where is my baby!*"

The last sentence belted from her throat at a high pitch, and afterward, she crumbled to her knees and wept, the black, cold coffee soaking into her pajama pants. "Oh … oh my god, Shawn. I can't live like this. Without her. I'd rather be dead."

Shawn let himself fall beside her, and he pulled her in and held her, let her sob into his shoulder. He wanted to cry too, but he had cried so much over the past two months, only anger was left. His wife's words still rang in his skull, and part of him wondered if she was right.

No, no. I miss my daughter. No matter how … difficult she was. No matter how frustrated I got. She's my goddamn daughter!

Shawn wasn't sure how long they stayed that way on the floor, Erin clinging to him as if they were on the edge of a cliff with strong winds slamming against them. At some point during her cry, she had fallen asleep, and Shawn didn't have the heart to wake her. Sleep didn't come easily these days.

The phone rang.

Every time that fucking thing rang, Shawn's chest tightened, his stomach dropped. So far, every time it rang there was no good news on the other end. Just useless information. Detective Hudson ensuring them that everything that could be done was being done. If it wasn't that, it was reporters, even a few prank callers.

Erin jerked awake, slapped him hard on the chest again and again. "Answer it. Hurry up, Shawn, and answer the goddamn—"

"I'm going." He raced toward the cordless, unable to keep his hopes from rising. A deep breath, then he answered. "Yes?"

Detective Hudson's voice swam into his ear. But the words he was saying couldn't possibly be true. After all this time …

The man kept talking, but Shawn didn't hear another word of it. His mind just kept repeating those first three words that were spoken.

We found her.

Oklahoma. They had found her in Oklahoma. A seven hour drive from Austin.

It took Shawn five to get there, and though Erin was always the kind to tell him to slow down, be careful, you're going to kill us, she didn't say a word as he weaved his way through traffic to get to their little girl.

Alive. She was alive. That's what the detective had said.

"A man was walking his dog, heard the screaming. Thirteen of them. We found thirteen children, but only nine alive."

And Lily was one of the living. Shawn knew it wasn't right to be glad that the other kids were dead and not his daughter, but he was happy about it nonetheless. He couldn't imagine what the other parents must be going through, but he forced himself not to think about it.

My baby girl is alive. She's alive and that's all that matters.

"Turn left here," Erin had said. She hadn't stopped shaking the entire trip, didn't say a word that wasn't directions she was getting off her cell phone.

Shawn didn't blame her. Until they actually saw Lily, it still didn't seem real. Felt like some kind of cruel trick.

Detective Hudson stood by his car. He had driven from Texas as well, a day before calling Shawn and Erin. "Wanted to make sure it was the real deal," he had said. "Wanted to see her for myself first." The man had been good to them, had actually given a shit. Shawn thought Detective Hudson wanted to find their daughter as much as they did.

Shawn hadn't killed the engine before Erin was opening her door and racing toward the detective. She screamed and bawled as she went, and just watching her, Shawn couldn't stop the tears from flowing. But after all the time he spent crying, these tears were different. These were tears of relief, a relief so heavy and strong it nearly crushed his ribcage. He stayed in the car, found it hard to open his door as he watched the detective take Erin into his arms, whisper something to her, and then guide her to the back seat of his Lincoln.

The door was thrown open. Erin dropped to her knees and wailed, then threw her arms into the car.

Shawn saw the tiny hands—covered in a layer of black filth—grip the back of Erin's head as the two of them hugged, Erin's body shaking as she clutched their daughter in her arms and bawled harder than ever.

The scene swam in Shawn's tears, and all he could do was rest his forehead against the steering wheel, cry, and thank God.

"I want to see it."

Detective Hudson pursed his lips, placed his hand on Shawn's shoulder. He shot a look toward the house where forensics was going in and out, taking pictures, bagging up evidence. "Can't do it, Shawn. Even if this was my jurisdiction, it'd be damn near impossible. Probably not much to see by now anyway."

Shawn shrugged the hand away, stared past the detective toward the house. The house where his daughter was held captive for over two months. Where twelve other children were held for God knows how long, four of them now cold and rotting.

"I want to see where that sick fucking bastard was holding my baby. Show me."

Erin held Lily in her arms and whispered into her ear. Lily looked as happy as ever, her smiles and giggles coming as easily as they always had. Besides the layer of grime on her skin and her slightly thinner frame, she looked okay.

It was Shawn's turn to grab the detective's shoulder once it dawned on him. "Did he … with my daughter … did he … ?"

"No. We had her checked out before you guys got here. The other kids too. No sign of sexual abuse of any kind."

Shawn kept his hand on the detective and squeezed, lowered his head. "Thank God for that."

"The man posed as a crossing guard. From what we can tell,

he traveled from town to town, volunteered at the schools. Most of the kids came from Texas, two from Oklahoma. Not a single one from the same town. Who knows how long he's been at it though."

"A crossing guard. Son of a bitch."

"Shawn," Detective Hudson started as he ran his hand over his graying hair. "It's not pretty in there. The smell … I don't see any reason why you should see it. You've got your daughter. You've got Lily, unharmed and—"

"Unharmed? My daughter might be … special. But she isn't stupid, Hudson. Unharmed? She'll be fucked up the rest of her life over this shit!" Shawn winced at the volume of his words, shot a nervous glance at Erin and Lily. Erin ran her fingers through Lily's hair, glaring at Shawn through slits, but Lily just smiled, played with Erin's cell phone.

"What I was going to say is, I've got video. Shot it on my phone, so it's not the best quality, but you can see the inside of the house, can even see the bastard as they were pulling his ass out of there. Was screaming some shit about finishing his work, how much pain and death there would be if—"

"Show me. I … I just need to see it. For my own sake. Please."

The detective smiled at Erin over Shawn's shoulders, gave her a slight nod as if they had some secret between them, then led Shawn to his car.

The video started outside of the house. An officer approached Hudson, told him he couldn't be there, and even after Hudson flashed his badge, the officer didn't look happy about it. But then they dragged the man out of the front door of the house, and his screaming got the officer's attention. Hudson moved closer, the video shaky as he trotted.

The man looked to be in his late fifties, possibly in his sixties. The white whiskers covering his face looked sharp, coarse. His eyes were wild, as red as painted toenails. The cords in his neck bulged and stretched as he tried to fight himself free from the officers on either side of him. A thin man. The kind of man who could only victimize children because he couldn't overpower anyone else.

"No!" he screamed as he kicked and bucked. *"You have to let me finish … you have to! So many will die if you don't let me finish my work!"*

"Jesus," Shawn said, balancing the phone in his palm.

As the man grew closer to Hudson and his camera phone, his gaze oozed over and stared, seemed to be glaring right at Shawn.

"Monsters," he growled. "Monsters, all of them. You don't understand what you're doing! If I don't kill them … if I don't kill them, thousands will die! *Thousands!*"

As the officers pushed him forward, he continued to scream. Reporters were there, trying to get statements, but were ignored. When the man was shoved into the back of the police car, he smashed his face against the glass, smearing it with tears and saliva as he kept shouting and begging. The look in his eyes made Shawn's stomach twist with dread.

He thinks Lily is going to hurt people … kill people?

Shawn thought about the way his daughter made him feel when he was around her. Yes, he loves her, of course he loves her, but there was always something … there. In the pit of his gut. Something he didn't even think she was aware of. Something Shawn didn't know how to explain even to himself, but it was something that always bothered him.

You're … you're glad this happened. Aren't you?

The footage showed the officers get in, wave off the reporters some more, and then drive away. Then it cut to the house just as Hudson had been entering.

"They tried to give me shit about going inside too, but I can be a persuasive son of a bitch," Hudson said, then pointed at the small screen. "Brace yourself, Shawn, okay? This shit is … well, it's fucked up is what it is."

Shawn didn't respond, but tightened his grip on the phone, tried to swallow some spit to moisten his throat, but couldn't get any down.

The house was a story and a half, the upstairs area a small loft. It was here that the children were kept, cages lining the back wall like some kind of animal shelter. Dog bowls sat in the corners, some still containing whatever slop he had been feeding them. Looked like oatmeal with raisins, but then the raisins started moving and Shawn realized they were flies. Clear water bottles hung from the cage, the same kind used for pet hamsters or mice. More flies cut through the air, crawled along the walls and ceiling, dove in and out of the dog bowls and scuttled across the floor.

"Fucking son of a bitch …"

Detective Hudson didn't say anything, just sighed and shoved his hands into his pockets.

The floor was padded with cardboard; the middle section stained a dark brown. The flies were there too, sucking up what they could. A few maggots scooted over the stain. A hospital gurney sat in the center of the room, thick leather straps hanging off the sides. The gurney's metal frame was spotted with dried blood. A tray sat on top, an array of surgical tools lined up neatly on its surface. Each one freshly painted with blood.

"He had been working on a young boy when they caught him. They didn't make it in time to save the kid," Hudson said.

On the other side of the room, across from the cages, were sheets of college-ruled notebook paper stapled to the wall. Each page had names written on them with a neat hand. The video showed some of the names, lingered there long enough for Shawn to read them, but they meant nothing to him.

The papers were arranged in columns, some shorter than others. The page at the top of the column had a name written in larger, bolder font, underlined.

"Those are the children's names at the top there," Detective Hudson said. "But so far nobody knows what any of the other names mean."

The video showed all of the names as it scanned the wall from left to right until finally coming to rest on the paper with Lily's name written at the top.

"Other kids maybe? That he was planning on kidnapping?" Shawn said.

"That's possible. If that's the case, thank God we found the motherfucker. Excuse my language."

Thank God indeed. There had to be thousands of names written on these pages. And as far as the length of the columns, Lily's was the longest by far, stretching down to the floor and then back up again. The names were tiny, hardly legible, while the other pages were easier read.

If I don't kill them … if I don't kill them, thousands will die! Thousands!

Shawn didn't know what it meant, but he had enough. He handed the phone back to Hudson, stared blankly out the windshield.

"Listen. You've got a lot on your mind, all of you do. Why don't you let me put you guys up in a hotel, get you some dinner, hmm?"

"You don't have to do—"

Hudson held a hand up. "Don't say another word about it. Now come on. The three of you need to be together, and I don't want you trying to drive home tonight."

After a few more seconds, Shawn nodded, smiled. He rushed toward his family and hugged them, picked up his daughter and peppered her face with kisses.

Back home, things went back to normal. The experience seemed to have brought the family closer together, and Shawn and Erin's relationship hadn't been so good since they were newlyweds.

They watched Lily closely, wondering when the PTS would start, or when she would lash out at them. But that never happened. She seemed completely fine, and for some reason, that worried Shawn even more.

"You should have seen it," Shawn said to Erin in bed one night. "Dog cages. He must have killed those other kids in front of the live ones, too. There was this gurney ... and the tools ... oh Jesus, Erin."

Erin lowered his head to rest on her breasts, ran her fingers over the back of his head. "She's home now. Don't think about it, Shawn. It's going to drive you crazy."

Don't think about it?

"The man. The things he was saying when they were dragging him out of that house. I just keep hearing it again and again in my head and ... I don't know. How is it I'm in worse shape than our daughter is?"

"A father is supposed to feel pain when his child does. It just means you're a good dad, that's all. Now enough of all this for tonight. It's time for you to be a good husband now."

She kissed him, slipped her arms out of her nightie. Though Shawn let himself melt into her flesh, and though it felt damn good, his mind was elsewhere.

And it wouldn't stop until he had some answers.

"You sure about this?" Detective Hudson said as they pulled up to the prison. The man had offered to drive Shawn out there, and Shawn had agreed. He hoped they could bounce some theories off each other on the drive over, but the two of them remained quiet for the most part.

"It's driving me crazy. What he said about the children. How thousands would die. I can't get his voice out of my head."

"He's just a crazy asshole, lost in his own fantasy. Don't subject yourself to this, Shawn. There's nothing this man will tell you that will help, I promise you that."

"And Lily. I thought she'd be ... I don't know. Messed up after everything, you know? But she's not. She's completely fine, as happy as could be. I asked her about it, and she remembers everything, even told me how the man would hurt the other kids.

I didn't tell Erin that part. When she said it … she was smiling.
Like she was remembering a trip to Disney World or some shit."

"Okay, so what're you saying? That your daughter … enjoyed
it? Because if that's what you mean, if you're buying into this shit
that asshole was saying—"

"I don't know what the fuck I'm saying, okay? I'm confused
and pissed off and scared. I don't know what else to do. I figure if I
can talk to the guy, maybe it could help. Maybe he'll say something
to help me understand."

After a few moments, Hudson nodded. "You want me to go
with you?"

"I think I better do this alone. Erin doesn't even know I'm
doing this. Told her you had some more questions for me, that I'd
be at the station all day. I'd appreciate if you kept this between us,
Detective."

He nodded. "I won't sit here and tell you I know what you're
going through. Because I don't. Never had any kids myself. If you
need this, I believe you. Just be careful, all right?"

"I will. And thank you."

After going through all the procedures—filling out paperwork,
handing over everything in his pockets, walking through the metal
detector, getting patted down—he was led into a room with gray
walls. There was a thick glass partition separating Shawn's side
with the other, and a phone on both sides. Shawn took a seat on
the orange plastic chair, wiped the sweat from his palms onto his
jeans. His heart thundered in his chest, and he started to wonder if
this really was a bad idea.

Maybe I should just walk out right now. Go home to my family.

A door opened up on the other side of the glass, and a guard
walked in backward … followed by the crossing guard. The man's
whiskers had grown to give him a full white beard, his pink bottom
lip in the center of it. He wore an orange jumpsuit, the handcuffs
biting into the flesh of his wrinkled, spotted wrists and hands.
Another guard followed, and they set the man at his seat across

from Shawn, said something to the man before stepping back, but still only a few strides away.

Shawn and the crossing guard stared at each other for a full minute. Shawn knew this man's name was given to him at some point, but he couldn't remember it. Just *crossing guard* stuck with him.

The man picked up his phone first, his hands quivering, mouth moving up and down like he was tasting something.

Shawn hesitated for a moment, then grabbed the phone and pressed it to his ear.

"I know who you are," the crossing guard said. "You don't see it. You don't know what she'll do."

Shawn almost dropped the phone. The man had whispered the words as if telling a secret. He breathed heavily, stared at Shawn with panic in his eyes.

"Why do you say that?" Shawn said. "What makes you think my daughter, or any of those kids, would ever hurt anyone? You're the monster here, you fucking bastard. You hear me? Not my little girl!"

The guards behind the man started forward, but Shawn took a deep breath, apologized to them with his eyes, held up his hand to let them know everything was fine. They held back, but looked ready to pounce on the inmate.

The crossing guard licked his lips, his eyes never leaving Shawn's for a second. "You're trying to convince yourself, not me. Because you know. Deep down, you know I'm right." He leaned forward. "Don't you see? By killing them, I would have saved so many lives. Thousands of lives. You think that made it any easier for me? I'm no monster ... but I'm cursed with the sight. I can see what they'll do, those kids. But that didn't make killing them any easier."

The tears started and the sight of them made Shawn want to break through the glass and strangle that asshole.

The crossing guard cleared his throat.

"But I did it because it had to be done. To save countless other lives. With those kids still out there … there's going to be so much pain. So much death. Oh God, help us all."

"My daughter … she's only seven years old. How could she possibly—"

"Not yet. I don't know when it'll happen. I just know that death surrounds Lily. More than any other child. She … she scared me," the crossing guard said. "Watched me. Always watching and smiling."

"Keep my daughter's name out of your mouth. You fucking piece of shit."

The man stood up, pressed his forehead against the glass. He dropped the phone, but Shawn could still hear his voice in his head, piercing, like needles in his brain.

"You have to stop her. You have to see. Finish it, Shawn. Finish what I started with Lily and the others. And there's more out there. So many more. There will always be more."

The guards were trying to wrestle the inmate away from the glass partition now, but couldn't budge him as he glared at Shawn.

And then the heat was there. Like his head was in a microwave.

Shawn backed away from the glass, grabbed his head with both hands and screamed. The heat was so intense he expected flames to shoot from his mouth.

The partition shattered, raining thick pieces of jagged glass all over the floor. In that same exact moment, the fire went out in his head and Shawn dropped to his backside, grimacing, moaning and massaging his temples. Blood poured from his nose, trickled from his ears.

The crossing guard leaned forward, ignoring the guards as if they were nothing but a couple of annoying flies.

"Now you see. Finish it."

The man picked up a piece of glass and pressed it to his throat, sawed back and forth until he worked his way from one ear to the other. Blood poured out in sheets, and the guards were finally able to move him, calling for help and scrambling to stop the bleeding.

Shawn just sat there, trembling, clenching his teeth as his head throbbed and pulsated.

Part of him wanted to rush home, be with his family, hold his girls in his arms and never let them go again. The other part of him was terrified to see them.

"You gonna be all right, Shawn?" Hudson said as they pulled into the driveway of Shawn's home. "You sure you don't want me to come inside, talk with Erin about what happened? Shit, man … don't you think she should know?"

The sun had gone down a couple of hours ago. He knew Erin would have questions.

Shawn opened the passenger door. "I'll tell her. But not right now, okay? I just … I just need some time. My fucking head is killing me, my thoughts are all over the place. Give me a day. I'll tell her tomorrow."

Hudson twisted his fists over the steering wheel. "Goddamnit, Shawn. I told you it wasn't a good idea. Shit … "

"Just … Tomorrow, okay? Thanks for the ride." Shawn shut the door, patted the hood. He heard the car reversing and driving away as he strolled toward the house.

Now you see. Finish it.

He wrapped his fist around the knob, could hear Erin and Lily laughing from inside. The sound of his daughter's laughter filled him with happiness, and in that moment, he knew everything would be okay. The crossing guard was just some crazy asshole. And now he's dead. *Good riddance.*

He walked in and went into the kitchen for a glass of water. Erin stood at the stove, mixing a big pot of spaghetti sauce with a wooden spoon. She smiled wide, wiped her hands on her rear as she rushed toward him, wrapped her arms around him, and planted a wet kiss on his lips.

"How'd it go? What did the detective want?"

"Just more paperwork. Nothing much. Boring really." He smiled, kissed her again. "It's good to be home. Where's Lily?"

"In her room. She kept trying to get a taste of the sauce, and I kept slapping her hand away. She's been asking for my spaghetti for days."

"It smells amazing. Let me go say hi to her, then I'll help out."

She rose to her tiptoes and kissed him on the forehead. "No need. I got this. Go play with your daughter. She was asking for you today. Seemed upset about something."

"Really?"

Shawn decided to skip the water. As he walked down the hall toward Lily's bedroom, he realized his headache was gone. The violent throbbing had ceased completely.

Lily giggled from the other side of the door. Shawn smiled, sighed.

When he opened the door, he immediately shrieked, tripped backward and slammed the back of his head against the wall. He sat there, staring into the room, at his daughter sitting Indian-style in the center, bouncing her Cabbage Patch doll up and down, up and down, smiling so wide, giggling.

The smell was the worst part. Like spoiled, burnt pork and hair. Thick and greasy and making the back of Shawn's throat sting with acid.

"Hi, Daddy," she said. "Did you see the bad man? The crossing guard?" She smiled again, wider than before.

Festering corpses surrounded her. Piled one on top of the other. Their flesh was charred, cracked to show the dark red beneath. Hairless. They were piled from the floor to the ceiling, so packed into the room that Lily hardly had any room to play.

Men and women of all ages. And children. Children younger than her, their faces twisted and frozen in anguish, their eyes liquefied and running down their blackened cheeks, sizzling and smoking as the jelly flowed.

The babies looked like roasted whole chickens, thrown in

sloppy piles all around her. Smoke filled the room as it swirled off the broiled flesh.

And Lily just bounced her doll and laughed. Happy as ever.

"What's the matter?" Erin called as she ran down the hall. She took one look at Shawn's face and her run became a sprint. She jumped over Shawn's legs and into the room.

Shawn tried to stop her, to warn her, but he couldn't do anything but stare at the genocide stuffed within his little girl's bedroom.

Erin didn't acknowledge the bodies. It looked like she was about to collide with the wall of cooked flesh, but instead, she walked through it as if it were nothing but a projected image. She knelt beside Lily, hugged her, rocked her, as she stared at Shawn.

"What the hell is your problem?"

So much pain. So much death.

Now you see. Finish it.

I will, Shawn thought. *I have to.*

CAROLE GILL

RAISED

London 1816

He loved the dead. Children mustn't play with dead things but he did. He always had. When he was small they were like toys to him, but when he was older they were no longer toys.

It began with a bird; just a pretty little robin that he used to feed. When it lay stiff and dead he wept. His older brother buried it and put a flower on top of the grave. "Now you may remember it always," he said.

But young James didn't wish to be parted from his little friend. *I will dig it up and keep it.*

He had seen things rot. In fact he found it fascinating and had often inspected rats that were burst open by maggots. His father was horrified and ordered him beaten. The servants thought the child a little mad, as mad as his mother they whispered.

The truth was they didn't like the mother. She was from America and was a flighty and stupid woman, and they suspected a bit touched.

They may have been right because lately it seemed even to James that his mother was worse than she had been. She was excitable and often screamed for hours on end.

He had never been close to her. A nanny carried him in on occasion and when he grew older he did stop in a time or two. But lately that had stopped.

"James, your mother is ill. There will be no more visits. She needs her rest. Do you understand?"

"Yes father," he said, even though he didn't really understand. "Will she be alright?"

His father didn't answer; he only smiled briefly, not a good smile but a twitchy, nervous one before patting the boy on his head.

The child was distraught and had no one to go to now that his older brother had unexpectedly died.

"Like the hand of God," the servants whispered.

He overheard the doctor tell his father it was a fever of unknown origin.

Whatever it was, James was not prepared nor was he willing to be parted from his brother. He loved him so much that he sat up all night with his brother's corpse, eventually climbing into the casket in order to be close to him.

He thought his brother greeted him and he was comforted. It felt good until forceful hands pulled him away.

"Master James! You are bad! You wait here!"

His father was summoned. Now, if he ever recalled the first moment he was regarded as insane, this was it. His father stared at him for a long time without speaking. At last he did: "James. I am confining you to your room until after the funeral."

How he screamed and pleaded. How he begged. "But Father! I want to attend. Please! I will never see him again..."

His father said nothing. Even when he took his son's hand and they marched up the stairs not a word passed between them not even when they passed the insane mother's room.

He didn't really mind having to stay in his room. His toys were there; even his dead bird. It was no longer stiff in fact it barely resembled a bird now. It was rotted and dried out. Mummified would have been the correct term, but James hadn't yet heard of that word.

The truth was it had been half eaten by maggots despite James having guarded it well.

Naturally, it proved to be impossible and the carcass was tainted, at least that was how he thought of it. How he would have liked to reverse the decay but of course he couldn't.

It was a strange house, that handsome house in Mayfair where the mad woman lived.

But if folks both upstairs and downstairs knew a mad woman was there they knew too her mad son was touched as well: servants do gossip.

"The boy ain't right in the head. Just like his mum. Poor mite."

Poor mite indeed it gave them such pleasure to discuss the strange little boy.

Eventually a tutor was hired. The father wished for the boy to get a good education.

"You will go to Oxford as I did. And you will make something of yourself."

His father was a barrister and if he had hopes of peculiar young James becoming one as well, he soon realized how unlikely that would be. He was too quiet and solitary aside from anything else.

It was when the tutor told him of the awful smells in James' room (James father never went in) that his father made an educated guess. This he did after discovering the cause of those odors; all those dead things.

He found the bird which started it all, but he found more. He found dead and rotting mice and rats. Cats and dogs, three rabbits and what looked like a human arm: all of which was badly decomposed.

"Where did you get all of this?!"

James was determined to stand up for himself. His madness had begun to have a calming effect. "Well father, I like to study things..."

That was it, wasn't it? He thought of his most unusual and strange predilection simply as a desire to learn about life (well dead things really)!

"Indeed." His father said trying desperately hard not to sniff the air.

"Well, James, I think it is time for you to go to boarding school."

James wasn't displeased. There was no reason to stay. His much loved collection of dead things had been discarded. His room had never felt more empty nor his heart.

And so he went to quite a posh boy's school. But he wasn't happy there in fact he was miserable.

They smelled a rat. Not one of his dead ones, but they (the bully boys that made up nearly all of sixth form) sensed something not quite right about James.

It was sorted out though; the boys were punished because James' father happened to make a handsome donation to the school.

James was no longer bothered. In fact he found himself sharing rooms with another strange boy whose father had also made a donation.

This boy took a very personal interest in his new roommate but when James showed him what for he took the hint. Still, he promised he would always adore James. In fact, he became his little slave.

Years passed as they do and James eventually enrolled in

medical school. He acted consistently normal. His secret life appeared to be over, when in fact, it was just beginning.

His father was pleased about his interest in medicine as he considered it to be quite a respectable profession. And so James was enrolled.

He found the school to be very much to his liking. He particularly enjoyed the medical dissection theatre.

How he loved to see the bodies. He'd have preferred them not to be dissected, he much rather have touched them whole and perfect. But that was not the purpose for which they were brought in.

"Young men, you see the cadaver of a man. He is approximately twenty five years of age. The cause of death was hanging."

Yes, the poor wretch had been hanged at Newgate.

James studied the man from top to bottom. Quite a well endowed fellow he thought. In fact he compared himself with this cadaver and found he was sadly wanting; wanting some inches!

A fear began to set in then. That he would be no good with women. Actually he had already tried. He had fondled a kitchen maid but when it was put up or shut up she laughed at him.

"Oh young sir!" she cried, her face nearly purple with merriment. "That is a small willy in't it?"

Yes, it was small. Small and useless and eventually hardly used at all. And he didn't want it to be. He wanted to work the life out of it. He knew he could go to prostitutes but he didn't like being laughed at. Yes he was rather worried about that.

It was a morgue attendant who suggested for a couple of guineas he could have a good feel. "And they won't say *nuffink* either, Guv, nor will I. You can touch 'em where you like for as long as you like!"

And so he did. And that's really where this story begins.

He was Dr. James Mitchell, his father long dead, his mother having been put in a private madhouse years ago.

The good doctor still resided at the family home but he worked there too. His dissecting room was there, on the ground floor—so easy for his men to pass through a cadaver for medical study. Yes, he was in his element.

There were a lot of cadavers too despite the fact that few were now obtained legally. Yes, things had changed. There were less executed felons now and so the objects of study had to be acquired differently.

If Knox had Burke and Hare—James had Gritter and Potts; not grave fillers as Burke and Hare were, but grave robbers. They were filthy and horrible but expert at what they did. They spoke about *cribs* and *larges* and *smalls*.

"I don't care about the *cribs*—where you get them, but I do wish them to be larges."

Both fiends winked at one another. "No, Guv, 'course." One said as he removed a louse from his hair and studied it. "You wants *larges* only. We understands."

"Quite right," James agreed. "I want adults!"

"And am I right in saying you wish them to be of the female persuasion?"

This was said as Potts nodded his head toward a naked female cadaver.

James quickly covered her. "Yes, that is correct."

"There, you see, sir. We knows what you want. We are specialists, we are."

They began to leave then, but not before Gritter turned around. "Now about our money sir..."

James sighed. "Ah yes. I shall have it for you next time."

Even as he said it he doubted he would. After all, he had a former servant who had been black mailing him for years.

What a troublesome wretch the man was. A leech sucking the doctor dry, why over the years James was certain he had taken hundreds, perhaps thousands of pounds from him.

If only he had the stomach for murder. But the thing was he

was no murderer. Oh, he was tempted. He felt certain Gritter and Potts would be only too thrilled to help him out with it too.

However, he felt that would only eliminate one problem by replacing it with another. They'd have something on him! Perhaps they'd start asking for money also. No. James would not risk it.

Since he did not wish to think of it, he decided to engage in his favorite pastime—studying a female cadaver. It gave him so much pleasure in fact; he studied her until the following morning and all through the night, too.

She was very special this one, nice and fresh. Not like the others, those he kept in one of the outbuildings. He had quite a few cadavers actually. They were laid out on shelves. Good for viewing and *studying*.

He sometimes wondered if anyone could smell anything as he no longer could. He had grown so used to death's scent.

Yes, there was a definite odor despite the fact that they were full of the doctor's own arsenic based embalming solutions. It was remarkable how aggressive decomposition could be slowed down.

There were twelve of them at present; ten ladies and two gentlemen. His study concerning the male cadavers was purely cursory. It certainly was not sexual although their sexual organs were of great interest to him. It was a size issue.

He had thought both men to be of normal size which cheered him a bit. At least they weren't overly endowed.

It pleased him to compare his own organ with theirs. He had stinted a bit on the preserving solution he used which caused some shrinkage. Naturally it delighted and reassured him.

The women were in worse shape for they had been carefully *studied*. Now they were all destined for burial and frankly, the sooner the better.

There was a fellow, a bit simple but strongly built who came around when needed, and for the price of a few beers was quite happy to take the unwanted (used) cadavers off Dr. Mitchell's hands.

Of course he had to remind him as the poor fellow could not hold a thought in his head for too long.

"We're going to have to add a few to the big one, Arthur."

That referred to the mass grave that now existed in the back garden.

Yes, the stenchy ones had to go. Alice was the only enjoyable one left.

Ah Alice! She had been with him for three days and was starting to reek a bit despite his solutions.

"I am sorry, Alice!" he said. He had no idea what her name really was, poor thing but he liked the name, Alice and enjoyed calling her that while he *studied* her.

Finally, when he grew tired he sighed. "I will bid you good night, Alice." Then climbing up to his bedroom, he paused. There was something lying on the floor, something that looked like it belonged to his mother. He picked it up; his eyes quickly filling with tears.

"Mother..."

It *was* hers! It must have been one of her necklaces. "Oh poor you. Poor Mummy!" he wept.

Yes, she was gone now. He had paid forty a year to keep her boarded in a private madhouse. Her room, they told him, over looked a garden. The truth was it over looked an alley where prostitutes took their clients.

If Adena Mitchell born and raised on a Virginia plantation had ever realized where she was, she'd have died of shame. Her isolation from reality was a blessing for her.

Feeling sentimental, he took the necklace to his room and put it on his bureau. He would have put it back in her trunk, but because he was tired, he would tend to it the next day.

Sad really because had he done that, he'd have seen that her trunk had been pried open and stripped of all jewelry and anything of value.

One of the thieves had spit on the necklace and rubbed it on his shirt to see if it looked valuable. He shouldn't have done that because that one action let out the bad magic. It woke the Djinn. And that's why everything happened as it did.

James never knew the thieves were actually Gritter and Potts, mightily aggrieved with him over unpaid wages. Yes, his own men—the two grime encrusted grave robbers lousy with lice would be responsible for an apocalyptic occurrence at the doctor's house.

James never heard the necklace rattle. Nor did he see it move. It was old African magic that caused it; very powerful, too.

The necklace was given to the strange little Adena by the slave woman, Sabaah who cared for the child. If others believed the child to be afflicted, Sabaah knew the poor little thing was possessed by demons. That was why she made her the necklace and blessed it too. She wanted protection for the child.

But the thing was Adena didn't have demons in her at all. She was mad from a mad family. This, the slave woman didn't realize. Nor did she know that the protective spell would change if the necklace was tainted by evil, in this case Gritter and Potts' touch.

She died long before Adena grew up, long before the trunk was packed with her belongings and with the necklace carelessly tossed inside by one of the family.

Adena's parents were long dead and the aunts that took care of the estate couldn't wait to get rid of the niece who embarrassed them.

She was being shipped off to England in the care of an aunt, palmed off to marry some cousin.

Money takes care of most things and the prospective groom didn't care if the wedding took place quickly. The bride's money paid for the rest of his schooling and an elegant house too.

As for the bride, Edward had little time for her. Well truthfully she grew ever more distant.

Eventually, they had two sons. Following the death of the first born, whatever tenuous grasp on reality Adena had, was soon gone.

In time she didn't know who she lived with nor did she recognize anyone.

And so the private madhouse beckoned. And the sad events rolled on all of which culminated in the very last night of James' life.

He slept soundly on that particular night. Had he been awake, he'd have seen the necklace lift off the bureau. He'd also have heard the sound of evil laughter for it was the Djinn himself who laughed.

Something did wake him. He heard a door open and close. His hearing wasn't that good but he did hear that. He rushed to the window. He didn't want the cadavers in the shed found.

When he saw the door to the out building open, he gasped. But then something moved in the garden.

He had just put his hand on the door handle when he heard what sounded like murmuring.

"James...James...!"

There was a smell too of rot and something else; that almond smell of arsenic.

The rot was so overpowering, he began gagging. He only stopped when he heard the footsteps.

Somehow he knew it was his men. Those dead men he had poked and prodded. Those men with their genitals shrinking more in death and delighting him,

I'm sorry ... I shouldn't have done that!

Yes, perhaps not. But it was too late now.

It's too late, James they are coming for you.

But I never hurt them.

Ah but you touched them. You held them!

But surely they couldn't feel anything! They were dead.

Maybe not dead, maybe resting?

Not resting now! They were at the door. He felt their presence, he *heard* them. He heard something else; he heard a door open downstairs. Could it be the dissection room?

He was horror struck. When something brushed against his bedroom door he nearly fainted and when the door opened, he screamed.

He was hiding under his bed by then. That bed where he took the women, his sleeping beauties as he called them.

A pair of small feet appeared. They looked alright. He just knew they belonged to Alice. It had to be Alice because she wasn't rotting badly yet.

"Alice?"

His question asked in a small voice, the voice with no greater pitch than a young child would have—a very frightened young child.

The figure bent down and a pretty face suddenly appeared; pretty, with its even features and its flat eyes. Yes, flat because the whites were dried up.

"James..."

Her voice was soft but strangely discordant. Of course he realized this was the first time he heard her voice.

Perhaps this is how the dead sound.

"James..."

There was more sound, more voices, muddled and feint sounding calling his name. Some were angry others not.

"James ... we have come for you."

"No!"

He put lit a lamp. Yes, it was better now. He could see he was safe and alone. He laughed to himself. But then the necklace rose up and began floating toward him!

He was backing up when something touched him. "James."

He turned although he didn't want to. That is his head turned as though someone had turned it. He saw them then! There were too many to count.

"Come with us."

They were like shadows.

But shadows don't rot nor stink.

They were lifting him up, high over their heads, as though he weighed nothing.

"It's a dream, isn't it?" he cried. "I'll wake up and I'll know it isn't real. Things like this can't happen!"

He thought they laughed, but it didn't matter, he was screaming anyway. Down the stairs they carried him. He heard the horrible shuffling of their rotted feet.

He recognized the hall. He heard the clock strike three.

"Help me!"

"Oh but we are, we are you'll see!"

They carried him through the hall, to the back kitchen and towards the open door. The moon was shining, lighting up the garden. He could see the earth splitting apart, spewing up so that the entire burial pit was revealed; that one great pit where all the specimens were!

Suddenly, he had one lucid thought. They were taking him *there!*

"No, please! *No!*"

As they brought him closer, he could see all the movement from *within*; all the hands that were reaching out to take him, hands mostly without flesh, skeletal fingers reaching up for him.

They dropped him in and he felt the bones, *and* the maggots, from the newer corpses. He smelled the putrid sweetness and he felt the sting as they bit him for they were already feeding.

"James...!"

Muddled voices calling him, or was it just in his head, not that it mattered. What mattered more were the dead fingers tearing his night gown from him.

"Touching you now..."

When he was naked, they probed his secret places. He felt their teeth and bones prodding him and tasting him.

They pulled him into their world, the world that had so intrigued him.

"You're ours now ... now and forever and ever...and we will touch you and love you for all eternity ... all of us together... enjoying death, relishing it, coming alive in its grand rottenness."

DANE HATCHELL

THE 'TAKERS

The 'takers are scheming behind the door. I wonder what instruments of torture are on their carts? Listen to them, cackling with delight. No doubt reliving some horrific scene perpetrated under their callous hands.

I spied a 'taker wearing the most unusual of necklaces the other day. It best resembled a chain of fingernails linked together with hair. Did the collection belong to one suffering soul or was it a tally of all the victims whom had resisted?

Is it my turn to be tested now?

The door handle rattles. I immediately shut my eyes as I always do, leaving the right eye open barley enough to warn me of an attack.

As I suspected. It's one of the Pawns. She's in my room and immediately pulling at the desk drawer to see if it's locked. Ha! They never fail of their thieving ways and test it at every chance. I'm glad I don't have any gold teeth in my head for her to pry out.

The drawer contains a few fragments of my life before I was so unmercifully forced into here. My only possessions being a box of old photographs from happier times and an inexpensive locket my wife, Gloria, used to wear around her neck. It opens to show our photographs in each half facing each other. She said we were kissing when it's closed. Gloria was romantic in that way. God, I miss her so.

Yet, the Pawn would remove that thread still binding me to my loss love if I failed to lock the drawer. Her arms are scarred and embellished in black ink. Her caste is an ignorant bunch that shunned education as youths. They preferred to revel in disobedience until the passage of time brought them into adulthood and left them with a future that led to nowhere.

The 'takers see her caste as an easy crop to harvest. Being hungry and without hope, they become Pawns and thus slaves to the meager wages offered.

Each Pawn wears the same maroon colored uniform. I imagine it is to remind me of blood to keep me in my place. That, or if I get out of line and receive a beating, help hide the stain of mine.

She's reaching toward my head. If she goes for my throat, well, let's just say I have a surprise in my hand waiting for her.

At first, she puts her fingers to my forehead. It's oily and sweaty as it is most of the nights. Why does she repeat this ritual over and over? Is she just some mindless robot, repeating actions without thought?

Now her hand drifts down my chest. Please don't go to my right hand. I … I don't want to do something to spoil my plans.

Thank goodness! She's only checking my pulse rate on my left wrist and not doing one of her invasive searches. That comes later. When she'll be back and attempt to strip away any remaining dignity I cling to. She only does that to erode my resolve.

She leaves the bedside while I hold back a deep sigh of relief. The light comes on in the bathroom followed by water splashing in the sink. There's nothing for you to steal in there either, stupid Pawn. I wonder what trap will lay in wait set by her mischievous hands?

That's how they operate. Little things they do that add up to wear down the individual. Throwing my soap away, hiding my toothpaste, and even taking my supply of paper towels I had hidden from obvious detection. Order must be kept according to their set standards. They want to force me to become just like them, a mindless automaton with a single purpose. Individuality be damned!

The light goes out and large feet scrape the floor. She is either too lazy or too fat to lift them off the ground without sliding them.

Oh, no. A Rook has entered the room. They're changing the routine and are trying to get inside my head. Rooks are much craftier than the Pawns. I must put on my best game face.

"Are you awake, Mr. Jaffe? It's time for your medicine," he says, with all the warmth of a toad sitting in cold potato salad.

I open my eyes pretending to unravel the cover of sleep. I go to speak, but my throat is dry. My vocal cords have never fully recovered from the day I was imprisoned. I was less disciplined then and shouldn't have screamed as much.

I nod my head yes, knowing the consequences of resistance.

His hand conceals a syringe loaded with some vile chemical that does nothing other than make me itch all over. At least it doesn't have any effect on my mind. God only knows what they're incubating inside me. They've probably infested me with a new strain of flu, or some other virus. Using me as the proverbial guinea pig for a new medicine they can charge the poor and needy a thousand times more than the cost of production.

'Guinea pig.' Ironic isn't it? That's what I've become. Oh the outrage from radical groups at the testing of animals in labs for research. What about me! What about the lab testing of humans? How can the 'takers get away from their merciless acts?

"Be still, now. This will hurt a bit."

Again, pretending to care about my well-being. One small step at a time; deception, hidden in deception, hidden in deception. He wears a white uniform, trying to convey 'the good guys wear white.' I know better. Rooks should be wearing black. Black to reflect the image of their soul. Self-serving, condescending bastards, all of them.

"Time for your pills. Open wide."

God only knows where his fingers have been. I take the pills so I can maintain some control over my mind. I am helpless against needles and don't want to give any reason to substitute injections for pills.

"Okay. Here's some water ... there. All down, Mr. Jaffe?"

I nod my head yes, closing my eyes as if sleepy. The Rook makes no haste in his departure. He has others in my wing to administer his dark wares.

The knife I stole from the cafeteria slips out my right hand. It falls to the floor under my bed, well out of my limited reach. I spit out the pills and wipe my tongue on the sheet, scraping off any residual that had begun to melt.

There are four pills in all. The pale green pill is for 'high blood pressure.' I know better, having no problems with my blood pressure before my capture. It is nothing more than a pill meant to emasculate me, removing sexual desire. The 'cholesterol pill' is strictly for my discomfort, making my body sore all over. I assume the goal is to compound the effects of my already failing body. The white pill is to help me sleep during the night. I take that pill as sleep in any form and for any amount of time is a priceless reprieve. The last, the one I most fear, is the gold colored 'anxiety pill.' That's the stealer of souls. Meant to extract the essence of everything God intended for me to experience during my short time remaining on Earth.

I shake my head at those who willingly line up with mouths open and pasty white tongues poking out ready to receive the anxiety pill. They act as if it will save their soul. It is the Devil's version of the Eucharist. The pill numbs the mind from the highs and lows of life, turning the symphony of sensations to one unvaried note.

That's not how life is meant to be experienced. The savor of life is spiced with as many tears as it is with laughter. The depths of despair give substance to the thrill of victory. The good cannot be known unless the bad is experienced to contrast.

The gold pill takes all that has meaning away.

I will not succumb to its power!

I hide three of the pills as I always do and swallow the white pill to put me to sleep. The ceiling churns in folds of black pudding as my eyelids grow heavy. I know it's just my mind playing tricks. At least it's not a coffin closing down. I thus retain a pittance of hope and a chance of escape.

I awake wearing a clean set of nightwear, having only faint memories of the Pawn who sought to break my short respite in the land of dreams. A new Pawn is in my room now, checking her charts, and making a quick inventory of my sparse accommodations.

"Mr. Jaffe. It's morning. Breakfast is being served," she says with a song in her voice. She is new to my wing. Perhaps new to the Institution. Her vibrancy won't last. Even in the short time I've been here I know that. "I'm not hungry." I've not had any mind-altering effects from eating the food but the fewer the 'takers to notice me the better.

"It's morning and you haven't had anything to eat since dinner last night," she says.

"I'll just take a little fruit in my room. Bring it to me, please."

She looks over that confounding chart. Always with the charts! Use your mind woman and make a decision on your own!

"Mr. Jaffe, your program requires you to get out of your room during the day. We can't have you hiding like a bear in his cave, can we?"

See, it's so obvious how the program operates. When I am alone my mind is the sharpest. I'm spared from the influence of the distractions around me. There's no one to tell me what to think, how to think, and when to think it.

They see me as a square plug in a round hole. Getting me out around others is supposed to knock off my sharp edges and subject me to the influence of the mindless herd. To become an empty-headed beast hailed at the ringing of a bell.

"Time to get up. Come on."

I take her hand and pull myself up. She reeks of dollar store perfume and urine, or perhaps the urine odor is wafting in from the hallway. It's hard to get away from, as is the pungent stench of feces.

"I can go to the bathroom by myself," I say.

"Take careful aim. Don't miss the pot," she mocks.

This girl is playing her part well. I guess they're using their best actors to try and win me over.

I take the three pills I hid in the pillowcase and drop them in the toilet. I pull my diaper just low enough to give me room to maneuvered my penis over the bowl and relieve myself. They force me to wear a diaper. What do they think I am, a child? I would have no bathroom issues if I could keep them from shooting that toxin into my veins.

I finish my business and wash my hands, careful not to touch anything and contaminating them with God-knows-what's-left from the other inmates who lived in my room before.

She is waiting with a wheelchair, still sporting her deceitful smile. "Let's go, Mr. Jaffe."

"I'd rather walk."

"I'm sorry. Your chart says your medicine can make you dizzy. Have a seat," she says, thinking if I didn't she would find someone to force me. I can read it all in her eyes.

I sit down and fold my hands in my lap, mentally preparing myself for the 'gauntlet.'

I cement my gaze straight ahead while I ride down the hall, ignoring the horrible odors and moans that come from open doors along the way. I fight back some of the images of what I have witnessed during my other trips, struggling not to let it break me down.

The wing opens into a receiving area lined with other unfortunates bound to the confines of the wheelchair. Some have mechanical apparatuses forcing them to stay alive.

One poor woman continually babbles without uttering a sound. Another sits with her face frozen in a blank stare into eternity. A man melts into his seat with his head cocked and drool streaming down his chin. There is more, each and every one with the light of the soul gone from their eyes.

That's what they want to do to me. That's what I'm up against. They're rubbing it in my face, taunting they're going to make me just like the others. But they won't! I will not surrender!

I keep my eyes pointed toward the floor, not wanting to bring the ire of some hotshot Rook waiting to make a name for himself by breaking the will of a renegade.

The three other inmates assigned to my eating table are already here. Barbra is removing the utensils from the plastic wrap. The other two, Margret, and Carrie, are so full of the anxiety drug their eyelids droop halfway over their eyes. You would think them asleep at first glance. I've never seen them in any other state of awareness.

The food is placed before us with the grace of a disgruntle city employee feeding mutts at the pound. Oatmeal slops over onto my eggs and mystery sausage.

With her tasks complete, the Pawn continues to serve the rest of the room in the least amount of time possible. I'm sure she'll reward herself at the end of the maze with a cigarette on the patio. My dining companions reanimate to life and begin eating with the mechanics of Disney World robots.

After I cut a piece of sausage with my knife, I put it to my nose and give it a sniff. I go to put the sausage back down, but then I see the Queen from the corner of my eye. I heard them call her Gurov. Must be Russian for 'sadist in charge.' She's standing with her arms folded, just waiting for an excuse to make an example of me, I bet. I'm determined not to give her an opportunity.

The sausage tastes only a little worse than it looks. At least it's not tough. The eggs and oatmeal are without flavor. I eat a few bites and spread the rest around my plate.

My God, I think more food is thrown away here than is eaten. The waste must really cut into the profit margin. I wonder how long it will be until meal portions are cut in half.

Why is the Queen still staring at me? I can feel those beady black eyes pricking into my back. Uh oh, a Rook is talking to her. It's the same one that came to my room last night. What kind of work hours does this madman keep? He's hiding his mouth behind a clipboard so I can't read his lips. Damn him! How did he learn my secret?

Both are leaving now—good. It will give me time to think things out further. Where's that Pawn that wheeled me in? I'm ready to get back to my room. Oh, there she is. Gathered with her pack, deciding who gets the largest share of the spoils no doubt.

Looks like the strategy session is over. They're peeling away like flies heading for a fresh pile of dung.

"I see you've finished eating, Mr. Jaffe. Was is good?" she says, making 'good' a two syllable word.

I nodded with half-opened eyes, trying to make her think I'm sleepy and ready for a nap.

"Do you know what today is?"

Oh, no. Please don't tell me the Cloggers are coming again!

"It's Wednesday, and it's time for Bingo!"

Another of their mind games. A covert way of testing how much of my soul still shines within. I've played the game for them many times and never once did I rise and call 'Bingo.' I'm sure the prize for winning is an extra dose of anxiety pills. That'll teach us inmates for exhibiting cognition.

"Okay, Mr. Jaffe. Time to go," she says, falling in line with the multitude of other wheelchairs heading to a large room across the hall. The tables are all set with cards ready to play the game.

What's this? That Rook and the Queen are waiting by the doorway. They're putting on masks of deceit. Little do they know I can see their true faces a million miles away.

The Queen is reaching out with those bony fingers … .

"Good morning, Mr. Jaffe. We've just got the results back from earlier tests. I'm afraid you're not well enough to play in today's game. We wouldn't want you to injury yourself with all the excitement, would we?" the Queen says, daring me to challenger her. My only regret is I left my knife from breakfast on the table.

Didn't she realize the fallacy of her argument? It is stress that drove evolution, creating all that lives. When does a plant flower best? Why, when it's under stress and afraid it will no longer survive. It flowers to bear seeds in order to propagate. The incredible beauty of a pearl is a product of stress. The oyster surrounds the irritant that invades its shell with layers of calcium carbonate creating one of man's greatest treasures. The mold of mediocrity must be broken in order for the next achievement of mankind to soar. It is stress from the challenge that perpetuates man into the future.

Without saying a word the Queen and her obedient Rook turn and walk down the hall. My Pawn doesn't hesitate following, with no concern of the consequence as she pushes me toward my untimely fate.

I should have known. We're heading straight for the King's office. I wonder if the Knights are on standby to haul me off to the morgue if I don't survive my interrogation.

And there he is waiting just inside the door, King Rathbone. He's ready to swoop down on me like a starving vulture. The Rook and Queen bow as they enter. The Pawn rolls me in and waits with her gazed fixed to the floor until dismissed.

"You may leave," the King says, shooing the debris out of his office.

The Queen puts on a phony smile while the King looks over another insidious chart before issuing his sentence.

The Rook casually sneaks behind me. I'm surrounded by a den of jackals.

"Mr. Jaffe, we've been perplexed by your test results over the past week you've been with us. We are forced to conclude the medications we have prescribed have not found their way into your system as intended. Do you have any idea why?" the King asks.

I know he knows the answer. He's playing his game with me. I can play games too. "Perhaps the Lord above protects the pure in heart from the Devil's snare."

The King and Queen look at each other. I don't think they're used to someone holding up a mirror for them to look into.

"Your blood pressure is in a very dangerous range. If you don't take your medicine you could have a stroke at best, or even die at worst. Why don't you want us to help you?" the Queen asks.

"You can help me best by bringing me home so I can care for myself. I've done so for the last ten years of my life. I'm quite capable of continuing on my own," I offer, drawing a line in the sand.

"There comes a time in everyone's life when they come face to face with the consequences of aging, Mr. Jaffe. I'm afraid the time for you is now. I'm sorry. I truly am. But you're not as well as you think. You need others to help with your daily routine. That's why you're here and why we are too," the Queen says, stepping to my side and taking my right hand in hers.

Her hand is soft like my Gloria's. Her fingers long and delicate, radiating special warmth only a woman can impart to a man. It reminds me of my wedding day, when Gloria and I held hands while the Pastor had us repeat our vows. It was a magical moment. One where the heavens opened and all the angels of God gathered in respect, sanctioning our commitment that would bind us until the last star in the universe ceased to shine.

"There, there, Mr. Jaffe. Don't be upset. The Doctor is here to help you. We are all here to help you. You just need to let us care for you," the Queen says.

I didn't realize my tears until she spoke, snatching me to the present. She is a smart one, finding a crack in my defense.

I cast her hand out of mine. "I'm not fooled. I know what you're up to. I know what all of you are up to. But I'm not going to give in. I might be an incubator for your horrible experiments, but I'll never call you Master. I'll die first!" I raise my fists, ready to take my final stand.

"Mr. Jaffe! Please, calm yourself. Your condition—it's affecting your mind," the Queen lies to me.

The King turns his back and hides from my view while he prepares the abomination of desolation.

I grab onto the wheels of my chair and attempt to back my way toward the door. The Rook abruptly brings my escape to a halt from behind. The King turns with a syringe swelling with the blood of a demon dripping in his hand. The Rook wraps his arms around me, pinning my arms to my side.

Striking with the dance of a cobra, the single fang of the syringe plunges into my vein and pumps its deadly venom into my arm.

I curse it with everything that is righteous, trying to defuse the bomb hurtling toward my brain.

The Queen drones on in the background with her reassuring words of my future.

The demon slams against the gate to my soul. I feel it buckle under the onslaught and redouble my efforts to block it out. I am chilled by the demon's cold laughter.

The Rook hadn't anticipated my revolt. He relaxes his embrace allowing me to spring from my chair. My head bucks under his chin. I lunge at the King with all the intentions of taking his life and send him to the fiery pits of Hell.

The Queen screams, giving me a burst of confidence as my

fingers dig into the King's soft throat. We crash to the floor, and soon the Rook is frantic in his attempt to tear me off the King.

The demon punches through my last layer of free will as a speeding bullet through paper. The assaulting wind invades my inner sanctum seeking to snuff the flame of my soul.

As a man, I am the greatest creation of the universe's fifteen billion years of evolution. I give it its very existence possessing the ability of its comprehension. No other creature on earth can make that claim. Now before my eyes, I see the universe's glory start to unravel one strand at a time. The adornments of life's pageantry are plucked away one by, leaving me with a world painted in black and gray.

The demon relaxes in the confines of all that is me. It reaches out with its crooked claws and pinches out my flame.

The scent of fresh-cut grass lingered in the air as Sherry Jaffe Nichols strolled toward the front doors of Whispering Oaks Guest House. Quaint wooden rockers and lovely park benches offered respite under the shade of the entrance awning.

The doors opened to the lobby with a nurse's station seconding as a reception area. Lined in a row, guests of the House sat in wheelchairs, staring blankly at the glass walls to the outside world. Aides dressed in maroon tended to the needs of the infirm; a never-ending task that brought little thanks for their yeomen efforts.

A male nurse dressed in white rolled her father from his early morning doctor's visit coming toward the lobby.

Sherry headed the two off before turning down the hall leading to his room.

"Hey, Dad. I'm here to see you," she leaned over and touched his shoulder. "How's he doing today?" she said to the nurse.

"He's doing very well, I'm pleased to say. It took my friend here a few extra days to adjust." The nurse patted Mr. Jaffe on the shoulder. "But now that Doctor Rathbone has his medication straight, he's become quite the happy camper."

"Mrs. Nichols, it's a pleasure to see you again," Mrs. Gurov, Head Administrator of Whispering Oaks said, extending her hand.

"Hello. The nurse was just telling me Dad is settling in."

"Yes, finally," Gurov laughed. "He was a handful for all of his Caretakers at first. But like the rest, adjusted to the daily routine. Elderly people just love to find a routine and stick with it."

"That's great," Sherry said, and then turned her attention back to her father. "How are you feeling, Dad?"

The old man's head continually twitched back and forth. His mouth was open, showing his bottom teeth. "Huuhhhh?"

"I said, 'How are you doing today?' Are you feeling well?"

He lifted his fishlike eyes to her face and searched for the right words in his mind. "Fine … ."

"I'm so glad you're doing better. You had me all tied up in knots your first week here. I thought you were going to hurt yourself. I told you if you just gave it some time you'd get to like it here. This is a perfect home for you."

"And guess what, Mr. Jaffe? Today is Wednesday, and you know what that means. Bingo at two o'clock," Gurov said.

"B … Bingo?"

"Yes, Dad. Bingo. They tell me you're on a winning streak," Sherry said.

"Bingo … ." Jaffe dropped his head, looking to the floor, almost having a meaningful thought come to mind.

Almost.

JACK DANN

CAMPS

As Stephen lies in bed, he can think only of pain.

He imagines it as sharp and blue. After receiving an injection of Demerol, he enters pain's cold regions as an explorer, an objective visitor. It is a country of ice and glass, monochromatic plains and valleys filled with wash blue shards of ice, crystal pyramids and pinnacles, squares, oblongs, and all manner of polyhedron — block upon block of painted blue pain.

Although it is mid-afternoon, Stephen pretends it is dark. His eyes are tightly closed, but the daylight pouring into the room from two large windows intrudes as a dull red field extending infinitely behind his eyelids.

"Josie," he asks through cotton mouth, "aren't I due for

another shot?" Josie is crisp and fresh and large in her starched white uniform. Her peaked nurse's cap is pinned to her mouse brown hair.

"I've just given you an injection, it will take effect soon." Josie strokes his hand, and he dreams of ice.

"Bring me some ice," he whispers.

"If I bring you a bowl of ice, you'll only spill it again."

"Bring me some ice ..." By touching the ice cubes, by turning them in his hand like a gambler favouring his dice, he can transport himself into the beautiful blue country. Later, the ice will melt, and he will spill the bowl. The shock of cold and pain will awaken him.

Stephen believes that he is dying, and he has resolved to die properly. Each visit to the cold country brings him closer to death; and death, he has learned, is only a slow walk through ice fields. He has come to appreciate the complete lack of warmth and the beautifully etched face of his magical country.

But he is connected to the bright, flat world of the hospital by plastic tubes — one breathes cold oxygen into his left nostril; another passes into his right nostril and down his throat to his stomach; one feeds him intravenously, another draws his urine.

"Here's your ice," Josie says. "But mind you, don't spill it." She places the small bowl on his tray table and wheels the table close to him. She has a musky odor of perspiration and perfume; Stephen is reminded of old women and college girls.

"Sleep now, sweet boy."

Without opening his eyes, Stephen reaches out and places his hand on the ice.

"Come now, Stephen, wake up. Dr Volk is here to see you."

Stephen feels the cool touch of Josie's hand, and he opens his eyes to see the doctor standing beside him. The doctor has a gaunt long face and thinning brown hair; he is dressed in a wrinkled green suit.

"Now we'll check the dressing, Stephen," he says as he tears away a gauze bandage on Stephen's abdomen.

Stephen feels the pain, but he is removed from it. His only wish is to return to the blue dreamlands. He watches the doctor peel off the neat crosshatchings of gauze. A terrible stink fills the room.

Josie stands well away from the bed.

"Now we'll check your drains." The doctor pulls a long drainage tube out of Stephen's abdomen, irrigates and disinfects the wound, inserts a new drain, and repeats the process by pulling out another tube just below the rib cage.

Stephen imagines that he is swimming out of the room. He tries to cross the hazy border into cooler regions, but it is difficult to concentrate. He has only a half-hour at most before the Demerol will wear off. Already, the pain is coming closer, and he will not be due for another injection until the night nurse comes on duty. But the night nurse will not give him an injection without an argument. She will tell him to fight the pain.

But he cannot fight without a shot.

"Tomorrow we'll take that oxygen tube out of your nose," the doctor says, but his voice seems far away, and Stephen wonders what he is talking about.

He reaches for the bowl of ice, but cannot find it.

"Josie, you've taken my ice."

"I took the ice away when the doctor came. Why don't you try to watch a bit of television with me; Soupy Sales is on."

"Just bring me some ice," Stephen says. "I want to rest a bit." He can feel the sharp edges of pain breaking through the gauzy wraps of Demerol.

"I love you, Josie," he says sleepily as she places a fresh bowl of ice on his tray.

As Stephen wanders through his ice blue dream world, he sees a rectangle of blinding white light. It looks like a doorway into an adjoining world of brightness. He has glimpsed it before on previous Demerol highs. A coal-dark doorway stands beside the bright one.

He walks toward the portals, passes through white-blue cornfields.

Time is growing short. The drug cannot stretch it much longer. Stephen knows that he has to choose either the bright doorway or the dark, one or the other. He does not even consider turning around, for he has dreamed that the ice and glass and cold blue gem-stones have melted behind him.

It makes no difference to Stephen which doorway he chooses. On impulse he steps into blazing, searing whiteness.

Suddenly he is in a cramped world of people and sound.

The boxcar's doors were flung open. Stephen was being pushed out of the cramped boxcar that stank of sweat, faeces and urine. Several people had died in the car, and added their stink of death to the already fetid air.

"Carla, stay close to me," shouted a man beside Stephen. He had been separated from his wife by a young woman who pushed between them, as she tried to return to the dark safety of the boxcar.

SS men in black, dirty uniforms were everywhere. They kicked and pummeled everyone within reach. Alsatian guard dogs snapped and barked. Stephen was bitten by one of the snarling dogs. A woman beside him was being kicked by soldiers. And they were all being methodically herded past a high barbed-wire fence. Beside the fence was a wall.

Stephen looked around for an escape route, but he was surrounded by other prisoners, who were pressing against him. Soldiers were shooting indiscriminately into the crowd, shooting women and children alike.

The man who had shouted to his wife was shot.

"Sholom, help me, help me," screamed a scrawny young woman whose skin was as yellow and pimpled as chicken flesh.

And Stephen understood that he was Sholom. He was a Jew

in this burning, stinking world, and this woman, somehow, meant something to him. He felt the yellow star sewn on the breast of his filthy jacket. He grimaced uncontrollably. The strangest thoughts were passing through his mind, remembrances of another childhood: morning prayers with his father and rich uncle, large breakfasts on Saturdays, the sounds of his mother and father quietly making love in the next room, yortzeit candles burning in the living room, his brother reciting the "four questions" at the Passover table.

He touched the star again and remembered the Nazi's facetious euphemism for it: Pour le Semite.

He wanted to strike out, to kill the Nazis, to fight and die. But he found himself marching with the others, as if he had no will of his own. He felt that he was cut in half. He had two selves now; one watched the other. One self wanted to fight. The other was numbed; it cared only for itself. It was determined to survive.

Stephen looked around for the woman who had called out to him. She was nowhere to be seen.

Behind him were railroad tracks, electrified wire, and the conical tower and main gate of the camp. Ahead was a pitted road littered with corpses and their belongings. Rifles were being fired and a heavy, sickly sweet odor was everywhere. Stephen gagged, others vomited. It was the overwhelming stench of death, of rotting and burning flesh. Black clouds hung above the camp, and flames spurted from the tall chimneys of ugly buildings, as if from infernal machines.

Stephen walked onward; he was numb, unable to fight or even talk. Everything that happened around him was impossible, the stuff of dreams.

The prisoners were ordered to halt, and the soldiers began to separate those who would be burned from those who would be worked to death. Old men and women and young children were pulled out of the crowd. Some were beaten and killed immediately while the others looked on in disbelief. Stephen looked on, as if it was of no concern to him. Everything was unreal, dreamlike. He did not belong here.

The new prisoners looked like Musselmänner, the walking dead. Those who became ill, or were beaten or starved before they could "wake up" to the reality of the camps became Musselmänner. Musselmänner could not think or feel. They shuffled around, already dead in spirit, until a guard or disease or cold or starvation killed them.

"Keep marching," shouted a guard, as Stephen stopped before an emaciated old man crawling on the ground. "You'll look like him soon enough."

Suddenly, as if waking from one dream and finding himself in another, Stephen remembered that the chicken-skinned girl was his wife. He remembered their life together, their children and crowded flat. He remembered the birthmark on her leg, her scent, her hungry love-making. He had once fought another boy over her.

His glands opened up with fear and shame; he had ignored her screams for help.

He stopped and turned, faced the other group. "Fruma," he shouted, then started to run.

A guard struck him in the chest with the butt of his rifle, and Stephen fell into darkness.

He spills the ice water again and awakens with a scream.

"It's my fault," Josie says, as she peels back the sheets. "I should have taken the bowl away from you. But you fight me."

Stephen lives with the pain again. He imagines that a tiny fire is burning in his abdomen, slowly consuming him. He stares at the television high on the wall and watches "Soupy Sales".

As Josie changes the plastic sac containing his intravenous saline solution, an orderly pushes a cart into the room and asks Stephen if he wants a print for his wall.

"Would you like me to choose something for you?" Josie asks.

Stephen shakes his head and asks the orderly to show him all the prints. Most of them are familiar still-lifes and pastorals, but one catches his attention. It is a painting of a wheat field. Although the sky looks ominously dark, the wheat is brightly rendered in great broad strokes. A path cuts through the field and crows fly overhead.

"That one," Stephen says. "Put that one up."

After the orderly hangs the print and leaves, Josie asks Stephen why he chose that particular painting.

"I like Van Gogh," he says dreamily, as he tries to detect a rhythm in the surges of abdominal pain. But he is not nauseated, just gaseous.

"Any particular reason why you like Van Gogh?" asks Josie. "He's my favourite artist, too."

"I didn't say he was my favourite," Stephen says, and Josie pouts, an expression which does not fit her prematurely lined face. Stephen closes his eyes, glimpses the cold country, and says, "I like the painting because it's so bright that it's almost frightening. And the road going through the field" — he opens his eyes — "doesn't go anywhere. It just ends in the field. And the crows are flying around like vultures."

"Most people see it as just a pretty picture," Josie says.

"What's it called?"

"Wheatfields with Blackbirds."

"Sensible. My stomach hurts, Josie. Help me turn over on my side." Josie helps him onto his left side, plumps up his pillows, and inserts a short tube into his rectum to relieve the gas. "I also like the painting with the large stars that all look out of focus," Stephen says. "What's it called?"

"Starry Night."

"That's scary, too," Stephen says. Josie takes his blood pressure, makes a notation on his chart, then sits down beside him and holds his hand. "I remember something," he says. "Something just —" He jumps as he remembers, and pain shoots through his distended stomach. Josie shushes him, checks the intravenous needle, and asks him what he remembers.

But the memory of the dream recedes as the pain grows sharper. "I hurt all the fucking time, Josie," he says, changing position. Josie removes the rectal tube before he is on his back.

"Don't use such language, I don't like to hear it. I know you have a lot of pain," she says, her voice softening.

"Time for a shot."

"No, honey, not for some time. You'll just have to bear with it."

Stephen remembers his dream again. He is afraid of it. His breath is short and his heart feels as if it is beating in his throat, but he recounts the entire dream to Josie.

He does not notice that her face has lost its colour.

"It's only a dream, Stephen. Probably something you studied in history."

"But it was so real, not like a dream at all."

"That's enough!" Josie says.

"I'm sorry I upset you. Don't be angry."

"I'm not angry."

"I'm sorry," he says, fighting the pain, squeezing Josie's hand tightly. "Didn't you tell me that you were in the Second World War?"

Josie is composed once again. "Yes, I did, but I'm surprised you remembered. You were very sick. I was a nurse overseas, spent most of the war in England. But I was one of the first servicewomen to go into any of the concentration camps."

Stephen drifts with the pain; he appears to be asleep.

"You must have studied very hard," Josie whispers to him. Her hand is shaking just a bit.

It is twelve o'clock and his room is death quiet. The sharp shadows seem to be the hardest objects in the room. The fluorescents burn steadily in the hall outside.

Stephen looks out into the hallway, but he can see only the far white wall. He waits for his night nurse to appear: it is time for his injection. A young nurse passes by his doorway. Stephen imagines that she is a cardboard ship sailing through the corridors.

He presses the buzzer, which is attached by a clip to his pillow. The night nurse will take her time, he tells himself. He remembers arguing with her. Angrily, he presses the buzzer again.

Across the hall, a man begins to scream, and there is a shuffle of nurses into his room. The screaming turns into begging and whining. Although Stephen has never seen the man in the opposite room, he has come to hate him. Like Stephen, he has something wrong with his stomach, but he cannot suffer well. He can only beg and cry, try to make deals with the nurses, doctors, God and angels. Stephen cannot muster any pity for this man.

The night nurse finally comes into the room, says, "You have to try to get along without this," and gives him an injection of Demerol.

"Why does the man across the hall scream so?" Stephen asks, but the nurse is already edging out of the room.

"Because he's in pain."

"So am I," Stephen says in a loud voice. "But I can keep it to myself."

"Then stop buzzing me constantly for an injection. That man across the hall has had half of his stomach removed. He's got something to scream about."

So have I, Stephen thinks; but the nurse disappears before he can tell her. He tries to imagine what the man across the hall looks like. He thinks of him as being bald and small, an ancient baby. Stephen tries to feel sorry for the man, but his incessant whining disgusts him.

The drug takes effect; the screams recede as he hurtles through the dark corridors of a dream. The cold country is dark, for Stephen cannot persuade his night nurse to bring him some ice. Once again, he sees two entrances. As the world melts behind him, he steps into the coal-black doorway.

In the darkness he hears an alarm, a bone-jarring clangor.

He could smell the combined stink of men pressed closely together. They were all lying upon two badly constructed wooden shelves. The floor was dirt; the smell of urine never left the barracks.

"Wake up," said a man Stephen knew as Viktor. "If the guard finds you in bed, you'll be beaten again."

Stephen moaned, still wrapped in dreams. "Wake up, wake up," he mumbled to himself. He would have a few more minutes before the guard arrived with the dogs. At the very thought of dogs, Stephen felt revulsion. He had once been bitten in the face by a large dog.

He opened his eyes, yet he was still half-asleep, exhausted. You are in a death camp, he said to himself. You must wake up. You must fight by waking up. Or you will die in your sleep. Shaking uncontrollably, he said, "Do you want to end up in the oven; perhaps you will be lucky today and live."

As he lowered his legs to the floor; he felt the sores open on the soles of his feet. He wondered who would die today and shrugged. It was his third week in the camp. Impossibly, against all odds, he had survived. Most of those he had known in the train had either died or become Musselmänner. If it was not for Viktor, he, too, would have become a Musselmänner. He had a breakdown and wanted to die. He babbled in English. But Viktor talked him out of death, shared his portion of food with him, and taught him the new rules of life.

"Like everyone else who survives, I count myself first, second and third — then I try to do what I can for someone else," Viktor had said.

"I will survive," Stephen repeated to himself, as the guards opened the door, stepped into the room, and began to shout. Their dogs growled and snapped but heeled beside them. The guards looked sleepy; one did not wear a cap, and his red hair was tousled.

Perhaps he spent the night with one of the whores, Stephen thought. Perhaps today would not be so bad . . .

And so begins the morning ritual: Josie enters Stephen's room at quarter to eight, fusses with the chart attached to the footboard of his bed, pads about aimlessly, and finally goes to the bathroom. She returns, her stiff uniform making swishing sounds. Stephen can feel her standing over the bed and staring at him. But he does not open his eyes. He waits a beat.

She turns away, then drops the bedpan. Yesterday it was the metal ashtray; day before that, she bumped into the bedstand.

"Good morning, darling, it's a beautiful day," she says, then walks across the room to the windows. She parts the faded orange drapes and opens the blinds.

"How do you feel today?"

"Okay, I guess."

Josie takes his pulse and asks, "Did Mr Gregory stop in to say hello last night?"

"Yes," Stephen says. "He's teaching me how to play gin rummy. What's wrong with him?"

"He's very sick."

"I can see that; has he got cancer?"

"I don't know," says Josie, as she tidies up his night table.

"You're lying again," Stephen says, but she ignores him. After a time, he says, "His girl friend was in to see me last night. I bet his wife will be in today."

"Shut your mouth about that," Josie says. "Let's get you out of that bed so I can change the sheets."

Stephen sits in the chair all morning. He is getting well but is still very weak. Just before lunchtime, the orderly wheels his cart into the room and asks Stephen if he would like to replace the print hanging on the wall.

"I've seen them all," Stephen says. "I'll keep the one I have." Stephen does not grow tired of the Van Gogh painting; sometimes, the crows seem to have changed position.

"Maybe you'll like this one," the orderly says as he pulls out a cardboard print of Van Gogh's Starry Night. It is a study of a village nestled in the hills, dressed in shadows. But everything seems to be boiling and writhing as in a fever dream. A cypress tree in the foreground looks like a black flame, and the vertiginous sky is filled with great blurry stars. It is a drunkard's dream. The orderly smiles.

"So you did have it," Stephen says.

"No, I traded some other pictures for it. They had a copy in the West Wing."

Stephen watches him hang it, thanks him, and waits for him to leave. Then he gets up and examines the painting carefully. He touches the raised facsimile brushstrokes and turns toward Josie, feeling an odd sensation in his groin. He looks at her, as if seeing her for the first time. She has an overly full mouth which curves downward at the corners when she smiles. She is not a pretty woman — too fat, he thinks.

"Dance with me," he says, as he waves his arms and takes a step forward, conscious of the pain in his stomach.

"You're too sick to be dancing just yet," but she laughs at him and bends her knees in a mock plié.

She has small breasts for such a large woman, Stephen thinks. Feeling suddenly dizzy, he takes a step toward the bed. He feels himself slip to the floor, feels Josie's hair brushing against his face, dreams that he's all wet from her tongue, feels her arms around him, squeezing, then feels the weight of her body pressing down on him, crushing him …

He wakes up in bed, catheterised. He has an intravenous needle in his left wrist, and it is difficult to swallow, for he has a tube down his throat.

He groans, tries to move.

"Quiet, Stephen," Josie says, stroking his hand.

"What happened?" he mumbles. He can only remember being dizzy.

"You've had a slight setback, so just rest. The doctor had to collapse your lung; you must lie very still."

"Josie, I love you," he whispers, but he is too far away to be heard. He wonders how many hours or days have passed. He looks toward the window. It is dark, and there is no one in the room.

He presses the buzzer attached to his pillow and remembers a dream …

"You must fight," Viktor said.

It was dark, all the other men were asleep, and the barrack was filled with snoring and snorting. Stephen wished they could all die, choke on their own breath. It would be an act of mercy.

"Why fight?" Stephen asked, and he pointed toward the greasy window, beyond which were the ovens that smoked day and night. He made a fluttering gesture with his hand — smoke rising.

"You must fight, you must live, living is everything. It is the only thing that makes sense here."

"We're all going to die, anyway," Stephen whispered. "Just like your sister … and my wife."

"No, Sholom, we're going to live. The others may die, but we're going to live. You must believe that."

Stephen understood that Viktor was desperately trying to convince himself to live. He felt sorry for Viktor; there could be no sensible rationale for living in a place like this.

Stephen grinned, tasted blood from the corner of his mouth, and said, "So we'll live through the night, maybe."

And maybe tomorrow, he thought. He would play the game of survival a little longer.

He wondered if Viktor would be alive tomorrow. He smiled and thought; If Viktor dies, then I will have to take his place and convince others to live. For an instant, he hoped Viktor would die so that he could take his place.

The alarm sounded. It was three o'clock in the morning, time to begin the day.

This morning Stephen was on his feet before the guards could unlock the door.

"Wake up," Josie says, gently tapping his arm. "Come on, wake up."

Stephen hears her voice as an echo. He imagines that he has been flung into a long tunnel; he hears air whistling in his ears but cannot see anything.

"Whassimatter?" he asks. His mouth feels as if it is stuffed with cotton; his lips are dry and cracked. He is suddenly angry at Josie and the plastic tubes that hold him in his bed as if he was a latter-day Gulliver. He wants to pull out the tubes, smash the bags filled with saline, tear away his bandages.

"You were speaking German," Josie says. "Did you know that?"

"Can I have some ice?"

"No," Josie says impatiently. "You spilled again, you're all wet."

". . . for my mouth, dry . . ."

"Do you remember speaking German, honey? I have to know."

"Don't remember, bring ice, I'll try to think about it."

As Josie leaves to get him some ice, he tries to remember his dream.

"Here, now, just suck on the ice." She gives him a little hill of crushed ice on the end of a spoon.

"Why did you wake me up, Josie?" The layers of dream are beginning to slough off. As the Demerol works out of his system, he has to concentrate on fighting the burning ache in his stomach.

"You were speaking German. Where did you learn to speak like that?"

Stephen tries to remember what he said. He cannot speak any German, only a bit of classroom French. He looks down at his legs (he has thrown off the sheet) and notices, for the first time, that his legs are as thin as his arms. "My God, Josie, how could I have lost so much weight?"

"You lost about forty pounds, but don't worry, you'll gain it all back. You're on the road to recovery now. Please, try to remember your dream."

"I can't, Josie! I just can't seem to get ahold of it."

"Try."

"Why is it so important to you?"

"You weren't speaking college German, darling. You were speaking slang. You spoke in a patois that I haven't heard since the forties."

Stephen feels a chill slowly creep up his spine. "What did I say?"

Josie waits a beat, then says, "You talked about dying."

"Josie?"

"Yes," she says, pulling at her fingernail.

"When is the pain going to stop?"

"It will be over soon." She gives him another spoonful of ice. "You kept repeating the name Viktor in your sleep. Can you remember anything about him?"

Viktor, Viktor, deep-set blue eyes, balding head and broken nose called himself a Galitzianer. Saved my life. "I remember," Stephen says. "His name is Viktor Shmone. He is in all my dreams now."

Josie exhales sharply.

"Does that mean anything to you?" Stephen asks anxiously.

"I once knew a man from one of the camps." She speaks very slowly and precisely. "His name was Viktor Shmone. I took care of him. He was one of the few people left alive in the camp after the Germans fled." She reaches for her purse, which she keeps on Stephen's night table, and fumbles an old, torn photograph out of a plastic slipcase.

As Stephen examines the photograph, he begins to sob. A thinner and much younger Josie is standing beside Viktor and two other emaciated-looking men. "Then I'm not dreaming," he says, "and I'm going to die. That's what it means." He begins to shake, just as he did in his dream, and, without thinking, he makes the gesture of rising smoke to Josie. He begins to laugh.

"Stop that," Josie says, raising her hand to slap him. Then she embraces him and says, "Don't cry, darling, it's only a dream.

Somehow, you're dreaming the past."

"Why?" Stephen asks, still shaking.

"Maybe you're dreaming because of me, because we're so close. In some ways, I think you know me better than anyone else, better than any man, no doubt. You might be dreaming for a reason; maybe I can help you."

"I'm afraid, Josie."

She comforts him and says, "Now tell me everything you can remember about the dreams."

He is exhausted. As he recounts his dreams to her, he sees the bright doorway again. He feels himself being sucked into it. "Josie," he says, "I must stay awake, don't want to sleep, dream . . ."

Josie's face is pulled tight as a mask; she is crying.

Stephen reaches out to her, slips into the bright doorway, into another dream.

It was a cold cloudless morning. Hundreds of prisoners were working in the quarries; each work gang came from a different barrack. Most of the gangs were made up of Musselmänner, the faceless majority of the camp. They moved like automatons, lifting and carrying the great stones to the numbered carts, which would have to be pushed down the tracks.

Stephen was drenched with sweat. He had a fever and was afraid that he had contracted typhus. An epidemic had broken out in the camp last week. Every morning several doctors arrived with the guards. Those who were too sick to stand up were taken away to be gassed or experimented upon in the hospital.

Although Stephen could barely stand, he forced himself to keep moving. He tried to focus all his attention on what he was doing. He made a ritual of bending over, choosing a stone of certain size, lifting it, carrying it to the nearest cart, and then taking the same number of steps back to his dig.

A Musselmänn fell to the ground, but Stephen made no effort to help him. When he could help someone in a little way, he would, but he would not stick his neck out for a Musselmänn. Yet something niggled at Stephen. He remembered a photograph in which Viktor and this Musselmänn were standing with a man and a woman he did not recognise. But Stephen could not remember where he had ever seen such a photograph.

"Hey, you," shouted a guard. "Take the one on the ground to the cart."

Stephen nodded to the guard and began to drag the Musselmänn away.

"Who's the new patient down the hall?" Stephen asks as he eats a bit of cereal from the breakfast tray Josie has placed before him. He is feeling much better now; his fever is down, and the tubes, catheter and intravenous needle have been removed. He can even walk around a bit.

"How did you find out about that?" Josie asks.

"You were talking to Mr Gregory's nurse. Do you think I'm dead already? I can still hear."

Josie laughs and takes a sip of Stephen's tea. "You're far from dead! In fact, today is a red-letter day; you're going to take your first shower. What do you think about that?"

"I'm not well enough yet," he says, worried that he will have to leave the hospital before he is ready.

"Well, Dr Volk thinks differently, and his word is law."

"Tell me about the new patient."

"They brought in a man last night who drank two quarts of motor oil; he's on the dialysis machine."

"Will he make it?"

"No, I don't think so; there's too much poison in his system."

We should all die, Stephen thinks. It would be an act of mercy. He glimpses the camp.

"Stephen!"

He jumps, then awakens.

"You've had a good night's sleep; you don't need to nap. Let's get you into that shower and have it done with." Josie pushes the tray table away from the bed. "Come on, I have your bathrobe right here."

Stephen puts on his bathrobe, and they walk down the hall to the showers. There are three empty shower stalls, a bench, and a whirlpool bath. As Stephen takes off his bathrobe, Josie adjusts the water pressure and temperature in the corner stall.

"What's the matter?" Stephen asks, after stepping into the shower. Josie stands in front of the shower stall and holds his towel, but she will not look at him. "Come on," he says, "you've seen me naked before."

"That was different."

"How?" He touches a hard, ugly scab that has formed over one of the wounds on his abdomen.

"When you were very sick, I washed you in bed, as if you were a baby. Now it's different." She looks down at the wet tile floor, as if she is lost in thought.

"Well, I think it's silly," he says. "Come on, it's hard to talk to someone who's looking the other way. I could break my neck in here and you'd be staring down at the fucking floor."

"I've asked you not to use that word," she says in a very low voice.

"Do my eyes still look yellowish?"

She looks directly at his face and says, "No, they look fine."

Stephen suddenly feels faint, then nauseated; he has been standing too long. As he leans against the cold shower wall, he remembers his last dream. He is back in the quarry. He can smell the perspiration of the men around him, feel the sun baking him, draining his strength. It is so bright …

He finds himself sitting on the bench and staring at the light on the opposite wall. I've got typhus, he thinks, then realises that he is in the hospital. Josie is beside him.

"I'm sorry," he says.

"I shouldn't have let you stand so long; it was my fault."

"I remembered another dream." He begins to shake, and Josie puts her arms around him.

"It's all right now, tell Josie about your dream."

She's an old, fat woman, Stephen thinks. As he describes the dream, his shaking subsides.

"Do you know the man's name?" Josie asks. "The one the guard ordered you to drag away."

"No," Stephen says. "He was a Musselmänn, yet I thought there was something familiar about him. In my dream I remembered the photograph you showed me. He was in it."

"What will happen to him?"

"The guards will give him to the doctors for experimentation. If they don't want him, he'll be gassed."

"You must not let that happen," Josie says, holding him tightly.

"Why?" asks Stephen, afraid that he will fall into the dreams again.

"If he was one of the men you saw in the photograph, you must not let him die. Your dreams must fit the past."

"I'm afraid."

"It will be all right, baby," Josie says, clinging to him. She is shaking and breathing heavily.

Stephen feels himself getting an erection. He calms her, presses his face against hers, and touches her breasts. She tells him to stop, but does not push him away.

"I love you," he says as he slips his hand under her starched skirt. He feels awkward and foolish and warm.

"This is wrong," she whispers.

As Stephen kisses her and feels her thick tongue in his mouth, he begins to dream.

Stephen stopped to rest for a few seconds. The Musselmänn was dead weight. I cannot go on, Stephen thought; but he bent down, grabbed the Musselmänn by his coat, and dragged him toward the cart. He glimpsed the cart, which was filled with the sick and dead and exhausted; it looked no different than a carload of corpses marked for a mass grave.

A long, grey cloud covered the sun, then passed, drawing shadows across gutted hills.

On impulse, Stephen dragged the Musselmänn into a gully behind several chalky rocks. Why am I doing this? he asked himself. If I'm caught, I'll be ash in the ovens, too. He remembered what Victor had told him: "You must think of yourself all the time, or you'll be no help to anyone else."

The Musselmänn groaned, then raised his arm. His face was grey with dust and his eyes were glazed.

"You must lie still," Stephen whispered. "Do not make a sound. I've hidden you from the guards, but if they hear you, we'll all be punished. One sound from you and you're dead. You must fight to live, you're in a death camp, you must fight so you can tell of this later."

"I have no family, they're all —"

Stephen clapped his hand over the man's mouth and whispered, "Fight, don't talk. Wake up, you cannot survive the death camp by sleeping."

The man nodded, and Stephen climbed out of the gully. He helped two men carry a large stone to a nearby cart.

"What are you doing?" shouted a guard.

"I left my place to help these men with this stone; now I'll go back where I was."

"What the hell are you trying to do?" Viktor asked.

Stephen felt as if he was burning up with fever. He wiped the sweat from his eyes, but everything was still blurry.

"You're sick, too. You'll be lucky if you last the day."

"I'll last," Stephen said, "but I want you to help me get him back to the camp."

"I won't risk it, not for a Musselmänn. He's already dead, leave him."

"Like you left me?"

Before the guards could take notice, they began to work. Although Viktor was older than Stephen, he was stronger. He worked hard every day and never caught the diseases that daily reduced the barrack's numbers. Stephen had a touch of death, as Viktor called it, and was often sick.

They worked until dusk, when the sun's oblique rays caught the dust from the quarries and turned it into veils and scrims. Even the guards sensed that this was a quiet time, for they would congregate together and talk in hushed voices.

"Come, now, help me," Stephen whispered to Viktor.

"I've been doing that all day," Viktor said. "I'll have enough trouble getting you back to the camp, much less carry this Musselmänn."

"We can't leave him."

"Why are you so preoccupied with this Musselmänn? Even if we can get him back to the camp, his chances are nothing. I know, I've seen enough, I know who has a chance to survive."

"You're wrong this time," Stephen said. He was dizzy and it was difficult to stand. The odds are I won't last the night, and Viktor knows it, he told himself. "I had a dream that if this man dies, I'll die, too. I just feel it."

"Here we learn to trust our dreams," Viktor said. "They make as much sense as this . . ." He made the gesture of rising smoke and gazed toward the ovens, which were spewing fire and black ash.

The western portion of the sky was yellow, but over the ovens it was red and purple and dark blue. Although it horrified Stephen to consider it, there was a macabre beauty here. If he survived, he would never forget these sense impressions, which were stronger than anything he had ever experienced before. Being so close to death, he was, perhaps for the first time, really living. In the camp, one did not even consider suicide. One grasped for every moment, sucked at life like an infant, lived as if there was no future.

The guards shouted at the prisoners to form a column; it was time to march back to the barracks.

While the others milled about, Stephen and Viktor lifted the Musselmänn out of the gully. Everyone nearby tried to distract the guards. When the march began, Stephen and Viktor held the Musselmänn between them, for he could barely stand.

"Come on, dead one, carry your weight," Viktor said. "Are you so dead that you cannot hear me? Are you as dead as the rest of your family?" The Musselmänn groaned and dragged his legs. Viktor kicked him. "You'll walk or we'll leave you here for the guards to find."

"Let him be," Stephen said.

"Are you dead or do you have a name?" Viktor continued.

"Berek," croaked the Musselmänn. "I am not dead."

"Then we have a fine bunk for you," Viktor said. "You can smell the stink of the sick for another night before the guards make a selection." Viktor made the gesture of smoke rising.

Stephen stared at the barracks ahead. They seemed to waver as the heat rose from the ground. He counted every step. He would drop soon, he could not go on, could not carry the Musselmänn.

He began to mumble in English.

"So you're speaking American again," Viktor said.

Stephen shook himself awake, placed one foot before the other.

"Dreaming of an American lover?"

"I don't know English and I have no American lover."

"Then who is this Josie you keep taking about in your sleep?"

"Why were you screaming?" Josie asks, as she washes his face with a cold washcloth.

"I don't remember screaming," Stephen says. He discovers a fever blister on his lip. Expecting to find an intravenous needle in his wrist, he raises his arm.

"You don't need an IV," Josie says. "You just have a bit of a fever. Dr Volk has prescribed some new medication for it."

"What time is it?" Stephen stares at the whorls in the ceiling.

"Almost three p.m. I'll be going off soon."

"Then I've slept most of the day away," Stephen says, feeling something crawling inside him. He worries that his dreams still have a hold on him. "Am I having another relapse?"

"You'll do fine," Josie says.

"I should be fine now. I don't want to dream anymore."

"Did you dream again, do you remember anything?"

"I dreamed that I saved the Musselmänn," Stephen says.

"What was his name?" asks Josie.

"Berek, I think. Is that the man you knew?"

Josie nods and Stephen smiles at her. "Maybe that's the end of the dreams," he says, but she does not respond. He asks to see the photograph again.

"Not just now," Josie says.

"But I have to see it. I want to see if I can recognise myself."

Stephen dreamed he was dead, but it was only the fever. Viktor sat beside him on the floor and watched the others. The sick were moaning and crying; they slept on the cramped platform, as if proximity to one another could insure a few more hours of life. Wan moonlight seemed to fill the barracks.

Stephen awakened, feverish. "I'm burning up," he whispered to Viktor.

"Well," Viktor said, "you've got your Musselmänn. If he lives, you live. That's what you said, isn't it?"

"I don't remember, I just knew that I couldn't let him die."

"You'd better go back to sleep, you'll need your strength. Or we may have to carry you, tomorrow."

Stephen tried to sleep, but the fever was making lights and spots before his eyes. When he finally fell asleep, he dreamed of a dark country filled with gem-stones and great quarries of ice and glass.

"What?" Stephen asked, as he sat up suddenly, awakened from damp black dreams. He looked around and saw that everyone was watching Berek, who was sitting under the window at the far end of the room.

Berek was singing the Kol Nidre very softly. It was the Yom Kippur prayer, which was sung on the most holy of days. He repeated the prayer three times, and then once again in a louder voice. The others responded, intoned the prayer as a recitative. Viktor was crying quietly, and Stephen imagined that the holy spirit animated Berek. Surely, he told himself, that face and those pale unseeing eyes were those of a dead man. He remembered the story of the golem, shuddered, found himself singing and pulsing with fever.

When the prayer was over, Berek fell back into his fever trance. The others became silent, then slept. But there was something new in the barracks with them tonight, a palpable exultation. Stephen looked around at the sleepers and thought: We're surviving, more dead than alive, but surviving …

"You were right about that Musslemänn," Viktor whispered. "It's good that we saved him."

"Perhaps we should sit with him," Stephen said. "He's alone." But Viktor was already asleep; and Stephen was suddenly afraid that if he sat beside Berek, he would be consumed by his holy fire.

As Stephen fell through sleep and dreams, his face burned with fever.

Again he wakes up screaming.

"Josie," he says, "I can remember the dream, but there's something else, something I can't see, something terrible …"

"Not to worry," Josie says, "it's the fever." But she looks worried, and Stephen is sure that she knows something he does not.

"Tell me what happened to Viktor and Berek," Stephen says. He presses his hands together to stop them from shaking.

"They lived, just as you are going to live and have a good life."

Stephen calms down and tells her his dream.

"So you see," she says, "you're even dreaming about surviving."

"I'm burning up."

"Dr Volk says you're doing very well." Josie sits beside him, and he watches the fever patterns shift behind his closed eyelids.

"Tell me what happens next, Josie."

"You're going to get well."

"There's something else . . ."

"Shush, now, there's nothing else." She pauses, then says, "Mr Gregory is supposed to visit you tonight. He's getting around a bit; he's been back and forth all day in his wheelchair. He tells me that you two have made some sort of a deal about dividing up all the nurses."

Stephen smiles, opens his eyes, and says, "It was Gregory's idea. Tell me what's wrong with him."

"All right, he has cancer, but he doesn't know it, and you must keep it a secret. They cut the nerve in his leg because the pain was so bad. He's quite comfortable now, but, remember, you can't repeat what I've told you."

"Is he going to live?" Stephen asks. "He's told me about all the new projects he's planning. So I guess he's expecting to get out of here."

"He's not going to live very long, and the doctor didn't want to break his spirit."

"I think he should be told."

"That's not your decision to make, nor mine."

"Am I going to die, Josie?"

"No!" she says, touching his arm to reassure him.

"How do I know that's the truth?"

"Because I say so, and I couldn't look you straight in the eye and tell you if it wasn't true. I should have known it would be a mistake to tell you about Mr Gregory."

"You did right," Stephen says. "I won't mention it again. Now that I know, I feel better." He feels drowsy again.

"Do you think you're up to seeing him tonight?"

Stephen nods, although he is bone-tired. As he falls asleep, the fever patterns begin to dissolve, leaving a bright field. With a start, he opens his eyes: he has touched the edge of another dream.

"What happened to the man across the hall, the one who was always screaming?"

"He's left the ward," Josie says. "Mr Gregory had better hurry, if he wants to play cards with you before dinner. They're going to bring the trays up soon."

"You mean he died, don't you."

"Yes, if you must know, he died. But you're going to live."

There is a crashing noise in the hallway. Someone shouts, and Josie runs to the door.

Stephen tries to stay awake, but he is being pulled back into the cold country.

"Mr Gregory fell trying to get into his wheelchair by himself," Josie says. "He should have waited for his nurse, but she was out of the room and he wanted to visit you."

But Stephen does not hear a word she says.

There were rumours that the camp was going to be liberated. It was late, but no one was asleep. The shadows in the barracks seemed larger tonight.

"It's better for us if the Allies don't come," Viktor said to Stephen.

"Why do you say that?"

"Haven't you noticed that the ovens are going day and night? The Nazis are in a hurry."

"I'm going to try to sleep," Stephen said.

"Look around you, even the Musslemänner are agitated," Viktor said. "Animals become nervous before the slaughter. I've worked with animals. People are not so different."

"Shut up and let me sleep," Stephen said, and he dreamed that he could hear the crackling of distant gunfire.

"Attention," shouted the guards as they stepped into the barrack.

There were more guards than usual, and each one had two Alsatian dogs. "Come on, form a line. Hurry."

"They're going to kill us," Viktor said, "then they'll evacuate the camp and save themselves."

The guards marched the prisoners toward the north section of the camp. Although it was still dark, it was hot and humid, without a trace of the usual morning chill. The ovens belched fire and turned the sky aglow. Everyone was quiet, for there was nothing to be done. The guards were nervous and would cut down anyone who uttered a sound, as an example for the rest.

The booming of big guns could be heard in the distance. If I'm going to die, Stephen thought, I might as well go now and take a Nazi with me. Suddenly, all of his buried fear, aggression and revulsion surfaced; his face became hot and his heart felt as if it was pumping in his throat. But Stephen argued with himself. There was always a chance. He had once heard of some women who were waiting in line for the ovens; for no apparent reason the guards sent them back to their barracks. Anything could happen. There was always a chance. But to attack a guard would mean certain death.

The guns became louder. Stephen could not be sure, but he thought the noise was coming from the west. The thought passed through his mind that everyone would be better off dead. That would stop all the guns and screaming voices, the clenched fists and wildly beating hearts. The Nazis should kill everyone, and then themselves, as a favour to humanity.

The guards stopped the prisoners in an open field surrounded on three sides by forestland. Sunrise was moments away; purple black clouds drifted across the sky, touched by grey in the east. It promised to be a hot, gritty day.

Half-Step Walter, a Judenrat sympathiser who worked for the guards, handed out shovel heads to everyone.

"He's worse than the Nazis," Viktor said to Stephen.

"The Judenrat thinks he will live," said Berek, "but he will die like a Jew with the rest of us."

"Now, when it's too late, the Musselmänn regains consciousness," Viktor said.

"Hurry," shouted the guards, "or you'll die now. As long as you dig, you'll live."

Stephen hunkered down on his knees and began to dig with the shovel head.

"Do you think we might escape?" Berek whined.

"Shut up and dig," Stephen said. "There is no escape, just stay alive as long as you can. Stop whining, are you becoming a Musselmänn again?" Stephen noticed that other prisoners were gathering up twigs and branches. So the Nazis plan to cover us up, he thought.

"That's enough," shouted a guard. "Put your shovels down in front of you and stand in a line."

The prisoners stood shoulder to shoulder along the edge of the mass grave. Stephen stood between Viktor and Berek. Someone screamed and ran and was shot immediately.

I don't want to see trees or guards or my friends, Stephen thought as he stared into the sun. I only want to see the sun, let it burn out my eyes, fill up my head with light. He was shaking uncontrollably, quaking with fear.

Guns were booming in the background.

Maybe the guards won't kill us, Stephen thought, even as he heard the crack-crack of their rifles. Men were screaming and begging for life. Stephen turned his head, only to see someone's face blown away.

Screaming, tasting vomit in his mouth, Stephen fell backward, pulling Viktor and Berek into the grave with him.

Darkness, Stephen thought. His eyes were open, yet it was dark, I must be dead; this must be death …

He could barely move. Corpses can't move, he thought. Something brushed against his face; he stuck out his tongue, felt something spongy. It tasted bitter. Lifting first one arm and then the other, Stephen moved some branches away. Above, he could see a few dim stars; the clouds were lit like lanterns by a quarter moon.

He touched the body beside him; it moved. That must be Viktor, he thought. "Viktor, are you alive, say something if you're alive." Stephen whispered, as if in fear of disturbing the dead.

Viktor groaned and said, "Yes, I'm alive, and so is Berek."

"And the others?"

"All dead. Can't you smell the stink? You, at least, were unconscious all day."

"They can't all be dead," Stephen said, then he began to cry.

"Shut up," Viktor said, touching Stephen's face to comfort him. "We're alive, that's something. They could have fired a volley into the pit."

"I thought I was dead," Berek said. He was a shadow among shadows.

"Why are we still here?" Stephen asked.

"We stayed in here because it is safe," Viktor said.

"But they're all dead," Stephen whispered, amazed that there could be speech and reason inside a grave.

"Do you think it's safe to leave now?" Berek asked Viktor.

"Perhaps. I think the killing has stopped. By now the Americans or English or whoever they are have taken over the camp. I heard gunfire and screaming. I think it's best to wait a while longer."

"Here?" asked Stephen. "Among the dead?"

"It's best to be safe."

It was late afternoon when they climbed out of the grave. The air was thick with flies. Stephen could see bodies sprawled in awkward positions beneath the covering of twigs and branches. "How can I live when all the others are dead?" he asked himself aloud.

"You live, that's all," answered Viktor.

They kept close to the forest and worked their way back toward the camp.

"Look there," Viktor said, motioning Stephen and Berek to take cover. Stephen could see trucks moving toward the camp compound.

"Americans," whispered Berek.

"No need to whisper now," Stephen said, "We're safe."

"Guards could be hiding anywhere," Viktor said. "I haven't slept in the grave to be shot now."

They walked into the camp through a large break in the barbed-wire fence, which had been hit by an artillery shell. When they reached the compound, they found nurses, doctors, and army personnel bustling about.

"You speak English," Viktor said to Stephen, as they walked past several quonsets. "Maybe you can speak for us."

"I told you, I can't speak English."

"But I've heard you!"

"Wait," shouted an American army nurse. "You fellows are going the wrong way." She was stocky and spoke perfect German. "You must check in at the hospital; it's back that way."

"No," said Berek, shaking his head. "I won't go in there."

"There's no need to be afraid now," she said. "You're free. Come along, I'll take you to the hospital."

Something familiar about her, Stephen thought. He felt dizzy and everything turned grey.

"Josie," he murmured, as he fell to the ground.

"What is it?" Josie asks. "Everything is all right, Josie is here."

"Josie," Stephen mumbles.

"You're all right."

"How can I live when they're all dead?" he asks.

"It was a dream," she says as she wipes the sweat from his forehead. "You see, your fever has broken, you're getting well."

"Did you know about the grave?"

"It's all over now, forget the dream."

"Did you know?"

"Yes," Josie says. "Viktor told me how he survived the grave, but that was so long ago, before you were even born. Dr Volk tells me you'll be going home soon."

"I don't want to leave, I want to stay with you."

"Stop that talk, you've got a whole life ahead of you. Soon, you'll forget all about this, and you'll forget me, too."

"Josie," Stephen asks, "let me see that old photograph again. Just one last time."

"Remember, this is the last time," she says as she hands him the faded photograph.

He recognises Viktor and Berek, but the young man standing between them is not Stephen. "That's not me," he says, certain that he will never return to the camp.

Yet the shots still echo in his mind.

E. A. IRWIN

JUSTICE THROUGH TWELVE STEPS

Emotion raced down my spine as if electric eels swam in my blood. Pacing didn't alleviate the building fury making me antsy. I needed to rant. Release the pent-up sensations only a true cry of the wild afforded. Just touch something—preferably someone's neck while I watched my hands close around it with knowing certainty.

My fingers itched with discomfort born of indignation, their jointed structures desperate for exercise only hurting provided. I rushed from the building. The door slam reverberated in my brain, sending the eels to attack different limbs. A fantastic, incomparable surge of emotion. Good. Think about what to do with the flare-up. Start making a plan.

Dashing through traffic, I honed in on faces of the masses blocking my way. They kept smiling. Their faulted natures attempting to glue their subversive guilt to me the way they always did. Fools, all of them. Didn't they understand they were the problem? I flexed my fingers to make sure they worked—just in case.

I compelled myself to slow my steps lest someone think me crazed. Another element of the psyche everyone misunderstood. Crazed was a good feeling. It kept you safe among those who thought you should change and act similar to the multitude of the affable living lackluster lives.

My stomach clenched, the spasm shooting knowledge through my brain stem. Ideas infiltrated my mind. Bursts from a semi-automatic rifle, ready to inflict the world with my version of pain. Inwardly, I chuckled as I strode past a herd of pompous wannabes who thought themselves individuals in their disordered and dysfunctional lives. Dressed similarly. Drinking coffee from giant cups adorned with the same pretentious logo. Spewing the same boring propaganda this obnoxious world seemed to enjoy. Sheeple waiting for their next devoted shepherd of like mind. Pus-filled boils awaiting puncture were more interesting. A spray of brain bullets could take them all down if I concentrated. But what would be the fun in that? Eventually, one would wander from the herd and opportunity would deliver them into my care. Visions of a baby gazelle, taken down by a stealth cheetah, added extra longing to my captive thoughts.

The idea grew at a delicious, unhurried pace in direct contradiction to my desire to beat them into submission and show them what type of shepherd truly adored them.

Slowing to a stop, I leaned against a stone wall as drab as the day and eased my hands into my jacket pockets to lovingly caress a few special items. The wannabes grew restless, their empty cups becoming paper drums on which they beat out-of-synch rhythms I couldn't bear hearing. My casual gaze already aware which one would break first and flee. A leggy blonde tucked a stray piece of straw-like hair behind a multi-pierced ear, and then cast a sly glance my way. I winked. She subtly moved her head in a direction away from the group, indicating she was more than ready to wander from the herd.

A chuckle threatened to escape. I should have earned big bucks for my intuition since I was rarely wrong. Flashes of what I could do with her strobed across my brain as she said goodbye to her pack and sauntered to a nearby alley. Far too easy. A freebie I didn't have to work for, although I never really had to work too hard for my fun.

Sex spilled from her. An invisible trail betraying her need. I'd match her need and up the ante until my wants were thoroughly met. My breath quickened, along with my pace, as I avoided broken pallets and garbage lining the chuck-holed blacktop. Anticipation built while I sped toward a new adventure, my body already in tune to what my mind desired. Twitching fingers signaled the fun was about to begin.

Decayed fish, heavily laced with burned grease, stung the alley air. A side of hot and rancid body lard added a certain pungency only the nasally impaired could enjoy. But her scent drilled a hole through the stench. Need, like acid, could permeate almost anything.

My eyes slowly adjusted to the eerie darkness she'd entered. Some abandoned building a good architect never graced or upscale clientele ever visited. Her hunger willed me forward, my confident steps sure on the worn linoleum path leading through the labyrinth of low-rent offices. I avoided brushing against the striations of chipped paint adorning the walls lest they leave evidence on me or the walls' grimy texture. No sounds of life echoed through the halls except the pounding of the eels' building frenzy. The need to grab my body before it burst grew unbearable. Instead, I let my fingers play in my pockets and imagined what they would do next. *Slow your breathing. No need to hurry. Let the wannabe wait for you. You're her answer. This is why you're here.*

Almost there.

Almost.

Not quite.

Let this bitch be worth my trouble.

The door to office 137 stood open. The lone gazelle perched on an ancient metal desk that looked as if it had been resurrected from sometime during World War II—the losing side. Its battered appearance, upon closer inspection, matched the woman's haggard face. She smiled while rearranging her body into what I could only assume a provocative pose, although legs spread, exposing crotch-less panties, seemed more clinical than sexy.

"There you are. Thought I'd lost you."

Cheetahs developed excellent technique. "Nope. I'm pretty good at following scent."

She grinned broader and beckoned me forward. Apparently she also assumed I liked the smell of the wretched berry concoction slathered on her like second skin. I approached with caution, watching for telltale signs of skittishness and the need to escape. A slight sheen formed on her face and not from exertion. Yeah, she'd go the extra mile.

"Got a name, babe?"

She looked startled I'd ask something personal. "Yeah, my name's Dawn." She fidgeted with her top so I could get a closer look at her fake tits. "What's yours?"

Maybe I should give her a false name, but why? I liked my name. Believed in my name. I was my name. "Stewart. Were you born at sunrise, Dawn?"

Confusion painted her unattractive face. "No. Why?"

Stupid cow. Apparently subtle conversation was lost on her. Never mind. Want to play?"

Her expression relaxed. "Sure, show me what you got, Stewie."

Her eyes widened. Her mouth quickly resembled an *O* when I showed her a pair of surgical gloves pulled from an inside pocket. Her rapid eye blinks thrilled me as the snap of latex on my hands resounded in my head.

"Hey, what kind of game do you have in mind, Stewie?"

A faint tic attacked the corner of my eye. Covered the physical nuisance with a slow blink and remembered why I'd come. Smiling seemed genuine when I stared into her shadow-ringed eyes. Discovering, as I moved closer, my ideas were wrong about the shadow—just smudged mascara applied in tarry thickness resembling tacky spider legs. I seductively whispered in her ear. "I like to play doctor. Did you ever play doctor when you were a kid, Dawn?"

Had she ever been a child?

Did I care?

No.

Her breath came out in a rush as if she'd inhaled weed and couldn't hold it any longer. Stale cigarettes and Juicy Fruit gum hung in the air between us like a toxic balloon ... she relaxed more.

"Yeah, I played doctor when I was a kid. Figured you for a touchy-feely kind of guy when I saw you. Something about that look in your eye. You know, all serious and stuff. So, Doc Stewie, you just want to examine me or do you want to touch and explore?" She spread her legs wider. Her fingers fondled the hole in her panties, a burst of coarse laughter ended in a smoky cough. "Or do you want me to touch you?"

I pulled a syringe from a baggie inside my coat pocket and ran the capped end lovingly along her pasty cheek. Dawn licked dry lips. The vein at the side of her neck, wild and uncontrolled, throbbed as the pulse increased. Her needs on display as vulgar as her pose.

"All in good time. Let's play house call first. I can see you need my expertise. Why, I even have a prescription to alleviate your ailment." I dangled the syringe in front of her, and then dragged it across one of her breasts. The need to stick the needle into a nipple and see if I could pop the repulsive balls of silicon overwhelmed, but I refrained. I could tell she wanted to grab the syringe and stick it in any vein she could find. This was too fun.

She pushed hair off her shiny face and smiled. "You want me to suck you or fuck you, Stewie?" Her eyes drifted to my crotch. "You got a nice big piece of meat there. It's an extra twenty if I deep throat you."

"Ah, ah, doctor, please. That is if you still want to play."

"Okay, Doc. You gonna touch or what? An hundred extra and I'll do anal."

Shit, she sounded like a fast food drive through … one from column A and two from the bargain menu. As if I'd ever put my prized member in any of her diseased holes. "Definitely you're going to experience my touch." I stepped in front of her and backhanded her hard across the face. Spittle flew and hit the desk as her head swung hard to the right.

Dawn tried jumping from the desk. Maybe she was a gazelle after all. I grabbed her around the neck and pulled her back to that awkward pose.

"What the hell did you do that for? What did I do to you? Let me go. Now. You're insane!"

I stared hard into her eyes and squeezed her neck. "I'm far from insane. Don't ever call me Stewie. I abhor that name. And if you don't know what abhor means, it means I really, really hate it. Got that?"

She hesitated, nodded, and gasped for air.

"Good. Now, I've come to your home. You're in pain." I socked her in the eye, ricocheting her head in the other direction just to prove my point. "You're in unbearable pain." I knocked her body onto the desk before she could react to the face slam and beat her head against the grimy table top. Her eyes grew unfocused. A satisfying whimper escaped her dry mouth. I held her down harder. "But remember, I have a prescription for pain. Something you need. Something you crave. Something better than my dick in your face-hole for money. Your body's screaming for it right now. I hear it echoing through this place."

Her legs flailed as I struck them with a mini leather flogger I'd pulled from another pocket. My elbow dug into her chest, preventing her from rising. The eels swam in my blood in wild abandon until delirium edged me toward darkness. I was almost there. Almost. But not quite. Could the cow, Dawn, make me high?

Dragging the end of the flogger up her legs toward that crotch-less spectacle, I closed my fingers around her neck and pressed hard. Her screams muffled as I applied more pressure. "I can't hear you. Scream for me. Louder." I slapped her across the face with the leather fringe. "I want to hear you squeal. I want to give you something for the pain. But you have to let me know how much it hurts for me to gauge the medication."

Dawn's voice, or straggled sob, sounded faint. "Why are you doing this? Damn you to Hell for beating me. That's not what we came in here to do."

I shook my head in disbelief. "I'm the doctor. I ask the questions. You answer. You're the patient." The cap of the syringe loosened when I dragged it across her chest, leaving a gash as angry red as I felt. I quickly snapped it closed. "Answer me! Are you in pain?"

There was that tongue again. Drawing itself across those wretched parched lips. Disgusting to witness. Like some creepy snail popping out of its house and checking the desert landscape for water.

"Yes, I'm in pain." Her voice almost too faint to hear.

She writhed and yelped when I twisted her nipples. I pushed her back onto the desk while she struggled to sit. I loved hearing her howls and wished we'd been in a better place than this dilapidated building so I could enjoy the heightened frenzy in comfort. A place where I had access to instruments my patients would appreciate. I missed my tools right now. I had a feeling she would love my proficiency when I created something beautiful out of the mess of her worn out face and body.

She was almost there. I was almost there. Did she have what it took to go all the way with me? I hovered over her face. The air between us tense and almost full-bloomed. Not quite yet. Slight bruises formed from my handiwork. No blood spatters. Good.

Dawn had given up conversation well into the examination process. After a while it seemed as if I played with the dead, but no, she still had a lot of life left in her. "You still in there?"

Those swollen eyes just refused to open. Her head nod feeble and lacking its earlier enthusiasm for the game. "I'm sure you endure far more than this when fucking strangers in an alley. Now, scream for me one last time and I'll give you your pain medication. Then all the hurt will go away, just like your mama kissing all the boo-boos gone."

"I can't." That whiny sound returned.

Prying a blackening eyelid open, I stared into its hazel iris. "But remember, *you* asked me to come here. *You* needed me. And even after asking me to pay I'm giving *you* a freebie. Now, I said scream."

"I can't."

I longed for my tools. It would have made things far easier. I got closer to her ear and whispered as I dug my thumb into her eye socket. "I think you have one final scream for Dr. Stewart left in you."

Her shrieks filled my head with euphoric delight. I was getting there. I needed to fall over the edge of reason while I shot my load over her decaying body, but that wouldn't happen. I'd save myself for later when rage burst and covered me in its true rain of pain.

I inhaled with deliberation to steady my hands. "I'm ready to fill your prescription now. I know you're going to love the high this will give. It's what you live for. What you've craved for quite some time. The scarred tracks along your veins agree with me. No more pain now even though you've lived a life of agony pumping that smack into you. Huh. I made a kind of joke. Smack for a smack. I should put that on a business card."

I slapped her face a little to get her to respond, then pushed her to a sitting position. Her head lolled forward as she balanced with my help. Rubber tubing closed around her arm I'd pulled from a baggie inside my pants pocket. "I'm afraid you'll have to inject yourself with the medication though. After all, this is a self-serve pharmacy due to newly instituted health policies." How delicious this was getting.

She mumbled incoherently.

"You're not fulfilling your end of the bargain and game. I have your medication. I promised I'd give it to you and you don't want to disappoint the doctor with bad behavior. You might not get a lollipop at the end the house call."

She mumbled again.

"All right. I'll help you this time. But it will be the last time I help." I uncapped the syringe and slipped the cap into my jacket pocket. Flicking the slack veins into something resembling healthy took time, but eventually a vein cried out in commitment. As I drove the needle home, I heard a short intake of breath. Grabbing Dawn's other hand, I forced her to hold the syringe and move the plunger forward until all the liquid vanished into her. She had chosen this life; it was only fair her prints appear on everything bringing her joy.

I laid her back on the desk, needle still sticking obscenely in her arm, representing her form of needy sex. Her eyelids fluttered, the drug beginning its path of destruction. I'd have loved to remain and watch her fully enjoy the remnants of our time together - however, I had other pressing engagements.

After studying the scene for any signs of my presence I left Dawn and headed toward afternoon.

I glanced at the numbers 137 on my way out the door and chuckled.

The numbers added up to eleven. Two ones walking side by side.

Snake eyes.

A few twists and turns through the empty building and I found a side door exit which led directly into a street bizarre. Brilliant colors assaulted from paper lanterns and overly decorated umbrellas. Wind chimes clanked against each other in the wind. From hollow metal bongs to glass tinkling, each chime sounded as if clapping marionettes, strung together, acknowledged my presence and applauded my efforts.

I disappeared into the crowded stalls, picking my way through the throngs of people, trying to remain invisible in their midst despite the need to acknowledge my accomplishments. I snagged a small brass bell from a table and pocketed it. A memento of my time in this part of the city, where pain dissolved into pleasure and death grew into a prelude of life.

The syringe cap scraped my fingers holding the bell. A rush of excitement fed the eels still swimming through me. My pace quickened. I needed to get home before I exploded.

Once inside my domain, I immediately stripped to remove the city's refuse. I'd probably have to burn my clothes in order to get rid of Dawn's rotted stench. The muffled thud of the bell, when folding my pants, reminded me I had other things to tend to first. I pulled it, along with the syringe cap, from the pocket and entered my secret sanctuary.

Naked, I approached my altar with reverence and began lighting candles. One by one, flames came to life on pure white pillars until the room shone with the illumination of a million stars across a vast universe. The wall-length mirror revealed my brilliance. And as I placed the syringe cap in the straight line, with all the other treasures, my chest swelled with pride.

The bell's brass winked at me when it rang. Reassuring. Signaling the ritual could commence.

A pearl handled flogger lay in front of the mirror along with my surgical instruments in precise attendance surrounding it. All tools of my trade. Expertise studied long and hard to accomplish until I'd reached the pinnacle of success. Until …

Smooth and cold in my hand, I caressed the handle with love, and then dragged it across my face and down the length of my taut body. My legs grew weak from the intensity of excitement making the eels dance inside my veins.

At first the slap of leather across my arms tingled. A tease promising ecstasy to come. Soon the leather joined the eels' dance, thrashing against my back until they swam toward the skin's surface in a frantic urge to break free.

Leather beat on flesh. Quick and sure as I watched me, Sun of the Universe, bask in the mirror's glow. Scents of blood and melting wax stung senses as the flogger lashed like lightning. Lightheaded, my brain released Dawn and her vileness to the hinterland of so many I'd aided to similar fates. A chill and giddy laugh engulfed when I thought about her expecting heroin and getting not only a speedball, but a speedball infused with potassium chloride. I struck my legs harder. Rest in peace, Dawn of the dead.

The need for more pain crept along the edges of my brain. Muscles well developed glistened from exertion. Each sculpted mound honed to perfection by sheer determination and constant attention to detail few understood. Even my dick stood proudly, engorged and ripe, its head beginning to shine with the seeds of forbidden fruit. We would participate in our own private ritual later, when night stood still in anticipation of unspeakable acts done in the dark.

A face superimposed over mine. Taunting. Haunting. Damn that bitch to Hell. How dare she invade my sanctum with her all-knowing disdain? She'd tried to ruin my morning, but I'd outwitted her continued questioning as usual. But that look said it all. Her superior consciousness over my assumed inferior lack of one. I'd played her inept games for months and now she'd insulted me with her condescending presence. I thought I'd left her behind with the slam of her office door, but she'd never leave me alone. Rage rose in me. Now I was forced to act and make an unplanned visit before an important meeting.

I caressed the length of me as I'd caressed the handle of the flogger. With love and admiration for the power each instilled. Cleaning the head with a delicate touch, I sucked the liquid from my fingers—food for the gods to sustain me until night consumed us both.

My fingers twitched. I wasn't one of the colorless bland inhabiting the city merely taking up space.

I had purpose.

Depth.

Stark lighting did little to advance the ambience of a windowless room. Giant metal coffee urns belched and spluttered while brewing what smelled like sweaty gym socks strained through molding carpet. Plates of doughnuts and cookies lay in haphazard patterns on a battered folding table. The raisins in the cookies looked like shriveled rat shit pressed into brown goop. I skirted the losers milling around the table and opted for a seat on a folding chair at the back of the room. Listening to inane banter from these idiots could make my I.Q. drop at least a hundred points.

One more hour to endure. Ending the day with these blubbering social misfits lacking self-control wasn't my idea of anything exciting or interesting. My ultimate high kept being denied. Although, the previous several hours had amped the pleasure scale to a greater level.

Watching outside that bitch's office until she'd finished her inquisition of other patients had bored me. Nevertheless, necessary measures needed addressing. I'd stepped from the shadows, surprising her before she entered her car. Following hadn't been difficult since her sense of self always consumed her, causing her to lack the ability to discern the universe waiting to strike. Frankly, she should have known parking too far from her office, just to get more exercise, would eventually lead her into danger. Which it had. I smiled at that memory.

The expression on her face betrayed the calm and self-assured confidence she attempted bolstering. Still, she continued questioning my motives. Not only what was I doing next to her car, but every other imaginable question she'd asked before this appointed time in our game.

I'd endured a year of interrogation aimed at intentionally undermining my ego. A year of subterfuge on my part, making her believe her inroads to my psyche were sound and I didn't possess issues. Issues. As if I ever allowed my brain to dwell in that lowland of depravity.

My patients legitimately came to me for help. Granting their desires had been my greatest goal. Elevating my expertise to degrees I originally thought unattainable. I cared for their needs. Brought them peace of mind and fulfilled their forbidden dreams. Delivered what they craved with the cutting steel lying on my altar. None of them possessed issues. Why should I? They put their lives in my hands, undergoing procedures conventional medicine denied them. They'd requested the best: Dr. Stewart Prentiss—surgical genius and dedicated disciplinarian in distinct subcultures. Each patient understood these practices and accepted my aid where none existed.

Except one.

It wasn't my fault he'd changed his mind after genital amputation. Damn him for ruining my life and forcing me to see this inadequate psychiatrist two times a week. He should have been the one in therapy, not me.

I fumed as I thought about her always in charge of every situation. Constantly assuring herself she was in control. It was long past time to test her theories. Exhaling the breath I'd swallowed to slow my pulse, I balanced the ire and horror I could deliver. She'd stared blatantly into my eyes, daring me to back away. I knew her eyes were blue but bleached to non-existent gray in the moonlight.

I'd stared into them enough times during our gab-fests to hate the color. But, on the upside, the shade would soon match what I'd do to her face. Had she realized her sight and insight would end tonight?

Was she upset I'd spoiled her perfect state of mind?

Did I care?

Not really.

She no longer deserved an opportunity of telling me what she thought about any situation. No longer deserved my delegated attention to her prosaic attitudes. My fingers wrapped themselves into a ball meant for pain, striking her until she fell at my feet.

She looked at me in disbelief. So innocent, like a deer in the middle of the road watching oncoming headlights. Unlike the bitch I'd seen this morning at my pre-arranged hour. Bristling, I thought of her writing my words onto her omnipresent yellow-lined tablet of medical permanency to be placed in a file labeled Dr. Stewart's issues. Now she'd understand issues.

The final red curtain had dropped on Dr. Melissa Haven, allowing seething pain I'd held for years to explode in a ceremony of violence. What a rush for my own judgment and justice to be meted out on the good doctor. Her eyes remained fixed on mine as she entered eternity. I returned the blank stare with a conceited look. Guess I'd managed that issue just fine.

Someone's shitty tale of woe brought me out of reliving the enjoyment of the past few hours before I'd arrived in this den of iniquity. Why was it the masses felt compelled to share their misguided lives with other people, unless they were forced by the State, like me, to attend this charade? Wasn't it enough we had to live with them in our outside space and play nice when they deserved otherwise? My fingers flexed in time to the insistent patter of the complainer. These meetings pressed any tolerance I possessed into a tiny corner of my brain where I could cope with the mundane and its inhabitants. My altar called with almost audible shouts.

Legs re-crossed themselves across the aisle. A flash of plastic caught the glint of fluorescent lights when she moved. Upon closer inspection, I realized the shiny square held a bus pass attached to her purse. This had to be her first meeting. I would have remembered the bus pass and her. My gaze traveled the length of her legs, my interest piqued while imagining what treasures lay beneath her conservative floral skirt, and how I might explore the land beneath all those flowers. The obvious, uncomfortable way she shifted in the chair assured me she wanted to be elsewhere. Yeah, didn't we all?

She turned slightly in her chair. A nervous smile met my reassuring one. She twisted her hands as if wringing laundry … or something else. I smiled more genuinely. Long legs, clean hair, neatly dressed, a rose among the room of stinkweed. Perhaps she would like to experience something other than this gripe-a-torium aimed at weak people.

She didn't look weak. Or frightened. In fact, she looked healthy and vibrant. Strong. Ready to go the distance if challenged. Another gazelle for the cheetah to play with … Definitely not a wannabe. A woman who would enjoy all the magic I'd provide. Someone who might love visiting my inner sanctum during the blackest of night to experience that true call of the wild nothing else could match. I knew I could make her hands enjoy something other than worrying about the perfect space between her golden bracelets. I needed to stroke my dick and show her now *I* was the answer for her problems. Not this room full of hypocrites and losers waiting to hear her plight.

The bus pass was the ticket to ride. I owned one myself and could go anywhere in the city I desired. I could follow … after. Obviously, she had the same needs otherwise she wouldn't be here in this hellish basement. The eels returned with a vengeance as I thought of her voice filling the night's void with a siren's song for me alone.

Like magic, she'd appeared. Just for me.

I could share my instruments. She'd understand and love their touch on her flesh. After all, we shared the same desires.

I wondered how many rituals she was into. I'd fulfill all of them.

A lull in the wretched confessions forced my hand. I stood and assumed the slightly apologetic posture I'd practiced in my glorious mirror. Another act I'd maintained through these years of idiocy aimed at someone else controlling me.

I didn't stare at her, but knew she watched. Waited. Wanted. I felt the lack of breath from her as she held it in anticipation of my words delivered upon her with expert care. I'd give her something to listen to. Something to care about. Something to want to take home in the dark and stimulate—anything—other than these embarrassing and boring tales. Something to finally sate the eels, after they spilled their life onto hers, and came to rest in her braceleted arms.

"Hello, my name is Stewart, and I'm addicted to pain."

I knew the score by heart.

My ritual only a few hours away. Waiting for me in my sanctuary.

After the pretense of this meeting ended.

A chorus of cheerleaders for the group responded on cue. "Hello, Stewart. Welcome to our meeting."

LINDSEY BETH GODDARD

THE TOOTH COLLECTOR

"What's his motive?"

Jenny blew a bubble with her purple chewing gum, popped it between her pink painted lips and started chewing it again. She pushed a lock of curly blonde hair out of her eyes and pressed the crosswalk button, waiting.

"What do you mean by 'motive'?" Cynthia asked.

"I mean … investing in this idea of yours is a financial risk. What does he stand to gain?"

Cynthia took a deep breath. It tasted of exhaust fumes, but she didn't mind. It was a breezy day in April, and the afternoon was alive with the thrum of taxi cab engines and bustling pedestrians. It comforted Cynthia, strolling through the busy city, being in the middle of it all.

"He's going to double his earnings. That's what he stands to gain!" Cynthia's blue eyes lit up as she spoke, reflecting her emotions like two cerulean mood rings. "Combining our businesses is a win/ win situation. He sells movies; I sell CDs. The Internet is destroying our sales. It's the perfect time to work together … to buy that empty office in between our stores, knock down the walls and triple our floor space. We can redesign the layout, get some flashy advertisements, and hopefully attract some new customers." Cynthia watched the traffic light change. A new direction of cars rolled through the intersection. The corner of her mouth curled into a half-smile as she fantasized about her plans.

"Mommy!" A shrill voice penetrated her daydream. Kya tugged at her arm. "Mommy, look!" The girl flashed a proud, gap-toothed grin. Blood dotted her lips. Bubbly red saliva coated her teeth, pooling inside a fresh hole in her bottom gum. "It fell out!"

Cynthia crinkled her nose, eying the bloody tooth her daughter clutched in spit-covered fingers. She sighed. Kya was losing teeth faster than a tree shedding leaves in autumn. It was a wonder that her gums weren't entirely barren. And Cynthia hated handling the teeth—odd little pieces of human anatomy, porcelain smooth on one side, rough and blood-stained on the other. But a visit from the tooth fairy meant the world to Kya, so she was forced to play along.

The traffic light flashed "WALK" in bold white font. "We can go," Jenny said, ushering for Cynthia and Kya to come along.

Cynthia knelt down and smoothed the stray hairs that had fallen from her daughter's redheaded ponytail. "Honey, put the tooth in your pocket until we get home, okay?" The girl nodded, licking a drop of blood from her lip. Cynthia grabbed her hand, and together they crossed the street.

The April breeze blew a napkin from the table. It went dancing down the sidewalk into oblivion. Cynthia loved sitting on the restaurant patio, watching the city move around her. The sun warmed her skin as she sipped on her water. It had been a little too windy for dining, but they had managed.

Her salad was down to the last few leafy green bites when she heard Kya crying. "Oh no! Mommy! I lost it!"

She wiped her lips with a napkin, motioning for Kya to come closer. A half-eaten chicken tender platter sat on the table beside her salad. Kya had gobbled it down and excused herself from the table to play games on the sidewalk, like she did every time they ate lunch outdoors. But now the six-year-old was upset, visibly shaken and heading back towards the table in tears.

"Mommy! It's my tooth! I lost it!"

Cynthia smiled. "Yes, I know, sweetie. You put it in your pocket, remember?"

"No, it's not there!" Kya pulled her pockets inside out to expose the cotton lining. "See?" Her lip quivered as she glanced toward the crosswalk. "I think I dropped it."

Kya's orange pony tail bounced as she turned toward the street. Cynthia reached out a hand, but Kya swatted it away, taking a step toward the intersection. Cynthia grabbed hold of her just before she stepped out of reach. She spun her around to meet her eyes. Snot formed in the little girl's nose as she whimpered. "I've got to find my tooth!"

"It's okay, honey. We'll leave the tooth fairy a note."

Kya's eyes narrowed into thin slits. Her eyebrows came together, a deep wrinkle in the middle. She bit down on her bottom lip and stood motionless, staring up at her mother with a confused expression. "What would the tooth fairy want with a note?"

Cynthia offered Kya a tissue from her purse. She took it, gingerly wiping her nose. "A note ... to explain what happened. A nice letter that says 'Dear tooth fairy, I have misplaced my tooth, but I drew you a picture to thank you for everything you do. Love, Kya.' I'm sure she'll understand, and she'll like the picture so much that she'll leave you something special under your pillow."

Cynthia chewed her lip, hoping that Kya would accept this solution. She was a strong-willed child, very emotional at times, but a good kid at heart. Kya was an only child, with fiery red hair and intelligent, fierce green eyes that were a mystery to Cynthia. Brown hair and blue eyes were dominant in Cynthia's family. And Kya's father had been blonde with brown eyes. But the red hair must come from his side of the family. She would never know for sure, of course. The coward didn't stick around long enough to discuss the genetics of their child; he simply disappeared when he heard the word "pregnant".

Oh well. Cynthia fell in love with those emerald eyes the moment she held Kya for the first time. She loved being a mother, single or not.

She pulled the frowning child to her chest and hugged her, patting the small of her back. "It's okay. The tooth fairy will come." She gripped Kya's shoulders, gently squeezing as she looked her in the eyes and smiled. "Now go play. We'll head home in a bit."

Kya hung her head. "Okay," she muttered. She knelt down to scoop up the Barbie she'd left lying on the sidewalk. Ken was sprawled at her feet, too, but she didn't take notice. Instead she watched the cars in the street, eyes fixed on the crosswalk. Dirty tires rolled over the white painted lines. A gum wrapper skittered across the asphalt. For a moment, not a single car passed, and Kya squinted, scanning the ground for her tooth.

"Now back to this motive thing." Jenny smiled as she pushed her bowl of pasta to the side. "Like I said, everybody's got a motive. I'm just wondering why this guy is willing to risk such an investment with a partner he barely knows."

"What are you getting at?" Cynthia narrowed a suspicious eye at her friend, waiting for the catch.

"Well, look at you!" Jenny gestured toward Cynthia with a wave of her hand. "You're gorgeous. You're smart. You're *single*. I wouldn't be surprised if this guy is trying to *get to know you* a little better, if you know what I mean." Jenny winked.

Cynthia laughed, a little too high pitched. She didn't like where this conversation was going. She hadn't dated since Kya's father flew the coop. A relationship wasn't worth the pain it might cause if things ended badly, especially now that Kya's feelings were involved. Cynthia was still wounded. The emotional scars from being left to raise a child alone had never fully healed. "Abandonment issues" was putting it lightly, she knew.

"Do you think he's cute? Because I think he's cute. That's why I figured you two might, you know, hook up..."

Cynthia sighed. "My interest in him is strictly business." She leaned in, prepared to argue her defense, but the sound of squealing tires caught her attention before she could continue.

A silver Suburban skidded toward a BMW which had spun out of control and landed sideways in the road, blocking the intersection. The driver of the BMW had slammed the brakes and jerked the wheel, sending the sports car across the oncoming lane. One of its wheels was bent, and the tire hissed air as it deflated.

The Suburban plowed forward. The smell of burnt rubber hung in the air as the SUV slammed into the sports car with a loud crunch, leaving black skid marks in the lane. Shards of glass rained down on both vehicles. Some of it bounced off the wreckage and settled in the street as frantic onlookers rushed toward the accident. One of them screamed, "The child, the child!"

Cynthia's heart sank. She searched the sidewalk for Kya. No sign of her. She sprang from her chair, screaming "Kya! Where are you?"

She ran from the restaurant patio. One of her high-heeled sandals caught a crack in the pavement, and she stumbled, pushing her way through a crowd of onlookers gathered at the curb. One of them shot her a dirty glance, but the cold expression softened as Cynthia ran toward the scene of the accident.

Cynthia wailed, "No! God no!" A purple sleeve poked out from underneath the smashed BMW. And the tiniest bit of orange ponytail. Blood began to pool around the mangled form of a little girl, barely visible through the twisted metal in the road.

Traffic came to a stop. Ignorant motorists further back began to honk their horns. Shocked citizens helped a limping man from the SUV as Cynthia ran to where Kya was sprawled, pinned down by the wreckage. Blood leaked over the white painted crosswalk, mixing with splinters of broken glass.

She fell to her knees and reached for the tiny hand with pink painted fingernails. She called her name over and over. But the girl didn't respond. She lay in a twisted heap. Crimson splatters stained her clothes and streaked her little face. One of the BMW's tires had flattened a portion of her thigh. Her chest was crushed against the pavement.

Cynthia closed her eyes against the horror, but the smell of smoke rising from the engine and the sirens blaring in the distance assured her this was real. The sirens drew closer, and Cynthia opened her eyes. She stared in disbelief at her daughter's body beneath the car as hot tears welled in her eyes.

Then someone was there, kneeling beside her. Long, brittle strands of hair hung from the hood that covered its head. The tangled locks were mostly black, speckled with strands of gray and white. A breeze blew around the dark stranger, whipping its hair and ruffling the gray cloak. Cynthia saw a portion of its face through the obsidian shadows of the hood—two glittering red eyes, its gaunt cheekbones set too high above a crone-like nose. The gaping, toothless mouth grinned at her, wickedly.

She scrambled backwards, looking around, but no one else seemed to notice the strange figure in the billowing robe, kneeling before the wreckage beside Cynthia. It crouched over the upturned hand of Cynthia's dead child and ran a pale, bony finger down Kya's gore-splattered wrist. The spindly fingers roamed to the center of her hand and plucked a pearly, white tooth from the palm.

It smiled, exposing its putrid black gums, and looked Cynthia straight in the eyes. Its own eyes glittered like ruby marbles inside the darkness of the hood. It tucked the tooth inside the long black robe it wore beneath the cloak and then, atom by atom, particle by particle, the figure dissipated into thin air, fading like a desert mirage.

Cynthia, still in shock, could only hug her knees and cry, thinking, *She came back to find the tooth. It's all my fault. I should have been watching.*

Cynthia held the baby tooth. Teardrops rolled down her face and smeared her faded makeup. She wiped her eyelids with the back of her hand, leaving a trail of mascara and eyeliner on her cheekbone.

She reached out to grasp the tooth between her thumb and index finger. She felt the smooth porcelain, the roughness of the underside. This wasn't the tooth that Kya had gone searching for the day of the car accident. That particular tooth had never turned up at the scene, a thought that sent a chill down Cynthia's spine as she remembered the bony fingers reaching out to pluck it from her daughter's lifeless hand.

No, this tooth was special. It was the first one Kya had ever lost. They had saved it in a glass container with the word "Memories" painted in red cursive letters on the lid.

Cynthia snorted a miserable half-chuckle as she slowly shook her head. She used to hate handling these odd little body parts, but now it was all she had left. A deep wail seized her, rattling her shoulders. This was the first time she had cried in days. She had tucked her feelings away on the ride home from the hospital that fateful day, alone, without Kya. Now she sat at the foot of her unmade bed in the white slip she had worn beneath her funeral dress, makeup from three days ago smeared at haphazard angles from wiping her overdue tears.

All through the funeral service, she had wondered if there was something wrong with her. And then, afterward, as family and friends gathered together, sobbing in huddled groups, she felt as if the hushed voices were gossiping, accusing her. *Why is she not crying? What kind of mother is she?*

Something had snapped inside Cynthia at the sight of her child's casket. Her sanity was like a rubber band fastened to a brick. Her mind strained under the weight of her loss, the proverbial rubber band stretched thin by the image of Kya's six year old body lying dead. And then more bricks were added: making phone calls, planning the funeral, having to carry on like a functional human while she'd lost all desire to live. The rubber band inside her mind was pulled tighter and tighter until—*snap*. She went numb. She couldn't cry.

Until now.

She squeezed her eyes shut against the memories. A tear drop fell from her cheek. It splashed silently against the tooth she gripped in her fingers.

When she opened her eyes, a cloaked figure stood a few feet from the end of her bed. The cloak it wore ruffled, as if stirred by a breeze, its black robe billowing in the stillness of the bedroom. The long tangles of black hair, streaked with strands of white and gray, seemed to dance on a mystical draft. A feeling of sadness and misery pulsated from the figure as it stood in a whirlwind of dark energy.

She scooted back toward the headboard, putting as much space as possible between her and the strange presence that blocked the door.

"I can return her to you," it spoke in a deep, haunting growl. The wet tongue smacking against its toothless gums made the voice sound almost mortal, but the way it filled her mind, the words echoing through her thoughts, caused every hair on her body to stand up.

Cynthia gulped. There was no need to ask pointless questions such as "Return who to me?" She knew exactly what the ghostly visitor was proposing. The thought disgusted her. She squeezed her eyelids shut tight and wrapped her fingers around the bed post, repeating a mantra: "You're not real; you're not real; you're not real."

"Oh, but I *am* real. And I can return her to you. She will breathe. She will grow. Blood will pump through her veins. She will behave as she always did, age like any other child. She'll be every bit the girl she was before. I promise you." The dark entity moved closer without taking a step, hovering with the end of its robes barely brushing the floor.

"Impossible," Cynthia managed to whisper as fear clenched her windpipe.

The entity stopped its advance. It was motionless aside from the evil wind that churned around it, adding madness to its rotten aura. Loud, maniacal laughter filled the bedroom, reverberating off the walls. It rattled the picture frames. One fell to the floor, cracking the glass. The laughter bellowed through her mind, bouncing off the inside of her skull.

"What do you know of impossible?!" A pointed nose, like the beak of a predatory bird, jutted from the shadows of the hood, followed by two blood red eyes that held her captive with a frightening stare. "*My* task is impossible. Collecting teeth from the children."

Cynthia arched an eyebrow. "Who are you?"

The dark presence ignored her question, continuing instead with its own line of thought. "The children, they wish to make offerings to me. They *want* me to collect their teeth. But the parents, they lie. They put the teeth in the garbage, leaving false gifts beneath their slumbering heads." The stranger paused, forming a steeple with its alabaster fingers. "That beautiful tooth your daughter offered me and the sacrifice she made to deliver it … I was touched."

Cynthia's heart raced. "You monster. Don't speak of her. Don't *think* of her. I banish you back to Hell where you belong!" She wasn't done speaking, but when she closed her mouth, her upper and lower jaw fused shut. It was as if her teeth had been super glued together. She worked her jaw, trying desperately to pull her teeth apart, but it was fruitless. She couldn't speak another word.

"Funny you should mention Hell. I was there once." The menacing figure moved closer. A sour feeling emanated from the air that swirled around it, like a force field of wickedness ever stirring its long hair and heavy garments. The raspy, baritone words, accented by a wet, smacking tongue echoed through her head as its voice filled the room. "I was a sinner in my mortal life. A heartless man with no soul." Cynthia shrunk as close to the headboard as she could manage. One of her hands gripped the bed post, and the other still clutched Kya's tooth in a balled fist.

"I was a collector in my old life, much like I am today. But back then, I did it for pleasure. I took the children ... oh, so many children. I snatched them from their parents, locked them away. I removed their teeth, one by one, just to watch them writhe in pain."

Cynthia moaned in terror. She closed her eyes, repeating the mantra in her mind. *You're not real; you're not real; you're not real.* The creature's voice was louder than her own thoughts. It continued...

"Now if I wish to find a moment of rest and escape my existence of misery and pain, I must collect enough teeth to triple those that I stole. That is my punishment, to dwell in the deepest state of sorrow until my collection is complete. I cannot take the teeth by force. They must be offered to me as gifts from the innocent children of the world."

Cynthia opened her eyes. She sucked a startled breath through her nose. The dark presence floated inches from her face, its red eyes set deep in its withered face like sunken rubies. It squinted, and the dark circles beneath its eyes were like shadowy half moons. "I am a restless soul, haunting the realm between Hell and Earth." A long, curved nose hung over its thin lips as it grinned, the smile nothing more than a black hole in the darkness of the hood. "You can call me the tooth fairy," it said.

Tears streamed from her eyes as she strained the muscles of her jaw, fighting to open her mouth. She wanted to scream in its face. *What do you want from me?*

It pointed at her closed fist. "I want the tooth," it said. Cynthia looked at her hand. It was clenched so tight that sweat oozed from her palm. Her brow furrowed as she considered its request. "I know it means the world to you, so I will make an offer. If I return your daughter—the living, breathing, innocent Kya—will you promise me the tooth?"

Cynthia's blue eyes were wide. Her whole body shook. The muscles in her mouth relaxed, and she could mover her jaw, her upper and lower teeth no longer stuck together. Everything inside her screamed and argued against the word that escaped her lips next. "Yes."

Her stomach flip flopped, and her vision dimmed as the lights in the bedroom flickered. And just as quickly as the word "yes" left her mouth, the hideous creature vanished.

Cynthia remained still, knees pulled up to her chest, fingers white around the wooden headboard. Minutes passed, but she didn't move. She was suspended on a frozen wave of panic. The telephone rang and she jumped, yelping like a frightened puppy.

Her hands shook as she picked up the phone and placed the receiver to her ear. "Hello?"

"Cynthia ... how are you doing?" Jenny's voice filled the ear piece.

Cynthia broke down, sobs rolling from her gut. "Not good, Jen." Her breathing was panicked. She choked on saliva, coughing as tears spilled down her cheeks. "I'm not good..."

"Oh, honey. You are crying. That *is* good, don't you see? Let it all out, sweetie ... just let it out..."

Cynthia watched the tall, sinister man through the bars of the cage. His arms jerked in sketchy spasms as he tightened the ropes, like sheer madness pumped through his veins. Firelight glowed across his pale features. His nose, like the tip of a vulture's beak, cast a thin shadow over his frown. Long hair was gathered into an unruly ponytail and tied with a ribbon at the back of his head. Wilds strands framed his gaunt face as he peered down at his victim.

The little boy fought against his restraints. His short blonde hair was matted with sweat. Blood dotted the raw skin around his wrists and ankles. His chest rose and fell with each frantic breath. He squirmed, his puny body strapped to a wooden table beneath an intertwining network of thin ropes and chains. The boy could only whimper, exhausted, and listen to the fire crackle.

"Done fighting so soon?" The man's voice was chilling and deep, and a lisp caused his 's' sounds to drag. "I enjoy watching you struggle." He stood before a table filled with shiny silver tools. Orange flames reflected in the steel instruments as the fire licked at the hearth.

Cynthia wanted to cry out and beg him not to hurt the boy, but a cloth gag had been shoved in her throat. Guttural noises escaped her mouth as she grunted in protest, but no words formed. The dry piece of fabric held in her mouth by a knotted cloth seemed to suck all the moisture from her tongue.

The man selected a pair of dental forceps from the table. Firelight gleamed on the polished metal and he smiled, revealing slick gums ripe with decay. "I never knew my father. My mother was an absent whore." He turned toward the boy, approaching him in long strides. "Gum disease left me toothless by age twenty-two." He stepped closer, and the boy's eyelids disappeared as he stared wide-eyed at the forceps.

"My only comfort is the suffering of others." He pulled the gag from the frightened child's mouth. The boy's cries filled the chamber, bringing a smile to the man's face. "Ah, it's like music to my ears."

The boy tried to fight back. He turned his head to the side, but the man was too strong. He held his tiny head in place with one lanky hand as the pliers descended. The metal grips locked around an incisor, and his entire body jolted with pain. Blood spurted from the tender, pink gums as the tooth was deposited into a jar. One of many jars that lined the dirty shelves, every one of them filled with teeth.

Cynthia couldn't help but scream. It came out as a pathetic, muted whine, muffled by the gag in her mouth. It was enough to catch the madman's attention. He turned his dark, menacing eyes on her, and smiled that empty smile.

Then he laughed and pointed the bloody forceps at her. "For every joy there is a sorrow. Sacrifices must be made. You are next!"

Cynthia gasped. She bolted upright in bed. Sweat trickled down her spine and beaded on her forehead. A strip of light shined through a gap in the curtains. It was morning. She was in her own bed. Cynthia fell back onto her pillow, relieved.

The nightmare again. The same dream that haunted every night of sleep since making a promise to the dark stranger months ago. In the dream, she was locked inside a cage and forced to watch children plead for mercy at the hands of a monster. Tears rimmed her eyes. She didn't know what frightened her more: the heartless acts committed in those dreams, or the promise she had made to the monster who committed them.

She rolled over and rubbed the hard bulge at her midriff. Over the passing months, her abdomen had stretched to the size of a beach ball. She could feel little kicks and punches if she rested her hand there. It gave her a reason to keep living.

The encounter with the cloaked figure seemed like a distant memory. She wanted to lock it in the back of her mind and never think of it again, but her body was a constant reminder. And the dreams were beginning to plague her. Every night they came: visions of the madman carrying out his evil deeds. More than just dreams. They felt *real* somehow. Like she was trapped inside the dark memories of a stranger, witnessing the sins of his mortal life.

It all started with that terrible promise. The dreams were short at first, nightmarish snippets in between more pleasant dreams. But then, they started to last the whole night. That's when Cynthia realized she had missed her period. She knew it was ridiculous— she hadn't been with a man in years—but something inside her told her to take a pregnancy test. The two pink lines that appeared in the "results" window of the little plastic test sent her into a state of shock. She sat on the bathroom floor that seemingly endless afternoon and stared at the pink lines until they lost all meaning.

Cynthia stretched, groaned, and sat up. Hair long brown hair was a mess, tangled from a long night of tossing and turning. A wave of nausea washed over her when she tried to stand up. She bowed her head and concentrated on breathing, resting her hands on her knees. She didn't know how much more of this she could take.

The dreams had become more vivid over the months as her health deteriorated and her belly grew. The sick bastard had tricked her. He had promised to bring Kya back to life, but not in the form of an unborn child. The pregnancy was straining Cynthia physically, fraught with complications. She was always sick, constantly lacking energy, and haunted by the recurring nightmares. The only thing that kept her going was the hope that, somehow, she and Kya would be together again soon.

Cynthia leaned on the counter and rested her chin in her hands. She watched Jason work, enjoying the way his muscles moved beneath his skin. Fluorescent lighting made it easy to read the thousands of titles on the shelves. Wall-to-wall shelves of books, DVDs, and CDs, categorized by genre and kept in alphabetical order. They even sold iPods and e-Readers now. The shop was really coming along.

"Feeling any better?" Jason knelt before a pile of display rack pieces, his dark brown eyes fixed on her.

"A little," she said.

"Good." He pointed to the checkout counter where she leaned. "There are some saltine crackers under the register if you feel woozy."

Cynthia forced a weak smile. "Thanks."

"What do the doctors say?" He selected a Phillips head

screwdriver from the collection of tools on the floor and flipped a piece of particle board into a standing position.

"They say all kinds of things. My iron is low. My blood pressure is high. And that's just the tip of the iceberg." She paused, not wanting to sound so pessimistic, then added. "But they say the Pre-eclampsia is under control."

She pretended to straighten the merchandise on the counter, secretly watching Jason as she worked. She'd been so lonely lately. And he was so sweet. "Thanks for taking care of everything while I was sick," she said.

"No problem. We're partners." He positioned a metal piece over the particle board and set to work driving the screw into the hole. Cynthia bit her lip. She tried to view Jason as a business partner and co-owner of the shop, but her hormones went wild at the sight of him. He looked up at her. "You don't have to stay late with me, you know. I'm a big boy. I can lock up by myself."

"It's okay." Cynthia hesitated for a moment, then smiled and decided to continue. "I enjoy spending time with you."

Arching his eyebrows, he set the screwdriver on the floor. "You do?"

She blushed ... or maybe it was a hot flash. "Yeah."

Jason grinned. A crooked tooth near the front of his mouth made his smile all the more adorable. She loved the curves of his lips, the stubble on his chin, the sexy way he chuckled nervously as he ran a hand through his short, dark hair. "I like spending time with you, too." Jason stood up and approached the counter. Cynthia couldn't help but smirk, thinking *Jenny was right all along.*

Cynthia's heart sank at the thought of Jenny. She hadn't spoken to her best friend in weeks. Cynthia had broken an unspoken rule by refusing to talk about the pregnancy. They had never kept secrets from each other in the past. Jenny couldn't understand what had changed. Eventually, it drove them apart. Cynthia laughed as she remembered Jenny's theory about motives. "Everybody's got a motive" she had said.

"What's so funny?" Jason asked as he stood on the customer's side of the counter, smiling at her.

"I was just thinking … about motives."

He squinted one eye in a questioning gaze. "What do you mean?"

"I mean … This might sound stupid and conceded, but … well … I'm very curious about something…"

"You've got my attention."

"Before you decided to invest in the store … were you interested in me? I mean…as more than a business partner?"

Jason rested his knuckles on the counter and leaned in close to her. "Like a friend?" His lips curled away from his teeth in a teasing smile.

"Well, maybe…"

He brushed a lock of brown hair from her eyes and leaned closer. "Or maybe more than friends?"

"Maybe," she replied, his lips inches from hers.

He leaned in closer. She could feel his hot breath on her ear as he whispered. "You're very beautiful, you know. I suppose we all have motives, don't we?" He slid his hand to the back of her neck and pulled her into a kiss. Warmth danced over her skin, tingling between her thighs. It was a feeling of euphoria she hadn't felt in ages. Followed by a wave of nausea.

She pulled away. "Sorry…" Cynthia felt lightheaded. She fought back a gag and spoke with her eyes closed, embarrassed and nauseated at the same time. "It's not you. I'm sick" Her voice shook with the last word as she tried not to cry. Her perfect moment was ruined.

"It's okay," he said, putting his hand on top of hers. "We'll try again when you're feeling better." He smiled, and she couldn't help but smile, too.

The hospital bed rattled softly as a nurse wheeled Cynthia down the hall. The pain in her gut exploded. It felt like her insides were filled with broken glass and being clenched in a tight fist until her internal organs were shredded. She winced and tried to focus on taking deep breaths.

"You've lost a lot of blood from the hemorrhaging. What is your pain level?"

Cynthia's teeth were clenched, every muscle tense. "10," she managed to groan.

The nurse pressed an elevator button. It lit up, and the door slid open with a ding. "The doctor is meeting us upstairs for the C-section."

"Where's Jason?" Cynthia mumbled as the door slid shut.

The nurse leaned over her. She smiled, but there was something in that smile that Cynthia didn't like. Pity, maybe. A hidden sadness. Fear for Cynthia's life. "If you're speaking about the handsome man you came in with, he's in the waiting room upstairs."

Cynthia raised her head. Her vision was blurred by tears. Every movement she made brought a fresh wave of nausea. Straining to hold her neck up, she examined her lower half. Blood soaked through the fresh sheets that had been placed on the rolling bed. The stain spread across the white cotton fabric between her thighs, dark red in the center.

She let her head fall back on the pillow. The ceiling whizzed by in a blurry succession of drop tiles and fluorescent lights. She heard the familiar tone of Dr. Killburn's voice. "The room is ready for her." He bent down to greet her. He smiled, but the smile seemed vacant somehow … just like the nurse's had been. The creases around his eyes and furrowed brow told a different story.

Cynthia, feeling woozy, could only struggle to keep her eyes open and think, *Oh no, am I going to die?* As if reading her mind, Dr. Killburn responded. "Hello, dear. We're going to get you through this."

Pain burst through her abdomen, so sharp she cried out. Cynthia couldn't fight it any more. Her eyelids fluttered as she fought against the blackness that checkered her vision. Afraid that she might drop the tiny tooth clutched in her fist, she slid her hand beneath the pillow and tucked it there for safekeeping. Then she slipped into unconsciousness.

Cynthia huddled in the cage. Dirty shelves, covered in old dust and cobwebs, loomed over her as she peered through the bars. In each jar was a different set of teeth. She considered counting the jars, but the crackling of the fireplace drew her attention.

Little embers popped from the logs and turned to ash when they hit the cool air. The flames danced to one side, and she noticed two black eye sockets staring at her from the fire. A draft stirred the flames again, and she saw the rest of the skull, smiling at her from the blazing pit.

The table before the fireplace was nothing more than a wooden slat atop a box-like frame, sitting low to the ground. A wet rag sat in a crimson stain on the table. Next to the stain sat a bloody saw. Morsels of flesh still clung to the sharp teeth of the saw. Cynthia shuddered. So that's how he disposed of his victims.

Her eyes panned to the table on her left. Chains and ropes hung from the dirty wooden surface. Beside it, a tall, narrow table gleamed with metal instruments. She trembled. Would Cynthia end up on that table? She knew this was a nightmare, but somehow, she felt there was more at stake than just having a bad dream.

"Your time has come." Cynthia looked up, expecting to see the tall, sinister man from her dreams. Instead, she was greeted by the glittering red eyes of the cloaked figure, staring down at her through the darkness of the hood.

The dark entity unlocked the cage and seized Cynthia's wrists in its cold, bony fingers. It yanked her through the cell door, pulling her across the dusty floor. Her flailing limbs kicked up dirt as she struggled against its stone grip.

She was released. Her wrists throbbed where the circulation had been blocked. She scrambled to her knees, looking up at the lost soul in the dark, billowing robes. "For every joy there is a sorrow. Sacrifices must be made. That's what you tell me in my dreams."

The dark figure said nothing. It was motionless aside from the swirling aura of misery that surrounded it, filling Cynthia's heart with dread.

"You bring me the joy of returning Kya to the world," she touched her stomach and realized she was not pregnant in the dream. She didn't like the feeling of her empty abdomen and frowned, but continued. "So what is the sacrifice?" Her voice began to shake, eyes wet. "Am I going to die?" It was frightening to put what had been plaguing her into words. The pregnancy had been so rough. She was always ill. And now she was losing so much blood...

The cloaked figure reached behind its back and produced a large scythe that materialized out of the shadows that swirled around its presence. The dark power that pulsated like a force field of wickedness around the stranger seemed to spread through the atmosphere like toxic gas. The toothless, red-eyed face leaned forward. Its ghoulish nose poked from the shadows. "For every joy there is a sorrow. For every good deed, a dark one. And for every soul I resurrect, one must be taken." The blade of the scythe caught the firelight.

"Must it be mine?" She was desperate now, pleading. "Every night you show me the sins of your mortal life. You paint a picture of the monster you once were. But that's not who you are ... not anymore. Your soul wants to rest."

The creature's robes whipped around as the wind picked up speed. Its eyes glowed even brighter. Misery poured from its heart, filling the room.

"My friend Jenny says no good deed is done without a motive. I think she's right. You have a motive in resurrecting a child. A brand new set of baby teeth will await you. But there's no motive in sparing me. I have nothing to offer you."

The floorboards shook beneath her knees as its thunderous voice filled her mind. "There must be a death! A sacrifice from the child's own bloodline!" He raised the scythe high over her head with both arms.

"Wait!" she screamed. "You cannot take a tooth unless it's offered to you, is that right?" The cloaked figure hovered there, perfectly still, with the blade held over her head, its pointed tip angled toward the center of her skull. "What good will it do you, then … to bring her back, if you're not guaranteed a single tooth from her head?" Sweat dripped down her face. Her blue eyes shined with a devious thought. "I can promise you every last tooth in her mouth. I will offer them to you, willingly. Just hear me out. This sacrifice you require must be of Cynthia's bloodline?"

The tooth collector said nothing. Its hands shook in the air, rattling the scythe. The air around it spiraled into chaos.

"Her father deserves to die at the tip of that blade. Not me. Not the one who loves her." The dark soul continued floating with the blade aimed at Cynthia.

After a moment, it lowered the weapon. The cyclone of energy that swirled around it faded to an ominous wind. It leaned forward, out of the hood, and Cynthia could see its pale, withered lips and long, cadaverous nose. The skin was alabaster white and clung to the bone so tightly that its face looked skeletal.

"We must summon him to this world. Think of him," the soul growled.

Cynthia did. She thought of all the good times they had together, of how she hated him for leaving without so much as a goodbye. She thought of all the birthdays he had missed. She hated him for walking out of her life, but most of all for abandoning Kya.

The atmosphere began to pulsate around her. A dark force pushed outward from Cynthia's broken heart, spreading to the far corners of the room. The air was alive with energy. It danced in waves, gathering speed until a cyclone formed before the fireplace, spinning out of control. The center of the tiny tornado grew darker, larger, and then ... he was there.

His dark brown eyes grew wide with fear as he appeared in the circling wind. He was older than she remembered. Wrinkles had formed on his forehead and at the corners of his eyes. The youthful glow had faded from his skin.

The dark figure approached him, hovering above the floorboards. Its robes dragged along the dirty ground, leaving a trail in the dust. The fire crackled. The bones within it shifted. The skull's mouth fell open in a silent scream. Recognition dawned on the blonde man before the fire as his brown eyes locked on Cynthia.

"Cynthia?" He looked to the cloaked figure, then back to her. "Cynthia, what's going on?"

"For every joy there is a sorrow. You are the sacrifice!"

The blade of the scythe came down on his skull with a loud crack. His eyes turned white as they rolled back in his head. A gurgling noise escaped his throat, and he coughed, dribbling blood over his lips.

The tooth collector yanked its blade from the man's skull. Another blow punctured the temple with a wet pop. The lost soul turned its eyes to Cynthia, two rubies floating in a black abyss.

She woke up with Jason's fingers tucked in between her own. He smiled with his mouth closed and gently squeezed her hand. "Nurse, she's awake," he said.

Cynthia's pulse quickened as she came to. Her eyes were panicked. "Is she ... is she..."

"She's beautiful," Jason replied.

Cynthia's heart swelled. Her eyes filled with tears. "Where is she?"

A nurse appeared beside the bed. She cradled an infant, swaddled in a pink blanket. Wispy locks of orange hair covered the newborn's head. Cynthia opened her arms. "May I have her?"

The nurse smiled. "Of course."

Cynthia took the baby in her arms. The emerald green eyes stared up at her, and she fell in love with them all over again. "I'll call her Mya," she said, and kissed the baby's head.

CHARLEE JACOB

LOCKED INSIDE
THE BUZZWORD BOX

Archetypal vernacular.

Ignition: cognition. Congenital Divinity.

And DIVINITY is CANDY.

I was my father's greatest experiment.

He was Dr. Feamy, chief-of-staff at the Feamy Institute for the Terminally Insane. A specialty within a specialty.

He wrote: *The Terminals are incurable.*

They will die insane.

Their brains are maimed, their souls mutilated beyond repair. Yet it is this very damage which brings to them a new perception.

They rage against time and space because they have been able, psychocognitively, to see through the lies told by both conceptual entities.

Who was to ask questions when no one wanted to admit they had somebody like this in their family? And most standard mental facilities had their hands full with the rest of the unbalanced and unintegrated.

You think stuff like this only happens in movies – or in screwloose screwtapes, dictated by dickless wonders. Well, it's like when people donate the bodies of departed loved ones to science. They don't want to know that their beloveds are really being used in experiments with industrial acids or to test land mines. Out of sight, out of mind. Out of your mind. Out of my mind.

My mother, Mrs. Feamy, was catatonic. But perhaps he loved her because she was gentle. Never raised her voice in anger. Passive to his aggressive.

Relationships are all about needs, aren't they? They aren't always traditional.

He watched as she breast-fed me. When I was far past the time when even late milkers were weaned, he strapped me to her. He wouldn't feed me much for days so I'd be forced to suckle. As he read aloud from Freud and Jung as if from a family Bible.

Or he'd read from his own notes.

The Lacunae are the unoccupied rooms in Psyche's house. They are the desolate wastelands of the soul, suffering's offbeat rhythm, a concert of psychopaths as wolves serenading a moon invisible to all save themselves, save themselves...

SAVE THEMSELVES

They cannot save themselves!

Primal scene ... splinter personality.

Splinter Sphincter Sphinx.

S

P

L

INFINITIVE

T

I implied I was hungry (So Hungry!) by opening my mouth round as the swollen belly of a malnourished child (seen on a film loop of Ethiopian children on television) and crying.

He inferred – guessing is often a form of sublimated wish fulfillment – that my infantile needs could be met by connecting me to this gentle, silent goddess.

I sucked and wept, uncontented.

"Clanci," Dr. Feamy explained to me, his daughter and #1 test subject. "Do not be ruled by your shadow. Acknowledge your self object – which is your mother – and your ego integrated into it. If this is a dream and it is reality, you are the single being sustained in both environments at once."

No one else on the staff knew I existed.

And my mother, who was she? Only some nameless, homeless deity. Fertile womb, infertile consciousness.

A stone Venus, Willendorf variety.

Arms and legs atrophied unto withered. Big belly, wide hips, teets swollen bigger than a drugged smile. Face so obese, her features were all but lost in mounds of expressionless dough. Prehistoric statue, posable non-action figure, earth mother for the vegetative.

Feamy took notes, eyes shining like the naked light bulbs swinging overhead. I sucked.

Sometimes I watched as he maneuvered her into position. That managed to be simple enough with catatonics, for they readily became clay. Or terra cotta. (Although Willendorf's was limestone.)

A prominent gut was a decadent representation of fertility, whether or not the female possessing it happened to be pregnant. Perhaps a tendency toward flab with excess musculature, ligament and skin was in her genes. Not so Feamy, skinny as a speed addict, complete with bad skin and worse breath. From ever being vigilant among those who – perishing from the cruel perfidy of the elements of time and space (duration and limitless purgation) – were always plotting to thunder up behind him.

I recalled sometimes the way he'd painted her an orange red before squeezing himself between gigantic thighs and into her triangular zone. Perhaps he attempted to make another baby, so he might suspend it from the other nipple.

A pair of subjects, combining him into the perfect mesh of Krafft-Ebing and Mengele.

Oh, Mother Of Songs, listen!
Doctor, doctor, I declare
I see someone's dark despair.

One night he was reading from Freud as I nursed.
"An internal cathexis could only have the same value as an external one if it were maintained unceasingly, as in fact occurs in hallucinatory psychoses and hunger phantasies, which exhaust their whole psychical activity in clinging to the object of their wish."

I think I was thirteen.
His pager went off. He hurried out. A major emergency. The walls trembled.
"Damned full moons," I heard him bitch.
Left me there alone, strapped to the anatomy of a fossil.
Obvoluted oblivion/outrage/oral orexis.
So hungry.
Breathless when he returned many hours later. To find me engorged on full moon pies.
The old goddess was dead.
long live the new Terrible Mother.

Dr. Feamy used a closet in his personal quarters. Invented the box. For me.

Essentially, I sat in it, tubes and bags for waste affixed to the proper outlets. Miniature bicycle contraption for the exercise of my legs and one for my arms – not enough to make me active or create usable muscle, just sufficient I didn't completely atrophy as mother had.

And the wheels on the bus go round and round, round and round, round and round . . .

A large plastic hose for food delivered it whenever I wished, pumped straight from the hospital's kitchen. A smaller one gave me milk. I was used to milk, yes? The food was often a mixture of raw meat and angel food cake.

How mammary is memory? Encoding from common triggers shared by an atmosphere of psychoses or a function of association?

Two brain chemicals, neuropeptide Y and galanin control the passion for fat-ladened foods, creating the paraventricular nucleus buried deep within the hypothalamus, as a body in a body. Coincidentally, these are closely alongside those for sexual behavior.

Hypothalamus/hypnopompic.

Hippo/hypnogogue.

He provided a closed-circuit television system for my continued education. A series of small, flat screen TV's mounted on the closet door and also on the narrow ramparts to either side of the doorjamb, a couple even devoted to the textured texual.

1) I watched inmates' sessions with DAD.

DEAD minus the -{e}-, a choice of elimination, especially if the excised -{e}- was a symbol for ego. Oh, he'd be so proud.

I read from Carl G. Jung. "The Dionysiac religion contained orgiastic rites that implied the need for an initiate to abandon himself to his animal nature and thereby experience the full fertilizing power of the Earth Mother."

2) No wards in this place. Mostly single rooms, isolation. I watched

the never-serene personal moments of the Terminals' reflections. The round O's of their mouths and howls. I understood: they were hungry.

But for what? Appetite was reactive. The acute schizophrenic resulted from major trauma or a terribly stressful encounter.

Bones, blood, bread.

Fee Fi Fo Fum.

Steak and spongecake,

yum yum yum.

Frozen madonna in pieta,

an icebox rose.

Snootful of thorazine

makes her baby doze.

Terror or reverie:

when psychodramas mesh,

the difference between transcendence

and plain old flesh.

Sometimes I ran my wheels like a gerbil. Mostly I ate. Gustation (sense of taste) hallucination (sensory impression without justification by external stimulus).

3) I observed the soap opera of the electroshock room, personality disintegration, as those suffering from disorganized schizophrenia left the finer points of their kinesthetic dream experience on the other side, forever.

Mother visited me in here, somehow both of us fitting in the cramped box. She moved the feeding paraphernalia aside and guided my lips to her breast, riddled with worms.

I grew fat, waxing full as the moon.

I was a little worm inside this hippo hypnogogue. Now a maggot, I escaped, went underneath the door. Now an earwig, crawling into the auditory holes of staff and patients. Never quite reaching Dr. Feamy, yet his bedroom was but twenty feet from my closet cell.

"Have you ever considered having a baby?" Feamy asked me. January 1st, I believe it might have been. Out with the old year, in with the new. Infantile iconics.

"I am a baby," I said, squinting to make him appear small. Neglecting to add the obvious *I am your baby.*

"You are a grown woman," he argued but without rancor. His tone sounded more condescending, the superior medical intellect beaming upon an inferior bedlamite.

"A most lovely maiden."

"I am both. I am also a crone," I admitted. "The triad is supposed to be: Maiden, Mother, Crone. Mother I am not. She visited moments before you arrived. See?"

I stuck out my tongue, bared my strong yellow teeth to show him the invertebrate remains deposited by contact with Mommy's hallucination: hippo hypnogogue.

"Ah, I see the kitchen pumped in spaghetti," he noted with thinly veiled disgust.

"No."

"Rice pudding?"

"No."

"Coconut pie?"

"No."

"You would look very nice in terra cotta."

Strapped down and in, I couldn't even spit at him, the expectorant merely fouling my feeding tubes. And I certainly didn't want to try to projectile vomit at him, since – with those aforementioned tubes in place – I might aspirate said stomach contents into my lungs … and die.

There are those depressives obsessed with suicide, a terminus to their suffering. But that does not make them *Terminals*. We merely rush on.

Active, reactive, reactionary.

As he leaned close to me all I could do was spin my wheels. Round and round. Poor bus, a sad substitute for an old-fashioned manic run-amuck.

"Just as well you don't have a baby," he replied with a sigh. "You would probably eat the poor thing."

I countered, voice echoing flatly within the chambers of those sticky tubes, "Or, even worse, when it grew old enough, you would screw it. Oedipal fixation perhaps? Was your mother a mammoth primeval archetype?"

(No fixation had I on him. I was definitely not Electra.)

I then quoted Sophocles, *Where shall now be read the fading record of this ancient guilt?*"

Feamy just made a barely repressed face of progenital disappointment as I continued, "The red you smeared on Mother stained your cock and balls the same color. As if you were a signature bloody warrior, a male dominant hunter-gatherer clans over maternal agrarianism, a priest-master of ceremonies and sacrifices, an emblematic rapist. Mother Earth is the result of a conspiracy between time and space."

He saw his opening. "Yet you claim, Clanci, that you have inherited this empirical throne. If your paranoia is to have any basis within the centroversion of your theory, then which am I, your father? Time or space?"

He listened intently for my answer. I heard an ultra-soft click click, the whir of an incoherent nightingale.

He had a tape recorder in his lab coat pocket. White that garment was, the cyclical color of death. Because it was the color of ... Hey, is that a bone in your pocket or are you just mad to see me?

I read on one of the screens from a book by Paul Ricoeur. "What psychoanalysis recognizes under the name of identification is simply the shadow ..."

I watched the rooms full of fire, a movable feast. Sometimes the defectives within stared back at the cameras. They would touch their heads, palms to skull bone. Or, restrained, they would manage a sideways nod to show I was indeed inside there.

I heard a commotion in the quarters outside my box. Feamy had escorted a nurse to his chambers. I imagined her all in white, probably Moby's great-grandwhale. Her footfalls, even in crepe soles, were as heavy as the manacles such establishments as these once chained patients to the walls with.

They laughed and danced, excited little tremors passing through the floor and box door. There was music. Queen.

"Fat bottomed girls, you make the rockin' world go round!"

"What's that? Red body paint?" she screeched. "How kinky!"

Dear Mother of Sorrows, a message in transference:

Time and Space say, "Choke on this."

"How are you today, Clanci?" Dr. Feamy inquired as he opened my closet door.

Hmm, must be May 1st. The last time was April 1st, no day for fools.

"I'm slipping away," I replied. "Wandering the halls, visiting the others, eating my way through their brains. On the inside of the skull where you can't see."

"But you never leave this box," he pointed out, the soul of rationality (spy for time and space). "I'd know. I have a camera on you, too."

I smiled. "You observe this analysand ampersand avoirdupois. The real me skinnies out, goes under the door. You can't distinguish this. I'm really so thin, I've only got one side. The camera and you see only in three dimensions. You *may* behold the actual me. I will permit it under certain circumstances."

"And how would I accomplish such a feat? What are the requirements for attaining this special perception of divine dispensation?" he wanted to know.

"Renounce the other two dimensions and bow before me."

He grinned back. "Fusions of delusions. If your outer body remains here as you ... er ... go abroad, in your inner body, does your outer body possess any iconic memory of having witnessed the inner body on the closed-circuit?"

I couldn't nod. My head was vised so I couldn't slip from the food and water tubes. But I related, "I saw me, a narrow length of entrail with veins for arms and legs. A doll's head."

"And you visit the patients, eating through their brains?"

"Yes, but I will my entrail back, excreting out their collective scraps. Add these to the outer form which is really only a disguise."

"So, this repulsive mountain of flesh isn't actually *you*," Dr. Feamy said, obviously trying to obtain a deeper contact through the negative gestalt of insult.

"You cut me to the quick," I answered blandly.

He chuckled and arched an eyebrow. "Then you should endeavor to develop a thicker skin."

"I'm working on it. One masticated, plasticated, digested quilt square at a time."

He produced a needle.

"I must temporarily tranquilize you, Clanci," DAD ...D-{e}-AD sans the egomonstrative...informed me. "Have to clean the box."

He jabbed me in a very meaty upper arm. Only got the faux outer layer.

I pretended to slump, to stare and drool, to sleep moronic motoneuronic. Even in such states where the inner self is wired and hot-awake, we may cross a threshold into maturation mode.

Nurture or Nature, oldest phlick in the book.

The walls trembled. They shook. I opened one eye and saw figures on the closed-circuit televisions, tearing terminal ass through the corridors. Froth about the lips can be milky pearls or wet rubies. Figurative staff members torn to literal pieces.

D-{e}-AD heard me giggle and glanced at the cameras.

He cursed, "Fucking full moon!"

Oh, the lovely Rorschachs on the hallway walls. Making senseless of the sense. The world persecutes; only Heaven can heal.

Proximal Stimulus/activities of every sense organ/the wheels on the bus go round and round.

He always kept the door to the chief-of-staff's private quarters locked.

Extra meds the standing orders on evenings of total luna. Electromagnetic sensitivity a buzz saw through the most sensitive. Some orderly must have been selling the prescript bottles on the side. Until the roof rippled and the floor tilted.

Cosmic Locus ceruteus. The brain's anxiety universe.

On camera, slits revealing pupils which glittered, shiny. Feral/ferocity/this hospital is a feral city.

Getting through the door. Gnawing through it like rats, like relentless zombies on primal overdrive.

Dr. Feamy screamed.

Dead Dad. -{e}- reintegrated.

They caught sight of me, so huge in my box that they couldn't even release me without ripping out the surrounding walls. Big as primitive Venus.

Those wheels weren't enough to make me strong. Set upon the floor, I had to inch like a fat grub, needed to roll to reach the doctor's body. The invaders to Feamy's sanctum assisted by giving me a push and nudge here and there, as well as worshipful encouragement.

My! Not quite dead was D-{e}-AD? His eyes bulged, bloodshot as a moon returning from eclipse above a heavily polluted city. His mouth opened round, the symbol for my dominion. They had knocked out his teeth, pulling and twisting his tongue until it snapped off (quite unusual for him not to have drowned in his own fluids at that point), so this circle was also very red. I took it as a portent. Fixation was the hallmark of the most resolute destiny.

Heaven waited, so did Hell. The two were even the paradigm for the amalgamation of rapture and damnation. Both places were Terminal Wards. Whatever you'd been sent there for (or born there with), you couldn't be cured.

But you knew time and space were a crock of shit.

"What is the driving force behind all meaning?" I whispered to my faithful.

Hisses in crisp gray noise. Shrieks of shadow core.

"Sex!" "Kingdomcome!"

"Power!" "Demoncum!"

"Destruction!" "Fuckdom!"

"Apocalypse!" "Shitdeath!"

So many answers, projections out of phobic darkness. Contemplated in the aggressive eternities of a frustrated finality.

"No," I murmured. "The driving force is hunger."

And with my body massive and fem-grotesque, my faceless face … they knew I was right.

The orderly slapped the intercom to inform the new chief-of-staff. "Uh, Dr. Chevron? Something's happened to Clanci Feamy's room."

"In Clanci's room?"

"No, ma'm. 'To' the room."

Dr. Chevron was tired, irritable after weeks of trying to clean up after the tragic riot at the Feamy Institute. She sighed, wanting to return to the relatively normal abnormals at the State Hospital. "What's happened to it?"

"Miss Feamy ate it."

Chevron frowned. "What's that supposed to mean? How can someone eat a room?"

The orderly shrugged – a gesture only for himself. "She ate all the cotton batting, the floor padding down to the cement subfloor, and everything soft on the walls to about three feet up."

Dr. Chevron swallowed dry, feeling an unpleasant rasp in her throat. Suggestibility: a bad trait, considering her profession. "What's Clanci doing now?"

"Just sitting there. Like she's going to explode. Except … well – *you* know – she already has."

Oh, Mother of Extremity, of Terminus, Of the End. For you this bit of verse from Charles Baudelaire:

To you, virgins, demons, monsters, martyrs,
To you great spirits spurning reality,
Searchers of the infinite, devotees and satyrs,
Now full of cries, now full of tears,
To you whom to your hell my soul has followed …

Salvation was a sandwich, a scream muffled at its end by elliptical epileptoid epicureanism. (Try saying that ten times fast.)

My outer body coughed – a cotton candy hairball floatable as dandelion fluff.

But I was out. I had left the carcass mountain.

Did they suspect? Hell, no.

Was I a shadow this time? Or a worm/maggot/earwig? Was I a length of gut on legs of blood-highway?

Didn't matter.

Skinny stalked the corridors.

K. TRAP JONES

DEMON EYED BLIND

I can see him in there; swimming in my head. My blood shot eyes pierce themselves within their own reflection in this mirror. Entrapped inside me, the demon mourns for its release, but without any other person here, he knows his demise is approaching. The cool steel of the Glock handgun is pressed firmly against my temple. I have been bred for this as a demon hunter; everything in my life has led to this exact moment.

Dead to rights I have this demon. His entrapment was by the book; a precise calculation that has landed me within this gas station bathroom. Although, not the ideal setting for the suicidal ritual, it will have to suffice. I have been tracking this particular demon for years and have come close on many occasions to entrapping him, but their ability to host jump has drastically improved. They have become masters of manipulation and stealth, but we have also evolved.

With the characteristics of the demon embedded within me, I began the hunt many years ago. As a hunter, I should not fear the end. We are trained and developed for the purpose of luring the demons within our bodies and sacrificing ourselves for the greater good of humanity. Isolated, with no other host to jump into, the demon dies along with the hunter. It is written as law and carried out accordingly. There should be no hesitation on my part, but there is.

This particular demon is challenging my emotions to the point where confusion is setting in. Questions about my past linger before my eyes within the mirror. He is scouring my mind to find a weakness; siphoning through memories until he has enough ammunition to strike back. It is only a matter of time before he locates my fears and elevates them to levels that I am not accustomed to.

My eyes bleed with vengeance and my heart races to keep up with the rapid blood flow, but I cannot turn away from the mirror. I can see through the demon's eyes as he shuffles through my dreams and discards the ones that are not useful to him. Devouring them with his appetite to control my mind, I am losing control. I feel insanity gripping my spine and using my rib cage as a stepping stone for its own good. My thoughts wonder aimlessly through the field of emotions, but yet I cannot offer it any comfort or safety as the lure of the demon is getting more powerful with every memory that it feasts upon.

I know what my true fear is and I am trying to not fall victim to the demon's demands by bringing it to the center of my mind. Even though I am able to suppress that particular fear, he has already collected so many more. My eyes display visions of obscurity against the canvas of the mirror. I see myself being held underwater as I struggle for one last breath. I am trying to keep my mouth closed, but my lungs push them apart in search for air. The water flows through my lips like a newfound sinkhole. I can taste the coolness of the water as it pours down my throat and fills my stomach.

My throat convulses and vomit pushes its way upwards. I cannot look away from the mirror; the demon will not allow it. Instead, the vomit seeps down my chin and drips into the sink below. My own reflection appears again to reveal my eyes draining with tears. Sadness overshadows all of my emotions now. A depression suffocates the other weakened emotional states. A reflection of my own death is difficult to deal with, but I still hold my finger on the trigger, so the demon goes back to work in search of additional fears.

Within seconds, my lungs collapse as my throat winces for even the slightest of air. Within the reflection, the shirt I am wearing gets saturated with blood in the center of my chest. The hand holding the gun trembles greatly, but the barrel does not leave my temple. The mirror shows two elongated clawed hands tearing at the shirt from inside. With enough leverage, the claws rip apart the shirt and reveal the head of the demon protruding from my chest. I want to close my eyes, but I am not allowed to. If only to blink and have that split second of mental freedom: anything to help ease my troubled mind.

The demon's forked tongue slithers out from behind rows of jagged teeth. A piercing howl vibrates my chest as the demon unleashes a sound so high in pitch that the mirror begins to splinter along the edges. By some action other than my own, my neck bends downward to allow my eyes to look upon my chest. No blood, no torn shirt, no demon. My neck gets bent back upwards where my eyes stare at the mirror once again. The demon has almost exited my midsection and is climbing up to my shoulders. Its long tail is the last to exit my insides and curls around my arm. As it unravels, the sharpened edges easily slice into my bicep. The burning sensation is intense, but I keep telling myself that it is only a reflection and not real. But my mind cannot overlook the sheer amount of pain that it is enduring. The tail gracefully wraps around my neck and indents itself within the skin. I can feel the pressure, but the anticipation of what might be next is clogging any strength that I may have left. Perched upon my shoulder, the demon extracts its tongue and licks my face. The action disgusted me and he could feel my frustration and disappointment. Unraveling the tail at quick pace, the sharpened edges severed my neck and pushed me into an unstable arena where I was preparing to battle my own thoughts. I could only observe myself choke upon my own blood. I watched as my body slumped to the ground within a pool of my own blood. I felt the pain and misery of the reflection. My eyes swelled with tears at the choices I had made in my life; a flash of sanity within this sadistic world. I felt sorrow and pity for myself as I saw my body shiver upon the bathroom floor. I wanted more for my life; much more than to lie helpless on that grime infested tile.

My fixation upon the mirror was rattled by the sound of knocking on the door. I was able to turn my own head as if the demon had momentarily fled the scene. I could sense him slithering about within my mind; debating with himself as to what reinforcement to use next. All of his dreams would be answered if I only open the door. He would be able to host jump and flee to safety. He pleaded with me and nurtured my loving emotions by pushing aside the quest for fear. My heart flowed with passion as he drained thoughtfulness into my mind. There were high hopes that I would fall victim to the personal needs of others, but he apparently did not know me well enough.

The police had arrived at the gas station. I knew they would eventually come to the scene from the chaos that led to the bathroom. The hunting of demons is not a very pleasant occupation. Wherever the demon treads, death is not far behind. Within hosts, the demon can roam wherever it sees fit and partake in various chaotic actions that bleed the foundation of civilization.

The interactions between the demon trying to flee and the hunter trying to entrap can prove fatal for those who linger beyond their welcome. Outside, the police will sift through the dead and try to piece together a crime scene that they will truly not understand. The bodies collected on the pavement have no symbolic meaning. They served as the demon's flight pattern until he made one last dreadful jump into the very person that he was trying to avoid.

I tried to corner the demon with the least amount of people around, but they are aware of that tactic and stay primarily within heavily populated areas with multiple avenues of escape. Through the years, my demon has always being able to filter away and it was only a twist of fate that I was able to snare him. I sat on the bus across town with him in the back. Within a large man, he dwelled. I could tell by the mannerisms and overall nervousness of the individual. But, it was much more than that. I had watched the demon enter his body just moments before. I was led to a fresh crime scene with multiple decapitations. Through the throat by way of severing the head was my particular demon's favorite way of exiting a body. Everything was in place, the claw marks on the neck and amount of tearing that provided for him to gain release.

The kills were fresh; the blood was moist. I cared nothing for the victims as I surveyed the audience for the escape path. The nearest person followed by the next closest person. Over the years, I have been able to predict the path only upon fresh crime scenes. The path can be lost if enough time has passed. On those occasions, I need only wait for more decapitations in order to get a new scent on the trail. The police will label the deaths a homicide and search for a killer, but they never see nor arrest the entity in which they seek.

I studied the mannerisms of the bystanders. When a demon enters a new body, there is conflict within the mind; a brief confused state that reveals itself within the facial and body characteristics of the host. Upon exiting, there is also that same method of physical conflict. In surveying the crowd, I could see both the entry and exit paths of the demon. It is useless to combat the demon while he is in flight mode. Only death occurs to the innocent when provoked. Instead, I stalked behind him as he blended away from the crime scene through the funneling of human bodies.

The path led me to a bus stop where I witnessed that sudden burst of confusion upon the face of a man who was about to climb the steps and enter the bus. I walked through the aisle and sat a few seats behind the man. I carefully watched all of those within reach and saw no exit path. He remained within the man until the next stop. Still, not exit path, so I followed the man off the bus as he walked towards a gas station. Without warning, the man stopped and faced me. I quickly drew my gun. By law, I am entitled to kill the host if I deem that no other death may come about as a result. It is the last line of defense that I have never encountered before. Much like the other times before, the man searched around for others to jump into, but there was no one available.

With my gun drawn and pointed at him, I saw confusion within his eyes. There was a panic that I was never able to witness before. The moment did not last long, as I heard another bus approach. The man's eyes widened at the sheer amount of people getting off of the bus and walking towards us. They didn't care that I had a gun and even shunned my warnings. Within seconds, the demon fled the man and entered into an elderly woman just long enough to rip through her neck and jump to another. Mass chaos was the perfect getaway vehicle for demons. Everyone panicked and ran in different directions as more people came out of the gas station store from the sound of screaming.

Three were already dead with more lined up perfectly within the travel path. The demon's flight pattern was heading towards the gas station. Instead of following directly behind, I angled to the right and ran passed the man where the demon resided, knowing that the path would continue. Against the wall I waited until the line of corpses continued to fall. The bathroom door swung open to reveal another man standing as the demon dove within his body. Without much thought, I sent a bullet through the man's head as the demon quickly fled and jumped into me. Falling into the bathroom, I locked the door behind me.

Sarcasm reared its ugly demeanor and formed a judging grin upon my face as I could tell that the demon was pleading with me to unlock the door. Plagued by false promises and forgettable displays of pity, my mind became my own. I felt some scrapes of power, that of which I had not felt since entering through the door. I felt in control of the situation with the ability to suppress the demon's temptations for sporadic moments of time. It was my mind fighting back.

With confidence, I turned away from the door and back towards the mirror. I was not the victim anymore; the demon filled that role quite nicely. There was an eerie pause as we both collected our thoughts. A period of peace; an understanding and mutual respect for each other's ability.

The police are still pounding on the door as my eyes become fixated once again on the mirror. My hand clenches the gun tighter and presses the barrel deeper into my temple. He knows that his only option is for me to open the door; that is his only escape. If he kills me, he dies. If I kill myself, he dies. He needs me and I know this. If it was a game he wanted to play, then I would create the rules.

Bleeding my brain with his visions, he hit me hard with frustration and deception. None of these mattered to me until my free hand began to move without my consent. I witnessed the most evil grin form upon my face as I looked into the mirror. It was neither a vision nor a dream; it was real. I could feel my cheeks rise and my lips spread wider apart. He found a way to control my actions. As my hand reached for the door, I tightened my finger around the trigger, prompting the movement to halt. With mental threats pouring from both of us, we had reached a stalemate in our peace treaty.

My elbow cracked for more extension as my left foot began to slide over. He did not have full control over my physical actions, as I was able to pull back my arm briefly, but it had become a cat and mouse game of who could control more of the movement. It served as an internal struggle that pulsated my brain and contorted any rational judgment that I had remaining.

Small sparks filter through the hinges of the door as the police begin to melt the bolts. The grin formed upon my face once again as the reaching ended. It was only a matter of time before the door would be removed. The demon simply waited inside, showing me visions within the mirror of him filtering into the police as they entered; leaping through the crowd of bystanders and ultimately disappearing once again into the human population. An emotion lacking during my stay within the bathroom, unveiled itself; anger flowed through me at the thought of more innocent death. It coated my eyes with a sweet revenge that allowed me to control the situation and lead upon the path instead of following and chasing. I became the leader; I became the dominant one who makes the rules.

I am a demon hunter. I swore an oath to protect the human population against those that wish to cause chaos through possession of innocent victims. I have done honor by those who serve alongside me and battle their own demons on a daily basis. I have seen a path of death and destruction through my failures to properly entrap the demon and I am aware that the innocent blood is on my hands.

As the sparks continue to enter through the cracks in the door, my arm remains outreached for the lock with the gun pointed at my head. I am a demon hunter and inside dwells my demon. It is my game; it is my rules. All I have to do is what I have been professionally trained to do and everything resolves itself. All I have to do is pull this trigger.

D.F. NOBLE

PSYCH

Joseph Sloan watched the psychiatrist set up a video camera and rubbed his hands together. He felt nervous, awkward even, but there was a weight on his chest he had to get rid of. A weight that was killing him, driving him mad.

The psychiatrist, Dr Thomas Uldritch, was nice enough. An older man, with more gray than color in his hair and thick glasses, but unlike many in his profession he wasn't cold and clinical. He seemed to genuinely care, or at least gave off that illusion.

Uldritch clicked the record button and Joseph saw the red light come to life. The psychiatrist turned and sat down in a chair a few feet away, then pulled up a note pad.

"So," Joseph asked, "how do we start?"

"Just relax, Joe," Uldritch smiled, "and tell me everything you can remember. Start from the beginning. Take your time."

Joseph nodded. "Okay, well..."

I hear all kinds of crazy things. It comes with the job, working on a psych ward. Geriatric Psych to be specific. You get used to it. It just kind of rolls off of you after awhile. Takes a certain type to be able to handle this kind of work day in, day out.

I mean, people toss around the word crazy but half the time don't really know what crazy is. Real crazy. Out of your mind crazy. Deranged. Schizophrenia. Dementia. Madness. They are just words till you meet it face to face. Till you have to give crazy a bath, make sure it's clean, feed it, and tuck it in bed.

You can care but you can't stop to care, really care for too long. It's too sad. It's just too much weight. That's somebody's child, somebody's brother or sister, mother or father, and they are insane. For real, insane. Not acting, but to the core, mad.

I work nights. Twelve hour shifts at a hospital and like I said, I hear crazy things all the time. I'll be at the bar with some friends, listening to some doofus saying, "Oh man, I had the craziest weekend."

No. No, you didn't …

I've always considered myself a pretty strong person. Mentally, physically, there's not a lot I can't handle. It's … different now. The first time I got one, a panic attack, I thought I was dying. It felt like something was holding me down and sitting on my chest. I couldn't breathe. It was terrifying in ways that are hard to puts in words. But it wasn't just a panic attack out of nowhere...

It started with a patient. Her name was Cathy. Typical case, you know. Dementia. She was feisty, liked to claw and scratch. All that stuff. Anyway … I was scheduled to work an overnight with her. This was on geriatric psych, or just Geri for short as well call it. It's a temporary transition point for the elderly before they're moved to a home, and it's always full. It's always busy. There's nothing pretty about it, nothing anywhere close to what you might think a regular hospital room may be. There's one long hallway that leads to a lounge and cafeteria area, drab gray and white paint, with one TV all the patients have to share. Limbo, purgatory...

When I first came in, Cathy thought I was the Devil, a *lying* Devil to be exact. An hour later, I was an FBI agent and so on and so on. None of this really bothered me. I was there for her safety. To make sure she didn't pull out her I.V. or catheter.

So after awhile she's finally getting used to me being in the room with her and she's just a sweet old lady all of a sudden. She thinks I'm her grandson and then...then she starts making this weird face and looking at the vent up near the ceiling. She's tilting her head, you know like the way a dog does? Yeah, like that, and just hyper-focused on this vent.

Then she turns to me and whispers, "*Could you please close that?*"

So I humor her. I get up and act like I close the vent. I mean you can't really; there's no closing it. She says, "I can still hear him."

"Hear who?" I ask her.

She gets all white, like a sheet. Like the blood just drained out of her. Cathy's eyes are all locked on the vent. She isn't blinking, but she says real low, and I mean ... I guess you had to be there, but it was just so creepy.

She says, "My husband. He won't stop singing that song."

"Well that's sweet he still sings to you," I tell her. I mean, what do you say to that? But then she looks at me and God, this look, like I just spilled pasta on her carpet or something. This dirty look and she says, "He's dead."

So at this point, yeah I'm creeped out. Nothing major, but it gave me the shivers. I spent the next hour trying to get her to lie down and sleep, and everything went back to normal. Well, as normal as it can get, and I'm sitting across from her bed reading a book. There's just enough light from the hallway coming in the door and Cathy starts smacking at the air around her. Starts asking me if I see all these bugs.

Of course, there were no bugs, and I tell her that. I tell her it's just her medications and her eyes playing tricks on her, but there she goes, just slapping the air, trying to smack these bugs away. I figure she'd just wear herself out after a while. She wasn't hurting herself, and she's eighty-something, she'd have to tire herself out. But no, instead she sits up again in bed, and she's looking over in the corner of the room, that same weird way, her head all cocked to one side.

I'm watching her, ready to jump if she starts anything, and she says, "Why don't you come out of there, Robert, and sing to me?"

Yeah, I know. Weird. Like I said, I hear crazy shit all the time.

She gets real quiet, and I can tell she's scared. She sees something obviously, and she says, "Who are you?"

At this point I decide to butt into the delusion, interrupt it before it gets worse. Sometimes you can just tell when someone's about to snap. So I tell her I'm a caregiver, and I'm here to help her with anything she needs and—she just gives me a dirty look and goes back to staring in the dark corner.

If I didn't mention it before, we're sitting in this almost dark room. Me by the doorway, and the hall light, and her in bed.

"You're not my husband," she says. Not to me, but to the corner.

"Cathy," I said, "would you like a glass of water?"

This is classic misdirection, a friendly offer that can save me, the nurses, and any other techs a bunch of trouble and a psychotic episode.

Then she looks at me and says, "You stay in the light. It hates the light. Doesn't want you to see it."

"Okay," I said, "how about that water? You want a snack, Cathy?"

"It's not a man," she says matter-of-fact-like. "It wants you to think it's a man. But I see you. *I SEE YOU!*"

At that point, I had to turn on the lights. Not because I was all that creeped out, but for precaution. Just in case she tried to hurt herself. And when I did flip them on, instead of escalating like I figured she would, Cathy eased up, took a deep breath, and lay back in bed.

"It's gone," she sighed. "Ugly thing. Horrible. Bugs all over it."

I went to her side and she held her hand out, and I took it in both of mine, trying to comfort her.

"It was singing. *Singing with Robert's voice.* But Robert's dead."

"There, there," I comforted her. "Get some rest," I say, "it was a bad dream."

And after doing this awhile, her rambling and me soothing her, Cathy did fall asleep. I had a few hours of quiet time in a chair beside her, read a book, clocked out at seven, went home and went to bed. The crazy night with Cathy didn't even cross my mind on the way home. I was singing along with the radio, jacked up on coffee. I got home, showered, and passed right the hell out. Slept like a baby.

Later that day, as I prepared for my next overnight shift with Cathy, management gave me a call. Cathy had just passed. I could take the night off, they said.

I wished her well and hoped she was at peace and then, then I caught up on sleep.

That was a Monday night, and everything was fine still. Everything was normal.

Wednesday, I got the call. Geri again. Male patient, late seventies, dementia, possible Alzheimer's. Fall risk, agitated, and constantly wanted to get out of bed. All of this normal, just another overnight.

His name was Ernest and when I got there, they'd given him a sedative. Strong enough he should've been in a coma, but no, he was awake still. Sitting up in bed like he was waiting for me. I came in with a nurse, introduced myself and told him I was there to help with anything he needed, that I was there to keep him safe. If he wanted something to drink, something to eat, or to use the bathroom, just to let me know, and I'd help him out.

He said nothing at first, just looked at me with dull, glazed eyes.

Guy was high as a kite.

I helped the nurse change his depends, and surprisingly enough, he didn't fight with us. He settled back into bed, with me at my post, in the doorway with a book.

Then he mumbled something.

Out of reflex I asked, "Say again?"

I looked up from the book and noticed Ernest sitting up in bed. He was staring into the corner, into the shadows. Staring at a vent.

He said, "I like the melody, but I don't like the words much."

At that point I'm pretty sure I made a dumb face. I changed position in the chair, being suddenly uncomfortable. I must've made some noise because Ernest turned to me.

He asked me to close the vent.

The singing wouldn't let him sleep.

I'm not a real spiritual person; I'm pretty skeptical when in it comes to just about everything. But right then, yeah. Shivers. Shivers all up and down my spine. Was this some kind of joke? Did he pick this up from Cathy a day or two ago before she died? Was he even on the ward then??

Like a big dummy I asked, "What're they singing about?"

Big glazed eyes locked on me. Face, old and worn, weathered. Stringy beard, stringy white hair. A skeleton draped in skin...

"Being dead," he said.

Then he started arcing his finger through the air, like a conductor. Started humming a melody, something almost like a lullaby, maybe an old Irish song – reminded me of sailing for whatever reason.

I remember it clearly. I think everyone remembers a good fright. Or the fright's so good you black it out, bury it in your memory. My hairs stood on end and I stood up.

I don't know why, curiosity maybe, but I asked for the words. I wish I hadn't because now they're stuck in my goddamned head, like a damn radio pop hit. I asked for the goddamned words and he obliged me alright.

In his gruff old voice he began to haunt me with the tune. Etched the words onto the stone of my mind, carving in a curse. That's what it felt like. What it feels like.

It goes...

> *We dance between raindrops*
> *we frolic in fire*
> *we huddle in mass graves*
> *chained down with barbwire*
> *our faces without skin*
> *hold permanent grins*
> *we weren't ready to die yet*
> *so please let us in*
> *in*
> *in*
> *in*
> *so please let us in*

I went for the light switch so fast, I knocked the damned door shut, and for a terrifying eternity I fell into the dark. I knew I was just inches, maybe a foot from the switch, but spooked as I was, I made an ass of myself. Tripped over the chair, slid down the wall. All the while, the old man carried on this tune somewhere in the dark...

> *We watch from the shadows*
> *we envy your laughter*
> *the flesh that we once had*
> *that's what we're after*
> *open your mind like a door*

blown by the wind
we weren't ready to die yet
so please let us in
in
IN
IN!

By the time I managed to find the light, Ernest was repeatedly screaming, cackling – *"LET US IN! LET US IN!"* Thank God the nurse wasn't far off. As soon as the lights came on, Ernest shut up, and the nurse opened the door behind me.

"Everything okay in here?" she asked.

I looked over at Ernest, who was lying flat on his back, eyes locked on the vent in the corner, but otherwise calm. I swallowed hard and laughed a little bit at myself.

"Yeah," I told her. "Thought he was gonna have an episode and went for the lights, tripped on the chair, knocked the door shut."

She gave me a grin and we checked on Ernest. He stayed silent, didn't respond to our questions and just lay there, staring off. The nurse told me if I needed anything to just buzz her. If he started acting up too much again she'd see if he could take another sedative.

I told her thanks, and then I asked her when he'd been admitted.

"Earlier this afternoon," she replied. "Why?"

"Ah, nothing," I said and let her go back to her desk down the hall.

I settled back in, still laughing at myself and trying to quell the thoughts in my head. What was it with people on this ward hearing singing in the vents? If he'd just been admitted earlier today, there was no way Ernest heard any of Cathy's conversation with me the other night. Maybe it was something the patients had overheard in the lounge. Hell, maybe they were so bored they were plotting against the staff and trying to give us the heebie-jeebies.

Maybe the vent was channeling someone's radio from another floor, if that was even possible.

So I played detective, approached the vent and...

Nothing. Nada.

I took a seat back in my chair, opened my book, got maybe three pages in and heard Ernest say, "Keep that light on, mister. Please."

You bet your ass I'll keep the light on.

By the time I clocked out and got into my car, the night's little freak out episode was fading fast. When I made it home, I'd thought of a million other things I wanted to do, and then the things I had to actually take care of. I showered, and went to bed.

When I woke up, I had a voicemail waiting for me on my cell.

Ernest had passed, but they needed me to come in for another overnight. As I prepped for work and left, I laughed off a thought.

Hopefully there would be no more singing through the vent. Of course I was wrong. Big reason I'm telling you this now.

When I walked in, the client was already slapping at the air. *Great,* I thought, *bugs, right? What are they giving these people?*

"Sir, sir . . ." the guy started. Older black guy, thin as a rail. His name was Henry. He sat up in bed, well, tried to. Underneath the blankets I could see something was wrong. He was missing a leg. Henry grabbed hold of the bed railing and sat himself up. His eyes were wide, and his voice wavered, hoarse, just above a whisper.

"Sir, I need you to call the police."

"What's wrong?" I asked, setting my things down in a chair by the door.

"They're trying to . . ." he swallowed hard and looked around as if somebody was listening in on us, "they're trying to kill me."

"Who's trying to kill you? We're in the hospital, Henry. Do you remember coming to the hospital today?"

He scowled at me. "Boy, don't play me for a fool. I know where I'm at."

Henry glanced over his shoulder, quick. Once, then twice, squinting. I know where he was looking...

"Then why do you think someone's going to kill you? We don't do that at a hospital. We're just trying to help you."

His grip tightened on the bed rail. Knuckles white. "Something ain't right here. Place...this place is infested. I need you to call the police, do ya hear? Now help me get up outta this bed, we gotta get out of here."

"Whoa now, just hold up," I told him and placed myself in his way. He pulled his blanket off at this point and I could see the missing leg must have been amputated. Fresh gauze had been taped to it, and it was spotting through with red. "Just calm down a minute, Henry. Tell me who's trying to hurt you."

I could tell he was agitated with me already. Which is a great way to start off a twelve hour shift, but he rasped at me, "Same ones who told me you was coming, boy. The damned ones singing up in there."

And then Henry turned and pointed at the vent. My eyes naturally followed and that's when it hit home for me. It was like getting punched in the stomach ... or ... or if you've ever been on a roller coaster, the ones that just drop you down and make you think you're going to hit the ground. Your breath, it just freezes in you. I remember it was kind of like that...

I didn't want to believe it. But I saw it.

Fingers. Long, white, thin fingers, sliding back into the vent.

That's when I passed out.

When I woke up I was screaming, thrashing. I'd accidentally struck a nurse across the face, not hard, but hard enough another orderly put me in some odd headlock on the floor.

Looking up at the ceiling, it was the light that finally calmed me down.

God, it was terrible. At that moment embarrassment hadn't set in yet. I'd stopped struggling and there were people buzzing about me, asking questions, shining lights in my eyes, checking my pulse. I just lay there for awhile, catching my breath, trying to erase the memory of that vision I saw in the vent.

It couldn't be real. It was just a trick, a shadow or sleep deprivation. Something, anything, other than fingers sliding back into the vent grate.

I shivered.

Was I losing my mind? Was there actually something in there?

Eventually they got me talking, asked me what happened. All I could tell them was I had a panic attack, which isn't far from the truth. They gave me the night off, and one of the nurses even offered to drive me home. Nice people.

I drove myself home, stopping at a liquor store on the way and buying a fifth of vodka and something sweet to mix it with. I was going to drink myself to sleep and turn on every goddamn light in my house.

When I did finally get home, I sat in the driveway for some time. I thought I might have another panic attack just thinking about walking in and turning on the lights, about spending the night alone. I hadn't felt that kind of fear, just overwhelming *fear*, since I was a kid and thought there was a monster in my closet. That kind of fear that makes your hair stand on end – makes your body tingle and go all rubbery...

So I started drinking in the car. Just straight from the bottle. I turned on some oldies, some Mo-town, and sang along like an idiot till my spirits were better. After a bit I stumbled inside, turned on all the lights, and blasted the TV.

I thought, *maybe it's a lack of sleep, maybe it's the circumstances, and maybe anybody would have been freaked out, freaked out the way I was dealing with that shit.* I thought I was going to be fine for a while, I really did. I was almost finished with the vodka, making my way to the bathroom with all the lights on when I noticed a part of the hallway that wasn't completely lit up.

Just enough, a shadowy corner, and one thought that let me know I wasn't quite alright.

I thought, *tomorrow I'm going to go buy some more lamps. Need more light.*

That next morning I had a long conversation on the phone with my supervisor. They told me it was alright if I took some time off, they even had a counselor who I could talk to. They said all things, you know, to make me feel better – "It's okay, this is a hard business. You're not the first to be overwhelmed. You're not alone …"

You know, all that stuff.

Didn't realize the counselor thing was mandatory by the company if you had a freak-out on the job. Psychological Evaluation, right? Make sure I'm not gonna flip on the patients. It's cool, I understand....

Right. Anyway...

So I tried to relax. Tried to forget that damn vision … that hallucination at the hospital....

During the day I was fine. I was also very drunk. Self-medicating. Booze and comedy movies. I was thinking: man I wish I was back in my home town. I could go hang out with some old buddies, even pass out on their couch if need be.

And then it happened again. Except this time it wasn't with a patient. I was home … it was night and I was passed out and drunk and I know you're gonna say it was the alcohol but I swear, *I swear to God it wasn't.* I tried to tell myself it was … I did. I'd rather believe that...

I was passed out on my couch. The DVD I was watching was over, just playing on loop on the menu screen. It was night, but like I said, I had all the lights on. None of that woke me up...

It was the doorbell.

I groaned, got up, stretched and wondered who the hell was

at my door in the middle of the night. Maybe it was one of the nurses, or a co-worker checking up on me. I stumbled down the hall, looked out the window next to the door and...

There was nobody. Just an empty porch.

My first thought was, *Goddamn kids*.

My second thought was to open the door and catch one of 'em hiding in the bushes, and then I remembered the song...

> *Open your mind like a door*
> *blown by the wind*
> *we weren't ready to die yet*
> *so please let us in*
> *in*
> *in*
> *in*

My hand stopped at the door knob. The hairs on my neck stood up. It took damn near everything in me to check the window again, but I did. This time I prayed it was kids, kids lighting a paper bag full of dog shit on my porch, anything but emptiness.

I checked to make sure the door was locked.

There's a part of you, a little voice that makes fun of you at moments like that. *You're a grown man. What're you afraid of? Ghosts? Why would you need to lock a door against a ghost? What kind of sense does that make?*

It doesn't make any sense.

But that's the thing about madness, the thing about irrational fear. At that point you do whatever it takes to make you feel safe, whatever makes you knock out the heebie jeebies. I left the front door and returned to the living room. My vodka was gone.

I wanted more, but something told me I shouldn't open the door. That other little voice told me it would be bad if I did. It told me to wait 'til daytime, to crawl under the covers and go to bed and wait till daylight.

I felt trapped.

I lay back on the couch, knowing I had to distract myself. So I started watching the blooper reel and special features on the DVD. Eventually, I relaxed enough to sleep and as I began to nod off … I heard it, for the first time, and I know you'll call me crazy. You'll call it a lack of sleep or stress or … whatever. But I heard it.

I heard it coming from the goddamn floor vent.

Mister, it whispered.

I froze in place. My breath caught in my chest. Did I really just hear that?

It's so cold outside …

I remember my hands coming up, trying to cover my ears I think. I wanted to run, but I felt like a stone. It felt like the temperature dropped in the room, like it was freezing cold. I wanted to scream, but all I could do was look at that vent.

Let us in, mister. Please let us …

Ding-dong.

The door bell rang then and I finally I did scream. I screamed and screamed until I thought my mind was going to rip to pieces, like someone tearing paper; that's how it felt. All I wanted then was to get out, to run down the street screaming 'til someone called the cops and took me away to a hospital.

I stood up, I guess too fast, because I didn't make it far. My vision wavered, and my body felt like a wet noodle as I fell to the floor.

I lay there, paralyzed, trying to catch my breath. My vision started going black, but I remember the sounds clearly, coming up from the vent.

It was music. Old music, and tinny sounding, like from an phonograph.

It's 3 a.m.
And most of my friends are dead
the ones that are left

got a foot in the hole
but it's alright
I see them most every night
they knock on my window on the 2nd floor
they'll give you a fright
skin white with empty eyes
but I let 'em in
out of the cold

"I don't remember much after that," Joseph said. "I think it was just too much. I know the sun woke me up in the morning, and … well, I got up. I did what any sane person would do. I blamed it on a nightmare. I blamed it on the booze. But … but I couldn't shake the feeling, the feeling that something was wrong … that something followed me home from the hospital. What do you think, Doc? Am I crazy?"

"No," Dr Uldritch said. "Joe, I don't think you're crazy. I think if anyone experienced what you told me, I think they would be absolutely terrified. It's a haunting tale you just told me."

"So what do I do? How do I make it stop?"

"Well, first I need to ask you a few questions … Have you had any thoughts or desires to hurt yourself, or bring harm to others?"

"What? God no. I wanted to work in health care to help people, not hurt anyone."

"Okay," Uldritch nodded, and wrote something on his pad. "Would you be willing to spend the night in a facility, where someone could watch over you?"

Joseph paused. "Will they keep the lights on?"

The video session ended and the detective turned off the TV. He turned to Uldritch, the one who'd made the tape and asked him, "Is that it?"

"That was the one and only video," the shrink answered.

"Mr. Sloan never did come back in for another session. He called once more to schedule an appointment, but never showed up."

The detective scratched the back of his neck and chewed his lip for a second. "Did you prescribe him anything?"

"A sleep aid and Xanax for his anxiety," he replied, "but nothing serious … But can I ask you a question, Detective?"

"Shoot."

"Am I under investigation," asked the psychiatrist, "or frankly, am I a suspect?"

The detective stood and shook his head. "At this point, it's still just a missing person's case. With all the blood left behind, you'd think we'd have a suicide or murder on our hands, but without a body..." The detective shrugged, "So, no. But, try not to leave town without letting us know."

"That shouldn't be an issue," said the psychiatrist and stood to walk the detective out. "Call me if you need anything, anything at all."

"I'll be in touch," said the detective as he turned to leave the office. "Oh, one more thing … you work for the hospital, correct?"

The psychiatrist nodded. "My practice is private, but I offer free services to the employees of the hospital, yes. As you can see from Mr. Sloan, some of the things people deal with in the profession can be quite dramatic."

The detective shook the doctor's hand and thanked him for his help. As he opened the office door to leave, the shrink asked him one more question.

"Sir, if you don't mind me asking … what did you find at the house? It's a very curious case. Of course, it's confidential. I understand but..."

The detective's face was cold when he answered, his tone flat. "All the lights were on … It looked like he was boarding up all the vents in his house. Except for the last one. A vent in his bedroom. The overhead light looks like it burned out. Only place in the house not lit up … That's where we found the blood trail."

"Trail? A blood trail to the . . ."

"Yeah," the detective nodded, "to the vent."

ANNA TABORSKA

OUT OF THE LIGHT

"You have to read it with a bishop standing at each shoulder..."

Charles tore his eyes from the young man who was wearing nothing but a rubber glove, and looked around for the one who'd uttered those riveting words, "... to stop your soul from flying out of your body in fright." Rupert finished his explanation and, seeing as nobody seemed to be paying him any attention, fell silent.

"Excuse me," said Charles, overcoming his customary shyness. "What are you talking about?"

"*Liber Tenebrarum*," Rupert turned around, spotted the enquirer and positively beamed. "*The Book of Darkness*."

"What is it?" Whether it was the vodka jelly enhancing his enthusiasm or just his innate curiosity, Charles was completely captivated by the idea of such a book.

"I don't know," responded Rupert. "I've never tried to order it up."

"Where from? The Bod?"

"Yeah." The conversation broke up as someone passed Rupert the homemade bong that was going around the room.

The Garden of Eden party was getting pretty wild – even for Brasenose College, formerly host to a branch of the infamous Hellfire Club. A couple of tipsy girls from St. Hilda's had worked out how it was exactly that the bright yellow Marigold was staying on the manhood of the Brasenose student, and were now attempting to de-glove him. The host of the party evidently felt it his duty to liven up the proceedings, and organised a competition to see who could hang from a wooden beam without letting go for the entire duration of the Soviet national anthem. Male students lined up for their turn, but none of them, it seemed, could beat the scratchy tones of *Gimn Sovetskogo Soyuza*, which now blared from an old record player in the corner of the room. A physics and philosophy student shouted over the Red Army Choir in an attempt to impress a female colleague with his explanation of Schrödinger's Cat. And the extremely strong hash in the bong was beginning to claim its first victims.

But Charles wasn't really noticing any of it. All he could think about was the mysterious book and how he was going to order it up from the Bodleian Library stacks on Monday morning. The bong reached him and he inhaled deeply, then coughed up the thick bittersweet smoke. After just one drag his head began to reel and he passed the improvised pipe to the girl on his left. The room shifted and time seemed to split into disjointed shards. The lights fragmented into rainbows, and Charles's last coherent thought was that he was tripping, and what on earth kind of hash was it anyway? He struggled to keep his head together, but eventually gave up and lay on the floor – his upper torso on the edge of a bean bag.

As the bong continued making its rounds, the beam-hanging

competition was abandoned – no one even seemed to know who'd won – and the eulogy to the *unbreakable union of free nations* gave way to The Moving Sidewalks' cover of "I Want to Hold your Hand." It seemed to Charles that the music intermittently slowed almost to a standstill, then speeded up again, but he figured it was probably his fried brain playing tricks on him. He watched fellow students wandering in and out of the room – those who'd stuck to alcohol and were still able to wander. Some of them had paid attention to the theme for the evening and were dressed as Adam or Eve, or as strange, exotic creatures; most just wore the usual student uniform of the time – jeans and jackets for the boys; short skirts, hotpants or jeans for the girls. Rubber glove man had disappeared somewhere – possibly with the girls from St Hilda's.

After half an hour or so Charles's head began to clear, and he struggled to remember the name of the book. He looked around for Rupert, but couldn't see him anywhere. He panicked as his memory failed, but then it came back to him: something about darkness … *The Book of Darkness.* That was it! *Liber Tenebrarum.* He staggered out of the party and made his way back to University College.

It wasn't far from Brasenose to Univ. Then again, nowhere was particularly far from anywhere in Oxford. Charles passed the porters' lodge and headed through the main quadrangle to his building. On his way up to his room he passed a gated alcove with a small dome, under which reposed a marble statue of the naked, drowned Percy Bysshe Shelley. The poet had briefly attended University College before being unceremoniously kicked out for publishing a pamphlet on atheism, but, as is so often the case, became a revered alumnus as soon as he became famous. Had Shelley lived long enough to witness this turn of events, he may well have told his former college where to put their effigy of him, but he hadn't – and he didn't.

Charles saluted the poet and climbed up the creaking wooden

staircase to the rooms he shared with Algernon Pyke. Algy, as he preferred to be known, was having a little party of his own in the joint sitting-room. There was a lively discussion going on as to whether the centuries-old oak mantelpiece could be cut from the wall, taken out of college and sold as an antique without anyone noticing. Charles tried to tell Algy about the book, but his friend was too drunk to take in what he was saying.

"Here, old man," he said, thrusting a glass of effervescing liquid into Charles's hand, "have a G&T!" Charles downed the offering, made his excuses and retired to his bedroom, head spinning with more than just the gin.

Sunday passed uneventfully, apart from Algy's essay crisis – the result of a tutorial first thing on Monday. Charles wasn't due to produce an essay until Friday, so he spent Sunday mentally preparing for his trip to the Bod.

On Monday morning Charles was up and out before Algy had even woken up. He was outside the Bodleian at nine o'clock sharp and was the first one in. He sat at one of the computer terminals and typed *Liber Tenebrarum* into the library catalogue search engine. Nothing. His heart skipped a beat. *Book of Darkness*. Nothing. Charles started to feel nauseous. He had skipped breakfast and now his gastric juices were trying to digest his own stomach lining. Perhaps he'd made a spelling mistake; he tried again: *Liber Tenebrarum*. Nothing. Could it all have been a hoax? A joke at his expense? Rupert had seemed sincere, but perhaps he was just repeating some rubbish that someone else had told him. Charles hurried over to the librarian.

"Excuse me. I'm trying to order a book, but it's not in the catalogue..."

"The electronic catalogue?"

"Yes."

"Try the manual catalogue … Over there."

Charles thanked the man and hurried over to the vast row of

wooden filing cabinets that housed the manual catalogue. It was arranged by author. "Shit!" But then a thought struck him: he went to the *A*'s and searched under *Anonymous*. He was amazed at how many books there were with no known author. *L-A*, *L-E*, and then there it was: *Liber Tenebrarum*. Charles's head felt a little light as he read the faded entry: *Anonymous. Liber Tenebrarum (The Book of Darkness)*. And nothing more. He filled out a request slip carefully, pausing to wonder how the librarian would find the book among 120 miles of underground passageways with no shelf reference. It was the librarian's problem, not his – he told himself – and placed the slip in the request tray on the counter. The librarian had disappeared, and Charles knew that it would take a couple of hours for his book order to be processed, so, lost in thought, he headed out for breakfast.

"Excuse me," it was lunchtime, and the *Liber Tenebrarum* still hadn't been delivered. "I ordered a book first thing this morning, and I was wondering when I'll get it."

"Did you put your request slip in the tray?" asked the man behind the counter.

"Yes, I did."

"Before ten?"

"Yes."

"I'm sorry, but all the book orders from this morning have been processed. It must have gone missing somewhere. I'm afraid you'll have to fill out another request slip."

Crestfallen, Charles filled out another form, submitted it and went across the road to the King's Arms for a bowl of soup and a pint.

There was a female librarian on front desk duty when Charles got back. And still no book. After making enquiries, he was told to wait – that his order was probably being processed and would arrive soon. A couple of hours later he was told to fill out another request slip. When it came to dinner time, Charles made a fuss, which only served to make the woman behind the counter defensive – even a little hostile. He put in another request form and headed back to college, arriving late for dinner, having missed all his Monday lectures.

"Where have you been, old man?" Algy greeted him with a booming voice and a Pimm's and lemonade.

"I..."

"Have a Pimm's!" Charles took the glass and perched for a moment on a chair – the sofa being crammed full of Algy's friends from the English Department.

"How was your tutorial?" he asked Algy.

"Oh, you know, old man..." Algy gesticulated theatrically, "I managed to throw something down on paper in the nick of time."

"Good, good," Charles downed the pinkish brown liquid, nearly choking on a piece of cucumber, made his excuses and retired to his bedroom. Algy watched Charles go, a concerned look on his face, then forgot all about it and turned back to a heated debate on whether Alejandro Jodorowsky really gave his teenage Down's syndrome actors cocaine during the filming of *Santa Sangre*.

The rest of the week turned into an Oxford version of *Groundhog Day*. Every morning Charles went to the Bodleian Library and ordered the Book of Darkness. Every day the book failed to arrive from the archives. Charles made enquiries, complaints and more enquiries, but none of them ever got resolved. He missed lectures, and took to writing all his essays in the Bod, so as to waste no time in filling out a new request form each time a book delivery failed to deliver. He stopped going to tutorials for fear of missing the book should it arrive, but as he still handed in first-class essays and wrote very polite letters to his tutors giving a variety of plausible excuses for his absence, there were no repercussions. Algy expressed concern at Charles's long absences and his increasing unwillingness to socialise. Charles tried to explain about the book, but his roommate seemed unable to understand, and merely tried to talk him out of his daily trips to the Bodleian. This state of affairs continued for a month.

Then it was Fifth Week, and Charles sat at his usual spot in Duke Humfrey's Reading Room, staring at the wall and waiting for the next book order to be brought up so that he could confirm the absence of the *Liber Tenebrarum* and fill out another request slip.

Darkness had fallen outside. Shadows started to gather in the corners and around the wooden bookcases. Charles's lids grew heavy from the fatigue of endless waiting in the airless room, and he caught himself dozing off. He shook himself awake and decided that leaving his post for a bit of fresh air and a quick cup of coffee wouldn't make much difference in the grand scale of things. He pulled himself up and strode along the shelves of ancient tomes to the exit. A female student smiled up at him as he passed her desk, but Charles didn't even notice. He hurried out of the building and across Broad Street to the café in Blackwell's Bookshop. There was only one person ahead of him in the queue, but even the three-minute wait was too much for Charles. He burned his tongue on the takeaway coffee and, forcing the plastic lid down as best he could, rushed back to the Bod. He stood outside and tried to wait for his drink to cool enough to be potable, but his anxiety became insufferable, so he discarded the coffee and ran up the stairs back to Duke Humfrey's.

As he entered the reading room, Charles suddenly felt cold. He stopped for a moment and hugged himself. The silence in the room was profound, and Charles noticed to his surprise that the handful of other readers who'd been in the room twenty minutes ago had all left. As he took a step forward, the lamps in the library flickered. The late medieval reading room was perpetually gloomy, but now it seemed to darken even more.

Charles hastened towards his desk with a growing sense of unease. As he approached, he could feel that something about his work station wasn't right – something was different. A tangible darkness appeared to have congealed in a rectangular shape on his table and, as he reached his seat, he realised what that darkness was. A shiver passed through his body. He slid onto his chair and sat motionless.

Now that he had what he'd wished for, Charles felt bewildered, exhausted and more than a little apprehensive. He stared at the book and had the ludicrous feeling that the book was staring back at him. It was a fair-sized volume, but not quite as big as he had imagined. There was a musty smell about it, and the binding – in some kind of vellum or hide – appeared to be rough-textured and a grubby greyish-brown in colour. On closer inspection, Charles realised that the tome was covered in dust. He leaned over the book and blew on it. Dust particles rose in the air, making him cough, but the book remained filthy. There was something repulsive about it – something that sent a shiver down the young man's spine, bringing to mind the expression that 'someone had walked over his grave'; something that made him want to get up and run from the library without looking back. Instead he reached out his hand.

As his fingertips touched the cover, Charles winced and pulled back in surprise. The book was burning hot. Ridiculous! He touched it again, and of course it wasn't hot – it was cold – ice cold, but that was no doubt to be expected of a leather-bound volume that had been sitting for years in an underground tunnel somewhere. Charles took out his handkerchief and tried to wipe off the grime. As he did so, he noticed a small round protuberance on the front cover. He turned the book over and found a similar bump on the back. For some reason he remembered the time when Lucy from Staircase III had gotten drunk and let him fondle her breasts before changing her mind and throwing him out of her room. He could clearly remember the firm, soft, rough feel of her nipples … A dire thought began to stir in his mind, but he pushed it away before it could fully form. The bumps on the covers were just imperfections in the leather, or perhaps the binding had warped lying there in the cold, damp catacomb from which it had come.

Charles continued to rub the cover. He took a quick look around, checking that nobody had entered the reading room in the last few minutes, and spat onto his handkerchief. It was easier to wipe the dirt away when the material was moistened, and the book itself seemed to relish the fluid, and scrubbed up a glowing golden brown. The texture left a little to be desired; unlike other leather-bound volumes that Charles had seen, there were pores clearly visible in the leather – tiny follicles that brought to mind the hairs that had doubtless once grown from them. But apart from the consistency of the hide, and the pair of hardened protrusions, the book was really quite handsome. Charles wondered why he had been so repelled by it at first. He ran his hand lovingly over the front cover, stopping only when his index finger touched the bump. Then he opened it. As he did so, the temperature dropped by another couple of degrees, the lamp on his table dimmed a little, and a sigh seemed to echo around the room. Charles felt an inexplicable stab of fear in the pit of his stomach and threw a quick glance over his shoulder, but there was nobody there.

The *Liber Tenebrarum* was a volume of about two hundred pages – some of papyrus, some of course parchment, most of the finest vellum. It contained no introduction or contents list, but launched straight into text. As Charles tapped his desk lamp to stop it flickering, and leafed through the pages, he saw that the book was an anthology of sorts. It was full of what looked like anonymous stories, some of which contained geometrical shapes and drawings. The handwriting was diverse; the texts were written in different inks and in various languages. With some of the languages Charles was familiar; others he could only guess at. But he had always been an exceptionally talented linguist, and felt confident that the first three years of his degree in Classics and Modern Languages had prepared him for the challenge. There was no contents list or index at the back of the book either, but

Charles did find something that might be useful in making sense of the book as a whole – an Afterword from the editor:

Editoris humilis post scriptum

Vobis qui fatum vestrum perfecistis scribam ego iste, qui sum in tenebras e luce egressus, lingua Creationis angelica ut anima vestra quid lateat in insidiis cognoscat.

Latin was second nature to Charles and he could read the words without effort, but comprehending exactly what the editor had in mind was a different matter. Charles could sense a veiled threat in there somewhere, and smirked at the tacit scaremongering underlying the editor's pompous message.

Directly beneath the Latin was a drawing consisting of two signs, almost touching. On the left hand side of the first sign was a shape resembling a tick, immediately followed by an upright cross that stood on a horizontal line, which led to a vertical line. At the top of the vertical line was a tiny loop and a small uneven horizontal line, ending with an equally small and uneven line that sloped downwards at a shallow angle. The second sign started with a short horizontal line, which led to an uneven V-shape. The left wing of the V was crossed by a line that ended in a small circle; the right wing of the V extended a little higher than the left wing and ended in a tiny rectangle.

The diagram perplexed Charles, but he guessed that it must be a signature of some kind. He read the Latin one more time.

An afterword from your humble editor: To you who have sealed your fate from one who went out of the light into the darkness. I shall write in the angelic language of Creation that your soul might learn what lies in wait.

Charles wondered what the angelic language of Creation might be – presumably, the beautifully presented, perfectly geometrically arranged collection of unfamiliar characters that followed on from the Latin, below the signature. If it really was a language, then Charles would crack it soon enough. After all, he had every book ever written in English at his disposal, and a good many others besides. But he was going to read the *Liber Tenebrarum* in the order in which it was written – or at least put together – and that meant that he would need a Sumerian-English dictionary to tackle story number one. For that's what Charles instinctively felt the cuneiform writing to be: Sumerian.

For a moment Charles's confidence wavered, and he wondered whether the whole endeavour was beyond his capabilities. He glanced at his watch and realised that the library would be closing soon. He had to hurry if he wanted to put in a request for anything that might help him decipher the first story. He ran his hand over the book one last time and turned to leave. As he did so, he thought he detected movement out of the corner of his eye. He peered into the shadows between the bookcases, but saw nothing. He cast a final look at the *Liber Tenebrarum* and headed towards the exit. As he turned right towards the door, something rattled in the half-light behind him. Charles froze. The noise came again – the discordant metallic sound of a chain being shaken. Charles turned around slowly and looked towards the bookcases in the far corner. There was a chained book on one of them – a gimmick for visitors on guided tours of the library to see how books were originally stored. When the library was first opened, each volume was attached to its bookcase by a chain long enough for the book to be placed on a lectern and read standing-up. Not the most comfortable way to study, but that wasn't Charles's concern right now. He looked fearfully in the direction of the chained book, but the sound had stopped and there was nobody there. He hurried out of the reading room, made a quick search of the catalogue, ordered up a couple of dictionaries and a battalion of text books on transliterating and understanding Sumerian, and left the library. It was dark outside and, as he hurried back to Univ, he couldn't quite shake the feeling that he was being followed.

"Back from the Bod, old man?" Algy got up and poured Charles a vodka martini, complete with stuffed olive on a cocktail stick.

"Indeed," Charles accepted the drink gratefully and smiled at his roommate.

"A smile!" Algy was pleasantly surprised. "The first one I've seen since you embarked on your quest for the Holy Grail."

"Hardly," Charles downed the drink in one, grimaced, then smiled at Algy again. "But the book finally arrived."

"The book arrived?" Algy was thrown for a moment. Charles nodded. "Oh … the book arrived! That's fantastic news … Was it worth the wait?"

"I'm not sure … I think so. I haven't read it yet."

"Why not?"

"Well, it starts off in Sumerian." Algy stared at his friend in stunned silence, then poured them both another drink.

Charles slept badly that night. Shadows flitted about his room, the tree outside scratched unsettlingly at the windowpane, and Charles imagined that he heard something whispering incoherently in the far corner. He tossed and turned, and when he finally fell asleep a little before dawn, he dreamt about a darkness that was gathering around him: a shapeless, nameless darkness that brought with it madness, terror and a paralysing feeling of helplessness and despair. When his alarm clock went off at 7.30, he woke with a start, his heart pounding. He got dressed, forced himself to eat a hurried breakfast, and raced to the Bodleian for opening time. His anxiety only subsided once he saw that the book hadn't vanished. Indeed, it was waiting for him on his desk, along with his Sumerian dictionaries and textbooks.

In the light of day, the small round bump on the front cover looked more disturbing than ever. Charles opened the book quickly and prepared to tackle the title of the first story. Cuneiform, it seemed, was a polyvalent script, and a single sign could represent a syllable, a word or even part of a phrase – not to mention that it could mean a number of different things. Charles knew that at the time the story was conceived, people wrote on clay tablets, and he hoped that whoever had taken the trouble to copy the whole text onto the papyrus had done so without any mistakes. He took a deep breath and started with the first sign. He looked it up in one of the dictionaries and proceeded to jot down all its combinations and permutations in a notebook he'd brought with him. Once he had transliterated all the signs in the title, he puzzled over which meanings were the correct ones. The process took him all morning. By lunchtime he believed that he had the title of the first story.

A cloud passed over the sun beyond the vast stained glass window at the far end of the reading-room, and the soft golden light was replaced by shadow. Charles shivered and stared at the title. He looked over his notes once more, but came to the same conclusion.

How the Great God Namtar was Summoned for the Purpose of Punishing a Woman.

Tired and hungry, Charles decided to have a quick lunch. He left his notes in the library and went across the road to the King's Arms. The sandwich he ordered took far too long to arrive and, when it finally did, he wolfed it down and ran back to the Bodleian. Despite the insanity of deciphering the Sumerian, Charles was desperate to carry on. His only worry was that, at the rate he was going, it would take him weeks just to read the first story. But he was wrong. Any self-doubt he might have had regarding his ability to tackle the task at hand effectively was dispelled as soon as he immersed himself in the text. He'd look up signs, work out a few words, and the meaning of a sentence would come to him instinctively – almost as if the book itself were his guide. In fact, with each passing hour that Charles spent with the book, the faster and easier reading it became. But also with each passing hour, the heavier a weight seemed to oppress his soul.

By the end of the day, Charles had deciphered an impressive three pages of Sumerian, and was about a fifth of the way through the first story. But as he closed the book for the night and packed up his notes, any satisfaction he should have felt at a job well done was crushed by the nature of what he had been reading. The story was a sickening one that might flippantly be described as a 'failed-rape revenge' tale. Narrated in the first person, it related with obscene relish the actions of a man living in the city of Uruk in – Charles calculated – roughly the middle of the third millennium BC. Having failed in his attempt to rape a young woman, the narrator decided to summon Namtar – the demon deity of death and pestilence – in order to avenge himself. Charles had reached the part in which the man decided to procure several children and offer them up as a sacrifice to his chosen god. The brutal images of the attempted rape at the beginning of the story refused to depart Charles's tired brain. As usual, he was the last student to leave the library. He was making his way through the reading room, lost in dark thoughts, when the rattle of chains behind him made him jump. He spun round, but, as on the previous night, there was no one there. The clanking metallic sound came again – this time off to his left. Charles ran out of the room and bounded down the stairs to the exit. He hurried back to college, all the time glancing over his shoulder in a fruitless effort to spy whatever it was he thought pursued him through the night.

"How was the book?" Algy held out a margarita and frowned, disturbed by the return of the morose look in Charles's eyes.

"Fine." Charles downed the sour liquid gratefully. "Thanks, Algy." He threw Algy a wan grimace masquerading as a smile and retired to his bedroom, leaving his roommate perplexed and worried.

From that day on, Charles was in the Bodleian every hour it was open. By the end of his first week's reading, he'd finished the first story. The narrator, whom Charles had come to hate – even across millennia – described in depth the ritual that he'd used to call up Namtar from the depths of the Sumerian underworld. Namtar, it seemed, had under his command sixty demons that could enter the human body in the form of incapacitating diseases. Bribed by the unscrupulous narrator with the burning alive of three kidnapped babies, the hellish deity sent his minions to accost the man's love interest with mortifying sickness of the eyes, heart, feet, stomach, head, back and just about every other part of her young body. As the poor girl writhed in agony, then slipped to the floor, weak and exhausted, the triumphant narrator was able to force his way into her home and into her devastated body. All this described in minute detail and with a sadistic enjoyment that, even in cuneiform, made Charles sick to the stomach.

The second story was written in Aramaic – 'the language of Christ' as Algy aptly put it on the one occasion that he actually managed to wrest some information from Charles with regards to what he was reading. As with the Sumerian, the title took the longest to decipher:

The Art of Death by Crucifixion.

After that, each sentence started to come together faster than the last. Charles read with a growing sense of dismay what purported to be the adventures of one Gaius Cassius Longinus as he traversed the easternmost reaches of the Roman Empire. In actual fact, the story was little more than an instruction manual on how to crucify someone with the maximum amount of pain over the longest period of time. Longinus, according to the writer of the piece, travelled much during his service in the Roman Army, and took a particular interest in observing local variations on methods of public execution, finding crucifixion to be by far the most diverse.

The author briefly digressed into a discussion about building materials – the best wood to use and the best metal for nails – before listing all the different types of crosses and the various ways of attaching victims to them. These ranged from a single upright pole to which a person could be nailed by one nail through the hands and one nail through the feet, to the two-beamed X-shaped cross to which one was nailed through each hand and foot, and the popular double-beamed cross which consisted of an upright pole and a cross-beam. The latter had a number of its own variations, not least the possibility of nailing a person's feet to it with just one nail or two separate ones. And that was where, according to the unknown writer, "the student of this profound science will find much that is of interest and value." For victims could also be nailed to the two-beamed cross upside down, with either their feet together or spread apart, depending on whether the cross-beam was placed closer to the top or the bottom of the upright pole. The process could be livened up further by lighting a fire at the base of the cross or by enticing wild animals to attack the hanging victim. Such was the author's excitement at this point in the story that he (for Charles assumed the writer to be male) recommended certain embellishments to the practice under discussion. He suggested the possibility of hammering nails into body parts that weren't essential to the traditional process – such as eyes, breasts and genitalia.

After a page of wild and wanton speculation, the writer finally remembered the protagonist of his tale, and returned to Gaius Longinus, stating that the centurion's career came to a very unsatisfactory end. For, after witnessing the crucifying of a Nazarene preacher, Longinus broke a cardinal rule of any successful crucifixion (successful, according to the author of the piece): rather than prolonging the man's suffering, Longinus ended it – by running a spear through the preacher's side – a spear that would become a weapon of power, coveted by warlords in years to come.

Charles had a throbbing headache. He buried his head in his

hands and sat in silence until a librarian came and informed him and other stragglers that it was closing time. This time he rushed out before the other readers to spare himself the rattle of chains that so often escorted him out of the reading room. But as the other students scattered in different directions along Broad Street, and Charles was left on his own, he sensed somewhere behind him the oppressive presence that had never quite left him since he'd opened the book.

Every day that he spent in the reading room, the hallucinations – as Charles tried to think of them – persisted. He heard whispers and moans that none of the other readers seemed to notice; shadows with no discernible source moved around him, and the rattling of chains unnerved him when he was alone. But worse than the spectral sounds and shades was the feeling that there was always someone watching him – someone or something that he felt, but couldn't see.

The third story was Egyptian. It told of a high priest of the Temple of Seth who invoked the object of his worship by re-enacting the culmination of the story of Seth and Osiris using his own younger brother. The unfortunate fourteen-year-old was lured to the temple and precisely dismembered over a period of hours, starting with that part of Osiris that was never found. Charles's sensitive mind, which was taking in these unthinkable acts one hieroglyph at a time, struggled to retain that orderly functioning that we know as sanity. During the day, his head was full of the vile images transcribed by the authors of *The Book of Darkness*, and at night his dreams were a chaos of torture, rape and mutilation; or worse still – he dreamed of the darkness that was coming for him – a little closer night by night.

Charles became increasingly withdrawn. He skipped meals and started to look positively gaunt. He scuttled about college like a beetle that's just had the rock it was hiding under removed, unexpectedly finding itself exposed to the discomfort of bright sunlight. He would scurry back to the Bodleian at every opportunity, and was always glancing nervously over his shoulder and jumping at his own shadow. Charles's anxiety edged its way toward depression. Algy worried about Charles, but could not quite commit himself to the serious business of helping him. In any case, he would not have known what to do. So he looked on in a concerned, but increasingly distant manner.

Eventually Charles stopped attending lectures and tutorials altogether. He didn't pick up work assignments and failed to hand in essays. His college tutor summoned him and tried to ascertain what was going on. Charles said that he hadn't been feeling well. He negotiated to be allowed to stay in college over the vacation, to make up for what he'd missed. If he passed a penal examination at the beginning of the following term, no disciplinary action would be taken against him. Charles promised to work hard over the break and to pull his socks up next term. Whether he believed in any part of the promises he made to his tutor was dubious. His intention was not to work on his degree subjects; he merely needed a place to stay so that he could finish reading the book.

Charles explained to his parents that he had to stay up at college over Easter to study. They were disappointed, of course, but they thought they understood. Their son had always been an outstanding student, and they were very proud of him. Ever since he was little, he'd amazed everyone with his ability to learn languages. Wherever the family holidayed with little Charlie, he became fluent in the local lingo within a week. Back home he would insist on giving directions to lost tourists in their own language, he would point out mistakes in inscription translations at the British Museum, and was able to read the Latin on gravestones long before he started learning the dead language at school. So although they'd miss him terribly, they believed that he was destined for greater things, and left him to do what he had to do.

"You're mad!" Algy hauled the last of his suitcases into the corridor, and came back in to say goodbye. It was the last day of term, and Charles looked pale and listless. "It's that book, isn't it?" But Charles shook his head firmly.

"I just need some time to think."

"Well, don't think too hard – it's not good for you."

"Okay," responded Charles.

"And don't sell the mantelpiece without me!" Charles's attempt at a smile reassured Algy a little. "See you in six weeks, old man," he added, shaking his roommate's hand warmly. But as he turned to leave, Algy felt an inexplicable pang of sadness.

Charles was exhausted and traumatised. He no longer wanted to get out of bed. He no longer wanted to live. No longer wanted to read the book. But it was inside him now – in his blood and in his bones. It had crawled into his soul, where it festered. And every day it was there in the library, waiting for Charles patiently – like a faithful lover or an old friend. And when the young man tried to stay away, his body was racked with terrible pain and uncontrollable nausea. Like a sick junkie he dragged himself to the Bodleian every day, wishing with all his might that the book not be there, but desperate to read it to the end.

The fourth story was written in Arabic in the eighth century. It told of the terrible fate that befell a scholarly man named Abdul who accidentally found artefacts of power that allowed the opening of a gate into a world of ancient and evil gods. Abdul tried to warn mankind of "the terror that walks outside and crouches at the threshold of every man." His punishment was terrifying. He was torn apart by "jackal-headed demons, emissaries of the gods of prey that gnaw on the very bones of men," and devoured by the Maskim and the Rabishu. His immortal soul was snatched by "vulture-faced Pazuzu, horned master of all plagues, four-winged lord of the desert wind that brings madness, with rotting genitalia from which he howls in pain through pointed fangs," and condemned to an eternity of torture – unspeakable, but nonetheless described in detail by the story's unnamed author.

Charles was able to read the fifth story without a dictionary, as it was in Latin. It concerned the flaying of a live child, in order to use its skin to create a homunculus. As the procedure inevitably led to the victim's death, the child had to be raped first in order not to incur the wrath of the goddess Diana, who was known to inflict severe punishment on those who murdered virgins. Charles couldn't eat after reading this particular story and, when he finally got to his bed that night, he couldn't sleep either. He anaesthetised himself as best he could with the aid of the alcohol that Algy had kindly left him, and lay awake – his eyes tightly shut lest he catch a glimpse of whatever it was that crouched, whispering, beside his bed.

The sixth story, written in Hebrew, was entitled *How to Reincarnate by Force the Soul of a Murderer for the Purpose of Creating a Dark Golem.* The author presented a complicated ritual with a foul necromantic rite at its core, then went on to describe the slow and tortured deaths that the monster which was produced inflicted on the enemies of its creator.

The seventh story was a German language account of the actions of a Prince of Wallachia in the mid fifteenth century. Vlad Tepes needed no introduction as far as Charles was concerned, but the detailed account of the impalings, burnings, skinnings, boilings and drownings perpetrated on the Prince's orders was none the less upsetting to him. It seemed that no matter how far Charles delved into the book, reading about the acts of torture, perversion and murder contained within its pages became no easier for him. He took to scrubbing himself raw in the shower every night, but nothing he did could stop him feeling soiled or ease the self-hatred that grew with each passing day. Still he kept going back for more.

A month into the Easter holiday, Charles was over halfway through the book, and yet it seemed like the self-imposed torture of reading it would never end. The extraordinary eighth tale, written in Spanish in the sixteenth century, commenced in Mexico and followed the adventures of one Juan Sánchez el Rojo, a Spanish cleric happily carrying the one true faith to the heathens, and performing all kinds of exciting feats in the service of the Spanish Inquisition. So fascinated did the padre become by the finer points of the human sacrifice carried out by the Aztecs, that he decided to dedicate the rest of his days to a search for the most terrifying method of killing he could find.

His new hobby led him to undertake the extremely dangerous self-appointed mission of penetrating the hostile kingdom of England – on an assignment that made every nerve in his body tingle. For he'd heard tell of a strange new instrument housed in the Tower of London that could make a sinner confess to every wrongdoing under the sun, and make him suffer in a hundred different parts of his body at once; killing him only when the interrogator was done. Connoisseurs of such matters said of the device that it was "a companion piece to the rack," and yet worked "in a way that was opposed to it." Try as he might, the curious cleric was unable to glean any further information, so he decided to risk everything to see this fine machine in operation. As fortune would have it, the protagonist of this swashbuckling tale came from a family no less wealthy than it was well-connected. And so contact was established with members of a secret organisation of the one true Church who, despite their Catholicism, had access to the best guarded places in the possession of the English Crown.

And so it came to pass that, with much cloak-and-dagger activity, and a considerable amount of money changing hands, our adventurous friend was smuggled into the Tower of London – there to see with his own eyes the peculiar device known as the Scavenger's Daughter. For it was one Leonard Skeffington – alias Skevington – Lieutenant of the Tower of London during the reign of King Henry VIII, who was the curious thing's father and creator. Quite how his name devolved from Skevington to Scavenger is a question for scholars of greater learning than that of the unknown author of Juan's story – and indeed than that of the priest himself. Not that the brave cleric cared much for philological niceties – he had things of divine importance on his mind. If at first he was a little taken aback by the unglamorous appearance of the object that he'd travelled hundreds of miles to see, his insatiability for observing new modes of torture was amply rewarded when the bribed guard showed and explained to him how the thing worked.

This particular rack functioned on the basis of compression rather than stretching. The instrument was made up of a single iron bar that connected iron shackles fastening around the feet, hands and neck. It pushed the head and knees together, compressing victims – in a foetal position – until they bled from their orifices and their bones broke. The unnamed writer of the tale described how "the priest's eyes shone with excitement, and he shook the hands of his guides a dozen times, so inspired was he by what he had seen." His expedition had been worth the dangers, even though he narrowly escaped with his life. For the very next day after his momentous trip to the Tower, war broke out between England and Spain, and Juan Sánchez barely made it back across the Channel with his life. Providence had been smiling on him, he thought, as for many years to come no amount of secret societies would be able to smuggle a Spanish Catholic cleric into England, let alone out again.

The ninth story was written in the first person, in an elegant, feminine hand. The author described the difficulties a noblewoman faced in the corrupt, power-crazed Kingdom of Hungary at the turn of the sixteenth and seventeenth centuries. She wrote of the man she'd been forced to marry as part of a loveless political match, and of the hideous men of power who gathered like vultures around her person and her wealth after his death. She wrote of falling in love for the first time as a woman in her maturity, and of her heartbreak when she thought that her young lover had left her on the eve of their planned marriage. Unaware of the conspiracy to kidnap her lover and keep him from her, she became obsessed by the notion that she had been abandoned because she was not in the first blush of youth. The idea so consumed her that she contrived at all costs to regain and retain the supple beauty that her skin had once possessed.

As she watched the young women and girls in her service, the countess realised that their skin was aglow no matter how hard they worked. It was youth that gave their skin that sheen – the youth that flowed in the blood of their veins. From that day on the woman contrived to create an elixir of youth by mixing young blood with herbs and a little goose fat. The ointment worked, but only briefly. The amount of blood she was able to mix and smear on her face was insufficient. She needed more. Her devoted servants brought her girls – fresh-faced maidens whose blood was not only youthful, but pure. Her servants helped her cut the girls and trap the blood, but too much of it was spilt. She used her learning to invent elaborate devices to hold the girls still and cut them slowly, to prolong and maximise the amount of the blood that could be used. But her impatience got the better of her – she wanted more blood. More and more girls were brought to the castle and bled to fill her bath. But blood congealed so fast and in the end the best way was to lie in the bath herself and have a girl trussed up above her. On her signal, the girl's throat would be cut and the countess would revel in the scarlet shower. But still it was not enough.

She dispatched servants to seek out girls, and scouts to look for her young lover. But it was not her lover who burst into the castle in the middle of a moonless night – it was a party of her enemies, using the excuse of missing girls and whispered rumours to violate her sanctuary. And now her haven had become her prison, as a court of men tortured her faithful servants to death and walled her up in her own chamber. And it was there, sealed in her premature grave that she wrote her story, watching her skin age and wither, and waiting for death.

Dear reader,

the tenth story proclaimed,

take heed and steel yourself for the most brutal and lubricious of tales. For depucelation of innocents snatched from their mothers' arms and ignominious acts steeped in bile and blood. The hero – and villain – of our tale is a man of noble birth, who once rode with the Maid of Orléans. But there are no depths to which perverse vanity and profuse lust will not drag even the noblest heart...

The French story was written in black ink, with a fine quill. *De Sade*, thought Charles, but he felt no satisfaction at the possibility of having found a long-lost story by the notorious author, foreseeing the atrocities that lurked within. The tale concerned a fifteenth century baron who gave up an illustrious military career to pursue artistic endeavours. Like Nero, perhaps, he fancied himself something of a poet, and wrote a play consisting of 20,000 lines of verse about the Siege of Orléans, in which he had taken part alongside Joan of Arc. There were 140 speaking parts, and 500 extras were required. 600 elaborate costumes were made for the occasion, worn for one performance, then discarded – to be replaced by new ones.

The nobleman gathered as big an audience as he could to view his magnum opus, and provided all its members with unlimited quantities of food and drink at his own expense. Having already spent much of his fortune on the creation of an impressive chapel in which he presided in robes he'd designed himself, not to mention a lavish lifestyle, the baron found himself broke, with no friends to turn to. Enter an alchemist, a magician of some power, who befriended the young baron and persuaded him that his wealth could be restored by the sacrifice of children to the powers of darkness. But even the alchemist could not have predicted – or perhaps he could – the enthusiasm and wicked pleasure that the young nobleman would come to take in the rape and slaughter of the innocent. It was only when the baron kidnapped a cleric in an attempt to snatch back one of the castles he had been forced to mortgage, that a formal investigation accidentally uncovered his heinous crimes. The author never said whether the baron's Satanic pursuits restored his squandered riches, but he did describe with clinical precision the hanging and setting alight of the disgraced noble.

Back at college that night, Charles spent an hour under the shower, trying to erase the filth of the day, but – as usual – his cleansing ritual failed to purify. He lay awake with his eyes closed and his hands clapped over his ears to shut out the whispering of whatever was leaning over him.

The eleventh story described the rivalry between two magick lodges. The grand master of one of the lodges held an all-too-realistic ritual reconstructing the rape of a nymph by a group of drunken satyrs. The stated aim was to evoke a physical manifestation of the god Pan, who would then violate the wife of the grand master of the rival lodge. This elaborate plan was outlined with much pompous philosophising by an author writing in English and hinting at his own identity by calling himself the Brother Who Would Endure Until the End.

It took Charles a long time and a great deal of trouble to work out the language of the twelfth and penultimate text, even though it was contemporary. The story was written in the Nilo-Saharan language known as Fur. More of a vision than a story – the vision of a twelve-year old Sudanese boy, noted down by village elders who believed him possessed by a saint. In a childish tongue he spoke of the century past and the century to come: of chimneys that spewed out the smoke of millions in a Europe occupied by men in black uniforms with silver lightning flashes and death's head insignia. Of the House of Karaman in which women were raped and forced to bear the children of their violators. Of burning oilfields and children dying under rubble. Of men tortured for years in secret places with no windows by governments that spoke of freedom, and of earthquakes, giant waves and death-bringing snow that devastated the Land of the Rising Sun. The boy spoke of the militias that raged much closer to home, of the destruction of his village and his own death under the curved knife of a tribesman butcher. Lastly he spoke of the war of the three great religions: of the annihilation of one by two, then the destruction of one of the remaining two by the other, and finally of the end of days in accordance with a hadith interpreted by the captive Ottoman scribe of the Letters of Light – in the year 2129.

The script containing the boy's vision did not burn with his village – even as the boy himself burned – but was taken by a tribal Emir and militia leader as a memento of sorts, probably on account of its pretty animal skin binding. How the editor of *The Book of Darkness* had acquired it for his work remained a mystery.

Charles was at a very low ebb. Term-time would start in a week and he had no energy to face it. There was one piece left to read – the thirteenth text: the afterword by the editor.

Charles's research into what the angelic language might be led him to the work of sixteenth century English mathematician, astronomer and occultist Dr. John Dee. It was claimed that the angels spoke to Dee and taught him their language. Armed with a body of work by the magician and his partner Edward Kelley, along with an array of modern dictionaries and textbooks, Charles had a chance of finishing by the beginning of term, but somehow he couldn't see beyond the book. He could no longer remember a time before the book, and he couldn't envisage a time after it. He had come too far to stop now, but he felt as if all the energy had been drawn from him and he wasn't sure if he could muster the strength to carry on. He opened the book and was about to leaf his way to where he'd left off, when the pages started to turn rapidly past his fingers, stopping at his target.

To you who have sealed your fate from one who went out of the light into the darkness. I shall write in the angelic language of Creation that your soul might learn what lies in wait.

It dawned on Charles: the words contained no subtle threat; the editor was merely stating facts.

Having read a number of spirit invocation passages in the previous texts, Charles now knew that the line drawing beneath the Latin was the seal – or sigil – of an angel. He searched through the encyclopaedia of angels at his disposal until he found a sigil with the distinctive tick and cross-shape at the beginning. It was the sigil of Samael. He looked up Samael and frowned. "(Hebrew: סמאל) (also Sammael) Angel of death. One of the seven angels of Creation. Archangel of the planet Mars. Angel of seduction and destruction. Fallen angel, leader of the evil spirits, ruler of the fifth heaven. Also known as Satan."

The library was very quiet. There were no mysterious susurrations tonight, and Charles listened for a while to his own breathing and the steady beat of his heart. He dismissed the angelic signature as cheap theatricality on the part of the editor, and delved into the final piece.

At first glance the text did not appear to be in any language as humans understand the term. But the letters that formed it were the most beautiful that Charles had ever seen. They were arranged in 49 tables. Every table was made up of 49 by 49 squares, each containing a letter. Square by square – letter by letter – Charles started to decipher the script. Each element of each table had 49 different meanings, and the ensuing experience was like reading 49 diverse tongues, all of them reverberating in Charles's head at once.

It was like existing concurrently in 49 parallel dimensions, and opening 49 different doors at once. And each door uncovered before the unfortunate young man a deeper circle of hell. For the words that Charles read assaulted him with every suffering, every perversity, every darkest fear; with horror beyond even the most twisted human imagination. It was like looking into the most depraved heart and sensing every perverse, twisted, homicidal sensation at once. Charles saw in an instant the torture, rape, murder, mutilation and genocide of millions. He saw every war crime, every disease, every form of tortured life and painful death. And he not only saw, but smelt, tasted, heard and felt every twinge of every tortured nerve. For the reading was like synaesthesia – Charles's senses intermingled and fused together, so that he smelled simultaneously the fear of the victims and the arousal of the perpetrators, he tasted the screams of the damned, he heard the blood and bile that flowed from a million festering wounds, he saw intolerable pain, and touched the anguish and hopelessness of the human misery that raged before him. All this as plain as a canvass spread before him, behind him and all around.

The perfect letters of the perfect words told of the infinite abyss of fire waiting for his immortal soul; of the darkness that had caught up with him, and of suffering, despair, madness and horror without end. Charles read and understood.

When the librarian made her closing-time rounds of Duke Humfrey's Reading Room, and asked the studious young man in the corner to get ready to leave, he made no response. She thought that he'd fallen asleep at his desk, and touched his arm. He did not move. Bending over him in the half-light, she couldn't see that his eyes were open and staring. She shook his arm gently, crying out in alarm as his body slumped forward and his head hit the table with a lifeless thud. Dictionaries and textbooks fell to the floor, but *The Book of Darkness* was nowhere to be seen.

TIM JONES

PROTEIN

I wake to the stink of piss and shit, to cries, to moans — my own among them. My left arm is heavy and swollen with pain. My legs ache. I am in darkness. It is cold, very cold. The floor is rocking under me, rocking like the sea.

My right arm seems unharmed. I lift it cautiously, explore my face, feel the dried blood caked on my forehead and cheeks. My tongue flicks out, tastes copper, withdraws into my mouth. I am very thirsty.

All around me, voices are crying, pleading. Something skitters across the deck by my feet. I am standing, restrained by ropes, my legs half-bent, my head slumped forward. I lift my head and the pain intensifies.

As my eyes adjust, I realise that it is not completely dark. To my left, light filters in around a rectangle of metal. A door, then.

To my right, a groan, a grunt. The smell of shit intensifies.

I try to remember how I got where I am, and work out what might happen next. My head feels thick, fuzzy, thoughts circling just out of reach. I was walking, I was walking . . .

I was walking by the shore, looking for any edible jellyfish that might have washed up overnight. I saw the boats as they came around the headland, heard the noise of their engines, saw their livery. I ran to warn the others, but it was much too late for warnings.

The door opens, and a hammer of light beats on the anvil of my skull. In they come, big, strong, ruthless. I can make out four of them, one woman, three men. They seize two of us, one to my left, one to my right. The man to my left goes limp and does not resist. The woman to my right resists, twists in her restraints, tries to bite an arm. The big man in his silver and black uniform has a gun in his free hand. He raises the stock and crashes it once, twice, thrice onto her head. A dreadful crack splits the sudden silence. The woman slumps to the floor.

"Idiot," says the woman in silver and black as she helps the big man pick the woman up. "Do you enjoy picking splinters of bone from your teeth?"

They leave, dragging the limp woman, the still-struggling man, through the doorway. This time, my eyes are well enough adjusted to the light to make out steps beyond.

We are locked in the hold of a boat, and now, despite the continued pain in my head and my arm, memory is coming back. With it comes fear, a fear stronger than any I have known, even in the depths of the storms that seek to tear all land in two, because I know why they have locked us here, and what comes next. We should have kept a better watch, I think. We should have been born in better times.

Twice more the door opens, twice more a pair of us are seized.

The second time, in the light from the opened door, I see that Doc Bryant has been taken. He does not struggle. His face is set. He knows that all his knowledge of life before the Drowning, all those stories, are useless now.

Some pains increase. Others fade. Time crawls the long watches of the day. I drift away.

I wake to find strong hands upon me. I stare at close ranges into faces flushed with triumph and exertion. Their breath stinks.

Struggling will get me killed, and though not struggling will also get me killed, I choose the easier course. But my leg muscles cramp agonisingly: I cannot walk. When hitting me across the back of my calves makes no difference, my captors shrug and drag me out of the hold and up the steps. I whimper as my legs bang against the iron steps.

Sunlight floods my eyes. I keep them tightly shut as long as I can, but when I open them, I see all that I have feared: our island taken, our town burned, and death among the ruins.

We have lasted longer than most. Across the scattering of islands with which we traded, rumour has long spoken of the marauders from the frozen South, a people perpetually hungry for meat to stave off the cold and the six months' darkness. Once, there would have been seals beyond number for them to eat, and an ocean full of whales and great pale fishes. There were no seals now, and no whales, and no fishes: only creatures too small to see and the great fleets of jellyfish that prey on them.

As the frozen continent began its long unfreezing, the Antarcticans tore it apart for its treasures of ore and coal, built and bunkered ships, and sailed north. Across the Southern Ocean, island after island fell silent: some ships that approached those islands were never heard from again, while others returned to report scenes of burned houses and old, discarded bones.

Our island was the smallest, the furthest from Antarctica, a mere speck on the angry Southern Ocean, with the hidden treasures and deadly perils of the mainland only hours away. We told ourselves the marauders from the South would pass us by, that they would not find our island among all the miles of water. We were wrong.

They have built a great bonfire with wood salvaged from the ruins of our village, and they sit around it, exulting in their victory, their bellies filled with the flesh of my friends. At least my family, my sisters and my mother, did not survive the other dangers of this world long enough to suffer this fate.

A ring of stakes, as tall as a tall man, surrounds the bonfire and the revellers. They tie me to a vacant stake. Doc Bryant is next to me on my left, close enough that we can talk. On my right is a little girl I barely know. She is sobbing. I want to call to her, to tell her it will be all right: but we both know that is not true.

"More meat!" comes a cry from beside the fire. Four of them rise. They start towards the Doc and I, and in an abject moment I pray to whatever God has deserted us that they pick him, not me. They stop and look between the two of us, a tall woman and a short, stocky man.

"Too stringy," they say. And they make for the little girl.

"No!" I hear myself cry. It is as of little use as my earlier prayer, as little use as the girl's screams. What they want, they take. They drag her to the fire, and then, as I watch, unable to look away, they rip her arms and her legs off and place them, the fresh blood still spurting, on iron skillets that sit atop the fire. They sever her head, then pick up her still-bleeding torso and throw it to their snapping, snarling dogs. They take the brain somewhere I cannot see, somewhere I do not want to see. I begin to cry.

"They'll get what's coming to them," says the Doc.

"How?" I demand, both angry at the interruption and glad of the distraction, wishing I could wipe the tears from my face and the snot from my nose. "Who's going to stop them? Are you, Doc?"

"No, but at least I know what will. Look over there."

He points with the only thing free to point, his head. Following his lead, I see two figures shuffling about uncertainly between the ring of seated Antarcticans and the fire. One of them suddenly bursts out, for no evident reason, into a long peal of laughter.

"What's their problem?" I ask.

"Their brains are their problem. Eat enough people, and you eat someone who carries a disease of the brain – I've seen it before. The laughing disease, it's called, or the shaking disease. I'll wager these cannibals kill and eat their own when times are hard – the strong devouring the weak. But that only spreads it faster."

I watch as the contents of the little girl's sliced-open skull are shared around the fire, like a particularly fine delicacy. I watch as the wavering figures wander back and forth, sometimes coming near enough to us that I can see the spasms of shaking that animate their bodies, that I can hear their low mumbling. I see them reach for the delicacies being offered around the fire, and I see how they are fed scraps, just like the dogs. At times, they lurch towards us, and are driven back by our guards. And I feel a bitter satisfaction that in the end they will share our fate, and that their death will be slow and lingering.

The night wears on. The wind rises. At intervals, more wood goes on the fire, and more lives are taken. Still the Doc and I survive.

I see couples depart hand in hand from their stations by the fire, hear groans of pleasure from somewhere at my back, beyond the reach of the firelight. The shambling ones draw nearer to the fire.

"If they come for me before they come for you," says Doc Bryant, "keep your eyes peeled."

Approaching dawn is paling the sky, and I have begun to think that they have forgotten us, when they come for us: as always, two to each victim. We are the only two left on this side of the fire. There is no doubt what will happen. I feel surprisingly calm: at least the uncertainly is over, and the end is very close. Though I do not struggle, it takes the cannibals a long time to untie me: they are the worst for wear, or for wine. Soon this will all be over . . .

And then a man screams to my left, and it is not Doc Bryant. He must have kept something sharp with him when he was captured, one of his knives or needles. The heads of my two captors snap towards the noise, and I twist from their grasp and run, out of the circle of firelight, into the night.

I have no idea where I am running: the only destination in my mind is away. I can hear shouting behind me, but if Doc Bryant has also managed to escape, we are better off separated. He will have to take his chances, as I am taking mine. I reach the far side of the field in which the fire has been built – a field that was once a farm – and plunge into the thickets of bushes, parched and thorny, that cover the centre of our island and climb up towards its summit above the southern cliffs.

As I struggle on, I quickly become enmeshed, and then halt altogether, the unwelcome centre of a thicket. I cannot go forward. Going back will be hard enough. Thorns ahead of me and thorns behind.

I crouch and listen. Nothing but the wind, insects, the sound of distant surf.

Have the cannibals retreated to their ships? Are they about to depart – might they already have left? Most importantly, is anyone else left alive? If they are, it is my duty to help them — and besides, anything is better than this uncertainty. I need to know. As the night's stars slide down the sky, I extricate myself from the thorns and begin to creep downhill. Nothing stirs, no-one leaps out at me. I creep closer, only a fringe of trees between me and the outskirts of the village.

Then two of them appear round the corner of a house, a big redhead and a smaller, slighter man with blond hair. I duck back under cover and fight to remain still. How pink they are, how sleek – but the left hand of the blond trembles a little as he walked, and his head wobbles from side to side. His stride is not confident: he shambles.

"I say we don't bother," says the redhead. "I say we load up the meat and get out of here."

"We need more," says the shambling man. "More food."

"Where we're going, there'll be enough food for us all. Whole cities, full of soft people, not like this stringy lot."

"Might not be there," says the shambler. "Must eat more before we go."

The redhead looks at his companion. "You really have got it bad, haven't you?"

"No, good!" says the shambler. "Good if we eat."

"Come on, then. Let's see what's left to eat."

They turn back the way they came. As quietly as I can, I follow them. They are approaching the place of the feast.

"All gone," says the shambler. "All gone!"

He is right. There is nothing there now, nothing but ashes and bones.

Then, with shocking suddenness, the shambler turns on his companion, grasping him by the throat, trying to bite him. The redhead is taken by surprise at first, but then wrenches himself from the shambler's grasp, revulsion in his features – even these cannibals, it seems, can feel revulsion – picks up a bone, and bludgeons the blond man to death with it, hitting him over and over again until he is no more than a twitching mass of tissue and bone on the ground. The redhead hits him one more time, and he is still.

"Fuck," says the redhead. He turns on his heel and walks away.

I feel the shuffling behind me before I hear it, hear it before I see it, see it just in time to evade the hands that clutch for me, the nodding heads, the awful, vacant smiles. I move forwards, towards the village. Perhaps I can outrun them among the buildings …

I do not get the chance. The man has returned, and in his hands, he holds a long torch, its end a bundle of flaming rags. The shamblers ignore past me and go towards him, their hands outstretched, beseeching. He waves the torch at them when they come too close, then plunges it into the dry thatch of the nearest hut. It catches eagerly, and I can see other plumes of smoke rise from further away.

They are firing the village. They are firing the island.

The three shamblers advance towards the redhead again. He snarls and menaces them with his torch.

Then he sees me retreating towards the scrub. "There's that fucker who got away, boys!" he says. "There's your dinner!"

The shamblers turn their backs on the burning village. They look at me. They begin to run.

So do I.

At first, my desperation is enough to overcome my injuries and my tiredness, and I put on a spurt of speed that outpaces what they can manage. But as the island begins to slope upwards, I am soon reduced to a walk, to a panicked crawl, my legs burning, my sides heaving.

At the top of a small bluff, I dare a glance backwards, over the burning village, over the fire that has spread to the dry scrub, to the distant sea. Boats, dark and somber, are departing for the north. Refreshed, replenished, with bellies full of protein, the cannibal fleet has set off on its mission to conquer the mainland. I hope that wide land will swallow up the cannibals as effectively as it swallowed the civilisation that once lived there.

There is no longer anything I can do to affect that. I turn my attention back to my surroundings. For the moment, there are no signs of pursuit. Could I double back, make my way back to the village, scavenge for food and weapons amid the ruins?

A long burst of laughter, carried uphill on the breeze, tells me I cannot. My only option is to keep climbing: and as I turn to do that, a head, nodding, drooling, breaks cover not twenty feet from me. The face broke into a smile, into raucous, hysterical laughter. I turn and run, crashing through thorns and thickets, pulling myself up by twisted roots and tangled branches. Whenever I pause to catch my breath, I can hear them behind me, their progress as laboured as my own. But they keep at it. The cannibal fleet may have left our island behind, but the fleet's remorseless determination still animates these castaways.

I know there can be only one end to this, but still I keep climbing, though my lungs burn and my right leg is dragging behind me. I feel fingers clutch at my heel. I kick them off. I scramble another few feet, drag myself over broken rock, heave myself atop one more outcrop, and emerge abruptly onto the peak of the island. Two steps in front of me, the island terminates in a great cliff that drops sheer down to a fan of debris at its bottom. Built on that fan is a little fishing village, the one place that I hope may have escaped the attention of the cannibal fleet. Looking down at its ruins, I can see that it was the cannibals' first port of call.

Above me, the sky boils with cloud. Far below, the sea eats away at the island. It will never be satisfied until everything lies beneath the waves. I stand a footstep from eternity. Behind me, I hear noises, laughter, chitterings, bodies clinging to life until the last possible moment. They will do anything for another mouthful. They will do anything for protein.

Well, they are welcome to it. I stand with my back to the sea. I watch them come, their mouths drooling with hunger and anticipation. I wait until they are upon me, until feeble hands drag at my limbs, until yellowed teeth snap at my neck. Then I throw my arms around them and arch backwards, throwing myself off the cliff. Though they mewl and scramble to break free, I take two of them with me.

The third, stronger, eludes my grasp. I fix my gaze on him as I fall. Hands shaking, head nodding, he stands atop the cliff as the smoke of the burning island billows up behind him: Man, lord of all he surveys.

JAMES WARD KIRK

BLOCK

Block is a giant. Block's soul is diminished, however, so he slumps. His heart hurts and he sleeps on the floor of his home. When his heart hurts, when the oxygen to his brain slows, I show him the moon. His dark suit is tailored to fit, but doesn't, like the rest of him.

The murder scene is larger and bitterer than even Block. Blood can never completely be washed away from this kitchen. Some small part of this human sacrifice shall live here forever, even when the house is lost to time; some soft cell of her melting into the earth below, a specter eternal also haunting Block until he offers his mortality to the universe.

The partibus corporis of this woman, the parts that comprise the human body, are displayed for review. Next to each organ is a small yellow sign with a number embossed in black, quite in contrast to the red—but not all blood is red. Liver blood is as black as hell—perhaps God's comment upon the human condition. The numbers run high as nothing much remains inside Mary's habitus.

The refrigerator kicks on.

Her eyes stare at Block from atop the refrigerator. Her face, deftly removed, is placed perfectly around the eyes. She seems more curious than angry. Her heart is in the sink, with fresh apples. Her intestines hang from the ceiling like sticky flytraps and are already at work. The buzzing is loud. The woman's brain is on the counter next to the microwave, split in half, and smells like fresh mushrooms.

Block's feet are too large for crime scene covers. He reaches into his jacket pocket and removes a roll of green-black thirty-gallon plastic trash bags. He uses a shoestring to tighten one around each calf. He steps into the lake of blood, sending ripples like lunar tidal waves splashing against the floorboards. Block cannot avoid all the hanging entrails, and flies angry for being distracted form an anti-halo around his head. Congealed blood mixes with his hair, clings to his face and shoulder and as he turns away, I know a tear forms in his eye.

Block imprints her pain upon his soul, incapable of not, of not knowing, not absorbing; like hovering near a loved one, a cancer patient, and listening to the final murmurs of life.

"This is the twelfth of the first," he says. His voice is as big as his body, and in the other room, a paramedic began weeping.

Block bends at the knees as if in prayer. He removes a tongue suppressor and gently pushes at the stomach; he sniffs gently at the cut esophagus and says, "Peppermint schnapps." *This beautiful girl was just having a little fun, perhaps a first date.*

The Coroner tells Block he shouldn't have done that and Block tells her to go fuck herself. Block will read the woman's report, words surgical and clean as if she is above human sentiment. He has absorbed the facts he needs from this theatre of the absurd.

Block walks to the edge of the kitchen and removes the bags from his feet. He steps into the hallway. People move away from him like sheep and he their Shepherd. "What is Mary's last name?" He knows her name is Mary. All twelve of these poor souls are named Mary.

"Benevolentia," the Coroner says, still new and unaware of the anger residing within Block.

"Mary Benevolentia," says Block.

The Coroner starts, "It means . . ."

"I know what it means," Block says. "It's Latin for 'good will'."

The Coroner enjoys the last word. "The subject's liver is in the refrigerator. The time of death is compromised."

No, thought Block, its *Mary's* liver, and it's the time of life that is compromised.

Like his wife, Luna, she is strangled, purple-black bruises, with a scarf. Block places his right hand upon his chest. His heart hurts. Again, I show him the moon and the man on the moon smiles. Block shrugs it off, but he is transfiguring.

2.

Alexander Lystan is shopping for a silk scarf.

"For your wife?" asks the sales girl. She is perhaps twenty-six. Her red hair is the death of her. I love her.

"No," *It is for you.* "Which one do you like the most?" Lystan is tan, thin, and handsome. He is charismatic, like sunsets and prophets.

"That's easy," she answers, choosing a green scarf the color of spring grass. The Eiffel Tower is patterned into the silk scarf.

Lystan asks the girl for her name.

"Abby," she says. She has a name badge: Abby Grwanski.

How many Grwanski's are there in the phone book? He wonders, *surely not many*, and he is right; later he will find her on Facebook too.

Lystan gives the girl some cash and concludes his transaction. He neatly folds the receipt in half and places it in his wallet. Lystan has seventeen similar receipts at home pinned to his bedroom ceiling.

Lystan moves artfully toward his Vienne French Four-Poster bed. He is nude, semi-erect, and carries the scarf with him. He sighs as he lies down upon five thousand dollars in silk bedding. He ties the scarf tender and tight around his neck, a knot perfect for choking oneself. He takes his fully erect member in his right hand and begins strangling himself with the scarf in his left.

Lystan is not beaten as a child; he does not go hungry or want for things other children less fortunate than him envy. He is a bright and meticulous student and earns the praise of his teachers. Peers admire and like him, and seek his company and companionship. Girls want to kiss him.

He does not kill small animals. He loves Mother and Father.

He does not murder until one night under a harvest moon, in the company of a young woman from a neighboring university—a spontaneous event while he is trolling the streets for pleasure.

Lystan is quite bored with life. He absorbs the information his professors offer effortlessly, and in a short time understands their areas of expertise perhaps even better than they. He is comfortable materially. Money is no problem for him. Mother and Father take good care of him, when they visit and when away. Lystan wants for nothing but his lust is overwhelming and sovereign. He does not work.

Lystan and Amanda are sitting in a white convertible, the top down, fondling one another and Lystan is unable to achieve an erection. An idle thought excites him: he might enjoy taking her life. He begins the process, uncertain at first, fumbling around until he discovers that he truly enjoys the eroticism of his hands upon the girl's delicate neck. His erectile dysfunction problem is solved, as the natural life of the young woman flees him.

His orgasm is a life-changing event, for us all.

Sated, he looks about and finds no person has witnessed his murder. As he returns his attention to his date, he discovers the rub—moonlight reveals his fingerprints upon his lover's throat.

Lystan drags the young woman's corpse to a copse of fir trees and hides it there. He fumbles around in the dirt, comes upon a sharp rock, and obliterates her throat and his fingerprints. Returning to his car, he finds the woman's purse on the floorboard, and her red scarf. He uses the scarf to lift the purse, and his member stirs at the sensation of silk rubbing leather. He leaves the scarf and the purse beside the corpse.

The memory of the scarf elevates his spirits for several months. Then reminiscence is not enough.

Lystan researches serial killers. He does not delude himself. He understands his undertaking. The first to show himself on Google is the Green River Killer. Lystan turns away in disgust. He will kill regular women. How nice to begin with a policeman's wife? He trolls the local newspaper online and reads about a giant. My giant.

Lystan sat up on the bed, frustrated. He cannot climax. He has a man in mind. The man's name is Alexander Mort. Mort is stealing his limelight.

Lystan and Mort killed in harmony one night, a year ago, albeit on opposite sides of town and each unaware of the other, but Mort gets the headlines. Television is all-atwitter about the man named Mort. Mort is brutal. Lystan likes to think of himself as human. To discover his art regulated to the second page of the paper, a mere afterthought of reporters because of Mort, infuriates Lystan. He is chagrined that he and Mort share the same given name.

The police are bereft of information regarding Alexander Mort. Lystan is not. He has seen Mort. He has witnessed the work of Mort and reconnoitered the aftermath. Mort is a brutal, ugly and stupid man. Lystan resolves to assist the police; since they cannot locate Mort, then he shall support them in their endeavors. He has all the necessary information.

Lystan decides he will visit the public library, access a public computer, and send the giant all of the information he needs to apprehend Mort—all contained in a tidy email from a temporary anonymous account.

Lystan freshens up. He's decided one more night of surveillance is required before he greets his new lover Abby.

3.

Mort is comfortable in his lair. He lies upon an abandoned mattress. He thinks he is alone, but I wait.

He lives in an abandoned stand-alone wood frame building once owned by a Russian who sold tobacco out the front door and heroin out the back door. He lives here alone, having frightened away other would be squatters with a simple meeting of the eyes. One man did not look away from Mort's eyes and died.

Mort is not retarded, as Lystan suspects, but he is brain damaged because of poor nutrition as an infant and repeated punches and kicks to the head as a toddler. He is self-aware.

Mort is good with his hands partly because of growing up on a farm in California and working construction as a teen. He has secured his home from would be intruders. Police are content to leave it alone, as the building's outward appearance resembles any other well-kept building closed because of the poor economy. The windows are covered with thick plywood. The doors are secured with premium locks. Drug dealers and prostitutes do not frequent the corner—and this *is* a surprise to local police. As one patrolman said of the surrounding neighborhood, "You can't throw a rock in this area without hitting a whore or a drug dealer." Mort does not tolerate people near the building, transient or not.

Mort often sleeps in the chicken coop as a child, especially when Mary has masculine visitors. Sometimes they stay awhile but eventually they all leave. He does not mind sleeping with the chickens. The mild cooing of the sleeping chickens calms him. The stench is preferable to that encountered in the house.

At age five Mort's mother takes him between her legs. Mort's penis is huge, but it is not his member that visits her dark place. He is awkward at first, and struggles for breath, but Mother That Becomes Mary is an excellent if cruel tutor.

At age eight, and beyond Mort's understanding, his member becomes tumescent when servicing Mary; Mary is outraged: "How dare you!" She lights a cigarette and burns his penis. Mort never experienced another erection after that, not even upon awakening or if needing urgently to urinate, but the burning of his penis continues. A ritual develops.

Mort's penis is scarred from base to tip. When he touches its leather-like surface to urinate, he becomes furious. A rage builds. The rage becomes frenzy. He uses a phone book to find Mary, and his wrath is released with Mary's death.

For a while; alas, the rage builds like the need for inhalation. Mort will find Mary again and she will die like an exhalation— spent. In death, Mary is Momma again.

Mort moves to a sitting position. He is troubled regarding the last Mary.

She says, as the knife descends, as its point penetrates, "I forgive you."

Several minutes pass before her words come to life in his thoughts, like a ghost ascending from its grave. He is sitting, a kidney in each hand, and he hears her words echo in his mind like the "who?" of an owl.

No one has said these words to Mort. I try to tell him "I'm sorry" but he isn't ready.

Standing behind Mary's house, hiding in the shadows of the alley, Mort says, "I forgive you."

He looks back at the house and sees a man entering. Mort returns to the house and peers through a window. He sees a man standing there, holding a silk scarf. Mort gets to know this man named Lystan.

Mort stands and leaves the mattress. He urinates into a coffee can. He returns to his mattress and lies down again—and at that moment, another voice cracks through his consciousness.

The voice says, "I am God. I forgive you."

Mort brings his hands to his head and says aloud. "Thank you, God." Mort has heard of God. He is a kind man who lives in heaven. Heaven is a nice place.

God says, "I demand recompense."

"What does 'recompense' mean, God?"

"You must give Lystan to the giant."

"Okay, God." Mort knows the giant. He always goes to Mary. Mort thinks the giant wants to put the Mary back together again, and this is fine because the Mary is now cleansed.

Mort rises, and begins the work God has given him. Crucifixion comes to mind.

4.

Lystan sits in his car outside Abby's apartment building. Abby's apartment is at ground level. Lystan is happy about this as it will make his entrance and exit less dangerous. There is a copse of maple trees behind the apartment complex and a small lake. As Lystan contemplates the subtleties of variance between suffocation by silk and drowning, he sees Mort leave the apartment carrying Abby.

Lystan understands this is no coincidence. Mort must have some plan. Lystan is not concerned. Mort is a brute, and it follows that his plans are brutish. He watches without agitation as Mort disappears into the woods behind the apartments. He wonders if Mort can get home without interference from the police. He imagines Mort making the trek home with success, as Mort enjoys at least the cunning of a coyote carrying its prey. He knows where Mort lives, and even has a master key for the locks. Lystan is comfortable. He has planned their eventual congress.

Lystan starts his car and leaves for Mort's den.

He will wait in the rafters, like a bat.

5.

Block awakes from his slumber. The moon is bright for a moment, but then clouds move across like a sheet over a corpse. The floorboards beneath him creak, as he rises to his feet, as do his bones.

Block has not slept upon his bed since Luna died. Yes, I speak of me in third person as I am more than Luna the dead wife.

Block's hungry; he goes to the kitchen and finishes the remains of a pizza. He washes it down with tepid tap water.

Block checks the voice mail from his phone. *If you want to find Luna's killer, come to this address.* Block writes down the address, but memorizes it and forsakes the paper beside his phone as he leaves his home.

Block looks to the moon. A soft breeze scuttles leaves across the driveway. They sound like the scraping of bones.

Block looks at the Crown Vic assigned him by IPD. His Ford pickup truck is parked on the other side. He looks at the sky and with all of his agony wishes to see the moon shine. He is rewarded, and shines too; but the moon is quickly covered again by copper clouds, like pennies placed upon the deceased's eyes.

Block knows that if he chooses the truck he will die.

Block has lived too much, suffered the touch of madmen, tasted the ugly redolence of death, and outlived the only human being that ever loved him. Even for a giant, death cultivates life too dear to be abided; death draws final breaths like moths to a light. Death draws even giants.

Block arrives at Mort's warren in his truck.

The door is open and Block enters. He has a police-issued Glock in his right hand. Block takes in the scene before him. He sighs deeply, one of but a few sad exhalations.

Mort is nailed to a cross, a crucifixion in all ways realized. A spear protrudes from his side. A nude young woman lies at his feet, dead. She wears a silk scarf around her diminished neck.

There is candle light.

Block is not surprised when the man on the cross moves, but is surprised that it is not he that is addressed.

Block hears the man say, "God, have I recompensed?" He watches the man on the cross die, consumed within a shudder, his question answered.

Lystan emerges from the shadows. He holds two sticks, one in each hand. "Old Mort was a fool."

Block sees Lystan as one sees the world as it slips away forever. Block sees in the shadows surrounding Lystan, as appendages, or tumors, a beautiful cow, a dragon and a ram.

Lystan says, "I bring hell with me. You shall see."

Block places a bullet between the eyes of Lystan anyway. *Why not?*

Block's heart hurts, spasms, and he bends to his knees as his heart spasms again. He drops face-first upon the floor and before the cross. He pulls arms under him, puts his hands to his chest, as if cupping his essence. Block's heart stops and the giant dies. And I am gone from this place.

Lystan bellows. No one hears his cry.

6.

The giant sees radiance in the distance. I too shine brightly. He is in a line of people heading toward the light.

Block says, "The line to heaven is a long one."

The man just in front of him tugs at the giant's arm.

Mort says, "At least we're in it."

"You got that right," Abby adds.

I have made a home for my giant on the northern shore. We will watch the tide move in and out under a full blue moon. Then Block will hurt no more.

CHANTAL NOORDELOOS

THE DOOR

It all started with that goddamn door.

It was a Friday night when Mila, age seven, ran down the stairs as if something was chasing her. She threw herself at her bigger sister with such force that the popcorn Jen had been eating fell to the ground, like a rainfall of confetti.

"Take it easy," Jen laughed, trying to wrench free from the little girl's iron grip. She brushed the spilled popcorn back in the bowl. "What happened?" Mila refused to answer and she buried her face in her sister's shirt. Jen grabbed the remote and pressed pause.

"Young lady," Jen said, strict now, "you should be in bed."

Mila sobbed slightly and Jen forgot that she decided to be

strict with her. Moving to the new house had been hard on Mila. Their mother's marriage with Judd had been hard on both of them. Ever since their father and brother died, their mother had changed. That was over seven years ago, when Mila was nothing but a little bump in Mom's belly. Their mother stopped showing Jen any form of affection and she never even bonded with her new baby girl. Ten-year old Jen became both mother and sister to the newborn Mila. She kept looking after the little girl, even now, after their mother had remarried.

Mom moved the girls into Judd's house after the wedding. It was much bigger than their apartment. From the moment they first met, Jen decided she didn't like Judd. She wasn't sure why she disliked him. It could be because of the strange, quiet way he looked at her. Sometimes she caught him staring at her, and it creeped her out. *Maybe he isn't that weird; I'm just jealous because Mom loves him and spends time with him. Maybe I just want Mom to love us instead.* She found it easier to blame Judd. In her head she had labelled him 'the freak.'

Since moving, Mila had become more quiet and introverted than before. Jen had no explanation for her little sister's behaviour; as far as she could tell, there was nothing out of the ordinary. She watched Mila like a hawk. The girls didn't need to move to a different school; Judd's house was closer than their old apartment. Even Mom was home more often, though she still didn't bother with her daughters too much. Yet Mila's uneasy behaviour became worse.

Every night she experienced nightmares, often waking up screaming. Jen worried about her sister and she took her into her bed most nights, hugging her tiny body to her own, wishing she could take Mila away from here.

"It's the door," Mila said, her voice a soft whimper. "It scares me." Jen wrapped her arms tight around her little sister and sighed. She knew the door the girl was talking about, the one to the basement. Jen had to admit, it was a creepy door. Big and heavy like a bomb shelter door, partially hidden under the stairs that led to the second floor, which cast it in permanent shadows. It was *ominous*.

"It's just a door, silly girl..." Jen's tone was soothing and she stroked the unruly blonde curls. "It can't hurt you." Her lips touched the soft strands of hair and she hugged Mila even tighter.

"There is evil behind it," Mila said with the voice of an ancient woman. Her eyes were round and she stared into the distance. "I can see it in my dreams; old evil, looking for sacrifice."

Jen tried not to laugh. Mila sounded like a little old lady when she said things like that. "Don't be silly," she said, pushing Mila away gently. "Here, let me show you." She unfolded her legs and jumped up from the sofa. Mila, realising too late what was happening, cried out in fear.

"There is nothing behind that door," Jen said. She looked over her shoulder to Mila, who just stared at her. With quick strides she walked towards the door. Behind her she could hear Mila get to her feet. A strange feeling settled in her stomach when she approached the stairs. Suddenly she wasn't so sure anymore. *What if there was something down there?* Her stride wasn't as confident anymore, her steps were smaller.

"Don't go in," Mila pleaded. Tears filled up her big blue eyes, and Jen held back a little. She wanted to show her sister there was nothing scary behind that big door, but to be honest, she was a little afraid herself.

"You know what?" she said with the tone of voice of someone who was about to reluctantly compromise. "I will just open the door and turn on the light. We won't go in, okay?" Mila nodded, barely.

Jen felt her heart pound in her chest and her muscles cramp up as she brought her hand down to the door handle. *What is wrong with me?* she thought. The handle felt cool to her touch.

After taking a deep breath, she pushed.

"It's locked," she said with a mixture of surprise and relief.

"Why would it be locked?"

"To keep the monster in," Mila said. Her face looked wise beyond her years.

"Well, then you have nothing to fear." Jen ruffled Mila's curls and pushed her gently towards the stairs. "Off to bed with you." Her hand slipped into Mila's small hand and together they walked up the stairs to her sister's pink and white bedroom. The little girl quickly crawled between the pink and lavender princess sheets, pulling them up to her chin. Jen sat on the edge of the bed and tucked her in.

"We have nothing to fear from our dreams," Jen whispered. "We are the heroes in our dreams and if the bad guys win, all we have to do is wake up." She shot Mila an expectant glance. "Okay?"

The girl nodded in response, pulling up the sheets a bit further so that they covered her nose. Her big blue eyes peered at Jen over the sea of pink.

"I shall be downstairs, and I will watch over the door," Jen said, trying to sound as brave and noble as she could. "So, it won't hurt you." Mila nodded again.

"Good girl." She bent over to kiss her little sister on the forehead and noticed Mila was tense. A sigh escaped from the depth of Jen's chest; she knew this night would be filled with Mila's nightmares, but there was nothing she could do.

Feeling heavy-hearted, Jen closed the door behind her and walked down the stairs. On her way to the living room, where the movie she had paused was still beckoning, she stopped in front of the big door. She stared at it and realised the fear was creeping up into her stomach again. There was a noise. It was faint, but she could hear it, like something scraping, or perhaps dragging something behind that door. Jen knew she was imagining it. It was a big metal door. She had seen it opened only once, but she remembered thinking the basement was built to withstand war. There was no way she could hear something move around inside … and yet she did. The sound made her blood run cold.

She walked away, almost ran, away from the door. She jumped onto the sofa, landing a little clumsily on her leg, and quickly turned on the movie, the volume cranked up to drown out the scraping noise that still echoed in her head.

That night, Jen slept poorly.

"What's behind the door under the stairs?" Jen asked the next morning at breakfast. Judd, who read the morning paper while he was eating his eggs, did not look up. The egg-covered fork he held paused in mid-air.

"Basement," he muttered, his eyes fixed on the paper.

"What's in the basement that's so important that you have to lock it?" She had the sneer down well, she thought, but Judd refused to look up at her. It was like having a conversation with a brick wall. His body language frustrated her. *Asshole.*

"Basement's dangerous." The bite of egg disappeared in his mouth. "Loose shelves, sharp tools, that kind of stuff. No place for children." The paper rustled as he turned the page; he gave it a little shake to get rid of any creases.

"Dangerous?" She almost laughed at him. "I'm seventeen, Judd. I think I've passed the age where you had to protect me from the wickedness of sharp tools."

He gave no response and just shovelled another fork full of egg into his mouth.

"Mila is just a kid," her mom said, scooping eggs onto her own plate from the skillet. She looked pretty in her fuzzy pink bathrobe and her light makeup. "Keeping the door locked is in her best interest." Jen was about to argue, but her mother shot her a warning look.

"You have no business in that basement," Judd finally said. "None of you do." It surprised Jen that he even shot a glance at her mother. Mom didn't seem to notice, but Jen felt a very uncomfortable feeling stir in her stomach again.

"It's my stuff down there." Judd put down his paper and fixed

Jen with an intense stare. "And my stuff is none of your business." His words took the fight right out of her, and Jen just nodded wordlessly. That was the end of the conversation.

As the weeks went on, Jen realised she was a little obsessed with what was behind the door. The reasonable side in her understood that even Judd had a right to his privacy. *Maybe he had a hobby?* If the door hadn't made her so uneasy, she would have let it go. But sometimes she heard the scraping behind the door. Jen didn't even like walking past it.

It's just a door, she told herself. *You're acting like a baby.*

Mila seemed to get more afraid of it as time passed and Jen started to have nightmares herself. In her dreams she was locked in the darkness of the basement, and something was there with her. Something old and very evil… and it was hungry…

When the nightmares came, Jen paid more attention to what Judd did when he was home. She didn't look away when he stared at her with his cold grey eyes. His habits fascinated her. Judd's routine was pretty regular: he would get home, have a beer, go to his office and stay there until dinner. After dinner he would go out with their mom, and the two would return around eleven. This was most nights. He never went into the basement. *If his precious stuff is there, why doesn't he ever go down there?* The more she studied him, the more she was convinced something wasn't right.

There were small clues, like the books on the top book shelves in the small office, where Judd spent his time before dinner. Jen went through his stuff when she had the chance. She found old, leather-bound tomes with writing that looked ancient and foreign. Not Latin— Jen knew a little from school. Not that she was an expert, but it was enough to recognise Latin when she saw it, and this wasn't it. *This is older than Latin, much older.*

Within the brittle, age-stained pages, Jen found horrifying prints of wicked-looking demons who engaged in tearing up medieval human beings. The details on the pictures were horrifying, far more elaborate than anything Jen had ever seen. The ink was faded on certain pages, and the leather was crackled. One of the books had a thick, gold pentagram on the front.

I'll bet Judd is a Satanist, Jen thought. The tomes made her even more wary of her stepfather. She pictured him performing rituals in a long dark robe in the basement. In her mind's eye she saw Judd decapitate a goat and pour the blood on a sacred circle. *I'm being silly* again, she thought, *these books don't prove he's a Satanist. They could just be collector's items.* She wasn't convinced. *On the other hand, who would want to collect these sick books?* Besides the strange tomes, there was no proof that Judd did anything out of the ordinary, and she couldn't even see where he would find the time for rituals involving goat sacrifice. Judd was either working or with her mom; they were practically attached to the hip. *Unless Mom is a Satanist too.* Jen shook the idea off.

The books bothered her, and she couldn't stop thinking about them. However, no matter how much she looked at him, Jen couldn't find much fault in Judd's behaviour until one night, when she woke to go to the bathroom.

She heard someone walking down the stairs, and a rush of excitement fluttered through her stomach. It was Judd. Quietly she followed, and from the landing saw Judd opening the basement door and going in. *This was it.* Jen's heart pounded in her chest as she sat at the top of the stairs, waiting. She was so tense she forgot to breathe at times.

After about fifteen, maybe twenty minutes, she could hear his footsteps, and she quickly got up and scrambled to her room. By the time she reached it she was out of breath, but she could hear his footsteps go past her room over her soft panting. The door to the bedroom across from her opened and closed and Jen tried to calm herself down. *He goes in there at night.*

The next night she stayed awake and she was pleased to see that Judd went down to the basement again. She was right; the night before hadn't been an accident. Judd went down every night, and he waited until he believed everyone was asleep.

Why would he wait if he had nothing to hide? She knew there was something wrong with Judd. He was doing something in that basement that could not stand the light of day. *Your private things my ass, Daddy Dearest,* Jen thought bitterly, *you are up to something, and it is bad.*

She realised she was more afraid of her stepfather than she was of the basement. He did something down there, kept something down there. Part of her was convinced she knew what he was and why he needed his locked basement. It was bad and she knew Mila could feel it too.

I am going to find out what you have there, fuck-wit, Jen thought. *And when I do, I am going to call the police.* She considered calling the police now, but she doubted they would come for a teenager who complained about her stepfather locking the basement door. She needed proof. Jen promised herself she would be careful, but she wanted to find the proof.

One evening, when both her mother and Judd were out playing cards at their neighbour's house, she decided to investigate a bit more. The card games always lasted deep into the night, so there would be time. Jen made her way to the master bedroom. She caught herself walking quietly, but realised this was silly. Mila was playing in her room and her parents were out, yet somehow she felt scared.

The master bedroom was twice the size of her little room. A plain beige carpet covered the floor and there were mahogany wardrobes lining the wall. A large double bed stood against the south wall, and Jen could see her mother had tried to spruce the place up by adding some colourful orange and green pillows. It didn't help; there was something depressing and bland about the bedroom. It reminded her of Judd. *How can a man like that make you happy, Mom?*

Jen looked around before she started searching. She wanted to disturb as little as possible in this room, so it would be better not to randomly ransack the place. She moved very carefully. *Like a ninja,* she thought to herself and almost laughed out loud. It took her a while to find out Judd's hiding place for the key to the basement. He always used it at night, so Jen knew he had to keep it in his bedroom.

Where would someone hide a key they use every night? She wondered. Her eyes scanned the bedside table and she decided it was probably in there. The first drawer she opened was filled with clutter. Her fingers gently rummaged through boxes of aspirin, shoelaces, a pair of nail clippers, cough drops, tissues and other such items. *Nothing.* She opened the second drawer. It held another one of his strange books. This one looked newer but the way the spine was cracked and how it fell open easily indicated it was well-read. To her horror she saw a drawing of a beautiful, but terrible, naked woman with black eyes and wild flowing hair, straddling a man who screamed in horror. The woman held her own breasts, her nipples peeking through her fingers, her forked tongue licking her lips. The picture gave Jen the creeps.

On another page the same woman seemed to give birth to a grown man, who was also screaming. Perhaps she wasn't giving birth to him; instead of coming out of her body, he could be sucked in. The thought alone horrified Jen so much that she quickly closed the book. The image of the woman stuck in her mind's eye. There was something ancient about that creature and yet somehow familiar. *Is this who you worship, Judd? Is she a goddess, or a demon?*

After further inspection she found a small silver charm that resembled an eye. It hung from a leather thong. The whole thing looked evil. *Satanic,* Jen thought again. She dropped it into the drawer, feeling an irrational sense that the pendant could betray her somehow. When she looked up, Jen glanced at the picture on the night stand. Her eyes met the eyes of her mother's, who smiled up at her from the frame. She grimaced at it and suddenly noticed something. From behind the frame she saw something sticking out. It was a large metal key that looked like it might fit in the basement door. It wasn't a very clever hiding place; Judd's complacency worked to her advantage. Jen put the stuff in the drawer back more or less the way she found it and grabbed the key. *I'm going in.*

Before she went downstairs, she peered around the corner of the pink bedroom to see what Mila was up to. The little girl brushed the hair of one of her Barbies and she hummed a tune. She would be fine for a little while, and that would give Jen some time to snoop around.

The door looked even more ominous than usual when she walked up to it, as if the shadows played tricks on her. A cold sweat appeared on her brow and on her back. *You'll be fine*, she told herself, but she wasn't convinced. Her hands clammy, she put the key in the lock. It fit. Slowly she turned the key, and with one hand on the door handle, she pushed the door open.

Her eyes needed to adjust to the darkness. In order to turn on the light she had to step on to the little platform that led to the stairs. Jen took a deep breath and stepped inside. Her fingers trembled but she found the light switch. A sickly yellow light illuminated the basement below, creating deep and threatening shadows in the corners. The basement was empty. Spooky ... but empty. Jen threw her head back and let a relieved breath escape. Whatever she expected to find there, it wasn't there. Maybe she never heard something; maybe she heard rats ... who knew?

She considered taking a look around, but decided against it. *No need to go down there, in the dark.* There was nothing here to find. She turned around and a loud thump almost made her scream out loud. Shocked, she clutched her chest and looked downstairs again. At first she saw nothing, but then her eyes locked on something. There, in the corner of the basement, she could see another door. It was hidden in the shadows, behind a rack of shelves, but it was there. *Fuck.*

Hypnotised, Jen slowly descended the stairs. Another thump, causing her to flinch and start, but she walked on as if the door was beckoning her. The shadows seemed to move around her, but no matter how frightened she was, she had to know what was behind that door. A scraping sound, like a large metal chain dragging across the floor, made her stomach flip. For a moment she needed to dig deep inside herself to find the courage to open the second door, but open it she did.

And then she had to swallow back a scream.

In the middle of the room sat a teenage girl, of thirteen, maybe fourteen years old. She wore a filthy nightdress that must have been white once. Her hair was blonde and it hung in greasy tangles about her soot-stained face. The girl scrambled to the farthest wall of the small room she was in, a thick chain moving with her. Large eyes filled with terror looked at Jen between the tangles of her hair. A smell of faeces and stale body odour pervaded the room. Jen thought she also smelled vomit. The floor of the room was absolutely disgusting.

"Oh my God!" was all that Jen could say. Her heart felt like a lump of ice that sank to her stomach. She desperately searched for something comforting to say to the girl, but she just couldn't think of anything to say.

That bastard, she thought, *that evil, Satanic bastard.*

She thought of Mila's words: *"There is evil behind that door and it needs sacrifices."*

Was she his sacrifice?

What was he going to do with the girl?

What sick rituals was he going to perform?

This would be enough to call the police. She would see that he would be locked away for good.

"Are you going to hurt me?" the girl in the corner asked. She shivered.

"No," Jen could hear her own hoarse voice. "I am going to help you."

The girl looked at her, nodded and sat up a little. "Can you do my hands first?" she asked. "They hurt." She held up her hands to Jen, and to her horror the teenager could see that the girl had two large metal hooks protruding from her flesh. It took all of Jen's strength not to throw up right then and there. She swallowed back her bile, but could not force herself to move; she just stared in shock.

"Jen?" Mila's voice came from directly behind her and Jen spun on her heel, worried that Mila would be traumatised by the sight of the girl.

"Mila, go upstairs," Jen commanded, but the little girl peered around her and saw the other girl.

"The monster," she cried, her eyes wide. Jen grabbed her sister and forced the little girl to look at her.

"This is not a monster, Mila," she said, feeling strangely calm now. "This is a victim, a little girl who has been locked in our basement." They stared at each other and Jen knew she had to say what was on her mind. "She was locked up here by Judd." Mila blinked.

"Go upstairs and phone the police," Jen said calmly. "Tell them we are in danger and give them our address." Mila nodded slowly as if in a dream, before she turned around and ran upstairs. Jen squeezed her eyes shut and inhaled deeply before she turned to the girl who was cowering in the corner.

"Please help," the girl pleaded. "If he comes back, he'll kill me. Like the other girl." Her words were like punches, Jen could almost feel them hitting her gut.

Like the other girl.

She swallowed and stepped closer. The girl held up her damaged hands. Dried blood covered them, crusty and foul; the wounds looked as if they were festering. Thick yellow ooze escaped from skin riddled with pustules. It was the scariest thing Jen had ever seen. She wanted to faint; the room spun around her as if she were standing on a ship on a stormy night.

I can't touch that, Jen thought. *It's a hook in an actual hand. It runs through an actual human hand. The hand of a young girl.*

Something in the back of her mind egged her on. If she did

it quickly there would be time for squeamishness later; she could faint when the police came. Her eyes met the girl's. She could see they were wet and puffy from days of crying, but they were brave now and Jen had to be brave too. Determined, she grabbed the girl's wrist. She could feel her fingers tighten around the warm flesh; this girl was burning up. The skin was soft and swollen with pus. *Why hadn't the girl tried to pull them out herself? Maybe she had but she couldn't?* Jen wished she didn't have to touch the hooks, or at least not have to look at them as she did. If only she could grab the hook with her eyes closed … but she couldn't, she had to keep watching what she was doing. Another moment of eye contact, and the girl nodded slightly. She was ready, and so was Jen. She wondered if she had to pull fast or slow and decided slow would be better; fast would probably do more damage. This was after all a hook, not a band-aid.

Three, two … she counted in her head, *one.*

She pulled.

At first the hook did not move, and Jen felt a slow panic creep up from her stomach, like a desperate spider with long hairy legs. She pulled again, a little more forceful this time, and the hook started to move. The flesh around it gripped at the metal, and it got stuck on the bones of her hand, but it moved. Jen couldn't look at the girl's face; she was too afraid to see the pain there. She was more afraid of the pain than she was of the blood. Thick dark blood, tainted with infection, started to pour from the wound. Jen wondered silently if this girl would ever survive, if she would not simply perish from the infection. And she wondered if the girl would still want to live after this, if the trauma would not have ruined her life forever.

I'm so sorry, Jen thought.

The hook pulled free and the girl let out a small sob that spoke of pain and relief at the same time. Jen fell back slightly, hitting cold concrete. She groaned, trying to hold back the stomach acid that still pushed against the back of her throat. The hook was still in her hand, and with a grimace she threw it aside. Her clothes were covered in the girl's blood, and part of her just wanted to run and scream and cry, but the girl was already holding out her other hand.

This is one tough little bitch, Jen thought. And if the girl was tough, she had to be too. Feeling exhausted she scrambled to her knees and leaned towards the girl again. Jen didn't hesitate this time and she grabbed the second hook. It felt easier, faster, less scary. This looked like it was going to work … she was going to rescue this girl. Her hands were slick from blood and it was difficult to grip the hook, but she did it anyway. She felt pride now.

"You little cunt," the voice behind her said and Jen felt ice filling her up. Her stomach tried to escape through her throat, and her muscles cramped. She didn't see the speaker, but she could see his reflection in the girl's fearful eyes. He was here, and he was going to kill them both.

"You fucking little cunt."

Jen slowly turned around, feeling the fear tingle in her hands and in her cheeks. In the door opening was Judd with Mila behind him. Her eyes were big as saucers and Jen just gawked at her.

"You got Judd?" she asked, not recognising her own voice. It sounded so far away and so small. Mila nodded.

"He has to help us with the monster," she said, hiding behind her stepfather's muscled leg. Jen felt the tears well up in her eyes.

"Judd *is* the monster, Mila." The tears echoed through her voice, "He locks up little girls and he hurts them." Jen pointed at the girl behind her. "Look."

"Get away from her," Judd ordered. His voice was as dark as his murderous eyes. "Jen, get over here, now."

"Please," the girl cried, "Don't let him hurt me anymore." Jen still looked at Mila.

"You were supposed to get the *police*," she said, her tone accusatory. "You were supposed to help." Jen turned around and with a quick motion pulled the hook from the girl's hand. The girl cried out; she obviously wasn't prepared.

"You run," Jen ordered, hoping against her better judgement that Judd would not kill her because he married her mother. "You just run." The girl nodded and crouched into a starting position, cradling her wounded hands against her chest; she looked like she was about to bolt.

"Jen," Judd said again, "get your fucking ass over here."

And then Jen ran, straight into Judd. Her shoulder made contact first and she felt as if she had run into a brick wall. The man only took one step back, but he grabbed her with his large hands and threw her aside. Then he stood to face the girl, who had now got up.

"You're free." His words sounded more like a gasp. "Oh Jen, what have you done?"

Jen looked at the girl, she wanted to cry out to her to run, but the words died on her lips. The girl wasn't cradling her hands anymore, she was standing very still and very erect. There was something about her face that made Jen afraid now, something very dark. Jen realised it was the smile that frightened her.

"I'm free," the girl said. Her voice sounded old, not like that of a young girl at all, but like something ancient. Jen's head ached. *I heard it wrong, I must have. It's only a young girl.* The girl took a step forward and kicked the chain on the floor. Mila screamed and ran away.

Her eyes glanced to Jen and then she turned to Judd again. She moved a step closer and Judd tried to take a step back, but something had him glued to his spot. Jen could see him struggle, but his legs refused to move. There was fear in his eyes. The girl took another slow, deliberate step towards him, her dirty feet making a wet noise on the concrete. She was standing right in front of him now, and Jen could see that Judd was crying. The girl's hands, covered in blood, toyed with his shirt. Then she punched him, not hard, but her hand went through his shirt. Judd opened his mouth in a silent scream, puffing out nothing but air. The girl pulled her hand back, revealing a long strand of glistening intestine that she coiled around her hand. Slowly, she pulled. *Oh god*, Jen thought. *Oh god, what have I released?*

"I am free now, guardian," the girl said. "You have failed."

Blood flowed down Judd's abdomen, staining his jeans a dark maroon colour. Their eyes met; Judd's mouth was slightly agape with a mixture of horror and sadness. She looked at him, placidly at first, but then her features changed and she was staring at him the way a cat stares at its prey.

"Please," Judd said, his voice barely audible. "Please." The girl shot him a look of disgust and gave his intestines one final yank before releasing them. The coil of warm meat made a sickening sound as it slid down his jeans. They made a wet plop as they connected with the concrete. The girl watched the intestines for a moment and then she looked at the man in front of her. She smiled and released Judd from whatever spell he was under. With a groan, his knees buckled and he fell to the ground. The girl stepped over him with the nimble movements of a cat. She turned to Jen, who cowered in the corner. *I am going to die next*, Jen thought.

"You have freed me," the girl said simply. "I will allow you to watch as I tear humanity apart." There was a cruel smile on her lips, a smile that Jen had seen before in her dreams. Then the girl, or creature, turned slowly away from her. Something deep inside the earth trembled with each slow and deliberate step she took. The darkness swirled around her like a thick black mist, a mist which poured from the basement door into a world ignorant of its fate.

In the darkness of the basement, Jen wept.

I'm so sorry.

W. H. PUGMIRE

DARKNESS DANCING IN YOUR EYES

The scent of night evoked him. Enoch Blake awakened and wiped the dust from his eyes. He thought he must have slept longer than usual, for his brittle bones were unusually stiff and difficult to move, and some spider had woven a web between his parted lips. His mouth always remained open when he slept, so as to drink darkness. It was Enoch's little theory that the darkness helped to keep him reanimated over the length of decades in which he semi-existed. Looking around, he saw that much had changed within the chamber wherein his master had worked with spells and philters and alchemy. The mangy room looked as if it had been vandalized, and much of the chemical apparatus had been smashed. Books had been removed from shelves and now littered the floor; furniture had been overturned and broken. But some of the room's wrack seemed to be the ravages of time, resulting in discolored wallpaper and brittle window shades torn and tattered. His master's desk remained intact, as did Enoch's favorite thing in the room—the full-length oval upright mirror. The dark glass of that mirror beckoned him, and he lifted his limbs to a standing position; but he did not step too closely to the mirror, for he did not want to be beguiled by its reflected shadow – the reflection that was not his own.

He saw it there within the glass, a thing of depth and dimension; and as he gazed at the image it began to coil, and by doing so it seemed to pull more shadow into it, so that it expanded and reformed until it aped a human figure. Its danse was seductive—Enoch could feel that movement reflected in his eyes, his eyes in which the other creature saw its own mirror image. Enoch watched as the figure in the mirror faded, he could sense the coiled image take over his eyes completely and weave its influence behind his eyes and to his brain. He suspected that this presence was that which remained of his master, the alchemist, who had a penchant for working with glass, with transmuting the components of glass so that it become something novel, something different and outré. Enoch began to feel that transmutation in the chemistry of his orbs, which chilled and hardened, which transformed from living tissue into something sleek and artificial. He was almost afraid to blink, worrying that the violence of eyelid movement might shatter the crystal of which his eyes were now composed.

Exiting the room, Enoch Blake walked into the night. The edifice in which he had served the alchemist had once been an isolated apartment building on a hill above the city, once teeming with occupants; but as those inhabitants became the occult toys of his master, the building became more and more isolated, abandoned, forsaken. For a long time it had been he and his master only who walked the building's dusky corridors; and then his master had gone away, except for that particle of him that existed in the mirror.

The scent of night aroused him; it amplified his sense and filled him with weird appetite. Enoch walked the silent night until he entered the place that took hold of his imagination. Although he was almost vacant of memories, he sensed that he had known this place long ago; for its rotting slabs were familiar, as were its willow trees; and when the wind picked up and moved the limbs of those trees, the sibilant sound was a noise that he knew. Other sounds came to him, or perhaps these were memories of sounds, of things that crept beneath the graveyard ground, muttering to the sod above them. Hadn't he been among their brood, long ago, moving through the burrows they had manufactured, sifting at times through the debris so as to break through the surface and leer at the moon?

There was no moon in the sky this night, and the dim stars above were very few indeed. He liked the lack of light, and smiled at the darkness above him; for darkness reminded him of his master, the alchemist who had found Enoch's special bungalow beneath the graveyard ground and spilled queer salts and liquid onto the earth, stuff that mingled with the mire and, sinking, sifted into the texture of his remains, transmuting Enoch's charnel nature so that he lifted out of shadow, split the stuff of earth, and stood before his master on the cemetery sod.

He stalked upon that sod again and saw the frolicker who capered among the tombstones. He could not ascertain the dancer's gender, for its lowered head was shaved and its uniform of pale linen might have been meant for any sanatorium inmate regardless of sex. When the figure stopped its movement and raised its emaciated face to his, Enoch recognized a degree of lunacy with which he himself had once been familiar, in some epoch of his existence. Thus he approached the mortal and allowed it to look at itself in the mirrors that were Enoch's eyes. The being danced

before the daemon, as the sorcery in Enoch's eyes lighted upon
the cavorting creature and entered the texture of its tissue, which
began to darken as shadow and break apart. Enoch could smell
the transmutation, for the dancer was but a whisper away from
him; and he was unprepared when one pale and solid hand, not yet
transformed into darkness, fell to Enoch's face and smashed into
his eye, his eye that broke into tiny shards by the violence of the
blow. His vision became so blurred that Enoch could not relish the
sight of the mortal's body, now a mound of black spectral particles
that sank into the graveyard ground.

Enoch found his way home, to the abode where he had
assisted his master when that alchemist had lived, where he served
his master still in some unholy way. He wanted to weep for the
destruction of his eye, but he was fearful that the gathered tears
would wash away remnants of that orb, and so his eyes stayed dry.
The building, as he approached it, looked more neglected and
lifeless than it had ever seemed to him, like some forgotten crypt
that, embracing Enoch, would hide him forever from the mortal
world. As he climbed the stairs that took him to the building's
door, he could hear the rising wind that sang through crevices of
rotting wood and he remembered a time when he had more of a
mouth and could whistle in accompaniment to such wind; but time
had withered his mouth so that its lips were now but two flat flaps
of thin and useless membrane. It was strange to experience, as he
entered the ruined room that had been his master's sanctuary and
laboratory, an ache of depression that blossomed as deep despair.
Enoch stood in that lonesome place and smoothed what remained
of his hands over his face, his throat, his chest. He pressed one
hand to the place where once he could feel his heart beat. Nothing
pulsed there now. He remembered how his master would touch
the blade of a ritual dagger to Enoch's breast and scratch a sigil
into his flesh, and how his heart would grow in strength as the
alchemist's lips smoothed against the wound so as to sup upon its
wet red nectar.

Movement in the mirror caught his attention. Enoch approached the mirror and stood directly before it for the first time. He saw the squares of polished glass with which the mirror was composed, and he remembered watching his master manufacture those oblong pieces of treated glass in his laboratory. Enoch watched the dark figure that was not his reflection and sighed at the way that figure danced before him; and he was close enough to the glass so that he could discern the pinpoints of cloudy light that were the figure's eyes. Those eyes were familiar, and the sight of them brought memory to Enoch's withered brain. He remembered those times when his master had taught him the alchemy of danse, had taught him how ritualistic movement could conjure impossible things. And so he lifted those white things that had once been hands and clacked their talons together, and he moved in time to the rhythmic noise. And he could feel the dark thing in the mirror reflected in his eyes, the one that was whole and the one that was shattered. Overwhelmed by memory and emotion, Enoch brought one talon to his breast, to the place where he had once been able to detect his heartbeat, nearly toppling when he detected a slight palpitation. Ripping his talon through his thin tissue, Enoch etched a remembered sigil, and he could not keep from weeping as he saw the slim stream of blood that seeped from the wound. He wept, violently, and the shards of his shattered eye broke free and fell onto the floor; but he did not care, for the dark figure in the mirror reached for him, brought its phantom mouth to his bleeding breast and kissed the wound. Enoch began to sing, as the sad pathetic remnants of his mortal frame dissolved as darkness that spilled into the mirror.

ROY C. BOOTH AND AXEL KOHAGEN

JUST ANOTHER EX

I follow people. It's what I do. I find out what dirty little secrets they've been hiding from the good people whose trust they've betrayed, and then I report back to whoever is paying my retainer. And my expenses.

The linoleum floor of the coffee shop, never clean to begin with, is wet and dirty with tracked-in snow and gunk. Were this place patronized by anyone other than college students, there would probably be a broken neck a day. But college students avoid death, more through luck than skill, and life goes on as usual. Bland, whiny indie-rock music plays on the stereo, and the thick smoke in our section feels more like fog than felon.

Tonight I'm following Neal.

Neal is young to be married. Very young. Perhaps too young. He's a tall, lanky kid. Red hair. Freckles. But it looks like he made up his mind in a hurry from what I can tell by what I see. His wife's a real looker. Drop dead gorgeous. Her name's Rachel. Dark hair and long legs. One of those gals who looks good no matter she's wearing. She says he first started acting odd around Halloween, muttering about a bunch of crazy stuff, "thin veils" and such. Something spooked him. By Thanksgiving he was constantly looking over his shoulder, acting like someone was watching him, following him. He was barely around during Christmas, their first time through the holidays as man and wife. He used to be the most doting of souls and now he's gone four nights out of five, and they only make love with the lights out. She notices and confronts him. He says nothing's going on, but he's still all jittery, still acting guilty. She decides she doesn't feel like waiting for him to slip up, so she calls me.

Makes perfect sense.

The music changes to something nearly as whiny and formulaic as the last song, Neal seems to be hearing a different song than the rest of us. He looks suspicious, like a man with secrets. Dark secrets. For starters, he sits alone. In the corner closest to an exit, so he can see everyone. Without a book, for fun or for study. No notes. No writing of poetry. No headphones. Nothing to wile the time away with. Just a cup of coffee. I'm the one tailing him, and I'm blending in better than he is.

Of course, Neal and I both know he has a rather big secret. See, five years ago, the winter of his senior year at some podunk high school about twenty minutes away, Neal's girlfriend at the time slipped off a ledge into the Mississippi river and drowned. Tragic story. Neal was walking alone with her at the time she fell, and he reported it immediately. Said she had been trying to balance on the safety railing and had fallen to her death. Well, when they found the body - or rather, what they found of the body - it didn't offer any help one way or the other as to why happened, or if foul play was involved, and so no charges were ever pressed. Her parents were very vocal about accusing Neal, but he was sort of an All-American boy, good looks, good on the football field and on the baseball diamond, and folks in typical small town fashion pretty much ignored them.

Neal gets up to leave. His coffee is maybe two sips closer to empty than when he got it. He takes it over to a big plastic tub for dirty glasses, sets it inside, and goes back to put on his heavy coat. I keep reading my paper (something about an outstate playwright who does shows on zombies). In Minneapolis, in the winter, leaving takes just a little bit longer. There are scarves to don, coats to zip up, and gloves to wiggle into. I wait as he goes through this ritual, and after he gets out the door I slide my arms into my coat and leave the *City Pages* behind. I zip my coat as I'm walking, pull the hood over my head, and shove my hands in my pockets.

It doesn't take long to figure out which he's went, and I pick up the trail again.

Her name was Wanda. Hair dyed jet black. All accounts suggest she was bad news, and the people I talked to were only as sad as propriety seemed to demand. She did everything rebellious kids do, and then she kept going. She'd been arrested twice (once for drinking, once for trespassing). Not only that, but Wanda was growing up to be like her abusive mother. So when she started dating Neal, everyone worried about him, but no one would say anything, figuring he was sowing wild oats, he'd wise up, and the itch would just pass. Common sense would prevail and he'd move on. But they all heard. Everyone heard Wanda berate Neal about the smallest, most insignificant thing he had supposedly done wrong. And when she turned up dead, I guess they figured Neal had finally had too much. But they apparently didn't blame him too much.

Neal turns left when he should go straight. He and I are

walking down a long bridge over the Mississippi. It happened here. They had been visiting on a college day, see what the college scene was like firsthand. Wanda and he were going to get an apartment together, after graduation, and rumor had it he was going to propose around Christmas. The rumor was also that she was pregnant, but when they found her body they found out she wasn't.

There's a small boy standing in the walkway. That's weird enough as is, because it's below zero and the bridge is not sheltered from the wind. Plus, there are cars hissing by to the left and to the right, making it very noisy. Neal slows down and stops beside the boy, and bends over.

At first, I think that maybe he was just trying to to be a Good Samaritan, and help the little tyke out. Then, a car comes by from behind me and illuminates the blue hood of the boy's coat.

There is no head inside.

No neck. No shoulders. Just an empty coat hood. When the car passes and the lights are gone, I can make out the outline of a face in the moonlight. Then, there is another car and again the hood looks empty.

I stop, light up a cigarette, and stare out at the river. Filthy habit. I can never fully quit smoking 'cause of times like this. It's a good excuse to just plant yourself in one spot and stare. Sad, really, we need deadly sticks of carcinogenics to give ourselves an excuse to stand in one place.

The cigarette also helps me keep my cool. And I really need that right now.

Neal sits down on the cold cement and looks up at his boy. Neither one is saying anything, though I can tell Neal is beginning to get all emotional and cry. They seem like statues, back lit by the cold moon. He starts jabbering, oblivious to anything else going on around him. I flick away the cigarette and move in closer so that I can hear what he's rambling on about.

The boy turns and points at me.

Neal's eyes get all wild like he's about to freak out, and then he just slumps, like all the air has been knocked out of him. Soon he's got his head in his hands, and starts talking again.

The boy just stands there.

"I didn't kill her. S-she was trying to stand on the rail and she fell. But … she caught herself. Wanted me to help her back up. And I just couldn't. It had been an awful trip and she had been so mean to me and she said she never wanted me to touch our son. So I just watched as she dropped.

"It wasn't till she was about halfway down that I realized he was still in there. When they found her, and they didn't find him … I thought I had imagined the whole thing. I thought I was crazy.

"One night I heard him. I came out here and he was standing, waiting for me. He's a nice boy. Such a nice boy."

As we watch, the child disappears. Neal stands up.

"You saw him, right?" Neal asks.

I nod.

"You were at the coffee shop, too," Neal said. He thinks, but he doesn't believe. "Are you following me?"

"Of course," I said. "It's what I do."

He believes it. "Rachel. Shit. I thought it'd help, if I married someone good, you know, better. Worthwhile. A better person than her. But I keep seeing our kid, can't get rid of that. It's like I'm stuck between two families, but no one would believe me."

I shake my head *no*.

"Well, then, what's it like?" He's looking at me like he's now relieved he's been able to say any of this to someone, like a great burden has been lifted so now he get down to business.

"It's not that," I say. "Rachel didn't hire me."

"Oh," he says. "Are you just … ?" He isn't sure anyone would want to stalk him just for the fun of it.

I take a step forward. "Someone else did."

There is a loud, violent thrashing in the water below.

"Wanda did."

Neal's eyes get all wild again, and then he jumps up. "She's dead," he says. "She's dead, she . . ." His voice trails off, hands tightening on the rail of the bridge, looking down at the water. The cars are going by quickly now, their lights strobing all about.

"Yes, she is," I say. I pull a coil of piano wire out of my pocket.

"Did you ... ? You have to be related to her."

I'm now within arm's reach of him. "No. She just comes around a lot, where I live. Not far from the river." I point in the general direction for emphasis. "She told me all about you, what happened that night, how you watched her die."

"Oh." He's really scared now, his eyes bugging out, waving his arms about like a human windmill. "L-look, I can pay you, pay you enough to, y'know forget about all of this, and-and-"

"No. Sorry. No can do."

He begins to dart away, but I get the piano wire around his hand and jerk it hard. I had practiced at home, with a bag of sand. She had watched me do it, bobbing in the nighttime throb of the river and pleased. I've always been the kind of guy who would've killed to be with a girl like Wanda.

The piano wire is attached to a three foot pole, kept hidden under my coat, which I wedge firmly into the bars. The wire cuts into his hands and he wails, thrashing about, but he did not fall. Instead, Neal swung there, like a clipped marionette, with the piano wire biting deeper into his wrist.

He screams.

"She wanted you to drop slowly," I say. He can't hear me, pleading and blubbering up a storm, but I say it anyway. "So it wouldn't knock you out. So you'd be awake."

She blooms out of the river then, her black hair blacker and her skin a mottled muddy river brown. No eyes - those were gone long ago. Her teeth have fallen out, too.

Neal sees her and screams. He tries to crawl back up the piano wire, but I had greased it and he only falls, causing himself more pain. He dangles about twenty feet above her, and from where I stand, it looks like her watery mouth was opening big enough to swallow us all.

He looks up to me, hoping I'd see something true and human inside him. Hoping I'd realize he deserved a chance to try again. A chance to live.

I just let him drop.

He falls into the water wailing, and she takes him into her arms. They go under the waves in a splash and then there is nothing. I wait for her to come back up, to give me a look. Some kind of sign to somehow let me know I had pleased her, done right by her. But there is nothing, and the water quickly becomes still.

I was alone on the bridge.

Frustrated, I trudge to my car, which I had the foresight to park near the bridge. I let it warm up a bit and I wondered if I'd see her later, by the river. I try to convince myself Wanda would come back for me later, hoping against all hope. I tried, at least.

When I get home the snow is coming down even harder. I park the car, get out, and go down to the riverbank, looking for any sign of her in the river. Or anywhere else. I stumble back into the house and pour myself something to drink. Somewhere, Neal's flesh and blood wife is probably doing the same thing wondering where he is, too.

I have sliding doors that face the river, and in front of them I notice there is a small circle, about a foot or so in diameter, where snow is not collecting. The section of deck there is clear, like under a car that's just been moved.

There is a knock at that door.

I look out to the river. This isn't like her.

The knock at the glass door grows louder.

And then it hits me.

I open the door and something whisks by me, something clammy, cold.

I down my drink and look at the hazy, cool air hovering before me. It isn't enough that she used me to get her ex back. No. She wants me to take care of their brat as well.

Hope you're havin' fun, Neal, I think. *I hope you're havin' fun.*

I turn on the TV.

THOMAS A. ERB

SPENCER WEAVER GETS REBOOTED

"Be cool, or be cast out."

Some people look back fondly on their days of high school with distorted, nostalgic lens-filled memories of Friday night footballs games, the prom and backseat gropings. Unfortunately, for loner Spencer Weaver, all the dreaded halls had to offer were nothing but gaping, pus-filled scars – both on and deep under his pale skin. For the lucky few, the same halls of Carrigan Springs High School were paved with gold and they ruled them with cruel, iron fists over the unfortunate peasants. Spencer hated the school along with all of its troglodyte students. He couldn't get away from the backwater farm town soon enough.

Everyone viewed him as a loser; the fat geek, with enough loose skin to make his entire body look like a turkey neck-another genetic legacy from his absent mother. His last memory of her was her sitting next to him on the living room floor. She was crying. She cried a lot.

"Chief, Mommy's going away for a while and I want you to be good for Daddy while I'm gone, okay?" She sounded like a hundred marbles inside a jar of mayonnaise. Spencer could remember his father standing in the kitchen; balling his eyes out and doing a bad job at keeping the hysterical whimpers from his young ears.

"Mommy wishes she could stay sweetheart, but there's something Mommy needs to take care of. You make sure you pick up all your toys. Brush your teeth. Do well in school. Oh, my little Chief Thundercloud. Don't cry. I love you. Be a good boy for Daddy, okay Chief?" She kissed his forehead. He could still feel her lips to this very day. Then she stood up, smiled at him, walked away and out the door of their small trailer. She never looked back. That was the last time he saw or heard from her. That was until a few months ago.

"Spencer? Spencer? MR. WEAVER! You were saying ... about the monster?" Mrs. Deline's voice snapped him from his daydream. The classroom exploded with laughter.

"Uh ... wh–? Oh yeah, *Ghoul*! See, Keene wasn't just using the scary monster to kill and eat people. No, not at all. He used the ghoul to illustrate how evil a flesh-eating ghoul can live inside us all. Oh yeah, he also wanted to show that there are far worse monsters in the *real* world than any horror writer could ever imagine in their fictional one. See what I mean?" Spencer's words came out warbled and panicky. He looked around the room, never stopping at anyone. He returned to the teacher, who was standing at the front of his row, holding a heavily dog-eared copy of *Ghoul*. She smiled, nodded, and shot the rest of the class a harsh look that fell on blind eyes. He didn't care. She was the best teacher the school had and she always understood him. To her, it didn't matter what he looked like, how much he weighed, or that he came from one of the poorest families in town. She saw talent in him. That gave him hope. That was all he needed. While the rest of his class laughed and made comments, he and the teacher ignored them. Her room was like Lothlórien and he never wanted to leave its safe haven. As with the rest of his Murphy's Law-filled life, the bell rang as if on cue. He could sense salivating wolves outside the classroom door.

Spencer tugged absently at the bottom of his sweat-soaked *Doctor Who* t-shirt that clung to his frumpy body, like a second layer of skin. The long walk through the crowded halls was like running the *"Humiliation Gauntlet"*. Today wouldn't be any different. He turned up the volume on his iPod and stepped into the crowded hall. He absently bumped into Bekah Perkins, causing her to drop her iPhone in mid-text. She was one of the hottest girls in school and head cheerleader – a Lady Gaga wannabe and about as smart as a box of rocks. Making matters worse, she was the girlfriend to the biggest jock-douchebag in school – Justin Martin.

"Hey, fat ass, watch where you're walking!" Bekah shouted. Laughing, she shoved him, and then was joined by the gaggle of blonde-clones surrounding her.

"Sorry." He kept his head low and shuffled away, trying to ignore the name calling. He turned the volume up, letting RUSH tune her out, creating an emotional-anesthetic through his earbuds.

Have another Big Mac, lard ass!

Waddle, waddle, and waddle.

Now there IS the Deadliest Catch!

Got your harpoon ready, man? Weaver off the port bow!

Every joke was as lame and tired as the next one. But, there was one burning joke that was always on top of the Hit List, and it cut like a million Light-sabers: *"Hey, Weaver, how's Mommy?"* That was the worst one. The words were said far too often and never stopped hurting. It made him shutter with an all-pervasive dread; knowing that even if he moved halfway around the world, he might never be truly *free*.

Graduation was only two months away, then he was out of there. Away from the *Marque-De-Sade'* inspired hellhole, away from his workaholic father and painful life. He hoped he had it in his fractured heart to hang on.

He followed the cold-tiled walls, while keeping his head low and holding his book bag close, trying hard to disappear into the crowd. He was sure all the laughter was at his expense, but he kept his thick legs pumping, hoping to pass by unnoticed. His habitual thoughts were shattered away as his cell phone alerted: *Exterminate ... Exterminate.* He never used to get any texts or emails. Except from his best friend, Mikey Collins, who had moved to North Carolina last year. But, for the past three months, he had been receiving emails from someone very special. Someone he hadn't spoken to in years.

His Mother.

His slippery hands fumbled inside his front pocket and pulled out the phone. Yes, it was from his Mother. He clicked the open button and read the text.

Hello, Spenc. How's your day going?

Hi, Mom! Headed to lunch now. Just came from Mrs. Deline's class.

Oh, did she like your report?

Ah, Mom. I nailed it! She loved it! Come on. It's my favorite book. I told ya all about that right?

LOL ... Yes, sweetie. You did. Over and over and over again. ;o)

Oh. Yeah, sorry. I get stoked about that stuff. You know that. LOL.

I do honey. I do. How are things with that Martin boy?

The same stuff. He texted back. Shuffling forward as the line snailed along.

I'm so sorry sweetie. I wish your father would do something about him! I've been worried about you! I can only imagine just how tough it is for you.

Yeah, it sucks. It is what it is. Dad works nights now and doesn't have time to come in. He does the best he can. His sweaty thumbs slipped on the keypad as he felt a tap on his shoulder.

He looked up, his heart stalled, and his mouth instantaneously dried up as Anna Richmond stood before him, in all her Emo splendor. He felt his breath flee from his throat. He'd been crushing on her since the fourth grade. She was perfection – pale skin that danced with light brown freckles. She was a book worm like he was; with doe-like blue eyes that held Spencer in a Medusa-like state whenever she batted her long lashes, while sitting next to him on the bus every day. Her long, reddish-brown hair softly brushed against her tight blue jeans.

Frilly black and orange crepe paper streamers and posters, selling the approaching prom, served as a backdrop behind her. It was like another stake in the heart – a reminder that she too was just another unrequited crush, doomed to the same Shakespearean fate as all the others.

How's that girl you've had the hots for? Have you asked her the spring formal yet?

He clasped the phone shut and shoved it into the pocket. Lady Luck always seemed to find ironic humor in kicking him in the junk every chance the cold-hearted wench got.

"Hey Spenc." Her thin lips formed into a perfect smile that could convince him to hand over his soul. Her cutting in line was a drop in the Grand Canyon compared to what he'd do for her. He didn't have many friends. Although, he did seem to have a few girls that were drawn to him. They were the ones that rode his bus, using his comfy shoulder to cry on when they were scorned by some insensitive jerk, who just wanted to get in their pants. *He didn't care,* he told himself. He had read about Buddhist monks and their ideas of reincarnation. They reminded him of his very own *Wheel of Samsara,* where he was reborn every few bus rides, dying again at the end of the next tear-filled trip. He cared too much, that was his cross to bear for sure. A glutton for punishment was his fate. He was a sucker and they all knew it. He was such a "good listener" and a "great friend". A truer curse word has never been spoken he had always thought.

Despite all the girls that used him for all his mad Dr. Phil or Oprah-like therapeutic skills, one seemed different. She actually forced him to look into her eyes when he spoke and she really listened. She didn't just stare at him blankly, waiting for him to finish.

"Are you okay?" She smiled.

"Uh...yeah, I'm good." He smiled, hoping his red cheeks didn't give him away.

"You sure?" She laughed and nudged him as the lunch line inched forward. "You look like you're about to toss your lunch even before we've dined on its culinary goodness." Her laugh sounded like angels singing, making him smile.

"Yuppers. Right as rain, good lady. I didn't see you standing there." He looked at her and laughed again.

"Oh, I really liked your report today." She always made his otherwise lonely life manageable. With her, he could truly be himself – fat geekazoid or not.

"Really? You really dug it?" He smiled wide and brought his excited gaze to hers as she nodded fervently.

"Oh yeah. It was great. I don't read that gory stuff you like. You know I'm more of a *Twilight* girl." She patted her backpack where the latest sparkling vampire drivel meekly peeked out the top as if even *it* was embarrassed to be seen in public.

"Uh, yeah. I almost forgot your horribly bad taste in books." He let out a loud belly laugh, his head dropped, and his face felt on fire. An uncontrollable smile breached his round face.

"Haha … very funny. You're just a book snob!" She punched him in the arm and they both laughed. "You should laugh out loud more often. It suits you." She smiled and nodded again.

"Hey, is that our resident fat ass?" A deep, booming voice

shattered the din of impatient lunch line conversation.

Spencer could make out that voice above the din of all the other rednecks, Emo-head cases and gangsta-wannabes. That soul-wrenching, scrotum shrinking voice always sent the same black-as-the-abyss-doom cloud over him, chilling his blood as it insidiously enveloped him.

That voice belonged to Justin Martin.

Justin Martin was Satan incarnate. His worst enemy. He was his Darth Vader, Sauron, Kahn, The First and Lex Luthor. All piled up into a six foot six, two-hundred thirty pound jock. Martin and his inbred band of under-achieving Neanderthals had made Spencer's life a living hell since kindergarten.

Spencer cringed, as his smile and laughter ran hell bent for leather to the shadows of the hallway. He wished that just once, he could meld with the drab walls and disappear. Sadly, that wish had long ago been ignored. He gulped deep, following the line past the graffiti painted alcove where a payphone used to be.

Shit, Man! Please just leave me alone! Spencer bit his lip and tried to shrink his body as small as his big frame would allow. He even thought about trying to hide behind Anna. But being the scared nerd was one thing, a first rate coward who hides behind girls was a whole other kettle of social suicide.

"Don't let those Visigoths bother you, Spenc. They're just angry because someone forgot to shave their knuckles before their *walking upright class* today." Anna tried to make him relax, but Spencer was already curling up like a turtle stuck in the middle of the road, bracing for impact from the eighteen-wheeler speeding his way.

He tried to ignore the loud taunts by Sammy Garzono and the death stare from Justin Martin. His text alarm went off and Spencer fumbled for his phone.

It was from his mom. He clumsily shoved his cell phone back into his pocket.

A blur from his right startled him and he flinched back into the cold wall. Anna grabbed at him, trying to help.

"I see the circus is back in town." Bekah sneered at Spencer, as she clung onto Justin, burying her pink tongue into his mouth. Spencer looked away as she groped at the bulge in his jeans.

"Nah, babe. We're just having a nice chat with Weaver and his skank here." Martin ran his thick tongue along the faux-tan on his girlfriend's face, while his cruel gaze never left Spencer.

"Now, Weaver, I know a chunk of beef like you needs to eat, but for fuck sake, can't your lard ass wait your turn?" Martin peered down at him with a cocked eyebrow and a wide sneer.

"Ssss...Sorry. It's just ... " Weaver averted his eyes to the tight weave of the rust colored carpet. His cell phone buzzed again and the *Daleks* chimed loud in the hallway – a fitting soundtrack to his pubic hell.

"Apologies are like assholes, meat wagon. Everybody's got 'em." Sammy heckled from behind Martin, who just stood there like an intimidating wall of shitbagness. Justin crossed his big arms over his barrel chest and continued to stare down at Spencer. Bekah just laughed, her orange face lost in her iPhone.

"Sorry, guys. I didn't mean to ... I was just ... " He knew it was a waste of time to even bother.

"Ah, hell, J. It's a good thing we got here in time, cos if we didn't, *Fat Fuck* here might've cleaned the whole place out." Sammy laughed, looking like an Italian scarecrow, all the while hiding in the big kid's shadow.

Spencer's phone's text alert rang again. He fumbled to turn the ringer off.

"Somethin' tells me that fat ass here could easily pound down all the food those cow lunch bitches have in there. You weren't gonna eat all the food were ya?" The square-jawed jock bent down and grinned in Spencer's sweaty face, poking a strong finger into his heaving chest.

"Of course not. Why would–" Spencer's reply was cut short as Sammy popped his rat-like face around Martin's shoulder.

"Or maybe, he was tryin' to impress book bitch?" Martin ran his big hand through Anna's long hair and winked at her, eyeing her up and down like a piece of steak. He stepped between Spencer and the shaking girl, and grabbed her firmly at the waist with his big hands.

"Why don't you forget this shitbag here and come with us?" Martin blew her a kiss.

"Get your feces covered hands off me you vile excuse for a living organism!" Anna slapped at his hands and pulled away.

Spencer could feel his heart pounding and his face burning. The last thing he wanted was for this dirt bag to mess with Anna. He could take the abuse. Heck, the ass-kicking and continuous verbal abuse was an everyday occurrence. For *him*, not Anna. Spencer knew he would do anything to prevent that humiliation. Even if that meant pissing off the toughest bad ass in the entire school.

Spencer felt a lump grow the size of the Doctor's Tardis in his throat. He shot Anna a glance. Unfortunately, Martin, who usually was dumber than a box of rocks, caught the look and must have noticed the rage growing on Spencer's face. A wicked smile creased his broad face.

Martin caught Spencer balling up his thick fist and laughed aloud. "Oh, look who woke up with a set of balls today!" His big form loomed, but Spencer gave no quarter, as Anna tugged at his fleshy shoulder.

"Leave her alone." Spencer felt the sweat soaking through his shirt, his chubby knees feeling like a drunken puppeteer's strings. Only by the force of sheer will and livid anger, was Spencer able to keep up a strong front.

Martin exploded with a roaring laugh and his entourage joined in. He quickly regained his composure and stared into Spenser's wide eyes.

"You wanna go bitch?" Martin sneered, looming over Spencer.

"Fuck you, *Justin*," Spencer said. He heard the harsh words well before he realized they escaped his trembling mouth. Anna grabbed at Spencer's shoulder. He pulled away.

"Ha! Bring it!" Spencer found a strength he never knew he had. Most of the time, he deeply feared an ass kicking. Today, he didn't care. He didn't know if it was the romantic image of him defending his lady's honor or that finally, once in his life, his mother was there … after all these years his life made sense. Much to his surprise, her love did mean the world to him … almost as if it gave him purpose. Either way, after twelve long years, he'd had enough.

"Fuck 'em up, *J*!" Sammy's eyes seemed to grow to the size of Frisbees and he punched his boney fists together, salivating at the promise of geek blood.

"Ya should've just kept your mouth shut, bitch!" Martin grabbed Spencer by the shirt, clinching his other hand into an all-too-familiar cinder block sized fist. Sammy shoved Anna back with one hand away from Spencer.

"Knock it off. All of you!" a deep voice doomed, freezing everyone in the hallway. It had come from a tall man with bushy, salt and pepper hair and beard. Martin ignored the order pulled Spencer in closer.

"I said … *enough!*" Mr. Williams took up the space between the bully and Spencer, his chest about level with the young star athlete's chin. Martin's entourage stepped back and fell silent.

"Hey, Mr. W. Me n' Spenc were just messin' around, ya know." Martin said, his deep set, blue eyes never leaving Spencer.

"Is that so, Mr. Martin?" Mr. Williams crossed his thick arms over his wrinkled, plaid dress shirt and tie, which looked as uncomfortable on him as he did wearing it.

"Hell, yeah! Me n' Sammy here always joke around with good ol' Spenc." Martin's GQ smile glistened under the glow of the fluorescent lights, as he patted the wide teacher's shoulders.

"I'm afraid your cheap attempt at being charming only works on impressionable freshmen girls, Mr. Martin." The teacher's voice seemed to drop an octave. The entourage stepped back another step, accompanied by a bunch of hushed oooh's and aaah's.

Martin ignored the burly teacher and leaned around him. "Spence, tell our good teacher here that we were just messin' around. Right, *bro*?" His steel gaze intensified and made Spencer's skin turn cold.

"Ah. I see. Is this true, Mr. Weaver?" Mr. Williams asked with obvious disbelief, all the while keeping his calm gaze on the twitching jock in front of him.

"I see. The two of you and Mr. Spencer here are the best of pals? And, this is just a simple game of grab ass?" The teacher already knew the answer, but was always looking for ways to balance out the already overly unbalanced jock-to-academic quotient in the athletically driven school.

"*No*, Mr. Williams." Anna declared. She glared at Justin and Bekah. Anna knew that Spencer had too much pride to admit the bullying and she had had enough of the childish games.

"These ... these ... ignorant muck trolls have been terrorizing Spencer since ... since well ... forever! Spencer flinched at her harsh words and the painful repercussions soon to follow.

The entourage behind Martin suddenly wanted nothing to do with their tough leader. They seem to shrink and force the line to move along hastily – not being able to put enough space between themselves and the bomb that was about to drop. Mr. Williams had a reputation for not taking any crap from students, regardless of whom their parents were, their social status, or what New York State record they may have set in the past. Unless it was the tennis team.

"Well, Mr. Martin ... If I were you, I would knock off this tough guy bullshit." Mr. Williams leaned in close, grabbed the young man by his finely pressed Abercrombie & Fitch polo and forced his eyes to his.

"It is my advice that you and your dipshit crew get your lunch, find a table, enjoy your fine sustenance, and leave Mr. Weaver alone. Do you *feel* me?" Mr. Williams' jaw muscles tightened and it was obvious to Martin that the big teacher wasn't joking around, and as much as he wanted to knock the old man's teeth down his throat, he backed down and nodded. He averted his eyes, turned around, and shoved Sammy toward the lunchroom door.

Spencer could see the bully was trying to hide his bright red face. He felt Anna's hand on his shoulder and turned to look at her.

"Can't we ever just have a quite lunch?" She laughed, shoving him forward as the lunch line moved.

"Thanks, Mr. Williams." Spencer paused, feeling a wet tear form in his eye.

"Keep it moving." Mr. Williams winked and patted Spencer on the shoulder.

"Enjoy your lunch Mr. Spencer." He nodded slightly, then headed down the hall.

Ahead in line, Spencer could feel the violent gaze penetrating him like a laser from Martin, as Bekah whispered in his flushed ear.

"What will it be Spence, strawberry Jell-O or apple crisp?" Anna asked nudging him forward.

"Well, ya know me … I'm all about the apple crisp." Spencer tried to hide his fear and trepidation. This was just a small victory in a much larger battle, and knowing the worst was coming, was like carrying around a Kia Soul on his weary back. They made sure to find a table far away from Martin and his gaggle of idiots.

The rest of lunch period went as smooth as he could hope. They sat and talked about his book report and what colleges they were hoping to attend after they escaped the cesspool. However, he found it hard to ignore the constant "ding" from his cell phone alerting him of incoming texts from his Mother. His alone time with Anna was precious too, so he let the text go. It wasn't that distraction that caused his chest to clinch tight as Neil Peart's snare drum. As hard as he tried, he couldn't avoid the venomous stare from Martin, who was still fuming from his lunch line embarrassment by Mr. Williams. Even the constant tugs from his "picture-perfect" cheerleader girlfriend couldn't break the brute's intense stare. Bekah shot him death rays from her squinting eyes, when she wasn't busy texting on her iPhone.

The bell rang and lunch was over. It was time for Mr. Ralston's art class. The only other place where Spencer felt safe.

His cell phone text alert chimed again.

It made him smile as they rushed out of the cafeteria, trying to go unnoticed. He'd really gotten used to his mom's texts. They helped make things better.

While sixth period couldn't come fast enough, it was bitter sweet. The bus ride with Anna was always the highlight of his day, especially since douche bag Martin drove to school. Once he hit Whitney Pine's Trailer Park, he knew it was back to his reality. His Dad would already be at work and the trailer would be dark and empty. A silent testimony of what his young life had become. He shrugged off the thought and focused on the texts he had gotten from his Mother that day. It had been the only thing in his life that had given him strength and encouraged him to finish high school and get out of this Podunk town.

"Afterimage"

As he got off the bus, the same dark fumes ushered him home as he unlocked the flimsy, aluminum trailer door. Inside, it smelled of thick cigarette smoke, dirty laundry and stale beer. His Dad left for work about an hour before, but his true essence remained to welcome Spencer home. He went over to the rickety computer desk and pushed the power button on the eight-year-old Gateway. As the computer hummed and beeped to life, Spencer went to the fridge, hoping that his Dad had shopped and bought some Diet Coke. His body slumped and his breath eased out, as he read the note attached to the freezer portion of the old fridge.

Hey, Spence. I meant to hit the store for chow and soda today, but I overslept. There's still one soda left, cold cuts and bread. Sorry, bud. I'll see you in the morning. Have to go to work. Have a good one and remember to do your homework. – Dad

Spencer opened the old Frigidaire and took out the last soda and sandwich fixings. He sat down at the old table and made himself a *pauper's supper*, as he liked to call it. He glanced into the living room and noticed the glass pot pipe half shoved underneath the beat up Lazy-Boy. Surrounding it was an army of empty Keystone Light cans. He shook his head. He sat there for a long moment and stared at the only picture of his mom. Spencer had to force his father to leave up on the living room wall. He ate the tasteless supper, drained the can of soda, and rinsed it out in the sink. He placed it in the plastic bag with the other empties and jumped as lightening flashed through the filth-covered kitchen window. A late spring storm quickly and violently overtook the small town and pelted bullet-like rain drops down into the dry earth. It didn't come alone; syncopated thunder and more lightening rocked the trailer.

Spencer knew he should turn off the computer, but couldn't bring himself to do it. He was still in shock that she *friended* him on Facebook weeks ago after not seeing or hearing from her in over twelve years. He was scared and apprehensive at first and he still hadn't told his father. Spencer loved him, but his father had to work tons of overtime just to pay for this tenement on cinderblocks. He never had much time for Spencer, and although he felt horrible about it, sometimes he resented the old man for his absence. Then there was all the drinking and drugs. His Dad tried to hide it from him, but he wasn't seven anymore. Now with his mom back in the picture, life just seemed brighter. She made all the crap at school not so hard to take and he wasn't alone anymore.

He lived for her texts, emails and Facebook chats. He asked her about meeting a few times, even to just call him, but she told him she was busy with work and that there was some issue with her phone. She said it was cheaper and better for now to continue to communicate the way they had been. He didn't care, really. She could fill that old empty hole with complete happiness now that she was back in his life. Spencer had been thinking about asking if it would be okay for him to come live with her after graduation. She had told him that she loved the idea and that there were plenty of colleges near her. He thought it odd that she never told him where she lived, but did keep telling him that she wasn't too far away, and she didn't want to make his life more complicated with his father. He just really wanted to see her again. He noticed that the memory of her face and soft soothing voice had become like an old photograph, yellowed and faded by the cruel hand of time.

His cell phone had been silent since the end of the school day. He frowned at it, tossed it on the old computer table and logged onto his Gmail account. There was nothing but ads to make his erection bigger and pills to turn his keg into a six-pack. Like he had any need for that kind of crap. He had the sexual mojo of a Bedouin monk. He leaned back in the kitchen chair and let out an exhausted breath.

The living room was dark, save the blue haze from the monitor, as Spencer checked Facebook. His eyes sprung wide as he saw all the posts saying how Justin Martin was punked by big geek, Spencer Martin. He leapt up from the flimsy chair and punched the imaginary air. His victory dance didn't last long. His jaw slacked open as he read the very last post from Martin himself.

Hey all. No worries. It was my bad and I was a jerk to Spencer and deserved what Mr. Williams said. Maybe it's time we all stop and really take look and see how we treat our fellow students. I'm really sorry, Spencer!

The comments that followed were myriad of disbelief, jokes and huzzahs. It boggled Spencer's spinning mind at the sheer number of the replies and reposts. Deep down he really wanted to believe Martin's lamentation, but his scars, both on the surface and the ones much deeper, weren't so quick to believe.

He shook his head, stared at his Facebook page, and waited for his Mother to sign on. An hour passed and she didn't show up. He felt his hopes sinking and wished he hadn't guzzled down the last can of Diet Coke.

The pounding storm outside lulled him into a sound slumber.

"Fly By Night"

DING ... DING. The Facebook instant message alert startled him awake-causing him to fall from his chair.

He rubbed the sleep from his eyes and spastically grabbed at his cell phone, knocking it on the floor. It took a second to realize the sound came from the computer.

"Oh, for the love of God," he grumbled and squinted to focus on the screen. He nervously shook the mouse to wake up the computer, the sudden light from the monitor blinding him.

"Holy hell," he said. He gave his eyes a few seconds to adjust. Part of him hoped it was from Anna and the other part wished it were his Mom. His smile grew wide and he guided the mouse to the Reply section on the IM window.

Entre Nous sent at 8:17pm

"Hello honey, you there?"

He frantically glanced down at the clock on the bottom of the screen. It read 8:25. His heart pounded, thinking that he missed her. He cuffed himself on the head when he saw the little green dot was on, indicating she was still online.

By-Tor94- replied at 8:25

Hi Mom! I'm here!

The storm raged on outside and thunder rocked the old trailer as a lightening surge caused the computer monitor to flicker. He shot the storm a snarky look, mumbling a plethora of curse words and promptly returned to the screen.

Entre Nous sent at 8:27pm

Oh good! I thought I missed you. How was your day hon? I had a strange feeling all day and I was worried about you after your last text.

By-Tor94- replied at 8:28pm

Wow, Mom! Really? I did have a messed up day. I mean, the Ghoul report rocked and all but, it was the crap that happened in the lunch line that turned my day into a pile of dung beetle filled crap. LOL ;o)

Entre Nous sent at 8:30pm

Oh no! What happened? You okay?

By-Tor94- replied at 8:31pm

I almost had my butt handed to me today, Mom. You remember that guy, Martin that I've told you about a gazillion times?

Entre Nous sent at 8:31pm

Sure do! Did he HURT YOU?

By-Tor94- replied at 8:32pm

Almost! I don't know why he always needs to mess with me, Mom! I've never done anything to him. Or any of his troglodyte stooges. They always want to shove my face into locker or kick my ass!

Entre Nous sent at 8:34pm

You sure you're okay? Tell me what happened hon?

By-Tor94- replied at 8:34pm

That asswipe was putting his hands all over Anna and me …

Entre Nous sent at 8:34pm

She's the one you've been crushing on since elementary school right? :o)

By-Tor94- replied at 8:34pm

Yes, Mom! Geesh!

Entre Nous sent at 8:35pm

Sorry, sorry. :o) Then what happened?

By-Tor94- replied at 8:34pm

I told him to leave her alone and he grabbed me and was about to punch me but a teacher … Mr. Williams stopped him. Boy did THAT piss Justin off! It was a good thing too, because I was about to go all medieval all over his sorry butt. In front of Anna and the whole blessed school!

Entre Nous sent at 8:40pm

Oh honey! I am so sorry! I wish I were there for you!

By-Tor94- replied at 8:40pm

I know, Mom! I am just so tired of it all. That dumb, as a box of rocks Neanderthal and his bleach-blonde automaton, seem to get their thrills out of making my life hell. I tell you … there are times when I can see why so many kids go postal and bring guns to school. I am so damn tired of being nothing but a punching bag for their sick and sadistic entertainment. If he pulls that crap one more time, there won't be a teacher alive that will stop me from stomping his inbred ass. Along with Sammy the "douche bag" and the other "The Hills Have Eyes" rejects. I would love to kick their asses for once and then see how THEY feel! I can't get out of this redneck town fast enough, Mom!

He could feel his heartbeat in his temples. Sweat covered his as rage coursed through him like the spring rainstorm battering the thin walls. His twitching fingers tapped on the mouse, waiting for his mom to reply.

By-Tor94- replied at 8:44pm

You there, Mom?

Entre Nous sent at 8:45pm

Oh yes. Sorry hon, the storm here is mad crazy and is messing with my internet connection. I feel so bad. I love you so much. I wish I could beat them up for you! ;o)

By-Tor94- replied at 8:46pm

I know, Mom. I love you too! Just wish you were here! I have to admit. I would have loved to

*punch that bag of feces right in that smug jaw
of his. I bet you he's not as tough as he thinks
he is. Nobody has ever given him a swift kick in
the junk I bet. Well, beside that cheap skank of
his. LOL*

Entre Nous sent at 8:50pm

*I am so sorry that I've left you alone for
so long! Seeing what you have been through and
knowing that your father hasn't done much to
help. I've been struggling with something for a
while now.*

By-Tor94- replied at 8:51pm

*It's okay, Mom. Dad does … He tries. What are
you thinking about?*

Entre Nous sent at 8:53pm

*Okay … here goes. How do you feel about moving
in with me? I know we've talked about it and it's
your senior year. Would you want to come live
with me? It's not that far of a drive and I could
bring you to and from school until you graduate.
I know your father tries, but to be honest, we
both know you deserve a better life … I …*

Spencer quickly sat up straight and the old chair creaked loud.
He leaned back and just stared at his Mother's shocking offer on
the screen. His mind scrambled and tossed with the possibilities
of a new life away from this rotting cesspool. Pangs of guilt rattled
his chest at the thought of leaving his father. He knew he couldn't
stay here and be his caretaker for the rest of his life. He had big
dreams, and not one of those included him staying here, chained
to the hell-on-earth fate of a lifelong resident of Carrigan Springs,

New York. Without a second's more thought, he found his excited fingers typing.

By-Tor94- replied at 8:53pm

Mom! I'M IN! :O)

Entre Nous sent at 8:54pm

Oh, I am so happy, honey! I can't wait to see you. Now here is the tough part hon, if we are going to do this we need to do it tonight. Is that a problem? I can be there in an hour to pick you up. Is that okay?

Spencer slouched in his chair. He looked about the dark, rundown trailer that had been his home for the past ten years and the uneasy thought of leaving it behind *tonight* made his stomach roll. Sure, he hated the living daylights out of this dead end crap hole, and he would be leaving in a few months anyway, but to leave his father high and dry just didn't feel right. The more pervasive thought was that his Mom offered him a fresh start in a whole new world. Sure, he would miss the hell out of his father and Anna. However, he could always stay in communication with them both. Especially, Anna. She was just as addicted to computers and social networking as he was, and they would still have until the end of the school year to hang out and make plans. It really wasn't that difficult of a decision.

By-Tor94- replied at 8:55pm

Sounds perfect, Mom! That will give me time to leave a Dad a note and pack some stuff. Do you want to come here?

Entre Nous sent at 8:56pm

No hon, I don't think that's a good idea. Do you remember where the elementary school playground is? How about meeting there hon?"

By-Tor94- replied at 8:57pm

I sure do, Mom! You used to take me to play on the swings! I will be there within the hour! I cannot wait to see you! I love you, Mommy.

His spastic fingers typed the words before he was even aware. He didn't care. She *was* his mommy. The world be damned. A smile grew on his face and he thought it might split it in two. He hadn't been this happy in a very long time, if ever.

Entre Nous sent at 8:59pm

I love you too, Hon. A new life for both of us begins tonight! I promise to make up for all those years I've been gone! You won't be lonely anymore Spencer. I swear to you! "See you soon!

She signed off. Spencer felt as if he was floating three feet off the matted, beer-stained carpet. He had so much to do and so little time.

"By-Tor and the Snow Dog"

Spencer almost wept as he thought of his vast collection of old paperbacks and hard cover books. The stacks of books seemed sad as he closed his bedroom door. They had been his best and constant friends since he learned how to read, and leaving them behind felt like ripping out a lung through his foot. *I can find them again or, maybe Dad will ship them to me? Heck, that's if he even talks to me ever again.* Warm tears fled down his cheeks as the zipped up his backpack and slung it over his shoulder. He didn't want to hurt his Dad, but he knew that this was the best thing for everybody. His Dad wouldn't have to worry about him anymore or hide his addictions.

It didn't take him long to pack. It took him much longer to write the goodbye note. It was short and succinct. The way Spencer always wrote. He tried to convince himself that it was his economy of words "style" but the truth was he didn't know what to say. A simple *thanks for everything you've ever done for me Dad. I'm going to live with Mom. You have my cell number. I'll call you soon. I love you.* That seemed to suffice. He left the note on the fridge, closed and locked the trailer door, hopped down off the rain soaked porch and headed downtown.

He wiped away the tears and tried to ignore the piranha chomping away at his innards and cut under the many ancient, looming maple's that lined the fence to the playground. The wind picked up causing the maple leaves to rustle nervously and light raindrops delicately pattered the trees.

Spencer's sweaty hand absently brushed along the cold fence as he followed it behind the school toward the playground. *Hmm ... that's weird. No lights on ... probably more budget cuts.* He would be out of here soon and none of those trifling things would matter anymore. He clenched the strap of his backpack and turned behind the school.

Pitch-blackness soaked the playground, save an occasional lightning strike off in the distance. Normally he'd be freaked out, but somehow the thought of seeing his mom again and leaving this place held all those old fears at bay.

He knew the playground well, even in the dark. He passed the monkey bars, seesaws and within a couple of minutes felt the familiar chilly chains of the swings. He left the heavy pack on the damp sand and plopped onto the center swing. This was *their* favorite. The memory made him smile and warmed his insides.

His mind swam with the possibilities of his new life that couldn't start soon enough.

A howling wind swept down from the old cemetery that overlooked the school. He shivered and flipped open his cell phone, frowned. *10:16* the cold blue display read. She's late. "Don't worry. She'll be here," he whispered into the night air.

Another thirty minutes passed and Spencer's hope waned with every passing minute. He had texted and even called his Mother. However, both got no response. Tears fled his eyes and he grabbed the strap of his backpack, but then dropped it as his loud sobs bounced off the school's brick walls. His heart fractured and all hopes of happiness were lost. Suddenly, the entire playground was awash in yellow brightness.

The large security lights hummed and flooded the area. Spencer jumped and covered his eyes from the harsh light. All he could see were multicolored flashes of light.

"Weaver, just what I'd expect from a big fat baby!" Spencer knew that voice. He felt his world drop out from under him. His stomach cinched into a million knots. His head swam.

Justin Martin.

All around him, laughter filled his ears, as his assaulted eyes slowly began to function again.

"Come on. Why so quiet now? You've been a busy little boy with all the texting and IMing you do." Justin's large frame stood silhouetted atop the wooden play set. He squinted to see over fifty people surrounding him on all sides. All of them were rolling with mocking laughter and dark stares.

"Oh Mommy, I loooove you!" Justin laughed. His voice echoed off the brick walls of the school.

"What ... what the hell are y–" Spencer tried to speak, his voice failed.

"Your mommy ain't coming, shitbag. She never was." Justin stared down at him, his tone almost lyrical.

"Ain't that right, babe?" He motioned and Bekah stepped

forward with a thick stack of papers and wearing an evil sneer.

"Spence, I'm so sorry I left you all alone for all these years. I miss you so much," Bekah read from the stack. *In her other hand she held out a cell phone.*

"Who? Wh–?" Spencer whimpered out, slowly piecing it together. Tears raced down his flushed face. His bulging eyes wept and he could see that the hysterical crowd had their own stacks of paper.

"Fat ass, turn this way. I wanna get your good side," Sammy's words giggled out from in front of Spencer. He was holding a camcorder.

"I don't under … wha … " Spencer tried again, swaying in place

"Smile pretty, Tubbalicious. You're lard ass will be up on YouTube before you can say, *'You want fries with that?'* " The circle of laughter swelled around him as they all took turns reading all the *Mom* texts Bekah had sent to him.

Justin read Spencer's parts, over accentuating his most sensitive lines. This went on for an hour as the vile crowd's cruel laughter lolled and broke against Spencer like punishing ocean waves on jagged rocks. He fought to breathe, and every time he tried to get away, the crowd shoved him back into the *Swing Set Arena*.

"Oh, my favorite part is when you say you wanna kick my ass. Well, let's see what ya can do, bitch!" Justin hopped down from the wooden bridge and sauntered over to Spencer's quivering form. Bekah took over reading the taunting texts, acting as a sadistic soundtrack to Spencer's destruction, while Sammy made sure to get it all on video.

"I … I didn't..." Spencer's words were broken.

Justin grabbed Spencer by the hair and yanked him to his feet. The big teen leaned into Spencer's tear stained face and sneered.

"Kick my ass huh, bitch?" He said through clinched teeth.

Spencer twitched; overwhelmed, scared.

"Make sure you get this Sammy." Justin's cold gaze never left Spencer's wide green eyes.

The next thing Spencer felt was a testicular wrenching pain in his stomach and one final blow to his jaw. Coppery fluid filled his swelling mouth as Justin threw him to the ground. He knelt down next to Spencer's limp form.

"Never fuck with me, Weaver. *You* will always lose! You wanna know why fat fuck? Do ya? You are a loser and I *always* win." He stood up, put a boot into Spencer's stomach, and spit a wad of chew on his cheek.

"You're a damn joke. Why don't you do yourself and the whole world a favor and just put a cap in your own ass and end it all." Justin turned and walked toward the camera and held up double "devil horns" while his tongue flicked the cold air. The crowd erupted into a barbarous symphony of hatred.

Darkness took Spencer.

"The Pass"

He woke alone. He didn't know how long he had been out, but the cold rain still pounded him, as he lay in a puddle of watery sand. Every step he took was a new experience in pain. He couldn't stop crying. His world had been destroyed in a matter of minutes. His mother wasn't real. Those assholes; Justin and Bekah made it all up. Pain tore into every shred of his being. How could've he been so blind? So gullible? Cold rain escorted him all the way to his dilapidated home.

He threw the heavy pack on the couch and sobbed uncontrollably. He pulled the cell phone from his pocket and screamed as he chucked it against the wall. It shattered into pieces.

He plopped onto the chair and stared at the computer screen. His mouth agape; as all over Facebook, Sammy had already posted links to the freshly made video of Spencer's humiliation. It had already gotten over 3,000 hits and comments that echoed Justin's suicide solution. He watched it repeatedly. Spastic torrents rained. His mind filled with dark clouds. Long moments passed before he realized he had his father's .38 in his trembling hands. All he knew was that it felt good.

It felt right.

Brutal thunder and lightning strikes outside washed out the gun blast. While inside the dark trailer, the faint blue glow of the monitor cast dark shadows on the family portrait; now covered in splattered blood, flesh, bone and Spencer's brains.

"The Body Electric"

Spence ... Honey ...

Yellow and blue tendrils swirled and slithered around Spencer's mind. The voice, distant at first, then grew stronger and direct.

He knew that voice.

Chief, it's really me. You're with me now. We're together.

Mom? He cried out. It felt like a dream. Bright flashes of light surrounded him. His body swam among the sparks and pulses. Electricity bristled through him. His nervous system buzzed and surprisingly, no pain.

Yes. It's me. You've joined me. I've been waiting for you.

Where am I?

You're dead hon. But it's okay. We are together again. Pain and loneliness are forever gone.

His eyes focused and it seemed as if he were in a circuit board. Resistors, processors and conductors buzzed in busy action. Blue light flew through and all around him. The yellowish-blue image blipped and cam into full view.

Before him appeared a digitized image of his mother.

It is you!

If I'm dead ... that means you're ...

Dead. Yes, Chief. When I left, I killed myself. Your father didn't have the heart to tell you. But it's okay now. We are together.

Where are we?

We are pure energy. In death, we have returned to the universal source. We can flow through the world through anything that holds a current. Our souls are electric. It's beautiful hon. The internet is our freeway.

Really? Holy cow. That's amazing.

It is. What's even better? I can help you get even with those horrible kids that did this to you!

From his new vantage point inside the computer, he could make out his blood-covered lifeless form. His mind prickled with sadness, excitement and the potential of his new life.

Show me how, Mom.

"One Little Victory"

Justin Martin's bedroom was dark and filled with Nag Champa and pot smoke. The storm raged outside and bright flashes of lightening lit up the shadow-filled room. He sat in the old recliner with a handful of Bekah's hair in his hands. He jerked her head up and down on his lap, as she slathered and slurped between his hairy legs.

"*Am a doin' somf in' wong?*" Bekah sounded as if she was sucking on a slack flounder.

Justin's laptop screen lit up on the bed next to them. They'd been watching Spencer's video, repeatedly. It should have made him extra hard and Bekah liked it that way. However, he'd been having issues, lately. Bekah bitched and blamed the steroids. What did *she* know?

Can't bitch with your mouth full. He clinched his jaw and shoved her head violently down on his member.

She pulled away and wiped her mouth. She gave Justin a frustrated look. "What the hell's wrong?" She flicked his small, limp penis.

The laptop's screen flickered as a bolt of lightning struck a nearby tree flooding the room in white light. The smell of burnt ozone, singed maple filled their nostrils. They didn't even notice when the small red light of the webcam turned on the laptop.

"Nothin'. What you talking about?" He grabbed her head and tried to force her back down on him.

"Don't play that again, J. You haven't been able to get a hard on in months. You still shooting up with that shit?" She pulled away and sat back on her haunches.

"Ah, hell no! I told you I quit that shit." He covered his groin with his hand.

"Damn, J. It's bad enough you have a dick the size of elbow macaroni. The least you could do is get what you *do* have hard." She held her thumb and forefinger together, almost touching.

"Fuck that. I.. What the ... " His voice trailed off.

"What is it?" She asked.

"It's fuckin', Weaver." His voice almost a whisper. He was staring and pointing a shaky hand at the laptop screen on the corner of the bed next to her.

"What? Where?" She laughed.

He pointed at the computer.

"What the hell?" She huffed.

On the screen was Spencer, lumped over in his chair, his face looking like a deer splattered by a tractor-trailer. A bloody fleshy smile on his decimated face.

His voice crackled through the laptop.

I hope you enjoyed your little joke. Very funny. You got your wish. The best part ... I'll have the last laugh.

Another voice rang in their ears.

Oh and dear, you sound nothing like me.

They stared blankly at the screen.

The house went dark. Blue arcs shot and lurched, back and forth, between Justin and Bekah's electrified bodies. Every available watt now was surging through them. Their eyes bubbled and exploded out of their skulls. Their skin bubbled and blistered, popped and slid off their bones. They never even got a chance to scream.

The air smelled of burnt hair, flesh and charged ozone. Justin and Bekah's bodies where now just slushy, reddish, grey piles on the bed.

That felt great, Mom! I think Sammy needs a visit.

Anything for you, Chief.

SHAUN MEEKS

PERFECTION THROUGH SILENCE

The sound had been following him around for days. It was a soft, whispered tick. Almost like a pocket watch that's been muffled. It didn't come and go, or get loud then soft. It was just a constant, low sound that stayed with him wherever he went. At first he thought everyone could hear it, even asking some of his co-workers about the noise. They responded with head shakes and wary looks. Tom had always been a weird one in their eyes; the quiet guy who kept to himself and his questions about unheard sounds only made him seem stranger.

On the second day, he had gone home, stripped off all his cloths and went down to the root cellar of the house his grandmother had left him. The place was dark and earthy, smelling like the open grave that she had been lowered into nearly a year before. The cellar would be perfect because there was nothing down there aside from some vegetables and two wicker baskets. Nothing to tick, tick, tick.

Yet, as he stood naked on the dirt floor, darkness engulfing him, the ticking persisted, whispering insistently. He plugged his ears, digging his fingers in as deep as he could, his untrimmed nails cutting into the soft skin as he pushed past the limit.

The sound didn't stop.

It didn't get louder, or decrease at all, just continued to tick.

Tick.

Tick.

Days passed and sleep was nearly impossible. He would lie in his bed, eyes stuck on the white ceiling above his bed, his heart beating in rhythm to the constant sound. Exhaustion would eventually take over and he would fall into a restless sleep for a few hours here and there. But even in the world of dreams he found his new companion there in his head, reminding him of the torture waiting when he awoke. His body and mind became tired from the game. His inability to concentrate made driving a nightmare, so he started to use public transit to get to work, a task he hated more than the sound itself. The buses and subways were full of people that were fighting some kind of virus; others smelled as though they hadn't bathed in years and all of them stared at him, watching him with their small eyes and terrible thoughts.

He wondered if anyone on the bus or subway could hear the ticking, thinking he might be sick with some new virus that could infect other passengers, but deep down knew it was a stupid thought. If it was contagious, why had his co-workers been immune?

He knew that he was grasping at straws, that the sound and the lack of sleep was pushing him over the edge and he needed to do something about it before he started to really lose it.

On the fifth day since the ticking started, Tom went to see his doctor in hopes of getting some answers. He sat in the waiting room, looking at kids rubbing their runny noses and touching every single surface with their sticky, little hands; all the while their parents seemed too busy to notice. He wondered when parents had decided updating their social networks or stalking ex-lovers on those same sites had become more important than watching and raising their kids. No wonder the world was falling apart.

Still, Tom had more important things on his mind.

And in his ears.

After a forty-five minute wait, he was finally called into the doctor's office. Tom sat on the flimsy paper that covered the cracked, orange vinyl examination table, annoyed by the loud crinkling sound it made every time he moved. The doctor was peering into his ears, going left to right and back again. The hairy man smelled so strongly of salami, Tom wondered if he ate anything else.

"So, when did you start hearing this sound?"

"A few days ago. Saturday I think."

"So, more like five than three?"

"Sure."

"Hmmm."

Tom waited for the doctor to say something else, thinking that "hmmm" was not really an end to the conversation. He wanted to hear the news, good or bad, it really didn't matter. He just wanted to know what was torturing him.

"Can you describe the sound again, Mr. Knox?"

"Sure. It's a ticking sound, the same as an old clock, or a watch when you put it up to your ear. Like the gears moving slowly. Tick. Tick. Tick."

"Did anything happen around the time it started? Something traumatic?"

"No. Why?"

The doctor leaned against the table across from where Tom

sat, slowly pulling off his latex gloves and looking confused and worried. Tom didn't like that look. It was the same look the doctor had on his face when he told Tom that his grandmother was going to die in less than a day.

"There is nothing physically there. I don't see any damage, other than a few superficial lacerations to the skin. I don't see anything that could be causing this. Do you hear it now?"

"Yes. It never stops."

"Interesting. And does the volume ever change?"

"No." Tom said. He felt frustrated that the doctor was asking the exact same question he had asked when he first walked in. He didn't want to answer any of them; he wanted the doctor to give him some answers. "So if it isn't physical, what're you saying? I'm crazy?"

"Now, Mr. Knox, I'm not saying anything like that, but we have to consider some things, maybe even run a few tests. It could be that something happened, a sort of traumatic mental incident that caused this. It could be an old trauma trying to surface, or there could be something deeper than just inside your ear that is making the sound. Something physical. The mind and the ear are tricky things. I don't want you to think that I am saying you have any sort of mental issue."

"That's what it sounds like to me!"

"Well, I would like you to see two specialists. One is an ear, nose, and throat specialist and the other is a psychologist. My secretary will give you their numbers."

And then he was gone, leaving Tom and the ticking sound alone. He sat there for a moment, collecting his thoughts, wondering if maybe this was just a sign that he really was going crazy. If nobody else could hear it, and there was no physical sign of something wrong, what else did that leave?

Tom jumped off the table and left the doctor's office, bypassing the secretary as he went, not bothering to collect the phone numbers she held out for him. As far as he was concerned, he wouldn't need them. He knew there was nothing really wrong with him other than his mind screwing around with him. What could either of those doctors do to help?

He walked out onto the street and moved aimlessly amongst the midday crowds, his footsteps falling in time with the ticking in his head. He moved towards a construction area where two men were jackhammering concrete. He hoped the loud machines would drown out a bit of the noise, but the ticking increased just enough to still be heard over the din. Somehow, the sound in his head was able to compensate so that the volume stayed constant.

What is this? What the hell is wrong with me?

He walked away from the jackhammering, disappeared into the crowds, and thought about going home. Home was the one place he used to feel safe, where he could find some sense of security and belonging. He had been living there since he was eight; nearly twenty-one years in all. He had moved there after his mother and father died. He had been found by the police two weeks after that and was taken into custody by Children's Aid. But his grandmother quickly swooped in and took him away from the cold, white hallways of the building he had been forced to stay in, taking him into her warm and inviting house. Much of his life before coming to his grandmother's was a blur, and the parts he could remember seemed fragmented and he tried to push them out of his mind.

Part of him wished his grandmother could still be there with him, talking the way she used to, holding his hand and making him feel better when nightmares haunted him in those early years. She had done so much to help him, not just providing a place for him to live, but healing the trauma of being alone after his parents' death.

But she was gone, just like them. He had watched as her coffin was lowered into the dark earth where he knew she would become food for the things that crawled through the ground. That first night alone had been hard. He had never been in the house without her, and it seemed so vacant, so desolate. Tom knew he had to do his best to make do and come around, try to be self-sufficient, but it wasn't easy. She had been his rock, the one person he could turn to for anything.

And he needed her, more than ever.

As the sun began to drop and darkness slowly bled into the sky, Tom found himself at the cemetery where his entire family was buried.

Mom. Dad. Grandmother.

All three graves were side by side, with an empty spot next to his mother. That was where he would be planted once he was dead. He hated the thought of death, hated the smell of funeral parlours more than anything else. All those false scents in the air, lilies and air freshener used to cover up the smell of the embalming fluid and the rotting flesh that was all around. It was so bad for him that every time he passed by a funeral home, he had to hold his breath to avoid the panic attacks that threatened him with those familiar smells. He never told anyone about that, thinking they would call him crazy, but those smells brought old memories to the surface he would rather keep buried.

As he made his way through the rows of tombstones, careful not to trip on any of the small markers as the last of the light faded from the day, he wondered if that strange fear and reaction to funeral parlours should have been an early warning sign that there was something not right in his head. Unwilling to go down that road of thought, Tom began to hum a song his grandmother would sing to him when he first moved in with her. Those nights when he couldn't sleep, when being in a strange house, away from his mom and dad whom he'd never see again, made it impossible not to cry. On those nights, his grandmother would come into the room, turn on the night light and sing to him until he fell asleep.

Again, he wished she was there with him.

Then, he realized he was with her.

As he stood before the graves of his parents and grandmother, the ticking continued, but it seemed more of a background noise as he looked at the names of those gone. He went to his grandmother's tombstone, traced his fingers along her name and whispered to her.

"You would have made this better, Gran. You were the only one who understood me, took me in and helped me. Why can't you be here now? I need you so much. Why aren't you here?"

Tom lay down on top of her grave and curled into the fetal position and let his tears flow. For the first time in days he was able to ignore the ticking sound, almost to the point of not hearing it at all. He wasn't even aware that it had faded as he closed his eyes and whispered softly into the ground and cried for her.

"Hey! Wake the fuck up, ya bum!"

Tom's eyes flew open; he realized he must have fallen asleep and saw a man standing over him holding a flashlight, looking very angry. As the fog of sleep faded away, Tom was able to see that it was a security guard, flashlight aimed at him. He had no idea why a security guard sounded so angry, even if he had fallen asleep.

"Sorry. I was visiting my grandmother and ..."

"Sure you were, pal. Gates closed six hours ago, so why don't you just get up and get out before I arrest you for trespassing?"

"Six hours?"

Six hours?

The shock of it was almost too much. In the last five days, Tom had probably slept less than that in total and he realized he must have slept even longer, because there had still been a bit of light in the sky when he arrived. He couldn't help but smile, much to the guard's chagrin, as he stood up and noticed for the first time that the ticking had stopped. There was no way to explain it, but there it was.

Gone.

"I *am* sorry. I'll leave now."

The guard escorted him to the gate and let him out. Tom headed home with hope that he had cured himself, that the problem must have been how much he had been bottling up his emotions.

When his grandmother had died, he hadn't really grieved for her properly. He had gone to work the day after and only took a few hours off work on the day of her funeral. He was afraid at the time that if he cried for her, admitting she was gone and not coming back, the reality of it might hit him as hard as it did when his parents died. And if that happened, who would help him through it? He had nobody left; he was alone, and he had to accept it.

He thought he was going to be able to accept it now, to move forward and be his own man, especially now that the insistent ticking had finally stopped.

It was such a relief to him. The sound had kept him awake for so long, making him move through his days in a haze. He was happy to have it gone, and even happier to be home where he could get a few more hours of sleep before work.

Then, as soon as he stepped through the front door of his home, it started again. No softer. No louder. Not even a slow build up. The same as it had been for days.

"STOP IT! LEAVE ME ALONE!" He screamed, slamming his fists into the side of his head, pounding on his ears as hard he could.

Frustration filled him as he slammed the front door and ran to the bathroom. He continued to hit and scratch at his ears as he went, but the ticking didn't stop, just continued in the same pitch and at the same steady beat.

Tick.

Tick.

Tick.

Once in the bathroom, Tom grabbed a hand mirror and used it along with the one on the medicine cabinet to try and get a look inside his ear. He thought that maybe the doctor was wrong, that there really was something in there that was causing this, perhaps closer to the surface, and he had missed it. After all, the doctor was almost sixty, if not older, and wore glasses as thick as bullet proof glass. Not to mention he was a family doctor, and in Tom's opinion, family doctors were the guys who didn't do well enough in medical school to become specialists so they had to bottom out in a family practice, only able to refer them to a real doctor to get a real diagnoses. So there was a high probability he did miss something important. Tom had to find it and fix it.

He peered into his dark ear, and then began to probe it. First with a finger, and then a cotton swab. When he found nothing there, he picked up the metal nail file that was sitting on the back of the toilet, the one his grandmother used to use and he had yet to discard; then started digging inside the dark orifice. He winced as the rough metal made small cuts in the delicate flesh, and as it tore the scabs off the old ones his finger nails had made. Panic was filling him as he probed and saw blood oozing out of each of his ears, but didn't hear the ticking falter.

He needed something better.

After a quick run to the kitchen, Tom was back in front of the mirror trying to find the source of the sound, this time using a Phillips-head screwdriver to try and find what the source was. He moaned as he went deeper and deeper into each ear, listening to the strange whisper of the metal brushing against the inner ear hairs. The pain became worse with each push, blood streaming out faster and faster until the anger, frustration, and his own sheer will to stop the ticking made him act rashly. Frantic and determined, he used the screwdriver to repeatedly stab himself in his right ear, then his left, punching holes in the earlobe and cartilage, and burying it so deep that it punched through each of his eardrums. The smell of copper filled his nose, the sides of his head glistening red from his injuries.

But the ticking was still there.

Added to it was a low humming sound from his destroyed eardrums.

He was deaf.

He could still hear it.

Tick.

Tick.

Tick.

Tom screamed out loud, louder than he would have if he could hear himself properly, then collapsed to the cold, tiled floor, a pool of blood gathering under him. The shock from the adrenaline dump, and the blood seeping from his ears, caused Tom to pass out.

He knew he was dreaming.

He knew it was a dream because the ticking had stopped. The other clear sign was that he was no longer in his grandmother's house. Instead, he was back at home where he lived with his mom and dad, and he was only eight years old again, judging by the hands he held up in front of his face.

In the dream, he was lying in his own bed, his Star Wars pajamas stuck to his body from the hot night. He had been woken up. Not because of the heat though, but because of the sound of his mom and dad fighting; a thing they were doing far too often as of late. He heard his dad's voice booming, calling his wife a whore, a slut, and a worthless bitch. Tom winced as he stood by his bedroom door listening to them, hearing several loud smacks, a sound similar to when his dad took a belt to him from time to time. Tom could hear his mom crying, pleading for her husband to believe her, to trust her, begging not to be hit, and that made Tom tear up. He hated the sound of his mom sobbing more than anything else and wished that his dad would just stop. It had been so long since he heard the two of them laughing together and prayed for that as the smacking continued.

"Whose phone number is this then? Huh? One of your little fuck pals?"

"I was just showing Tommy his numbers. It's not a phone number."

"And I'm supposed to believe that shit, you lying cunt?"

SMACK!

"Hank, please!"

This was followed by his dad whispering and his mom crying harder and harder, until she screamed in a way Tommy never heard before, sending a cold chill down his spine despite the hot night, and then she made no sounds at all. The only thing Tom could hear after that was his dad laughing and mumbling to himself, and when that stopped, there was nothing. The house was utterly silent.

Tom sat against his door for what felt like hours before he went out to see if his mom was okay. He hoped his dad was already asleep, not wanting to get caught out of bed hours after he had been tucked in or else the belt would no doubt be pulled out on him. Just in case, he crept slowly, staying quiet as he went down the hall towards the kitchen where his mom usually sat to nurse her wounds.

When he got to the kitchen, she was there, but she wasn't nursing her wounds, nor was she alone. Tom nearly gasped when he saw his dad sitting in the kitchen with her, afraid that he was going to get up and beat him, just as he had beat his mom. But neither of them moved when he came in. Tom's mom was lying on the floor, the cat licking her face, and his dad was sitting close to her, his back leaning against the lower cabinets.

"Mom? Dad?" They didn't respond as Tom called out and walked into the kitchen. His eyes went from parent to parent, not sure what he was seeing, but knowing in his heart that it wasn't good.

Dad was smiling, but his eyes were shut. Dark liquid that looked like chocolate in the low light had spread down from large gashes on each arm. His mom was lying face down in a pool of that same dark water, the cat next to her, licking her face and the stuff she was lying in. Tom knelt beside her, the cat ignoring him as it lapped at the blood.

"Mom? Mommy?"

Tom shook her lightly, but she didn't respond.

He lay down beside her, confused and scared, but unable to grasp that his parents were dead. He curled up next to her cold body, her blood smearing his face. He cried to himself as the cat, Mr. Socks, went at the pool of blood. Tom watched him, mesmerized by the metal, heart-shaped tag hanging from the cat's collar, which hit the floor with a hypnotic rhythm.

Tick.

Tick.

Tick.

Disoriented, Tom woke up on the cold floor, blood dried on his face, and thought for a moment he was going to see his mom's dead face looking back at him; that Mr. Socks was still there, licking up her blood as the cat's tags clicked against the tiles. The same sound was still in his ears, still clicking and ticking, slow and steady, but he was alone. Just as he had been alone with the bodies of his parents for nearly two weeks. When the police had come in, Tom was close to death from dehydration, and he had seemed less than mentally stable. He had lain on the floor, curled up in the arms of his decomposing mother, having pissed and shit in his pajama pants, lost in a state of shock the doctors swore he would never overcome. This was the memory he kept from himself all these years.

His grandmother had thought differently, taking him to her house to try to help him find his way back, to heal him, to bring him out of the place he was trying to hide.

And it worked.

She would sit with him, sometimes for hours at a time, and try to pull him from the dark place he hid. She would take down her metronome that sat by the piano and make it move from side to side as she spoke softly to him. She timed her speech with the rhythmic ticking of the pendulum, told him to focus on it and the sound of her voice. She used this method to help him forget about his mom, his dad, and the nightmare of his life before her. In a way, she hypnotized him to forget that old life, making him only think of his new life with her.

The only person who knew how to fix me was her! And now that I'm broken again, she's calling to me, using the ticking to let me know that it's her!

Tom sat up, his head throbbing from the pain in his ears, and he knew what he needed to do. He took a mouthful of water and used it to swallow a handful of Advil to dull the pain. Then, after cleaning as much blood off of his ears and neck as possible, he changed his shirt, grabbed the screwdriver, and left the house. The slow metronome ticking was a steady companion, but he no longer let it bother him. He knew it was there for a reason. A beacon, in a way. The dream had reminded him of where the ticking had come from, where it had all started. A memory he pushed down so far and so deep that it took his unconscious mind to recall it. But Tom was sure that wasn't why the ticking was there. It wasn't trying to make him remember his mom and dad and those terrible days alone with their bodies. It was a calling, like the PING of a submarine, summoning him.

It was his grandmother.

That was why it had stopped for him when he was on her grave. He had found her and there was no need for it. Only she could make it better, just like she had before. She made it go away when he was a child, and the night before. She would do it again.

Tom was patient, knowing he only had to wait to make it all better. He had gone six days with the sound; what were a few hours more?

He hid, waited, and watched; as the security guard appeared and locked the gates to the cemetery, Tom came up behind him and jammed the screwdriver into the man's right ear, swirling it around, tearing apart everything in the man's skull. Tom couldn't hear if the guard had screamed at first, his world still silent aside from a low hum and the ticking, but he judged by the fact that nobody on the street had looked over; no sound had been made. He thrust his own body weight forward on the dying guard, knocking them both to the ground, and Tom slammed the screwdriver over and over again into his face. Because of the damage to his ears, Tom couldn't hear the bone screaming against the metal, nor did he hear the wet, meaty slaps as his fists continued to strike down on the pulpy, liquefying remains of the man's head. He only heard the steady hum of deafness and the ticking of his grandmother's call to him.

"I'm sorry for this." He whispered as he stood up, blood and brain matter dripping in thick globs from his hand and the screwdriver. "I wish there was another way."

Tom dragged the man's body over to a large area of bushes and did his best to hide him. He wished he could feel bad for the man, someone who might have a wife or kids, but he couldn't. Not when he himself had suffered so much and could only end the suffering by doing what he was going to do. The guard would have gotten in the way, kicked him out just as he had the night before. In his state, he believed killing him was the only way he could carry out his plan.

Once the body was hidden, Tom ran through the graveyard until he found the headstone that read "Norma Jean Knox". Without wasting any time, he began digging into the earth, pulling away handfuls of dirt and grass. He used the bloody screwdriver to soften the dirt as much as he could, but after a while, he threw it aside as madness and determination took over. He barely felt it as two of his fingernails on his right hand peeled back from the skin, and then one on his left did the same. There was no time to pay attention to the stinging as dirt mixed with blood and a fourth nail threatened to come off.

He dug.

Like a dog, his hands cut deep into the soil, going faster and faster as he felt sheer madness take over. The ticking was quieting, slowing, the deeper he went. For hours he dug into the earth, the smell of it so much like that of the root cellar he stood naked in days before, worms and other deep ground bugs bleeding from the soil as he went. He started to cry tears of relief as he got closer and closer to her, knowing she would save him from his own insanity; save him from the ticking that wanted to push him over the edge. He needed her arms around him, her comfort and her soft voice to make it all better.

Hours later, the top half of the coffin broke through and Tom cleared away enough dirt to open it. He struggled with the lid, his hands bleeding from six missing fingernails and several gashes. He grunted and finally pulled the coffin open; he was greeted by the smell of musty earth and decayed flesh. He didn't wince though, didn't feel the panic the funeral homes inspired. Instead, he welcomed it; reminding him of the days he had curled next to his mom's lifeless body. He fully opened the top half of the coffin and for the first time in a year, looked down at his grandmother.

More tears came at the sight of her. She lay on dirty white satin in her tattered ivory dress with the lavender flowers on it. The dress had been one of her favorites and he had been glad to pick out for her; it was what she would have wanted, even if it was little more than dirty rags when he pried open the coffin.

Worse than that was her once-beautifully pale and slightly plump face, now brown and grey; her cheeks sunken and lips peeled back, forming a skeletal grin. Her once-blue eyes were gone, no doubt eaten away by the bugs that now swarmed deep in the empty sockets, dancing in her faded memories. He wished that she still looked as she had, but he knew that everything changes. Just as he no longer looked like that eight year old boy she had rescued from the cold walls of that institution, she was no longer the same woman she had been.

But she was still his grandmother.

And she was still there to make it all better.

It wasn't until three in the afternoon the next day that the guard's body was found tucked into the bushes. The police came, took photos and fingerprints and tried to piece together what happened. The cemetery was closed to the public for a week as the police kept the scene open to investigators. It was on the third day that a warrant was put out for the arrest of Thomas Knox. They checked his work and his grandmother's house, but it only brought up more questions. The pool of blood and the nail file covered in his DNA made no sense to the detectives. They spoke to his doctor, who would only say he had seen Thomas recently and tried to refer him to a specialist, but would give no other information to the police without a warrant. It seemed as though Thomas Knox had simply vanished.

That is, until they opened up the cemetery to the public again and the groundskeepers found his grandmother's open grave. The detective in charge showed up, expecting to find the body stolen. He had heard of it happening before, something to do with separation anxiety. He was a little upset nobody had gone into the graveyard to investigate, but they were only looking at the crime scene and the grave was over a mile away from where the guard was found. He hoped to find some answers at the grave.

What he hadn't expected to find was Tom, still there, in the coffin with his grandmother. They were both lying on their sides, arms around one another. The detective felt nauseous at the sight of a nest of maggots bubbling out of Tom's one visible ear, with beetles crawling in and out of the smile on his face. Tom looked as though he had been happy to die there, buried with a near skeleton of a corpse. He wondered how far gone a guy would have to be to do something like that.

"Too bad we hadn't actually done a search this far into the cemetery," one of the uniforms said, looking down into the grave.

"At least I don't have to do anymore work for this. If they all killed themselves, it would make my job easier." The detective sighed and walked away from the grave.

"What should I do with this?"

"Stand there with your thumb up your ass until someone comes to cart him off to the morgue. Enjoy."

ADAM MILLARD

THE INCONGRUOUS MR MARWICK

He was out again, digging up his front garden with his gnarled, rheumy claws. Samuel had watched the mad old coot do this before; there was something deeply inhuman about the way he hooked his fingers into the ground, as if he believed himself to be an animal. Samuel watched, not with fear and apprehension like the rest of the kids in the street, but because Marwick intrigued him. Whilst his friends taunted the geriatric oddball, Samuel observed; a casual outsider trying to ascertain just what had propagated the man's absurd behaviour.

Samuel's father, a respected physician, believed Marwick

was mostly harmless. Sure, he didn't respond well to having shit pushed through his letterbox or graffiti-tags on his front door, but who *did*?

The cases in question were both, unfortunately, perpetrated by Samuel's friend, Kevin Jacobson. Kevin was the kind of kid who lacked boundaries. If an offer of cash-money was made in return for Kevin lopping off one of his own fingers, he would walk away with the money and a bleeding digit, without a doubt. Most of the trouble in the neighbourhood was down to Kevin, and more than half the japes inflicted upon Marwick were either by his own hand or a brainchild of his that he'd managed to offload on another impressionable fool.

The shit through the letterbox had been a mistake; Samuel wanted no part in the caper, and had stood across the street, raptly spying. Deep down, he had been as involved as Kevin; prevention would have been the only thing to eliminate him from blame, and from across the street – where it was safe and he could get a good head-start if required – he did nothing of the sort.

Kevin had crept along the front of the house like Fantômas. The only thing missing was a mask and a bag labelled *swag*. Samuel had wanted to call out, to tell his friend to abort the mission, that he had a very bad feeling about it.

But it was too late. Kevin delivered the package – an amalgamation of Mrs. Beetham's tabby and Roger Bernstein's Jack Russell – and quickly traversed the driveway, too scared to check across his shoulder, too excited to enjoy the moment.

If he *had* looked, he would have seen Mr Marwick fast approaching. Samuel had watched the old guy practically sprint from his house, swinging the bag of shit in that liveried right claw of his. He was completely naked – apart from a flat-cap which perched precariously on top of his balding pate – and he'd screamed in a manner usually utilised by the final girl in horror movies.

He'd chased them all the way to Birch Street before giving up the ghost and limping, breathlessly, back to his house. Kevin found it hilarious; Samuel felt nothing but utter shame.

"Is he pretending to be a dog again?" a voice asked. Samuel didn't need to turn to know that Kevin was there. "Makes you *sick*, don't it? They allow nutters like that to roam free. Look at him, he's eating the dirt now. *Eurgh*, that's gross!"

Samuel couldn't avert his eyes. It was like watching a car-crash in slow-motion. He knew it was wrong, but there was something grotesquely fascinating about it. Marwick loaded fistfuls of mud and grass into his mouth, chewing momentarily before letting it all fall out again.

"I heard he tried to eat a pigeon last week," Kevin said as he placed a friendly hand on Samuel's shoulder. Samuel, for some reason, found his touch overwhelmingly offensive and stepped aside. Kevin continued. "Managed to catch it in one of them traps he has set out in his back garden. Lindsey Baker's garden backs right onto his, and she saw him pulling its feathers out. Toying with it, she reckons."

Samuel shook his head. "Lindsey Baker's house doesn't back onto his garden, Kevin. She's two doors down; there's no way she can see over his fences."

"Why do you always have to stick up for him?" Kevin asked. "What is he? Your *granddad*?" He laughed; Samuel could see bits of breakfast still stuck to his teeth, which made him feel queasy.

"Why do you always have to *pick* on him?" Samuel said, knowing very well that it was because Kevin liked to think he was the cock of the neighbourhood, the funny one from down the street who always got the girls and never got caught. Truth be told, Samuel suspected Kevin would find himself in a prison cell before he turned twenty. His crimes were small now, but the time would come when shit through a letterbox would not be enough. When that happened it would be a car through an off-license window, or a knife through an old lady.

Samuel knew one thing for sure.

He didn't want to be there when Kevin made the transition.

"He's an *idiot*," Kevin retorted. "Look at him. Thinks he's a fucking cow, or something."

Samuel finally managed to overcome the strange compulsion to watch and turned away. "He's misunderstood," he said. "How would you feel if that was one of your grandparents? Would you throw rocks and spit *then*, huh?" Samuel already knew the answer. If it wasn't Marwick, if it was instead one of Kevin's own, Kevin would treat them just the same. Maybe worse. With kin you could get away with a hell of a lot more.

"He'd be in a home," Kevin shrugged, as if it was the simplest answer imaginable. "Somewhere he wouldn't be able to attack some poor fucker. The man's a hazard to society; anyone who eats their own front garden is."

As far as Samuel was aware, Marwick had never attacked anyone. There had been rumours of indecent exposure, but nothing violent. And Samuel, who tried to see the good in everyone, put the self-exhibition down to the fact that the guy didn't know what day it was; it was likely he didn't know whether he had pants on, or not, half the time.

"Anyway," Kevin continued, "wait until you see what I've got in store for him tomorrow. He won't know what hit him." He burst into a fit of laughter that was more frightening than anything old man Marwick had ever done.

Across the street, Marwick snapped his head towards them. Soil and worms dangled listlessly from his puckered lips. Had he heard Kevin's threat, or was he simply reacting to the uncontrollable laughter that followed?

"Leave him alone," Samuel whispered. He tried to look aloof, but it was difficult knowing Marwick's piercing blue eyes were watching him.

"Don't be such a pussy, Sam," Kevin said, patting his friend on the back. Once again, Samuel shrugged him off. "Anyway, you don't have to do anything. Just sit back and watch the fireworks. It'll be hilarious, dude."

Samuel was about to appeal one last time when Kevin turned his back and began to walk away. Marwick, across the street, scrambled to his feet, kicking up mud and dirt, and for a split second Samuel thought he was going to chase Kevin. He didn't. He made a strange mewling sound before rushing for his front door. Kevin was cruelly laughing and pointing as Marwick slammed the front door shut. The dead wreath that hung just above his letterbox swung to and fro, threatening to fall but never quite attaining enough momentum.

Just then it started to rain. Samuel took it as an omen and made for his own house.

Wait until you see what I've got in store for him tomorrow.

Those words repeated over and over in Samuel's mind; a stuck record that turned his blood to mercury. He hoped Kevin was exaggerating, but if he knew Kevin – he *did*, and it wasn't something he was proud of any longer – he had something epically boorish up his sleeve. Samuel didn't want anything bad to happen to the old guy, but he knew there was very little he could *do* about it.

"I could tell Dad," he mumbled to himself as he lunged through his front door and out of the rain.

He didn't notice Marwick's curtains twitching across the street, nor the dirty grinning lips beyond.

At dinner that evening, Samuel – somewhat laboriously – informed his father of Kevin's plot to deride Marwick the following day. Since he had no proof and wasn't sure exactly what his friend intended to do, his father responded in pretty much the manner Samuel had anticipated.

"Just don't get involved, Sam."

That was it. There would be no heroic intervention, no phone-call to Kevin's parents to report the news of their son's perverse scheme. Sam had been warned to keep his distance, as if that would somehow make it all okay.

"Dad, I don't know what he's gonna do, but I'm worried for the old guy. Kevin can be—"

"A pain in the ass," Samuel's father interjected. The way in which he slammed his mug down on the kitchen table suggested he was drawing a line under the conversation.

Samuel knew he was wasting his time. Marwick was going to be made a mockery of, whether he liked it or not. Standing up to Kevin wouldn't stop him. He was unyielding; the kind of kid who did what he liked whenever he felt like it. In fact, attempting to counteract would be the equivalent of friendship suicide.

No, there had to be something. Some way to keep the old guy safe without Kevin realising he had a part in it.

Samuel went to bed that night with a heavy head and a hollow heart. Sleep, or anything like it, was not forthcoming.

Marwick spent the morning standing in front of his own door, knocking as if there might be someone there to eventually welcome him. The door was ajar, and occasionally he would peer around it to check before quickly pulling out and proceeding to knock. Samuel kept his distance, slowly rolling the skateboard along on the opposite side of the street. If Marwick knew he was there, he didn't show it.

It was a bright morning; people walked around with permanent squints. The usual plethora of dog-walkers marched up and down the street, allowing their hounds to shit for all and sundry to tread in. Newspaper delivery-boys went about their rounds, their earphones pumping tinny garbage into their heads. Across the way, Mrs. Beetham and Miss Schofield palavered over their separating fence. Samuel couldn't quite hear the conversation, but several choice words drifted across, enough for him to know they were discussing the terrible paedophile-ring that had dominated the previous week's news. They did that a lot; prattled on and on about things that were of no concern to them. Their lives were so sad and pathetic that all they had left to talk about were asinine stories plucked from whatever shitty tabloid they had the misfortune of subscribing to.

And Marwick, the poor, misunderstood man from number thirty-four, was considered the odd one.

Samuel reached the end of the street and flipped his board up, catching it adroitly in his right hand. As he began to walk back towards his house, he saw that Marwick was no longer banging on his front-door. He'd moved along the front of the house and was now peering through a window, shielding his eyes from the morning sun. As Samuel approached, he could hear the old guy laughing.

Samuel often wondered what went through Marwick's mind. Did he see the world as everyone else did? Was he capable of seeing things others weren't? There was no way to know, or ever find out. Marwick was an enigma, a perplexing anomaly that no amount of psychiatric help or care would ever fathom.

His laughing grew louder, and Samuel felt a chill run the course of his spine, despite the blazing sun. He watched as Marwick did a little dance – a Leprechaun's jig – in front of his window. For a man of his years, he could certainly move; he was jaunty and lithe, as if he hadn't a care in the world, and Samuel wanted to scream across at him to be careful, to watch out for Kevin Jacobson who would be paying a visit later with his bag of tricks.

He couldn't speak. He hurried along the path, clutching his skateboard to his chest, trying to ignore the dancing eccentric in his periphery.

Wait until you see what I've got in store for him tomorrow, Kevin's voice said in his head, but it was no longer *tomorrow*. It was *today*, and Marwick was blissfully unaware that his day was about to take a turn for the worse.

That afternoon, Samuel made a point of calling for Kevin. The chances of stopping him were zero if he didn't at least know what he had planned. Kevin nonchalantly answered the door in his pyjamas; he looked like he'd just clambered from his pit.

"Hey,' Samuel said. "What're you doing in there? Have you seen the weather?" It was a valid question but – as much as it sounded like one – not an invite. Samuel didn't want to spend his day around Kevin, and not just because his father warned him against it.

"Late night," Kevin replied. "Mom and Dad were arguing all night. I think my dad's been screwing his secretary again."

Samuel snorted, then suppressed it as he realised Kevin wasn't joking. "Shit, man, that sucks."

"Not for my dad," Kevin yawned. "His secretary's stunning."

Now Samuel did laugh, and despite Kevin's apparent fatigue, so did he. Somewhere in the house, a vacuum cleaner whirred into life. Kevin rolled his eyes and stepped out onto the street, pulling the door to silence the incessant drone of his mother's frantic cleaning.

"She always does this after an argument," Kevin sighed. "I don't know whether she thinks the dirty words they call each other leaves a stain, or what. Dad's gone to work in a huff, and I'm left with old misery while she tears the place apart with a feather duster and a Hoover."

"So, you've got no plans, then?" Samuel asked. He honestly hoped that Kevin had forgotten his threat from the previous day, or that the sleepless night had taken the wind out of him. Marwick might have nothing to worry about, after all.

"Nah," Kevin said, yawning once again. "Video-games and low-budget horror."

Samuel sighed; this was the best possible result.

And then Kevin said, "Got to get my rest before tonight's main event." His mouth contorted into a wide grin, like something you might see carved on a pumpkin. Samuel's heart dropped down into his guts; Kevin hadn't forgotten at all. He was conserving his energy for whatever twisted trick he had in store. He had probably been up all night finalising things, making sure that everything went off without a hitch. If anything, his parents arguing and keeping him awake had given him more time to get things right.

Samuel had never felt so utterly helpless in his life.

"Eight tonight," Kevin said, rubbing his hands enthusiastically together. "Sean and Trucker are gonna be there." He said it as if it would somehow make the whole nightmare more appealing. Sean Rogers was an idiot, and Tommy "Trucker" Dale liked nothing more than seeing Marwick suffer, although he never got his own hands dirty.

And why would he need to when Kevin was more than happy to step up to the plate?

"You *are* going to be there, aren't you?" Kevin asked. It had never crossed his mind that Samuel would rather be somewhere – *anywhere* – else. "Please don't tell me you're thinking of hiding in your fucking bedroom when the fun starts. *Shit*, Sam, it's gonna be hilarious. The old fart's finally gonna realise that his crazy-ass behaviour has consequences."

He won't realise *anything*, Samuel thought. The man was vacant and so far mentally detached that it was impossible to determine just how he might react, or what he might do.

Samuel grimaced. "I'll be there, but don't expect me to do anything. And please, Kevin, don't do anything to hurt him. He might be freaky, but he's still a person."

"Yeah, yeah, whatever," Kevin said as he pulled his front-door open and stepped inside. The sound of the vacuum cleaner was gone, replaced by some shitty radio-station; Samuel could hear the rowdy voice of an overzealous sportscaster. "It's just a bit of *fun*, Sam. Crazy old fucker ain't gonna have a coronary."

Samuel was about to disagree when the door closed and he was left staring into frosted glass.

He had done what he could. It wasn't, by any means, enough.

Samuel and Sean watched from the bushes across the street. Trucker had somehow managed to drag his fat ass up the tree outside Mrs. Beetham's house. Sean held a crackling walkie-talkie in one hand; Trucker had the other. They were arguing back and forth over who would win in a fight: zombies or vampires. Samuel couldn't care less because neither were real. Mr Marwick was real, and something terrible was about to happen to him. *That* was all Samuel could think about.

Samuel had a walkie-talkie, too. His was on the same frequency as Kevin's, who was busying himself with something in Marwick's back garden.

No doubt putting the final touches to his master plan.

"What do *you* think, Sam?" Sean asked, snapping Samuel from his reverie.

"About what?" Samuel spat. He was not in the mood for bantering with idiots.

"A vampire could rip a zombie's throat out, *right?*"

"Have you heard yourself?" Samuel said. "It doesn't fucking *matter*. It doesn't matter who's hairiest, Bigfoot or Chewbacca. It doesn't matter if you think Star Trek's better than Star Wars. Sean, just tell Trucker to pipe down, will you, and stop arguing over stupid things, for fuck's sake!"

Sean released the button on his walkie-talkie; the annoying hiss, Samuel thought, was nowhere near as annoying as the two boys bullshitting each other. After a moment of contemplation, Sean pushed the button and said, "Trucker, be quiet now. Kevin's gonna do his stuff and Samuel's on the verge of crying over here."

Samuel shot him a reproachful glance. In the tree along the street, Trucker waved acknowledgement before turning his attention to Marwick's house.

Ten more minutes passed; the streetlights flickered to life. Samuel thought about radioing through to Kevin. It had been a long time since they'd last heard from him. *Too* long. But Samuel had visions of his friend stealthily approaching the house, the walkie-talkie suddenly crackling into life. They emitted a stifled hiss, but it would be enough to alert Marwick to the interloper.

Wasn't that what he *wanted?* To foil Kevin's plot? It would certainly put an abrupt end to the night's entertainment, as Marwick would emerge and chase him off, an unleashed dog with the scent of bacon beneath its nose.

"Fuck it," Samuel muttered. He pushed the button on the side of his walkie-talkie, and before Sean could stop him he began to speak. "Kevin, what's taking so long?"

Click. *Hisssssss.*

"What the hell are you *doing*, man?" Sean gasped. A look of utter disbelief had washed over him. "You're gonna drop him right in the—"

Samuel shushed him and they both glanced down at the crackling transceiver. Kevin would not be happy with the interruption; they waited for the inevitable barrage of abuse to begin.

It didn't.

Samuel and Sean stared into each other's fearful eyes, jaws slack and drooping as if dislocated. Sean was about to suggest going in after their friend when the hissing from the walkie-talkie ceased. Samuel heaved a sigh of relief; Sean patted him hard on the back.

The silence, however, was not broken by Kevin's angry voice. A shrill laughter pierced the night, a cackling that Samuel was all too familiar with.

Marwick.

Samuel dropped the walkie-talkie just as the fireworks began to light up the pitch-black sky. Both he and Sean rolled away from the bush, terrified by the sudden noise, mesmerised by the explosions overhead.

So that was what Kevin had been planning. He'd set up an entire display of fireworks in the old guy's backyard. He was probably out there now, trying to get them all lit before he was chased away by the deranged resident. Across the street, Trucker fell out of Mrs. Beetham's tree and landed with a thump on the pavement beneath. As he clambered to his feet he began to whoop and dance at the sight of the spectacle. Rockets and silver spinners, crackling starbursts and brocade plumes filled the night-sky; the resulting cacophony was enough to bring people out of their houses, no doubt fearing a terrorist-attack or something of that ilk.

Samuel and Sean staggered to their feet and waited for Kevin to come rushing from Marwick's backyard. They were amazed when the front door to Marwick's house flew open and Kevin ran, full-pelt, towards the street. He was completely naked and appeared to be bleeding from his neck. Rivulets of crimson ran down his bare chest. He was howling, or screaming, or both, but the noise of the fireworks rendered him inaudible to anyone farther away than his bewildered friends.

Samuel staggered backwards, pulling Sean with him. He'd realised something; he'd seen the silver pubic hairs in the glow of erupting fireworks.

It wasn't Kevin.

Marwick stopped still in the road, illuminated in reds and yellows and greens, and as he tore Kevin's face from his own to reveal the sickening grin beneath, Samuel could have sworn his heart stopped completely.

Kevin had been right all along. The guy was a maniac, a savage, a murderous old crone who'd had plans of his own.

The fireworks continued to explode, and Marwick continued to dance, swinging his antagonist's face around and around until the police arrived twenty minutes later.

CHRISTINE MORGAN

NAILS OF THE DEAD

A corpse-cart comes, heavy-laden and rumbling, wheels churning thick in the muck. The ox plods along with head lowered against rain mixed with spattering sleet.

I wait.

The driver and his boy keep their heads down as well, shabby cloaks wrapped around them, hoods drawn over their gaunt faces.

I wait and I watch.

They pay me no notice. Even the ox is oblivious to my lurking, hidden presence. If they had a dog with them, it might be another matter … some dogs are my friends; some, but by no means all.

The boy coughs. It is a wet, weary sound.

He is plague-stricken.

The sickness spread across the countryside like a savory rumor. Neighbor to neighbor, friend to friend. And, like a rumor grows greater and stronger in the telling, so too did this.

The driver says nothing, makes no gesture of comfort. He nudges the ox with the goad. The beast obligingly turns toward the funeral-pit that was, in days not so long distant, a rocky hollow at the village's edge.

They have a night of grim work ahead.

So do I.

The cart stops. The driver climbs down. His boy, still coughing, follows. They take hold of an old woman. Her fine, grey hair trails like cobwebs. Her limbs are bony sticks. Her fingers, deep-grooved from a lifetime of distaff and spindle, thread and loom, seem to scratch like hooked claws at the dark-clouded sky.

They lift her, and carry her, and swing her, and let her go.

Down the corpse falls, a stiff and brittle bundle.

Into the pit. One more for the pile.

Birds flap up, protesting at the disturbance. Gulls, mostly; Odin's ravens, greedy corpse-pickers that fancy themselves too noble for this feast. Rats scurry, squeaking and indignant. The lesser carrion-eaters, worms and beetles, go about their business.

A child is next.

This is the way of such things. The weakest are often first to succumb: the very old, the very young, the poor and the frail. But, ultimately, no one is safe. Lord or thrall, hall or hovel, no one is safe.

I continue waiting and watching as they unload the cart of its burdens. Bodies tumble like logs. Cold, dead flesh slaps and smacks onto the rain-slick, rotting mound below. The stench, already a tangible thing, worsens. The belch and sigh of released gases—decaying organs rupturing upon impact—it is a reeking, pale miasma hanging in the air, felt and tasted as well as smelled.

The boy stumbles, gorge heaving. He does not vomit, but as he gags and retches, he begins again to cough. He coughs until he drops, choking, to his knees. Blood-foam flecks his scabbed lips. The sound is terrible, thin and desperate wheezing gasps between each ragged lung-ripping spasm.

He collapses, face-purpled, watering eyes wide and pleading. His trembling hand outstretches. It is gore-streaked, filthy, grime caked under the nails in thick black crescents.

The driver, with a pained expression, turns away. He puts his back to the dying boy. His shoulders shake. At his sides, his white-knuckled fists clench. He seems to stare unseeing in the direction of the village, where scant, thin threads of smoke unspool from chimneys.

Then it is over. A final rasping gurgle escapes the boy's throat. His body goes limp. Rain washes the bloody foam from his lips. Sleet melts in his eyes.

I watch with great interest.

I am no stranger to death or the dead.

The dying, however, I do not often witness. I follow later, like the rats and gulls, like the worms and beetles, like the proud ravens and those dogs who are not so loyal as to refrain from feeding on the remains of their former masters.

I watch now as the driver covers the boy's face and wraps him in his cloak. He sets this one aside, treating it far more gently than the others in his care.

Working alone, he resumes the unloading. He lifts those he can, drags or hauls those he cannot. He grunts with effort as he tips the corpse of a large man over the rim of the carrion-pit; it rolls down the slope and lands on the pile with a noise like a sow flop-wallowing in deep mud.

At last, the cart is emptied. The hungry gulls wheeling above voice their approval and impatience. The driver places the boy's cloak-wrapped body with the others, then returns to his seat and goads the ox toward home.

When he is gone, it is time for me to do *my* work.

I descend among the dead. The rats and birds do not flee from my approach; their kind know me of old, and know that I am not here to interfere with their feeding. Indeed, the rats welcome me, because my scavenging helps clear the way for their own.

The rot-stench does not bother me. Nor does the unyielding rigor of flesh, nor the clammy feel of skin moist with coagulated oozings. I do not cringe from gaped mouths where worms crawl, or from the maggots that writhe and teem in sockets where sharp beaks have plucked out the milky orbs of sightless eyes. When I find a she-rat has birthed a litter of pink, squirming creatures in the eviscerated hollow of a man's belly, I do not disturb them.

I pick up the man's dead hand in mine.

A large hand, tough, strong, powerful, well-callused. The knuckles are scarred. A half-healed cut slices the base of the thumb.

The nails are very good.

Broad and thick; healthy, and long.

Not overly long, not protruding much beyond the tips of the fingers, but long just the same. Untrimmed for some while, several days at least.

Of course. As I had expected, and why I had come.

In times such as this, plague-times or other times of illness, disaster or despair, these little matters often go neglected. There are, folk think to themselves if they think of it at all, far more important matters to attend to. Trimming their finger- and toe-nails can wait. A day more or less—what difference would it make? Then they fall ill, and grow sicker, and die ... and those who survive are in no fit state to attend to grooming the dead.

All the better for me, and for my work and purpose.

I wear the tools of my trade on a ring at my belt. They clink and rattle as I move. Iron and silver, antler and tin, whale-ivory, wood, hammered brass and forged steel; from needle-fine pincers to sturdy gripping-tongs such that a blacksmith might use, my belt-ring of tools holds something for every occasion.

I choose the right one and begin as I always do: with the forefinger. I pry up the nail enough to wedge the bottom jaw underneath, then bear down with careful pressure until I have it in a sure and firm grasp.

Then I pull.

Not slowly, since I have many more yet to do, yet not in a quick, rude yank either. The sensation is one as much heard and felt as seen, a peeling separation, the faintest crackle of gristle as it parts from the bloodless, blue-grey flesh-bed beneath.

It is a well-practiced pull, a draw clean and smooth as a blade from a sheath.

I hold it up to examine and nod with satisfaction. No cracks, no splitting of the nail, no breaking, no jagged splinters left sticking up from the nail-bed; I have it entire. I tuck it into the bag slung around my neck.

I move on to the next finger. Then the third, and the smaller fourth. They are all clean pulls. Last, on that hand, I take the thumb-nail. Those, and the nails of the large toes, are always the most well-rooted, the most difficult to extract. They resist with tenacity, often trailing threads of sinewy tissue when they tear loose. Yet they are also the ones of most use and value.

The right hand done, I lower it and pick up the left. Already, whiskered noses twitching, some of the rats creep nearer. Their sharp little yellow teeth, made for chewing and nibbling, are well-suited for the eating of corpse-lips. They gnaw at the ear-lobes and the flared ridges of nostrils, but those parts are tougher, a less satisfying meal.

With the nails tugged from the ends of finger- and toe-tips, they are exposed, soft and unobstructed. The rats may readily strip the meat from the bones, just as a man at a feast-table might devour boiled pork from a pig's ribs. When I remove boots or shoes to get at the toes, this saves them the trouble of chewing through leather.

Yes, the rats know me. They like me. In a way, we are friends.

We meet in graveyards and barrows and burial-mounds. We meet in the gritty soot of funeral-pyres, sifting together through burnt wood and char-blackened bones. There, the rats find their meals cooked, if overdone. The nails I take from the ashes are hardened, baked like potter's clay, stained with a glaze of rendered fat and blood. These serve their own special purpose.

On the battlefields the rats and I often meet. So too the ravens, the wolves, and flies in roiling, buzzing green-black clouds. Sometimes, I see folk there, men and women, even children. They go searching for survivors or loved ones, or to snatch up what plunder they can from the dead: silver and gold, weapons, mail-coats and treasure.

I avoid them.

They know me, though not as the rats do. Not as friends. They fear me. They tell their stories about me, but not all they tell in the tales is true.

They think I am many.

But I am only one.

There is no great army of Naglings, no spirit-horde.

Only one. Only me.

Safne, I am called, or Nagl-Safne in full.

The Gatherer. The Nail-Taker.

Here in this pit, where plague-corpses have been dumped, is a bountiful harvest. The rain turns to sleet as dusk deepens toward night, but compared to the realm of my birth, the sleet is mild as bath-water. It has nothing on cold Niflheim, which itself has nothing on the Fimbul-Winter that will come.

And each nail that I pull helps to hasten its onset.

I take them all. Male and female, young and old. Even the tiny, fragile nails of babes, which must be done with the most exquisite deftness of touch.

Mothers tell their children not to bite their nails, or chew their hair. This, they say, will cause the remnants to amass in their gizzards, forming into knots like owl-pellets. "It will cause belly-aches," they'll tell them, "and the Naglings will find you, slice you open, cut out your gizzard and steal it as you sleep."

A ridiculous lie, but if it does keep them from biting their nails; so much the better. As long as they also neglect to trim them before they die.

Once the nails have been trimmed, clipped or cut, I can do nothing with the shreds and scraps left over. Those are useless to me. Useless to my purpose.

Most folk are mindful of that truth and will give care to their grooming. All the more so when they must face risk of death, as when men ready for battle or war. They are reluctant to contribute to the cause that I serve.

Plagues such as this, sudden and far-reaching, are therefore a windfall.

One by one, finger by finger, hand by hand, toe by toe, foot by foot, I pick bare the corpses in the funeral pit. The nails go into my bag. It is nearly full. I have been busy.

Last of all, I reach the cart-driver's boy. I unwrap the cloak. The life-heat has leached from his body, but the stiffness has not yet set in and the pallor barely greys his skin. He might almost be in a deep slumber.

He is not. He is dead. He does not flinch when I grip each nail in the tin pincers and peel them free. No beads of blood well up from the raw nail-beds.

I find when I remove his shoes that he is missing three toes on one foot. The flesh is gnarled with old scars where they had once been. A childhood injury, but one that had not unduly impaired him; I had not noticed him limping.

There are still two toes, two nails to take, and I do. Yet I consider it a sign, a sign as good as any. My bag is close to full. It is time to go.

I whistle for my hound. His name is Hrugbein, heap-of-bones. Though the runt of the litter, he is a great and ugly gangly thing, large enough to bear me upon his back. I swing astride, pressing my knees to his ribs and clinging tight to clumps of coarse, patchy fur.

We are off at a run. Ungainly as his gait may be, Hrugbein is fast-footed, taking us swiftly away from the village and plague-raddled land. We seem to fly along the road where souls trudge their hopeless journey. They avert their haunted gazes as we pass.

Torch-fires at the bridge burn a freezing blue-white, winter flames carved of the deep hearts of glacier's ice. The river rushes beneath us, a noisy tumult in the darkness. The guards stand aside, the gates open for us, the terrible snow whirls and chills, and we come to Eljudnir, the cold sleet-sprayed hall.

Eljudnir is the dwelling of the corpse-queen, pitiless Hel, keeper of the unchosen dead. Hel, daughter of Loki. Hel, half her body fair and beautiful and unblemished, the other half rot-black, skin sagging and sloughing with decay. Hel, the dreaded gloom-goddess.

Sloth and Laziness serve her, while Age and Infirmity manage the household. In the feasting-chambers, the tables are built of Deprivation, laid with Thirst's cups and Hunger's plates, and the knives are Famine. The beds, made of Sickness and Discomfort, are spread with blankets woven from Restlessness. Bladder-stones pebble the floors of the necessary rooms, where the boards are holed with Constipation, Flux and Cramping.

This is not a place of torture but of bleak and simple miseries. Ever damp, ever dreary. Noses drip. Skin itches. Joints and teeth ache. Mist and fog obscure all. Silence, sorrow, tedium and grief hold sway.

This is Niflheim, realm of Hel, who is my mother.

She is, and always has been, unsure what to make of me, her strange child; not son nor daughter, not both but neither. I, Nagl-Safne, grey and sexless, in my garment stitched from rat-skins, with the husks of beetles knotted into the lank locks of my hair. I with my belt-ring where the tools of my trade clink and rattle, and my gathering-bag slung around my neck.

I show it to her, the bag, brimming with nails of all sizes. She stirs through them with her own long, pale hand. The sound is a dry susurration that hisses and whispers, harsh utterances of loss, wistful sighs of the dead.

Hel nods to me. Half her mouth curves in a brief smile, displaying satisfaction but no warmth. The other half remains twisted in a fierce, downcast sneer.

It is sufficient for now. I am dismissed, given leave to go.

Nearby, upon a throne of chained honor sits Baldr, prince-hostage among the gods. His gaze follows me, solemnly, as I cross the wide somber hall. I raise the bag to him. I give it a shake, as a merchant might shake a weighty pouch of silver. I grin. He looks away. He knows that my work hastens the end of his imprisonment here, yet he cannot bear to well-wish that endeavor, for he also knows what else it will bring.

I clamber again onto Hrugbein's back. We ride forth from Eljudnir with such speed that the rime-frozen land becomes a blur. Over ice-fanged mountain peaks and chasms where waterfalls plunge, through a vast and still forest, we race and we ride; this path is familiar to us, for we have ridden it a thousand-thousand times.

It brings us to the home of the giants on the foaming eastern sea. It brings us to the shipyard where the most feared ship of all awaits completion.

The shipmaster is here as well, Hrym, my father. Ancient and decrepit he may be, and perhaps as mad as some say, but none can deny his skill. Such craft, such genius and artistry, none in the Nine Worlds have ever before seen.

Terror and pride rise in my blood as I behold again the hugeness of the unfinished *Naglfar*. From a distance, it might seem to be made of bleached birch-wood and bone. Only nearer does its true nature become clear.

Naglfar, the Nail-Ship.

The hull and deck planks; the rails, mast and oars; the prows sweeping up, defiant, beast-headed; it is built bit by bit, piece by piece, of what I painstakingly gather from the fingers and toes of the dead.

They are placed overlapping like snake-scales, like roof-shingles, like the rows of shields forming an army's shield-wall. They have give, one against the other, like scales as well. Like the links of a mail-coat, strong but flexible.

I bring my bag to Hrym at his sorting-table. He pours the bounty from it.

"Ah," he says, pleased.

He permits me to help. We sort the nails. We scour them clean in basins of sand, scrubbing the dried fluids, filth and flesh from them.

The nails of dead men are more prized for the hull, being larger and thicker, stronger, more durable. Yet those of women and children have their uses as well, in the finer fittings and for decoration. Most are yellow-white; some are char-blackened or otherwise stained. They are smooth or ridged, sharp or blunt, sometimes nicked or chipped. These variations in size and shape, color and texture, let them be worked into intricate patterns.

Few might even notice the beauty, and fewer still appreciate it. But I do. I watch with awe and admiration.

Hrym fits each nail into its place. Though he is a giant, with a giant's immense hands to match, he is anything but clumsy. His precision makes my own deftest touch look crude and ham-fisted.

Naglfar grows, by slow increments but ever-steadily, toward its destiny.

This is my role. This is my purpose. To provide these materials for the ship-builder's art. The nails of the dead; only they will do, and so they must be collected. For this reason, I venture among the rats and the ravens, the beetles and worms. For this reason, I haunt barrow-mounds and funeral-pits and tombs. I dig in grave-soil and the ashes of pyres. I lift cold, stiff hands to pry loose and pluck out these hard, thin little corpse-rinds.

This is why, when folk trim and clip their nails, when men attend well to their grooming before they brave danger or risk death, it delays our progress. It delays the inevitable.

But only delays it.

One day, the construction will be finished. The last nail will be fitted into the last crevice. The sails will be set. *Naglfar* will be sea-worthy.

Where a ship made of wood resounds with the creak and groan of its timbers, the noise of this one will be of myriad scratchings and scrapings, the brittle click and tick of nail against nail, moving over each other.

How it will leap over the sea, bend and crest upon the mightiest waves! How the froth will shatter against its prow, how the cut water will churn in its wake!

Oh, and what a great occasion that shall be! When Loki himself takes the helm; when armed and armored giants fill the oar-benches and monsters line the rails; when *Naglfar* breaks from its moorings and heaves strong toward the battle-surge ...

I have been promised a place on the ship, a ledge near the prow where I may perch and hold tight, the wind and brine-spray dashing into my face as we go. I will watch for the field that stretches a hundred leagues in each direction, and the assembled hosts will cover it completely from near end to far.

There, in the starless twilight of the final days ... as the earth shudders such that trees topple and mountains break ... as the sun and moon are consumed by wolves ... as the sky splits in two and the bridge breaks ... as the world first burns and then drowns as the gods march to war, as they march to fight and die ...

I will go forth among the fallen, the ring with the tools of my trade clinking and rattling on my belt.

Because my bag will be empty, and I want to take what I can before Ragnarok ends all.

WILLIAM TODD ROSE

THE GRAVE DANCER

Dust motes swirled in the shaft of light and the cooling fan hummed so softly, it was almost overpowered by the piston-like purr of the projector's workings. An elusive scent which could only be described as *warm* wafted from the vents, conjuring memories of elementary school nature films in a darkened classroom. This particular smell mingled with buttered popcorn and the lingering ghost of the joint which rested within the pinched grip of forceps on the coffee table. With the streetlights defeated by tightly pulled drapes, the fake wood paneling of the den flickered in the projector's glow, causing shadows to jump and dance along the walls and ceilings.

"Where'd you get this again?" Jamie Foxworth leaned forward

and plunged his hand into the crumpled bag Rosa offered; wincing, he yanked it back out almost immediately as his fingers wrapped around a kernel that felt like the microwave had transformed it into a fiery ingot.

"A safe in the back of the projection room at the Roxy." Paul Thompson hunched over the 8mm projector as he spoke, fiddling with a knob which sat just behind the lens. When the images, cast upon the sheet that had been stretched across the far wall, blurred into fuzzy blobs of light and shadow he frowned and turned in the opposite direction. "Thought maybe it was old porn, ya know? Something I could sell on eBay or somethin'."

For as long as anyone could remember, Paul's grandfather had owned and operated the only theater within forty miles of Willow Creek. A throwback to an age when marquees still sported the fluted, futuristic look of art deco, the Roxy had been an anachronism that refused to fade in an era of multiplexes and THX surround sound. The floors were sticky from decades of spilled cola and the seats so old the coiled springs felt as though they fused with the patrons' spines. Being situated close to the Elk River, it was common for rats to scurry through the darkness, picking at dropped popcorn and gooey Milk Duds while most of the audience remained blissfully unaware. Despite this, the old man had loved that cinema and kept it going far longer than was financially feasible. When he finally passed away, his memorial service had been held there; the black casket glistened in the footlights as the entire town filed down narrow aisles and onto the curved platform in front of the screen. They paid their respects and now the shutters were permanently drawn, the box office closed, and bits and pieces of the old cinema were auctioned to collectors who associated some sort of nostalgic glamour with these bygone days. For the first time in decades, the Roxy actually showed a profit… even if it took the scavenging of its musty carcass to do so.

"There. That does it." Paul nodded smugly and crossed his arms over his chest as he backed away from the projector and plopped onto the couch. He always sat so closely to Rosa that his elbow brushed her breast with the slightest movement and the blonde girl edged closer to Jamie, placing her hand on his thigh as if broadcasting an unspoken message: *I'm taken.*

The images on the makeshift screen had resolved into a black and white landscape. Scratches and squiggles jumped about erratically and particles of dust lent a grainy quality to the scene, making it almost seem as if a window through time had somehow opened within the small room. The edges were a dark border that threatened to seep into the frame, only to be pushed back time and time again by brighter areas whose radiance pulsed like the wavering light of a candle. Behind the imperfections in the film was what appeared to be a graveyard at night. Moonlight cast long shadows from the stoic rows of headstones and the treetops in the background swayed as if dancing with a wind that could be seen, but not heard. Every so often, dried leaves tumbled across the manicured lawn like creatures fleeing the approach of some fearsome predator and flowers spilled from a toppled vase as if the dead had rejected this offering.

"So what's this?" Rosa mumbled through a mouthful of popcorn. "Some kind of silent horror movie or something?"

"Nah... 8mm was specifically made for home movies. Less expensive than 16mm." Through summers spent working at the Roxy, Paul had absorbed an almost encyclopedic knowledge of the film industry. "I mean, there were a handful of productions released on 8mm. But even though the format was cheaper for the average Joe, it was actually *more* expensive for studios. Weird, huh?"

"Do you guys mind? I'm trying to watch this."

The unseen cinematographer was in motion now, moving through the graveyard at a slow gait which, in turn, caused the footage to become shaky and unsteady. Crypts and stone angels skewed at awkward angles as tombstones jittered and bounced. At one point, the film showed only the grass below as brown loafers slid in and out of the frame with each step.

"Christ, Jamie," Rosa sighed, "it's a *silent* film. God, you're so damn anal."

The cameraman seemed to be stalking a row of hedges that were like a dark wall against the night. As the shrubbery grew closer, his pace slowed and the angle dipped steadily lower, creating the illusion that the bushes loomed over this man like a pouncing predator. The rocking motion of the camera, however, betrayed the truth: for unknown reasons, the filmmaker had dropped into a crouch so low that he waddled toward his target like a duckling uncertain of its new legs.

"This is like some fucked up Blair Witch shit." Rosa scooped another handful of popcorn from the bag and gestured with it as she giggled.

Jamie glanced at his laughing friends with a frown, but any retort he wished to hurl was trapped within a throat that felt as though a cold, icy hand had closed around it. The hairs on the back of his neck tingled as they stood on end and chills crept along his arms. He wasn't sure why, but he felt as though his soul were retreating further into his body; as if it could somehow hide from the images playing out across the bed sheet and find a modicum of comfort within its skeletal cage.

But that was silly. After all, there wasn't anything particularly disturbing in the film. It was nothing more than some guy creeping through a graveyard at night. So why did his stomach feel as though its contents had soured, flooding his dry mouth with bitter acidity? Why was his jaw clenched so tightly that his teeth ached as if they were moments away from shattering?

"Paranoia," he thought with a glance toward the roach on the table. "You've just had too much weed, dude."

The idea felt like a lie the moment it flittered through his mind. To distract himself, Jamie reached for the popcorn and realized his outstretched hand trembled as it plunged into the bag. Eyeing Rosa and Paul, he assured himself that both were too busy chuckling to notice his obvious unease, yet he felt the warmth of a blush blossom in his cheeks none-the-less. He was being stupid: he'd sat through *The Exorcist* without batting an eye and hadn't so much as flinched when viewing *Saw*. So why did this ridiculous home movie leave him feeling like something slithered through the darkened room, something that wouldn't rest until it coiled around his chest and neck and fed upon the sweet fear oozing from his pores?

Onscreen, the cameraman sidled up to the hedges and a pale hairy arm extended into the frame. It pushed away the branches, forming a small hole in the shrubs. He must have leaned forward then, for the shot was suddenly bordered on all sides by scraggly limbs and branches. It was like looking through a tunnel of vegetation and, on the other side, the rolling knolls of the cemetery continued on, dotted with crosses and grave markers.

Jamie reflexively clenched his fist, crushing the popcorn and smearing butter across his already moist palm. He realized he was holding his breath, but was powerless to do anything about it. Even Paul and Rosa had settled down, each leaning forward as if they were peering over the shoulder of the filmmaker. No one spoke. No one moved. Only the clatter of the projector proved that they hadn't become frozen in time and space, as the scene momentarily slipped out of focus.

Rosa squeezed Jamie's thigh as if the fear had now passed into her as well and when Paul broke the silence, his voice was a thin whisper.

"Wait for it... wait for it... *there!*"

The film was thrown back into sharp focus and in the center of the scene was a figure which hadn't been present before. Silhouetted by distance and the moon, it seemed to be a woman. Long hair whipped in the wind from beneath what appeared to be a veil and a dress fluttered about her ankles like the wings of a demon as she danced and spun among the gravestones.

Jamie felt as though a valve had ruptured somewhere within him and the pressure gushed relief as he threw popcorn at the screen with a shaky laugh. "Bullshit! All that build up for a fucking hoax?"

"I dunno, dude," Paul insisted. "It might actually be her."

"Be *who*?" Rosa's brow knitted with confusion and she looked from side to side as she awaited an answer.

"If that's her, then I'm the Queen of England."

"I think it's really her. . ."

"Bullshit."

"Photographic evidence."

"Bullshit."

The dancing woman stopped as if suddenly aware she was being observed. Her shadowy figure turned so slowly it almost seemed as though the film speed had been cut in half. Even though her features were cloaked in darkness, it was obvious that she turned to face the hedgerow and finally stood as still as the memorials surrounding her.

"Guys," Rosa stammered, "who the hell are you talking about?"

A sense of dread and foreboding crept back inside Jamie and words dried up within his mouth. He was so tense that the muscles in his forearms quivered and jerked and the air in the room felt thin and dry. His heart thudded almost painfully and his gaze locked onto the screen as color drained from his face. Rosa's questioning was nothing more than incoherent babble, as vague and indistinct as if being heard underwater.

A single idea had lodged in Jamie's mind, hijacking his train of thought like an emotional terrorist demanding attention. It was irrational and preposterous, but its tenacity refused to be ignored.

She's looking right at me.

He couldn't see her eyes, but he could feel them: both hot and cold at the same time, chilling his flesh even as her stare pierced him with white-hot needles.

Right at me....

The woman walked forward, her steps as slow and deliberate as an executioner approaching the gallows. As she moved, she seemed to pull shadows to her. They stretched out from graves and trees, snaking across the ground like unfurling tentacles of darkness. When they reached her legs, the shadows appeared to wrap around her, enshrouding the woman in a gloom so complete that even though she was closer to the camera her appearance remained concealed in obscurity.

"What the fuck?" Rosa's voice sounded as if it came from a great distance, as nebulous as the memory of a dream.

Being further away, Paul's reply filtered through Jamie's trance-like state in disconnected snippets. "…illusion…. moonlight behind clouds …."

The woman had covered half the distance between her and the cameraman. Even though the wind still whipped through the trees, her hair and clothing remained undisturbed. It was as if she walked between worlds, existing yet immune to the physics and trappings of reality. Would this ability allow her to pass right through the bed sheet like the creepy little girl in *Ringu*? Was she not only looking directly at Jamie… but coming for him as well?

Beads of sweat dotted his forehead as his fingernails dug tiny crescents into the arm of the couch. The part of his mind that clung to rationality and logic made a thousand excuses: *the weed had been laced with something, PCP or some other hallucinogenic that distorted his perceptions like a fun house mirror; or maybe it was all an elaborate prank set up with clever editing, a practical joke Paul dreamed up in the midst of a drunken binge.* Yet nothing could explain the chill that had seeped into Jamie's bones. It was as if ice water flowed through his veins and a panicked little voice in the back of his mind whispered, *Run. Run now. Fuck Paul, fuck Rosa, just run!*

But he could only watch as the woman on the screen grew closer. And closer still.

Within moments, she'd be completely visible. So close that no amount of shadow could conceal the madness that surely burned within her eyes. So close that if she reached out, her cold fingers would brush his face and the reek of decay would waft from her gaunt body, filling the den with the stench of unearthed graves and coffins bloated by decades of rain.

At that moment, Jamie may have as well been dead. The pounding of his heart simply ceased and no air passed through his lips or nose. A nameless terror paralyzed his body to the point that even his muscles no longer trembled. He could only watch and wait for the end.

The woman raised her right arm so smoothly it almost seemed as if the limb were lighter than the air around it and would float away into the darkness. Her index finger uncurled… and was it just the house settling or could he actually hear the bones crack and pop as she pointed directly at him? Was that the cooling fan in the projector? Or a strong wind whispering through pine boughs in a graveyard that bridged not just past and present, but also life and death?

A sharp clattering shocked Jamie's system as efficiently as chest paddles. With a jolt, he gasped for air as his heart made up for lost time; beating as if he'd just sprinted half a mile at full force. Tears stung his eyes as the room wavered in and out of focus and his hands patted his chest and thighs, reassuring a mind deluged with emotion that he was still solid, still real. Still alive.

The graveyard and woman were gone, replaced by a bright rectangle of light against the white sheet. Behind the sofa, the end of the film slapped against the spinning take-up reel and for a moment the trio sat in silence, each one watching the screen as if half expecting the woman to burst back into view like the killer at the end of a slasher flick.

It was Rosa who eventually broke the silence, speaking in a stilted tone as if in shock: "Okay, guys. Seriously. What the *fuck* was that?"

Unlike Paul and Jamie, Rosa hadn't been born in Willow Creek. She'd been transplanted to the small, rural community when she was sixteen, leaving behind the lights and bustle of her beloved Chicago. Because of this, she'd never heard the tales local fathers told to their children. She'd never laid in bed with the covers pulled up to her chin, wondering if the raspy scraping coming through the walls was a tree branch brushing against the side of the house… or something else. For the children of Willow Creek, every stray shadow was a potential threat, every unexplained thump thump – approaching footsteps. For generations they'd scrambled inside at the first sign of dusk, not daring to be caught alone in the dark. Until, that is, they were old enough to realize there was no more truth in these stories than in Santa Claus or the Easter Bunny. Yet the legends never truly left them and within time their own children were subjected to the same horrors that had been described so graphically to them in their youth.

"That," Paul explained, "was The Grave Dancer."

Some claimed she was a farmer's wife who'd went insane during the Great Depression, killing her husband and children before dedicating her soul to Satan and taking her own life. Others said she'd been around much longer than that; they asserted the Cherokees had passed down stories of her long before the white man ever dreamed of crossing the ocean westward. In the mid-50s, it had even become fashionable to cast The Grave Dancer as a being who'd fallen from the stars, a cosmic castaway who hunted the indigenous population while dreaming of the day she would return home.

These stories of her origin were as varied as the reports of those who claimed to have seen her. But there were some details which remained so consistent that they leant an aura of credibility to an otherwise wild tale. She would appear as either a haggard crone with breath that stank of the grave or a beautiful, young maiden whose dark eyes twinkled with lust. In either incarnation, her clothing was always the funeral garb of a bygone era: a ruffled, black dress of lusterless cloth draped her frame, the form-fitting bodice fastened by a row of dark buttons all the way to a neckline with only the hint of a collar; with her face obscured by a thin veil, an appearance of Victorian propriety surrounded her as thickly as the scent of mildew wafting from the folds of cloth. It was said that the musty odor crept into clothes and hair as she danced, carried like spores on the currents of air displaced by her whirling body. Hot showers and shampoo were no match for this dank stench; it was as if the fetor had infused the follicles themselves, coating each cell with a patina of mildew that lodged in the back of the sinuses like stale dust. If, that is, the observer had been fortunate enough to survive the encounter. A lingering scent of age and decay, common wisdom dictated, was a small price to pay for your immortal soul.

"Shit, guys, this is so fucking *cool*!" Rosa sprang from her seat and paced about the room, her hands fluttering like the wings of a baby bird attempting flight as she babbled. "Why am I just now finding out about this? I mean, it's right here in front of our faces. *Right here!*"

Paul and Jamie exchanged a glance and an entire conversation was held with nothing more than the arching of eyebrows and a shrug.

"Um... what's right here?" Jamie's stomach still felt as if hard ball of ice had settled into its core and his words trembled slightly. If his girlfriend noticed, she gave no sign. Her round face practically glowed as excitement sparked in her eyes.

"A real life mystery, man. Scooby Doo-type shit. I mean, you hear about this crap on Monster Quest but you never think it could happen to you."

Taking the forceps from the table, Paul held them to his pursed lips but then paused. "So what, then?" he asked. "You sayin' you want to go look for this thing?"

"Hell yeah!"

Jamie felt as though the darkness closed in around him. Like a camper alone in the forest with the fire quickly dying out, he could sense predators in the shadows, drawing ever closer as the ring of light and safety steadily diminished. He wanted to leap from the sofa and snatch Rosa into her arms, to yank her so closely that their noses would nearly touch as he shook her and screamed: *Are you crazy? Have you lost your friggin' mind?*

Instead, he wrapped his arms around himself and tried to chase away the chills that prickled his flesh with brisk rubbing. But the cold was bone deep, as if his very marrow had been flash frozen, and the sense of doom haunting him refused to dispel so easily.

Paul had finally lit the roach and the smell of marijuana flooded the room like the spray of a perfumed skunk. Holding the smoke within his lungs, he offered the forceps to an oblivious Jamie and tried to speak amid the flurry of coughing that ensued.

"Fuck." He finally sputtered as he wiped tears from his watering eyes. "Why not? It ain't like there's anything else worth doin' in this mausoleum of a town. Whatcha say, Jamie? You in, dude?"

Jamie was anything but in. His mind flashed back to the footage on the screen, the flickering grayscale images of the woman. The certainty that she'd been peering into his soul. That she was coming for him.

But what would Rosa think? The girl was so psyched by the idea of an honest to God paranormal investigation that she bounced from foot to foot like a kid in a candy store. She'd clapped her hands and squealed when Paul said he was game and now she clasped those hands in front of her breasts as if in prayer as she targeted her boyfriend with an exaggerated pout.

"Please, please, please, *please*... let's do it, baby. Come on. Please. For me?"

If he refused, what would she think? That he was just another ignorant hick, as superstitious as any medieval villager? That he was weak? He'd seen the way guys in town looked at her; and occasionally he'd notice an expression of approval pass over Rosa's face as her eyes momentarily locked with an admiring gaze. He was lucky to have a girl like her and he knew it.

"There's nothing out there." Jamie told himself. "The Grave

Dancer isn't real. We'll tromp around for a while, get the munchies, and go home. Don't be such a fucking baby."

His inner voice sounded like a coward trying to muster a facade of courage and his heart pattered distress calls in frantic Morse code. He perched on the edge of the couch like a statue frozen by indecision, moving only his eyes. They darted to Rosa, taking in her smooth skin and silken hair at a glance. The curve of her hips and lips so soft they were like kissing velvety rose petals; the way she sometimes touched the side of his face with her long, graceful fingers as she smiled: *could he really risk losing this woman?*

In the end, fear of being alone won out over fear of the unknown. Even then, however, Jamie was unable to voice his consent. Somewhere deep inside, it felt as though a pit had opened within him. He felt his resolve tumble into this void like clumps of dirt falling into an unearthed grave. They were devoured by darkness so complete, that light may have as well never existed at all. Lurking within this impenetrable gloom, he sensed something hidden and monstrous. Something that longed for a taste of life.

Something that smiled when, against every instinct he had, Jamie reluctantly nodded his agreement.

Woodlawn Cemetery sat on the outskirts of Willow Creek, welcoming rare visitors with rows of the dead. Some of the older markers were beautifully elaborate, carved into the shape of tree stumps so realistic it almost seemed as though a petrified forest had once stood upon the spot. These were inscribed with the names of soldiers who'd given their lives in the war between the states, indicating a lineage which could afford such extravagant embellishments. Others, however, were rough hewn slabs as white as bleached bone. They pierced the ground like a child's drawing of teeth and moss crept over their cracked and crumbling facades. The elements had worn the faces of these stones smooth, ensuring the skeletons below were nothing more than lost children of history. Nameless and forgotten, they moldered within their graves, staring up through the earth as they waited for the vibration of footsteps to chase bugs from hollow sockets.

The tires of Paul's used Subaru crunched over the gravel road bisecting the cemetery and its headlights splayed shadows from the line of gravestones in its path. Newer markers flared brilliantly, as their glossy surfaces reflected the light and the darkness beyond was perforated with blue pinpoints of color from the solar powered night lights above the graves of children. The hatchback crept along this road, proceeding through the fog with what felt like reckless abandon to Jamie. He stared straight ahead, pretending to be lost in the intricately layered music playing softly from the stereo. Paul had been on a *Tool* kick lately and the dark, almost hypnotic, tones seemed a fitting soundtrack. The music hinted at things there, but not seen. It peeled back layers of reality, bridging the gap between the worlds of science and alchemy, and Jamie regretted taking those final tokes from the joint. He was fear incarnate by this point, nothing more than primal emotion wrapped in a human skin.

There was no turning back now.

There was only the cemetery and darkness. The silent stones and silhouetted trees, leafless with the coming of autumn. Color had been stripped from this landscape: blacks, whites, various shades of brown and gray… the dead had no need for anything more. Theirs was a drab kingdom devoid of anything remotely hinting at life. The withered wreaths of Memorial Day had long since been removed, the dried leaves driven back into the forest with leaf blowers; even the grass seemed drained and lifeless, flirting with hints of green only in rectangular plots leading up to markers.

Jamie knew they weren't meant to be there. This was not their world and its secrets were best left buried. Yet Rosa and Paul giggled like a pair of giddy schoolgirls as the car came to a stop. In the center of a cul-de-sac encircling a gnarled oak, the headlights went dark and the engine ticked in the cool, night air. Jamie watched as if from the haze of sleep as his friends flung open their doors. His soul had gone on strike and cowered behind the picket line while his hands betrayed him by lifting the lever on his own door. The legs which swung out into the darkness were not his. They couldn't be. *His* legs would never take place in this mutiny. They'd never lead him from safety into danger. And yet there he was, exposed in his environment by the warm blood surging through his veins.

From this elevation, Jamie could just make out The Roxy. Dark and silent, it was just another tombstone, marking the spot where an old man's dreams had died while the rest of town lived on. The lights of Willow Creek formed diffuse halos in the fog and hidden insects chirped their praises to the night. A distant hound brayed, its howl sounding like a lonely plea mocked by echoes. These things were less than three miles away. But to Jamie, it felt as though he gazed across a vast chasm; he knew once crossed, there was no guarantee you'd find your way back. The streets and houses would look the same. The businesses would be exact copies of what they'd once been. Even his friends and family would be reasonable facsimiles of the real thing. But he would know.

If you don't wanna find darkness, don't go meddlin' in the affairs of the dead.

His grandmother's voice recited her favorite expression in Paul's mind, and he could picture her small mouth pulled so tightly into a frown that wrinkles stretched her face. She wouldn't approve of this. She'd never openly welcome him into the light, knowing exactly what he was up to.

Rosa and Paul had fanned out, each walking away from the car at opposite angles. They called to each other through cupped hands as tendrils of fog curled around their legs like a misty python.

"We see anything and we holler." The fog robbed Paul's voice of its usual richness, leaving the words muffled and flat.

"First one to see her wins a dime bag." Rosa laughed. She skipped among the stones like an unknowing child, so secure with her misplaced trust in the world that thoughts of tragedy never crossed her mind.

The innocent suffer, too.

Jamie knew that to be a universal truth. Yet, he still allowed his feet to carry him further into the cemetery. The fog ate his companions slowly, dissolving them from solid beings into nothing more than vague shadows which played at being human. And then they were gone entirely, leaving Jamie to wander the necropolis alone.

He knew she was out there. He could feel her in the darkness, pulling him to her as if their fates were tethered by invisible strings. His feet knew the way and the toes of his tennis shoes became glossy as they parted dew slick grass. The world blurred and warm tears stung his eyes, but he cried silently. The human body had no sound for what he felt, no vocalization that could convey the frustration of being held prisoner in his own body.

He didn't want to see her. He didn't want to be taken into her waltz and held close to maggot-ridden breasts. He didn't want her festering lips to part or to taste the stench of decaying organs as she leaned in for a kiss. He somehow knew she'd flicker in and out of reality, shifting between corpse-like hag and lusty vixen like a double exposed film.

Though his flesh recoiled from her embrace, his body continued on.

She was just over the next hill now.

Waiting, but still unseen.

Hysteria seized control and Jamie laughed between his tears as if he'd just gotten the punch line to God's epic joke. His voice echoed in the darkness, alternately wavering with madness and breaking with emotion.

"Cut, man. Cut. I said fuckin' *cut*!"

Paul and Rosa called his name from somewhere beyond the veil of fog, sounding like travelers lost in the forest. With each step, their voices grew more distant and lost their tenuous grasp upon reality.

"That's a fucking wrap people!"

Words were barely distinguishable as language now and snot bubbled from clogged nostrils. Cresting the hill, Jamie looked down upon her and his shrill screeches startled a flock of birds into flight.

His friends would come running, of course. That's what people did. And like a trapdoor spider, she would be waiting for them as well. The end credits had begun to roll, and those poor bastards didn't even realize it yet. Perhaps in that, if nothing else, he was lucky.

With that, Jamie Foxworth closed his eyes and allowed the darkness to rush in.

RAMSEY CAMPBELL

WELCOMELAND

Slade had been driving all day when he came to the road home. The sign isolated by the sullenly green landscape of overgrown canals and weedy fields had changed. Instead of the name of the town there was a yellow pointer, startlingly bright beneath the dull June sky, for the theme park. Presumably vandals had damaged it, for only the final syllables remained: MELAND. He mightn't have another chance to see what he'd helped to build. He'd found nothing on his drive north that his clients might want to buy or invest in. He lifted his foot from the brake and let the car carry him onwards.

Suppressed gleams darted through the clogged canals, across the cranium of the landscape. The sun was a ball of mist that kept failing to form in the sky. The railway blocked Slade's view as he approached the town. He caught himself expecting to see the town laid out below him, but of course he'd only ever seen it like that from the train. The railway was as deserted as the road had been for the last hour of his drive.

The road sloped towards the bridge under the railway, between banks so untended that weeds lashed the car. The mouth of the bridge had been made into a gateway: gates painted gold were folded back against the wall of the embankment. The shrill darkness in the middle of the tunnel was so thick that Slade reached to turn on his headlamps. Then the car left its echoes behind and showed him the town, and he couldn't help sighing. It looked as if the building of the park had got no further than the gates.

He'd bought shares in the project when his father had forwarded the prospectus, with Slade's new address scribbled across it so harshly that the envelope had been torn in several places. He'd hoped the park might revive his father and the town now that employment, like Slade, had moved down south. Now his father was dead, and the entrepreneur had gone bankrupt soon after the shares had been issued, and the main street was shabbier than ever: the pavements were turning green, the net curtains of the gardenless terraces were grey as old cobwebs, the displays in the shop windows that interrupted the ranks of cramped houses had been drained of colour. Slade had to assume this was early closing day, for he could see nobody at all.

The town hadn't looked so unwelcoming when he'd left, but he felt as if it had. Nevertheless he owed the place a visit, the one he should have made when his father was dying, if only Slade had known he was, if only they hadn't become estranged when Slade's mother had died … "If only" just about summed up the town, he thought bitterly as he drove to the hotel.

The squat black building was broad as four houses and four storeys high. He'd often sheltered under the iron and glass awning from the rain, but whatever the place had been called in those days, it wasn't the Old Hotel. The revolving doors stumbled round their track with a chorus of stifled moans and let him into the dark brown lobby, where the only illumination came from a large skylight over the stairs. The thin grey-haired young woman at the desk tapped her chin several times in the rhythm of some tune she must be hearing (dum-da-dum-da-dum-da-dum), squared a stack of papers, and then she looked towards him with a smile and a raising of eyebrows. "Hello, may I help you?"

"Sorry, yes, of course." Slade stepped forward to let her see him. "I'd like a room for the night."

"What would you like?"

"Pardon? Something at the top," Slade stammered, beginning to blush as he tried not to stare at her vacant eyes.

"I'm sure we can accommodate you."

He didn't doubt it, since the keyboard behind her was full. "I'll fill in one of your forms then, shall I?"

"Thank you, sir, that's fine."

There was a pad of them in front of her, but no pen. Slade uncapped his fountain pen and completed the top form, then pushed the pad between her hands as they groped over the counter. "Room twenty will be at the top, won't it?" he said, too loudly. "Could I have that one?"

"If there's anything else we can do to make you more at home, just let us know."

He assumed that meant yes. "I'll get the key, shall I?"

"Thank you very much," she said, and thumped a bell on the counter. Perhaps she'd misheard him, but the man who opened the door between the stairs and the desk seemed to have heard Slade clearly enough, for he only poked his dim face towards the lobby before closing the door again. Slade leaned across the desk, his cheeks stiff with blushing, and managed to hook the key with one finger, almost swaying against the receptionist as he lunged. Working all day in the indirect light hadn't done her complexion any good, to put it mildly, and now he saw that the papers she was fidgeting with were blank. "That's done it," he babbled, and scrambled towards the stairs.

The upper floors were lit only by windows. Murky sunlight was retreating over ranks of featureless white doors. If the hotel was conserving electricity, that didn't seem to augur well for the health of the town. All the same, when he stepped into the room that smelled of stale carpet and crossed to the window to let in some air, he had his first sight of the park.

A terrace led away from the main road some hundred yards from the hotel, and there the side streets ended. The railway enclosed a mile or more of bulky unfamiliar buildings, of which he could distinguish little more than that they bore names on their roofs. All the names were turned away from him, but this must be the park. It was full of people, grouped among the buildings, and the railway had been made into a ride; cars with grinning mouths were stranded in dips in the track.

Surely there weren't people in the cars. They must be dummies, stored up there out of the way. Their long grey hair flapped, their heads swayed unanimously in the wind. They seemed more lively than the waiting crowd, but just now that didn't concern him. He was willing the house where he'd spent the first half of his life to have survived the rebuilding.

As he turned from the window he saw the card above the bedside phone. DIAL 9 FOR PARK INFORMATION, it said. He dialled and waited as the room settled back into staleness. Eventually he demanded "Park Information?"

"Hello, may I help you?"

The response was so immediate that the speaker must have been waiting silently for him. As he stiffened to fend off the unexpectedness the voice said "May we ask how you heard of our attraction?"

"I bought some shares," Slade said, distracted by wondering where he knew the man's voice from. "I'm from here, actually. Wanted to do what I could for the old place."

"We all have to return to our roots. No profit in delaying."

"I wanted to ask about the park," Slade interrupted, resenting the way the voice had abandoned its official function. "Where does it end? What's still standing?"

"Less has changed than you might think."

"Would you know if Hope Street's still there?"

"Whatever people wanted most has been preserved, wherever they felt truly at home," the voice said, and even more maddeningly "It's best if you go and look for yourself."

"When will the park be open?" Slade almost shouted.

"When you get there, never fear."

Slade gave up, and flung the receiver into the air, a theatrical gesture that made him blush furiously but failed to silence the guilt the voice had awakened. He'd moved to London in order to live with the only woman he'd ever shared a bed with, and when they'd parted amicably less than a year later he had been unable to go home: his parents would have insisted that the breakup proved them right about her and the relationship. His father had blamed him for breaking his mother's heart, and the men hadn't spoken since her death. The way Slade's father had stared at him over her grave had withered Slade's feelings for good, but you prospered better without feelings, he'd often told himself. Now that he was home he felt compelled to make his peace with his memories.

He sent himself out of the room before his thoughts could weigh him down. The receptionist was fidgeting with her papers. As Slade stepped into the lobby the bellman's door opened, the shadowy face peered out and withdrew. Slade was at the revolving doors when the receptionist said "Hello, may I help you?" He struggled out through the doors, his face blazing.

The street was still deserted. The deadened sky appeared to hover just above the slate roofs like a ghost of the smoke of the derelict factories. Even his car looked abandoned, grey with the grime of his drive. It was the only car on the road.

Was the park somehow soundproofed so as not to annoy the

residents? Even if the rides hadn't begun, surely he ought to be able to hear the crowd beyond the houses. He felt as if the entire town were holding its breath. As he hurried along the buckled mossy pavement, his footsteps sounded metallic, mechanical. He turned the curve that led the road to the town hall. Among the scrawny houses of the terrace opposite him, there was a lit shop.

It was the bakery, where his mother would buy cakes for the family each weekend. The taste of his favourite cake, sponge and cream and jam, filled his mouth at the thought. He could see the baker, looking older but not as old as Slade would have expected, serving a woman in the buttery light that seemed brighter than electricity, brighter than Slade had ever seen the shop before. The sight and the taste made him feel that if he opened the shop door he could step into memory, buy cakes as a homecoming surprise and walk home, back into the warmth of having tea beside the coal fire, the long quiet evenings with his parents when he had been growing up but hadn't yet outgrown them.

He wasn't entitled to imagine that, since he'd ensured it couldn't happen. His mouth went dry, the taste vanished. He passed the shop without crossing the road, averting his face lest the baker should call out to him. As he passed, the light went out. Perhaps it had been a ray of sunlight, though he could see no gap in the clouds.

Someone at the town hall should know if his home was intact. There must be people in the hall, for he could hear a muffled waltz. He went up the worn steps and between the pillars of the token portico. The double doors were too large for the building, which was about the size of the hotel, and seemed at first too heavy or too swollen for him to shift. Then the rusty handles yielded to his weight, and the doors shuddered inwards. The lobby was unlit and deserted.

He could still hear the waltz. A track of grey daylight stretched ahead of him and showed him an architect's model on a table in the middle of the lobby. He followed his vague shadow over the wedge of lit carpet. The model had been vandalised so thoroughly it was impossible to see what view of the town it represented. If it had shown streets as well as rides, there was no way of telling where either ended or began.

He made his way past the unattended information desk towards the music. A minute's stumbling along the dark corridor brought him to the ballroom. The only light beyond the dusty glass doors came from high transoms, but couples were waltzing on the bare floor to music that sounded oddly more distant than ever. In the dimness their faces were grey blotches. It must be some kind of old folks' treat, he reassured himself, for more than half of the dancers were bald. Loath to trouble them, he turned back towards the lobby.

The area outside the wedge of daylight was almost indistinguishably dim. He could just make out the side of the information desk that faced away from the public. Someone appeared to be crouched beside the chair behind the desk. If the figure had fallen there Slade ought to find out what was wrong, but the position of the figure was so dismayingly haphazard that he could only believe it was a dummy. The dancers were still whirling sluggishly, always in the same direction, as if they might never stop. He glanced about, craving reassurance, and caught sight of a sliver of light at the end of the corridor—the gap around a door.

It must lead to the park. He almost tripped on the carpet as he headed for the door. It was open because it had been vandalised: it was half off its hinges, and he had to strain to lift it clear of the rucked carpet. He thought of having to go back through the building, and heaved at the door so savagely that it ripped the sodden carpet. He squeezed through the gap, his face throbbing with embarrassment, and ran.

He was so anxious to be away from the damage he'd caused that at first he hardly observed where he was going. Nobody was about, that was the main thing. He'd run some hundred yards between the derelict houses before he wondered where the crowd he'd seen from the hotel might be. He halted clumsily and stared around him. He was already in the park.

It seemed they had tried to preserve as much of the town as they could. Clumps of three or four terraced houses had been left standing in no apparent pattern, with signs on their roofs. He still couldn't read the signs, even those that were facing him; they might have been vandalised—many of the windows were smashed—or left uncompleted. If it hadn't been for the roundabout he saw between the houses, he might not have realised he was in the park.

It wasn't the desolation that troubled him so much as the impression that the town was yet struggling to change, to live. If his home was involved in this transformation, he wasn't sure that he wanted to see, but he didn't think he could leave without seeing. He made his way over the rubble between two blocks of houses.

The sky was darker than it had been when he'd entered the town hall. The gathering twilight slowed him down, and so did sights in the park. Two supine poles, each with a huge red smiling mouth at one end, might have been intended to support a screen, and perhaps the section of a helter-skelter choked with mud was all that had been delivered, though it seemed to corkscrew straight down into the earth. He wondered if any ride except the roundabout had been completed, and then he realised with a jerk of the heart that he had been passing the sideshows for minutes. They were in the houses, and so was the crowd.

At least, he assumed those were players seated around a Bingo counter inside the section of the terrace ahead, though the figures in the dimness were so still he couldn't be certain. He preferred to sidle past rather than go closer to look. The roundabout was behind him now, and he thought he saw a relatively clear path towards where his old house should be. But the sight of the dungeon inside the next jagged fragment of terrace froze him.

It wasn't just a dungeon, it was a torture chamber. Half-naked dummies were chained to the walls. Signs hung around their necks: one was a RAPIST, another a CHILD MOLESTER. A woman with curlers like worms in her hair was prodding one dummy's armpit with a red-hot poker, a man in a cloth cap was wrenching out his victim's teeth. All the figures, not just the victims, were absolutely motionless. If this was someone's idea of waxworks, Slade didn't see the point. He had been staring so hard and so long that the figures appeared to be staggering, unable to hold their poses, when he heard something come to life behind him.

He felt as if the dimness in which his feet were sunk had become mud. Even if the sounds hadn't been so large he would have preferred not to see what was making them, wheezing feebly and scraping and thudding like a giant heart straining to revive. He forced his head to turn, his neck creaking, but at first he could see only how dark the place had grown while he had been preoccupied with the dungeon. He glimpsed movement as large as a house between the smudged outlines of the buildings, and shrank into himself. But it was only the roundabout, plodding in the dark.

He couldn't quite laugh at his dread. The horses were moving as if they could hardly raise themselves and yearned to fall more quickly and finally than they could. There were figures on their backs, and now he realised he had glimpsed the figures earlier, in which case they must have been sitting immobile: waiting for the dark? They weren't going anywhere, they were no threat to him, he could look away and make for the house—but when he did he recoiled, so violently he almost fell. The torturers in the dungeon were stirring. They were turning their heads towards him.

He couldn't see much of their faces, and that didn't seem to be only the fault of the dark. He began to sink into a crouch as if they mightn't see him, he was close to squeezing his eyes shut as though that would make him invisible, the way he'd believed it would when he was a child. Then he flung himself aside, out of range of any eyes that might be searching for him, and fled.

Though the night was thickening, he could see more than he wanted to see. One block of unlit houses had been turned into a shooting gallery, although at first he didn't realise that the six disembodied heads nodding forward in unison were meant to be targets. They must be, not least because all six had the same face—a face he knew from somewhere. He stumbled past the heads as the six of them leaned towards him out of the dark beyond the figures that were aiming at them. He felt as if the staring heads were pleading with him to intervene. He was so desperate to outdistance his clinging dismay that he almost fell into the canal.

He hadn't noticed it at first because a section had been walled in to make a tunnel. It must be a Tunnel of Love: a gondola was inching its way out of the weedy mouth, bringing a sound of choked slopping and a smell of unhealthy growth. Slade could just distinguish the heads of the couple in the gondola. They looked as if they hadn't seen daylight for years.

He swallowed a shriek and retreated alongside the canal, towards the main road. As he slithered along the overgrown stony margin, flailing his arms to keep his balance, he remembered where he'd seen the face on the targets: in a photograph. It was the entrepreneur's face. The man had died of a heart attack soon after he'd gone bankrupt, and hadn't he gone bankrupt shortly after persuading the townsfolk to invest whatever money they had? Slade began to mutter desperately, apologising for whatever he might have helped to cause if it had harmed the town, if anyone who might be listening resented it. He'd only been trying to do his best for the town, he was sorry if it had gone wrong. He was still apologising breathlessly as he sprawled up a heap of debris and onto the bridge that carried the main road over the canal.

He fled along the unlit road, past the town hall and the sound of the relentless waltz in the dark. The aproned baker was serving at his counter, performing the same movements for almost certainly the same customer, and Slade felt as though that was his fault somehow, as though he ought to have accepted the offer of light. He mustn't confuse himself with that; he must get to his car and drive, anywhere so long as it was out of this place. It occurred to him that anyone who could leave the town had done so—and then, as he came in sight of his car, he thought of the blind woman in the hotel.

He mustn't leave her. She mustn't be aware of what had happened to the town, whatever that was. She hadn't even switched on the lights of the hotel. He shoved desperately at the revolving doors, which felt crusty and brittle under his hands, and staggered into the lobby. He grabbed the edges of the doorway to steady himself while his eyes adjusted to the murk that swarmed like darkness giving birth. The receptionist was at her desk, tapping her chin in the rhythm of the melody inside her head. She shuffled papers and glanced up. "Hello, may I help you?"

"No, I want—" Slade called across the lobby, and faltered as his voice came flatly back to him.

"What would you like?"

He was afraid to go closer. He'd remembered the bellman, who must be waiting to open the door beside the desk and who might even come out now that it was dark. That wasn't why Slade couldn't speak, however. He'd realised that the echo of his voice sounded disconcertingly like the voice on the hotel phone. "I'm sure we can accommodate you," the receptionist said.

She was only trying to welcome a guest, Slade reassured himself. He was still trying to urge himself forward when she said "Thank you, sir, that's fine."

She must be on the phone, otherwise she wouldn't be saying "If there's anything else we can do to make you more at home, just let us know." Now she would put down the phone Slade couldn't see, and he would go to her, now that she'd said "Thank you very much"—and then she thumped the bell on the counter.

Slade fought his way out of the rusty trap of the revolving doors as the bellman poked his glimmering face into the lobby. The receptionist was only as sightless as the rest of the townsfolk, he thought like a scream of hysterical laughter. He'd realised something else: the tune she was tapping. Dum, dum-da-dum, dum-da-dum-da-dum-da-dum. It was Chopin: the Dead March.

He dragged his keys out of his pocket, ripping stitches loose, as he ran to his car. The key wouldn't fit the lock. Of course it would—he was inserting it somehow the wrong way. It crunched into the slot, which sounded rusty, just as he realised why the angle was wrong. Both tyres on that side of the car were flat. The wheels were resting on their metal rims.

He didn't need the car, he could run. Surely the townsfolk couldn't move very fast or, to judge by his observations, very far. He fled to the tunnel that led under the railway. But even if he made himself venture through the shrilly whispering dark in there to the gates, it would be no use. The gates were shut, and several bars thicker than his arm had slid across them into sockets in the wall.

He turned away as if he was falling, as if the pressure of the scream he was suppressing was starving his brain. The road was still deserted. The only other way out of the town was at the far end. He ran, his lungs rusty and aching, past houses where families appeared to be dining in the dark, past the town hall with its smothered waltz, over the bridge towards which a gondola was floundering, bearing a couple whose heads lolled apart from each other and then knocked their mouths together with a hollow bony sound. The curve of the road cut off his view of the far side of town until he was almost there. The last of the houses came in sight, and he tried to tell himself that it was only darkness that blocked the road. But it was solid, and high as the roofs.

Whether it was a pile of rubble or an imperfectly built wall, it was certainly too dangerous to climb. Slade turned away, feeling steeped in despair thick as pitch, and saw his house.

Was it his panic that made it appear to glow faintly in the midst of the terrace? Otherwise it looked exactly like its neighbours, a bedroom window above a curtained parlour beside a nondescript front door with a narrow fanlight. He didn't care how he was able to see it, he was too grateful that he was. As he fled towards it he had the sudden notion that his father might have changed the lock since Slade had left, that Slade's key would no longer let him in.

The lock yielded easily. The door opened wide and showed him the dark hall, which led past the stairs to the parlour on the left, the kitchen at the back. The house felt more familiar than anything else in the world, and it was the only refuge available to him, yet he was afraid to step forward. He was afraid his parents might be there, compulsively repeating some everyday task, blind to him and the state of themselves—though if what was left of them could be aware of him, that might be even worse.

Then he thought he heard movement in the street, and he stumbled to the parlour door and pushed it open. The parlour was deserted, the couch and chairs were as grey as the hearth they faced, yet the stagnant dimness seemed tense, poised to reveal that the room wasn't empty after all. The kitchen with its wooden chairs that pressed against the bare table between the oven and the sink seemed breathless with imminence too, but he was almost sure that he heard movement, slow and stealthy, somewhere outside the house. He scrambled back to the front door and closed it as silently as he could, and then he groped his way upstairs.

The bathroom window was a dull rectangle that gleamed faintly in the mirror, like a lid that was opening. The bath looked as if it were brimming with tar. Even that was less dismaying than his parents' bedroom: suppose he found them in the bed, struggling to make love like fleshless puppets? He felt as if he were shrinking, reverting to the age he'd been when his father had shouted at him not to open their door. His hands fluttered at it now and inched it far enough to show him their empty bed, and then he dodged into his room.

His bed was still there, his chest of drawers, his wardrobe hardly wide enough for him to hide in any longer. He shouldered the door of the room closed tight and huddled against it. He felt suddenly as though if he went to the bed he might awaken and discover he had been dreaming of the town, just a nightmare about growing up. He mustn't take refuge in the bed, it would be too like retreating into his childhood—and then he realised he already had.

He'd been left alone in the house just once when he was a child. He'd awakened and blundered through the empty rooms, every one of which seemed to be concealing some terror that was about to show itself. He remembered how that had felt: exactly as the house felt now. He'd retraced the memory without realising. Then a neighbour who'd been meant to keep an eye on him had looked in to reassure him, but he prayed that wouldn't happen now, that nobody would come to keep him company. Surely his house couldn't be where they felt most at home.

"Never fear," the voice on the phone had advised him—but Slade had. The night couldn't last forever, he told himself desperately, pressing himself against the door. The sun would rise, the bars would slide back to let the gates open, and even if they didn't he would be able to see a way out. But he felt as if there was nowhere to go: he couldn't recall the faces of his colleagues, the name of the London firm, even the name of the street where he lived. He didn't need to remember those now, he needed only to stay awake until dawn. Surely the rest of the town was too busy to welcome him home, unless it was his fear that was bringing the movement he could hear in the street. It sounded like a wordless crowd that could barely walk but was determined to try. They couldn't move fast, he thought like a last prayer, they would have to stop when the sun came up—but clearer than that was the thought of how endless the night could seem when you were a child.

AUTHOR BIOS

Scathe meic (Uí) Beorh is a writer and lexicographer of Ulster-Scot ancestry raised in New Orleans. At the age of 25, he was spirited away to Hollywood for several years before being set down on the East Coast of Florida at St. Augustine where, apart from yet another spiriting, this time to Ireland for a year and a day, he has lived since 1990- and today with Ember, his lovely and exceedingly creative wife.

His books in print include Children and Other Wicked Things (James Ward Kirk Fiction, 2013), Black Fox In Thin Places (Emby Press, 2013), Always After Thieves Watch (Wildside Press, 2010), Pirate Lingo (Wildside, 2009), Emhain Macha Dark Rain (RS Press), The Pirates of St. Augustine (Wildside), Golgotha (Punkin House), and Dark Sayings of Old.

He also helms the three periodicals Haunted Magazine, Beorh Quarterly, and Mad March Hare. His dilectus sanctus is Thérèse of Lisieux.

Amazon:http://www.amazon.com/Skadi-MeicBeorh/e/
B0039STGZU/ref=ntt_dp_epwbk_0

Roy C. Booth hails from Bemidji, MN where he manages Roy's Comics & Games (est. 1992) with his wife and three sons. He is a published author, comedian, poet, journalist, essayist, optioned screenwriter, and internationally awarded playwright with nearly 60 plays published (Samuel French, Heuer, et al) with 810+ productions worldwide in 29 countries in ten languages.

He is also known for horror/fantasy/science fiction collaborations with R Thomas Riley, Brian Keene, Eric M. Heideman, William F. Wu, Axel Kohagen, and others (along with his presence on the regional convention circuit). See his entry on Wikipedia, his Facebook page, his publishers' sites, and his Amazon Author Page:

Amazon Author Page: http://www.amazon.com/Roy-C.-Booth/e/B00A7CVLNG
Website: https://www.facebook.com/roy.c.booth?fref=ts

Ramsey Campbell. The Oxford Companion to English Literature describes Ramsey Campbell as "Britain's most respected living horror writer". He has been given more awards than any other writer in the field, including the Grand Master Award of the World Horror Convention, the Lifetime Achievement Award of the Horror Writers Association, the Living Legend Award of the International Horror Guild and the World Fantasy Lifetime Achievement Award. In 2015 he was made an Honorary Fellow of Liverpool John Moores University for outstanding services to literature. Among his novels are The Face That Must Die, Incarnate, Midnight Sun, The Count of Eleven, Silent Children, The Darkest Part of the Woods, The Overnight, Secret Story, The Grin of the Dark, Thieving Fear, Creatures of the Pool, The Seven Days of Cain, Ghosts Know, The Kind Folk, Think Yourself Lucky and Thirteen Days by Sunset Beach. He is presently working on a trilogy, The Three Births of Daoloth – the first volume, The Searching Dead, appears in 2016. Needing Ghosts, The Last Revelation of Gla'aki, The Pretence and The Booking are novellas. His collections include Waking Nightmares, Alone with the Horrors, Ghosts and Grisly Things, Told by the Dead, Just Behind You and Holes for Faces, and his non-fiction is collected as Ramsey Campbell, Probably. His novels The Nameless and Pact of the Fathers have been filmed in Spain. His regular columns appear in Dead Reckonings and Video Watchdog. He is the President of the Society of Fantastic Films.

Ramsey Campbell lives on Merseyside with his wife Jenny. His pleasures include classical music, good food and wine, and whatever's in that pipe. His web site is at www.ramseycampbell.com.

Website: http://www.ramseycampbell.com/
Amazon: http://www.amazon.com/Ramsey-Campbell/e/
B000APEIRG/ref=ntt_athr_dp_pel_pop_1

Lily Childs writes dark fiction, horror and chilling mysteries with the occasional dally into pulp fiction and twisted crime. She has a novel or three on the way - all set in the south of England where she lives, a stone's throw from the sea.

Her short story collection *Cabaret of Dread: a Horror Compendium* is available in paperback or ebook through Amazon, with the second volume in the collection set to be published in late 2013. Author of the *Magenta Shaman* urban fantasy short stories.

Lily's gothic horrors, ghost stories and nerve-janglers have appeared online, in print and in ebook anthologies such as *The Demonologia Biblica* from Western Legends Press (2013) which features her Victorian demonic tale, *The Twistweaver's Son*. In 2011 many of her poems were published in *Courting Demons – A Collection Of Dark Verse*, and in the same year her psychological crime thriller *Carpaccio* was nominated for a Spinetingler Award for Best Short Story on the Web.

You can read more of her fiction, dark verse, reviews and interviews on her website (see link below). She is also the Horror Editor at award-winning e-zine Thrillers Killers 'n' Chillers.

Website: http://lilychildsfeardom.blogspot.co.nz/
Amazon: http://www.amazon.com/Lily-Childs/e/
B003YBVE3O/ref=sr_tc_2_0?qid=1383086178&sr=1-2-ent

 **Lincoln Crisler's** body of work consists of over thirty short stories, two novellas and editorship of two anthologies, most recently Corrupts Absolutely?, an anthology of dark superhero fiction. His work has appeared in a variety of print and online publications, to include HUB Magazine, Shroud Publishing's Abominations anthology and IDW's Robots vs. Zombies anthology. He is a member of the Horror Writers Association.

A United States Army combat veteran and non-commissioned officer, Lincoln lives in Augusta, Georgia with his wife and two of his three children. He enjoys music, cooking, web design and comic books. Lincoln and his wife own a virtual assistant business, Crisler Professional Services. You can contact him at lincoln@ lincolncrisler.info.

Amazon: http://www.amazon.com/Lincoln-Crisler/e/ B002UD1BWG

 **Jack Dann** is a multiple-award winning author who has written or edited over seventy-five books, including the international bestseller The Memory Cathedral, which was #1 on The Age Bestseller list, and The Silent, which Library Journal chose as one of their 'Hot Picks' and wrote: "This is narrative storytelling at its best... Most emphatically recommended."

Jack Dann's work has been compared to Jorge Luis Borges, Roald Dahl, Lewis Carroll, Castaneda, Ray Bradbury, J. G. Ballard, Mark Twain, and Philip K. Dick. Library Journal has called him "a true poet who can create pictures with a few perfect words" and Best Sellers said, "Jack Dann is a mind-warlock whose magicks will confound, disorient, shock, and delight."

Dann lives in Australia on a farm overlooking the sea and "commutes" back and forth to Los Angeles and New York.

Website: http://www.jackdann.com/
Amazon: http://www.amazon.com/Jack-Dann/e/B000APG6E4/ref=sr_tc_2_0?qid=1383092306&sr=1-2-ent

**Robert Dunbar** is the author of several novels and a collection of short stories, and his essays about literature and film have appeared in numerous publications. For more information, visit his site at: www.DunbarAuthor.com.

"The catalyst for the new literary movement in horror." ~ *Dark Scribe Magazine*

"One of the best authors working in dark fiction today." ~ *Literary Mayhem*

"Easily one of the best dark fiction writers around." ~ *The Black Abyss*

"In a class all his own." ~ *The Aquarian Weekly*

"A literary craftsman, a stylist." ~ *Shroud Magazine*

"Spearheading the movement to infuse the modern horror genre with more literary sensibilities." ~ *Serial Distractions*

Website: http://www.dunbarauthor.com/
Amazon:http://www.amazon.com/Robert-Dunbar/e/
B003ZO61WY/ref=sr_tc_2_0?qid=1383256182&sr=8-2-ent

Thomas A. Erb is a genre fiction writer exploring all shades of darkness and light and the varying definitions of heroism. Refusing to pigeonhole his writing, Thomas continues to craft tales that blur the lines of dark, fantasy, thriller, weird western, science fiction for both adult and young adult audiences. His first novella, 'Tones of Home' was published in May of 2013 by Crowded Quarantine Press (UK). He is also an editor and his first anthology, 'Death, Be Not Proud' has been published through Dullahan Press/Dark Quest Books.

Thomas is also an artist/illustrator of murals and comic book/graphic novels. His art is heavily inspired and influenced by the golden age of comic books such as: Jack Kirby, John Buscema, John Byrne to more modern artists Bart Sears and Jim Lee. His painting gurus hail from the traditional artists: Da Vinci, Michelangelo, Durer, to fantasy painters and illustrators ranging from Frank Frazetta to Norman Rockwell.

Thomas is a member of the Horror Writer's Association and you can find out more here:

Website: http://www.thomerb.com/p/home-page.html
Amazon: http://www.amazon.com/Thomas-A.-Erb/e/B0049D761A/ref=ntt_athr_dp_pel_pop_1

 **Brandon Ford**'s previously published works include Open Wounds, The Final Girl, Coffee at Midnight, and The Facility. He has also contributed to more than a dozen anthologies. He currently resides in Philadelphia and may be reached at the following link:

www.writerbrandonford.blogspot.com

Carole Gill has a deep and abiding affection for gothic horror. Her gothic vampire novels make up The Blackstone Vampires Series, which include:
The House on Blackstone Moor
Unholy Testament - The Beginnings
Unholy Testament – Full Circle
The Fourth Bride

Carole is widely published in a number of horror and sci-fi anthologies.

Website: http://carolegillauthor.blogspot.com/
Amazon: http://www.amazon.com/Carole-Gill/e/
B0032TTVVA/ref=ntt_athr_dp_pel_1

Lindsey Beth Goddard is a dark fiction author living in the suburbs of St. Louis, MO. She's managed to weasel her stories into such amazing anthologies as: Bleed (Perpetual Motion Machine Publishing), Mistresses Of The Macabre (Dark Moon Books), Nightmare Stalkers & Dream Walkers (Horrified Press), Night Terrors (Kayelle Press), Welcome To Hell (E-volve Books), and Mental Ward: Echoes Of The Past (Sirens Call Publications) and the e-zines/ magazines: Sirens Call, Dark Moon Digest, Flashes In The Dark, Hogglepot, Dark Fire Fiction, Infernal Ink, Twisted Dreams, and Yellow Mama. When not writing, she enjoys interviewing fellow authors, playing with her three children, and watching horror movies.

Website: http://www.lindseybethgoddard.com/
Amazon: http://www.amazon.com/Lindsey-Goddard/e/
B0072F9VEM/ref=ntt_athr_dp_pel_1

**J. F. Gonzalez** is the author of several acclaimed novels of terror and suspense as well as over eighty short stories and numerous articles. He's primarily known for the novels They, Primitive, Survivor, and as the co-author of the Clickers series (with Mark Williams and Brian Keene respectively).

Born in Los Angeles, CA, Gonzalez was raised in the nearby suburb of Gardena. Following graduation from high school in 1982 he attended college, and then dropped in and out for the next several years before quitting for good in 1986. In 1990, he co-founded Iniquities Publications and worked as the co-editor/publisher of Iniquities magazine and Phantasm magazine until 1997, selecting and publishing material that would later be reprinted in various Year's Best anthologies and winning awards. He worked as a full-time writer up until his passing in November, 2014.

Amazon: http://www.amazon.com/J.-F.-Gonzalez/e/
B001K7TRBU/ref=sr_tc_2_0?qid=1383095260&sr=1-2-ent

Dane Hatchell was born and lives in Baton Rouge, Louisiana. He works in the manufacturing industry by the shores of the Mississippi River.

He is the author of numerous short stores that have appeared in various horror and science fiction anthologies over the past several years. His first novel RESURRECTION X: ZOMBIE EVOLUTION debuted in 2012. He is the co-author of the action packed horror novel INSURGENT Z and the thrilling novella SLIPWAY GREY. He is a member of HWA.

Website: https://www.facebook.com/dane.hatchell?fref=browse_search
Amazon: http://www.amazon.com/Dane-Hatchell/e/
B003KAR05K/ref=sr_ntt_srch_lnk_1?qid=1383180915&sr=8-1

 **E. A. Irwin** resides in California, writes fiction and poetry, often crossing genre boundaries just to keep life interesting ... and because she can. Her motto: "Success lives between your ears."

Those who know her understand her intrigue of getting inside someone's head and deliciously digging around with shiny cutlery to find out what makes a person tick, or gives them ticks. She likes complex characters, plots, and being disturbed by what alters a character's normalcy. Loves it when all that falls onto on a page and someone says her writing came too close to reality.

Author of the short story series "Myth to Life: The Rise of Riley McCabe," she is currently working on the first full-length novel in this series. Her work has appeared in various anthologies, as well as print and online magazines.

Website: http://eairwin.webs.com/
Amazon: http://www.amazon.com/E.-A.-Irwin/e/
B002BTGZMU/ref=sr_tc_2_0?qid=1383259450&sr=1-2-ent

Charlee Jacob has been a digger for dinosaur bones, a seller of designer rags, and a cook – to mention only a few things.

With more than 950 publishing credits, Charlee has been writing dark poetry and prose for more than 25 years. Some of her recent publishing events include the novel STILL (Necro), the poetry collection HERESY (Necro), and the novel DARK MOODS. She is a three-time Bram Stoker Award winner, two of those awards for her novel DREAD IN THE BEAST and the poetry collection SINEATER; the third award for collaborative poetry collection, VECTORS, with Marge Simon. Permanently disabled, she has begun to paint as one of her forms of physical therapy.

She lives in Irving, Texas with her husband Jim and a plethora of felines.

Amazon: http://www.amazon.com/Charlee-Jacob/e/B00JI02IS0/ref=sr_ntt_srch_lnk_1?qid=1467845365&sr=1-1

 **K. Trap Jones** is an author of horror novels and short stories. With inspiration from Dante Alighieri and Edgar Allan Poe, he has a temptation towards narrative folklore, classic literary works and obscure segments within society. His short stories have appeared in various anthologies and magazines. His novel, The Sinner won the 2010 Royal Palm Literary Award. He can be found lurking around Tampa, FL. His novels include: The Sinner, The Harvester, The Charm Hunter, The Drunken Exorcist, The King's Ox and One Bad Fur Day.

Website: http://ktrapjones.wordpress.com

Tim Jones is a poet and author of both science fiction and literary fiction who was awarded *the New Zealand Society of Authors Janet Frame Memorial Award for Literature in 2010*. He lives in Wellington, New Zealand. Among his books are fantasy novel *Anarya's Secret* (RedBrick, 2007), short story collection *Transported* (Vintage, 2008), and poetry anthology *Voyagers: Science Fiction Poetry from New Zealand* (Interactive Press, 2009), co-edited with Mark Pirie. Tim is currently co-editing, with P.S. Cottier, an anthology of Australian speculative poetry.

Website: http://timjonesbooks.blogspot.com
Amazon: http://www.amazon.com/Tim-Jones/e/B004MGX7Z8/

 **James Ward Kirk** is a publisher and writer of horror and speculative fiction. His recent collection of short stories, "Death Anxiety" has won critical acclaim. You can find him on Facebook at James Ward Kirk Fiction.

His website is jwkfiction.com.

Axel Kohagen is a writer from Minneapolis, MN. He has a story published in Human Cuisine, and defined "horror" and "Stephen King" for The Encyclopedia of Men and Masculinities. His work has been mentioned in Rue Morgue Magazine. He recently finished his online serial thriller The HooseCows, about an independent league baseball league stalked by a murderer and haunted by ghosts. He currently plans to revise it and publish it in some form, probably electronically.

Website: http://axelkohagen.com/

 **Shane McKenzie** is the author of Infinity House, All You Can Eat, Bleed on Me, Jacked, Addicted to the Dead, Muerte Con Carne, Escape from Shit Town (co-authored with Sam W. Anderson and Erik Williams), Fat Off Sex and Violence, Fairy, The Bingo Hall, and many more to come. He is also the editor at Sinister Grin Press. He lives in Austin, TX with his wife and daughter.

Amazon: http://www.amazon.com/Shane-McKenzie/e/ B0073FH1GG/ref=sr_tc_2_0?qid=1383182865&sr=1-2-ent

 **Shaun Meeks** lives in Toronto, Ontario with his partner, Mina LaFleur, where they own and operate their own corset company L'Atelier de LaFleur. Shaun is the author of The Dillon the Monster Dick series (Earthbound and Down and The Gate at Lake Drive), as well as Maymon, Shutdown and Down on the Farm. He has published more than 50 short stories; the most recent appearing in Midian Unmade: Tales of Clive Barker's Nightbreed, Dark Moon Digest, Shrieks and Shivers from The Horror Zine, Zippered Flesh 2, Of Devils & Deviants and Fresh Fear. His short stories have been collected in At the Gates of Madness, Dark Reaches and Brother's Ilk (with James Meeks). To find out more or to contact Shaun, visit:

Website: www.shaunmeeks.com
Amazon: http://www.amazon.com/Shaun-Meeks/e/
B007X5KZLO/ref=sr_tc_2_0?qid=1467785768&sr=1-2-ent

Adam Millard is the author of twenty-two novels, thirteen novellas, and more than two hundred short stories, which can be found in various collections and anthologies. Probably best known for his post-apocalyptic fiction, Adam also writes fantasy/horror for children and Bizarro fiction for several publishers, who enjoy his tales of flesh-eating clown-beetles and rabies-infected derrieres so much that they keep printing them. His "Dead" series has recently been the filling in a Stephen King/Bram Stoker sandwich on Amazon's bestsellers chart. Adam is a regular columnist for UK horror website, This Is Horror.

Website: http://www.adammillard.co.uk/
Amazon: http://www.amazon.com/Adam-Millard/e/
B005G815QO/ref=sr_tc_2_0?qid=1383187637&sr=1-2-ent

 **Christine Morgan** recently relocated from the Seattle area to the Portland area, beginning a new, more-social phase of her life among the local horror/bizarro creative community. They like how she brings goodies to readings and events. In addition to her several books and dozens of short stories in print, she's a regular contributor to The Horror Fiction Review, the editor and publisher of the Fossil Lake Anthologies, and dabbles in many various other writing-related projects. Her other interests include history, mythology, cooking shows, crafts, superheroes, gaming, and spoiling her four cats as she trains toward eventual crazy-cat-lady status.

She can be found online at:

https://www.facebook.com/christinemorganauthor and https://christinemariemorgan.wordpress.com/

 **Billie Sue Mosiman** is the Author of sixteen novels and over two hundred short stories. Nominated for both the Edgar Award and the Stoker. Her latest novel is THE GREY MATTER from Post Mortem Press and an anthology, FRIGHT MARE-WOMEN WRITE HORROR.

Website: http://peculiarwriter.blogspot.com/
Amazon: http://www.amazon.com/Billie-Sue-Mosiman/e/
B000AQ0Z5E/ref=sr_tc_2_0?qid=1383257619&sr=1-2-ent

 **D.F. Noble** was born in Alton, Illinois. He grew up learning to draw and write stories in the hopes of becoming a comic book artist. He later transitioned into music and played with a band called Templit and went on to record two albums. After goofing off with some bizarre and commercial solo projects in the music field and tampering with film, he later connected with Kevin Strange and helped co-found StrangeHouse Books. From there he has written for various anthologies, including Tall Tales with Short cocks vol. 3, and the upcoming book "Queefrotica". You may also find his works in the Strange House anthologies - "Strange Sex", "Zombie! Zombie! Brain Bang!" and "Strange Vs. Lovecraft." His other works include, "Scary Fucking Stories," "Grownups Must Die", and his first novel "Beer Run of the Dead".

Website: http://donnobleauthor.wordpress.com/
Amazon: http://www.amazon.com/D.-F.-Noble/e/
B008NF5XS8/ref=sr_tc_2_0?qid=1383258333&sr=1-2-ent

Chantal Noordeloos lives in the Netherlands, where she spends her time with her wacky, supportive husband, and outrageously cunning daughter, who is growing up to be a supervillain. When she is not busy exploring interesting new realities, or arguing with characters (aka writing), she likes to dabble in drawing. In 1999 she graduated from the Norwich School of Art and Design, where she focused mostly on creative writing.

There are many genres that Chantal likes to explore in her writing. Currently Sci-fi Steampunk is one of her favorites, but her 'go to' genre will always be horror. "It helps being scared of everything; that gives me plenty of inspiration," she says.

Chantal likes to write for all ages, and storytelling is the element of writing that she enjoys most. "Writing should be an escape from everyday life, and I like to provide people with new places to escape to, and new people to meet."

Website: http://www.chantalnoordeloos.info/
Amazon: http://www.amazon.com/Chantal-Noordeloos/e/
B009XUB50W/ref=sr_tc_2_0?qid=1383258124&sr=1-2-ent

 **W. H. Pugmire** has been writing Lovecraftian weird fiction since the early 1970's. He has completed, with collaborator David Barker, a wee novel set in H. P. Lovecraft's dreamlands, which has just been accepted for publication. Wilum's second hardcover collection from Centipede Press, AN ECSTASY OF FEAR AND OTHERS, will be published late 2017.

His books include THE TANGLED MUSE, GATHERED DUST AND OTHERS, SOME UNKNOWN GULF OF NIGHT, UNCOMMON PLACES, ENCOUNTERS WITH ENOCH COFFIN (written in collaboration with Jeffrey Thomas) and BOHEMIANS OF SESQUA VALLEY.

Website: http://sesqua.net/
Amazon: http://www.amazon.com/W.-H.-Pugmire/e/ B002CQONYO/ref=sr_ntt_srch_lnk_1?qid=1383258513&sr=1- 1-spell

 **W.J. Renehan** serves as editorial director for New Street subsidiary Dark Hall Press, a publisher of first-quality Horror and Science Fiction. He is an alumnus of Dean College, SUNY New Paltz and the University of Rhode Island.

Website: http://newstreetcommunications.com/new_street_literary/the_art_of_darkness
Amazon: http://www.amazon.com/W.J.-Renehan/e/B00J7XWPKY/ref=dp_byline_cont_book_1

 **William Todd Rose** is a speculative fiction author currently residing in Parkersburg, West Virginia; he has been named by The Google+ Insider's Guide as one of their top 32 authors to follow. His short stories have been featured in numerous anthologies and magazines, and his work includes the novels Cry Havoc, The Dead & Dying, and The Seven Habits, alongside the novellas Apocalyptic Organ Grinder and Crossfades.

While Mr. Rose has been known to delve into the worlds of scifi and cyberpunk, his main affinity is for dark fiction with a particularly special place in his heart for zombie lit. He is currently at work on his next project

Website: www.williamtoddrose.com
Amazon: http://www.amazon.com/William-Todd-Rose/e/
B002UFOZZE/ref=dp_byline_cont_ebooks_1

Anna Taborska was born in London, England. She is a filmmaker and writer of horror stories, screenplays and poetry. Anna has written and directed two short fiction films (Ela and The Sin), two documentaries (My Uprising and A Fragment of Being) and a one-hour television drama (The Rain Has Stopped), which won two awards at the British Film Festival Los Angeles in 2009. Anna also worked on twenty other films, with actors such as Rutger Hauer, Scott Wilson, Noah Taylor and Jenny Agutter, and was involved in the making of two major BBC television series: Auschwitz: the Nazis and the Final Solution and World War Two behind Closed Doors – Stalin, the Nazis and the West.

Anna's short stories have appeared in a number of 'Year's Best' anthologies, and her debut short story collection, For Those who Dream Monsters, published by Mortbury Press in 2013, won the Dracula Society's Children of the Night Award and was nominated for a British Fantasy Award. A new collection of novelettes and short stories (working title: Bloody Britain) is planned for release soon.

Website: http://annataborska.wix.com/horror
Amazon: http://www.amazon.com/Anna-Taborska/e/
B00DRIPW96

EDITOR'S BIO

William Cook was born and raised in New Zealand and is the author of the novel *'Blood Related.'* He has written many short stories that have appeared in anthologies and has authored two short-story collections *('Dreams of Thanatos' & 'Death Quartet')* and two collections of poetry *('Journey: the search for something' & 'Corpus Delicti')*. He also writes non-fiction – his books *'Gaze Into The Abyss: The Poetry of Jim Morrison'* and *'Secrets of Best-Selling Self-Published Authors'* are available in both digital and print editions.

You can find him online at http://williamcookwriter.com and his books at: http://tinyurl.com/BloodRelatedNovel

FRESH FEAR CREDITS/ ACKNOWLEDGMENTS

I would like to thank a few people who have provided support and help in putting together Fresh Fear.

A special thank you to Vincenzo Bilof who helped with edits when I was confined to my bed with a bout of pneumonia. Thank you also to WJ Renehan who kindly provided the introduction, including a poignant excerpt from his wonderful study, The Art of Darkness: Meditations on the Effect of Horror Fiction. Bobby Hitt is due credit for permission to use his wonderful photo of Charlee Jacob. Big thanks to publisher, James Ward Kirk, for invaluable guidance and patience during the process of editing/ compiling Fresh Fear in its first edition and for his support of Indie Horror and dedication to the genre. Finally, massive thanks to all the fantastic contributors; including those whose stories aren't included here, but who took the time to submit work. And, of course, to you the reader who relishes those dark forays into the psychological world of fictional horror. Here you will find plenty to satiate your fears and fetishes.

I would like to especially thank talented photographer, Louis Blanc, for his generous permission to use his photography for the cover design.

COPYRIGHT/CREDITS

Grab a free copy of William's 250 pg collection,

'Dreams of Thanatos.'

Sign up now for the VIP newsletter at:

http://williamcookwriter.com/p/subscribe-now.html